IRISH TEXTS SOCIETY

CUMANN NA SGRÍBHEANN GAEDHILGE

Vol. LII

CATH MAIGE TUIRED

The Second Battle of
Mag Tuired

edited by

ELIZABETH A. GRAY

PUBLISHED BY THE

IRISH TEXTS SOCIETY

PRINTED AT THE LEINSTER LEADER LTD., NAAS, CO. KILDARE

1982

CONTENTS

INTRODUCTION

(I)

Cath Maige Tuired is the account of the epic battle between the Túatha Dé Danann and the Fomoire. A contest between the gods of pagan Ireland and their enemies, once also a supernatural race, it stands at the centre of Irish mythology; and although the conflict is set within the chronological framework of Irish pseudo-history represented by *Lebor Gabála Érenn,* the defence of Ireland by the Túatha Dé Danann is essentially timeless, a paradigmatic illustration of principles fundamental to the ordering and maintenance of human society. Often compared with the battle between Asuras and Devas of Indic tradition, and with that between Aesir and Vanir in Scandinavian mythology, *Cath Maige Tuired,* known as 'The Second Battle of Mag Tuired' to distinguish it from an earlier battle between Túatha Dé Danann and Fir Bolg, is of great value for the comparative reconstruction of the Indo-European mythological inheritance as well as for the exploration of Irish mythological tradition itself.

References to the tale abound throughout Irish literature, in learned tradition and in epic narrative, in bardic poetry and in folklore. Despite its importance, however, only two independent narrative versions of *The Second Battle of Mag Tuired* are extant, each represented by a single manuscript. The older version, based upon Old Irish materials, occurs in a sixteenth-century vellum manuscript, Harleian 5280, consisting of 78 ff. $9\frac{1}{8}$ in. by $6\frac{3}{4}$ in. The main scribe, Gilla Riabhach Ó Cléirigh, son of Tuathal son of Tadhg Cam Ó Cléirigh, probably wrote in the first half of the century, as his father died in 1512. Other hands that have not been identified appear at ff. 18b-20b, 45 11. 10-33, 58, and 58b; and there is a pen-trial by Maolmuire Ó Cléirigh, perhaps the son of a nephew of Gilla Riabhach. Inscriptions of ownership link the manuscript first to Hugo Casserly and then to Henry Spelman, one of the commissioners sent by James I to settle disputed Irish land titles. Bound with the vellum are seven paper leaves in the hand associated with Casserly. A full description of the manuscript and an account of its contents appears in Flower's *Catalogue of Irish Manuscripts in the British Museum.*[1] An edition and translation of *The Second Battle of Mag Tuired,* omitting obscure or obscene passages, was published by Stokes in 1891, and an edition of the lacunae was supplied by Thurneysen in 1918.[2] The present work includes an edition of the entire narrative,

---

[1] The details regarding the MS., its history, and the Ó Cléirigh family, are taken from Flower's discussion. See Robin Flower, *Catalogue of Irish Manuscripts in the British Museum* (London: William Clowes and Sons, 1926), II, 298-323.

[2] Whitley Stokes, 'The Second Battle of Moytura,' *Révue Celtique,* 12 (1891), 52-130; 306-308.

together with a translation that aims at completeness, although most of the obscure poetic passages remain to be deciphered. The early Modern Irish version of the tale, *Cath Muighe Tuireadh*, from the Royal Irish Academy MS. 24 P 9, written in 1651-2 by David Duigenan, is verbally distinct from the Harleian text, although the two overlap considerably in plot. It has been edited by Brian Ó Cuív, without translation but with an excellent English summary, and with full notes on major points of similarity and divergence.[3]

The Harleian narrative, drawing together materials from a variety of sources, begins with events that take place long before the battle itself, explaining the origin of the hostility between Túatha Dé Danann and Fomoire. While still living on islands north of Ireland, the Túatha Dé Danann ally themselves with the Fomoire, and Ethne, daughter of the Fomorian champion Balor, is given in marriage to Cían, son of the Túatha Dé Danann physician Dían Cécht. Soon afterward, the Túatha Dé Danann occupy Ireland, defeating its previous inhabitants, the Fir Bolg, in the first battle of Mag Tuired. In the course of the battle, the Túatha Dé Danann king, Núadu, loses an arm and therefore cannot continue to rule (§§ 1-13). The women of the Túatha Dé Danann, intending to strengthen the earlier alliance, propose to elect Bres, the illegitimate son of the Fomorian king Elatha and Ériu, a woman of the Túatha Dé Danann (§ 14). Here the narrative inserts an account of the circumstances of Bres's conception before revealing that after much debate the Túatha Dé Danann accept him as their king (§§ 15-23). The choice, however, proves disastrous, and Bres's reign offers a paradigm of incompetent kingship. Seeking only his own profit and having no concern for the well-being of his people, Bres ignores his subjects' proper social roles and status: practitioners of the arts receive no recognition from him, and the warrior Ogma is forced to serve as a supplier of firewood. The Dagda, master of druidry, becomes Bres's rath-builder, and is faced not only with his assigned task but with the loss of his food to the extortionate satirist Cridenbél. Through the counsel of his son the Mac Óc, the Dagda destroys the satirist by means of his own greed, at the same time causing Bres to utter a false judgement, and, after finishing Bres's fortress, chooses as the reward for his labour a single black heifer — a choice whose significance is made clear only at the end of the tale, when she leads home all the cattle taken from the Túatha Dé Danann as tribute (§§ 24-32).

At this point two distinct narrative strands are visible: in one

Rudolf Thurneysen, 'Zu irischen Texten. III. *Cath Maige Turedh*,' *ZCP* 12 (1918), 401-406.

See also the partial translation into German by Gustav Lehmacher, S.J., 'Die zweite Schlacht von Mag Tured und die keltische Götterlehre,' *Anthropos* 26 (1931), 435-459.

[3] Brian Ó Cuív, ed., *Cath Muighe Tuireadh: The Second Battle of Magh Tuireadh* (Dublin: Dublin Institute, 1945).

On David Duigenan, see Paul Walsh, *Irish Men of Learning* (Dublin: At the Three Candles, 1947), esp. 25-33.

(§ 25), the Túatha Dé Danann are immediately subject to demands for tribute from Fomorian overlords, including Bres's father Elatha; in the other, Bres himself is responsible for plundering his people (§§ 36-38). Both narrative traditions agree that the Túatha Dé Danann eventually meet to restrict Bres's avarice, following a satire made against him by the poet Coirpre, who has experienced the king's inhospitality at first-hand (§§ 39-40). Soon after, Bres flees to his father Elatha, asking for a Fomorian army to support his claims (§§ 41-51). The Túatha Dé Danann are free to restore Núadu to his former position, his own arm having been miraculously replaced by Dían Cécht's son Miach (§§ 33-35). Vastly outnumbered, and aware of the danger of Fomorian attack, the tribe gathers for a royal feast at Tara (§ 53).

Lug, the son of Cían and Ethne, arrives among the Túatha Dé Danann in the midst of this crisis, and claims the right to enter the feast, which is restricted to practitioners of different arts, because he is the unique master of every art. Hearing of this, Núadu invites Lug to enter, and after consultation with the tribe, gives him responsibility for co-ordinating their preparation for battle (§§ 54-74). Lug calls together representatives of the various arts to review their capabilities, sets the time of battle, and arranges for the provision of weapons (§§ 75-83). The narrative then turns to the adventures of the Dagda: his meeting with the Morrígan, their sexual union, and her magical attack upon the Fomorian king Indech (§§ 84-86). As various other preparations go forward, Lug sends the Dagda as ambassador to the Fomoire to gain a truce until Samain; and despite Fomorian hostility, which takes the form of monstrously excessive hospitality, the Dagda is successful, not only in his assigned mission, but in gaining the affection and magical aid of Indech's daughter (§§ 87-93). Before the conflict begins, Lug questions each member of the Túatha Dé Danann regarding his or her particular contribution to the war effort, revealing the superior skill and coordinated expertise of the tribe as a whole (§§ 94-120). There are preliminary combats, and the ability of the Túatha Dé Danann to provide weapons and heal the wounded astonishes the Fomoire, who commission Rúadán, son of Bres and Bríg, daughter of the Dagda, to kill one of the artisans responsible. Instead Rúadán himself is slain, but the Fomoire are successful in devising a scheme to destroy their enemies' well of healing (§§ 121-126). Despite this loss, the quality of Lug's leadership and the effect of their unmatched abilities in the arts ultimately bring victory to the outnumbered Túatha Dé Danann in spite of the loss of their king. Although the Túatha Dé Danann attempt to keep Lug from the battle for his protection, he escapes to join the fighting, encouraging his host with chanted spells; and at a turning point in the conflict, he faces his maternal grandfather in single combat, destroying Balor by casting a sling-stone at his evil eye, and thereby avenging the fallen Núadu (§§ 127-138).

The battle then becomes a rout; the Fomoire are driven back to the sea; and the remainder of the tale consists of various negotiations between victors and vanquished (§§ 139-164). Bres gains his life in return for information that will bring agricultural prosperity (§§ 149-161); the Dagda regains his stolen harp and harper, not by force, but through the power of music (§§ 163-164); and the Túatha Dé Danann recover all the cattle taken as tribute, through the lowing of the Dagda's black heifer (§ 165). Poets of both tribes prophesy a new age of peace and prosperity for the Túatha Dé Danann in Ireland, the victory is proclaimed (§§ 141, 166). The last words, however, are spoken by the Morrigan, and these prophesy the end of all things, even the newly-won freedom established by the second battle of Mag Tuired (§ 167).

(II)

Much of contemporary mythological analysis rests upon comparative, sociological, and structural methods shaped by the perspectives of Durkheim and Lévi-Strauss, and these methods are especially applicable to Irish myth, where the world of the gods reflects the organization of human society and illustrates the role of various social institutions in creating and maintaining social order.[4] In examining the relation between myth and social organization in many Indo-European traditions, Georges Dumézil and others have developed a New Comparative Mythology that emphasizes the structural role of inherited Indo-European ideological patterns.[5] In particular, Dumézil and Benveniste have explored a central set of Indo-European ideological categories, a tripartite system that includes (i) sacred or magical knowledge, associated with sovereign power; (ii) physical, especially martial, force; and (iii) a complex group of concepts dominated by the principles of fertility and abundance, but including such traits as beauty, pleasure, and prosperity.[6] To these

[4] Émile Durkheim, *Les Formes élémentaires de la vie religieuse* (Paris, 1912), available in English as *The Elementary Forms of the Religious Life*, trans. Joseph Ward Swain (New York: Collier, 1961).

A descriptive analysis of Lévi-Strauss's contribution to contemporary anthropology is offered by Edmund Leach in *Claude Lévi-Strauss* (New York: Viking, 1970).

Lévi-Strauss's own theoretical writing on myth is to be found primarily in *The Savage Mind*, trans. from *La Pensée Sauvage* (Chicago: University of Chicago Press, 1966) and in *Structural Anthropology* (New York: Basic Books, 1963). Theory and practice are joined in his series *Mythologiques: I Le Cru et le Cuit* (1964), *II Du Miel au Cendres* (1966), and *III L'Origine des Manières de Table* (1968).

[5] The phrase, 'New Comparative Mythology,' was coined by C. Scott Littleton, whose book, *The New Comparative Mythology: An Anthropological Assessment of the Theories of Georges Dumézil* (Berkely: University of California Press, 1966), is a convenient English guide to Dumézil, most of whose works have not yet been translated. Littleton also discusses other Indo-Europeanists such as Benveniste and Wikander who have used similar methods to study myth.

[6] Georges Dumézil, 'L'idéologie tripartie des Indo-Européens', *Collection Latomus*, 31 (1958).

Émile Benveniste, 'La Doctrine Médicale des Indo-Européens,' *RHR* 130 (1945), 5-12; 'Symbolisme Social dans les Cultes Greco-Italiques,' *RHR* 129 (1945), 5-16.

three central concepts (*fonctions*) correspond not only Indo-European social groups (the priestly class and the king, the warrior aristocracy, and the farmers and cattle raisers directly concerned with fertility) but also members of divine society who patronize and symbolize these special functions.

Dumézil himself has often turned to Celtic material for comparison and analysis, and his work has influenced current interpretations of Celtic myth by such scholars as de Vries, Le Roux, Mac Cana, Rees and Rees, and Vendryes.[7] In regard to *The Second Battle of Mag Tuired*, Dumézil has proposed that the tale represents the convergence of several wide-spread Indo-European myths.[8] One of these, he suggests, examines the contractual and magical aspects of sovereignty through the actions of two divine figures, the first, one-handed, the second, one-eyed. By his mutilation, the one-handed figure secures a contractual peace, while the one-eyed deity gains total victory through terrifying magic. For Dumézil, Núadu and Lug are the Irish equivalents of these two figures: Núadu's loss of an arm leads to a contractual settlement between Túatha Dé Danann and Fir Bolg (according to the independent and rather late tale, *The First Battle of Mag Tuired*), while Lug's chanting of spells with one eye closed ensures complete victory over the Fomoire for the Túatha Dé Danann.[9] A second myth present in the tale involves the integration of deities representing all three functions into a single divine society, following antagonism between the representatives of the first two functions, sacred power and physical force (the Túatha Dé Danann) and those of the third function (Bres and the Fomoire).[10] Yet a third myth shaping the narrative describes the struggle between divine society as a whole and its supernatural or demonic enemies, a myth appearing in Indic tradition in the war between Devas and Asuras.[11]

Dumézil's analyses have been followed or furthered by a number of Celtic scholars, especially de Vries, Le Roux, and Rees and Rees.[12]

---

[7] See in particular Jan de Vries, *Keltische Religion* (Stuttgart: Kohlhammer, 1961); the articles on Celtic, and especially Irish, myth by Françoise Le Roux in *Ogam*; Proinsias Mac Cana, *Celtic Mythology* (London: Hamlyn, 1970); Alwyn and Brinley Rees, *Celtic Heritage: Ancient Tradition in Ireland and Wales* (London: Thames and Hudson, 1961); and Joseph Vendryes, *La religion des Celtes*, in *Mana, Introduction a l'Histoire des Religions*, 2. III. (Paris: Presses Universitaires de France, 1948).

A notable exception to the current emphasis upon comparative methods, and one essential to any study of Irish myth, is Máire MacNeill, *The Festival of Lugnasa* (Oxford: Oxford University Press, 1962), which approaches myth through Irish folk narrative and folk ritual.

[8] Georges Dumézil, *Mitra-Varuna* (Paris: Gallimard, 1948) esp. 159-162; 179-188; and 'La Guerre des Sabines,' in *Jupiter, Mars, Quirinus* (Paris, Gallimard, 1941), I, 155-198.

[9] J. Fraser, 'The First Battle of Moytura,' *Ériu* 8 (1915), 1-63. See also Dumézil, *Mitra-Varuna*, 1948, 183-187.

[10] See Dumézil, 'La Guerre des Sabines,' in *Jupiter, Mars, Quirinus*, I, 155-198.

[11] Dumézil, *Mitra-Varuna*, 1948, 161.

[12] See note 7 above.

In *Keltische Religion*, 1961, for example, de Vries endorses Dumézil's description of Lug and Núadu as corresponding to Ódhinn and Tyr, the one-eyed and one-handed gods of sovereignty in Germanic tradition; his identification of Ogma as a second-function figure; and his interpretation of the tale as a conflict between Bres as representative of the third function and the Túatha Dé Danann as representatives both of sacred, sovereign power and of physical force.[13] And in *Celtic Heritage*, 1961, which includes an original and far-reaching application of Dumézil's methods to Irish and Welsh materials, Rees and Rees supported the association of Bres with the third function, and further examined the demonic aspects of the Fomoire in Irish tradition.[14]

In general, Dumézil's analysis of the tale as corresponding both to the mythic conflict between two groups of gods (I and II against III, in functional terms) and to the battle between gods and demons seems now to be well-established. There are some points, however, at which a close study of *The Second Battle of Mag Tuired* suggests development or re-evaluation of Dumézil's case that an Indo-European myth regarding the contractual and magical aspects of sovereignty underlies the one-handedness of Núadu and the temporarily one-eyed aspect of Lug. In the tale in its present form, Núadu's loss of an arm is not linked with a contractual settlement of peace; instead, he and his tribe drive their enemies into the sea, and no subsequent treaty is mentioned. Other details of the narrative do associate Núadu with the contractual or juridical aspect of sovereignty: for example, he enters an essentially contractual arrangement with Lug, acknowledging him as his superior for a temporary and symbolic period in exchange for Lug's assistance in preparing for battle. But Núadu is also clearly characterized as a warrior, a second-function figure, by his association with a remarkable sword (§ 5) and by his career as a whole, which seems to symbolize the costliness of warfare to the tribe, and to the warrior class in particular.

Núadu's complexity may be explained in terms of another 'trifunctional' pattern, separate from the two myths outlined by Dumézil, but conflated with them in shaping the narrative. Each of the successive kings of the Túatha Dé Danann (Bres, Núadu, Lug) appears to be associated primarily with one of the three functions: Bres, with the third; Núadu, with the second; Lug, initially with the first and ultimately with all three. This sequence as a whole demonstrates that the virtues which typify the three functions are among the qualities that define a king: he must be generous, brave, and just. These requirements are traditional: Medb, the euhemerized goddess of the sovereignty of Tara, demands that any king who marries her be 'without jealousy, without fear, and without niggardliness.'[15] Her qualifications are stated negatively, but require the

---

[13] Jan de Vries, *Keltische Religion*, 153-154.

[14] Alwyn and Brinley Rees, *Celtic Heritage*, 144.

[15] On Medb, see D. A. Binchy, 'The Fair of Tailtiu and the Feast of Tara,' *Ériu*

characteristic virtues of the three functions, for jealousy impedes justice, fear constrains courage, and niggardliness defeats generosity. As the tale proceeds, it becomes clear that Lug, unlike Bres and Núadu, is a royal model who brings together all three functions, synthesizing and harmonizing all the qualities that must be present in a king.

This tripartite exploration of kingship occurs within the symbolic context of opposition between the just sovereignty of the Túatha Dé Danann and the chaotic tyranny of Fomorian rule. At the same time, using the contrasted figures of Lug and Bres, whose kinship relations with the two tribes are precisely opposite, the tale examines the nature of maternal and paternal kinship, particularly in relation to tribal membership and personal allegiance. Other aspects of paternal kinship are presented in the differing father-son relationships of Elatha and Bres, the Dagda and the Mac Óc, and Dían Cécht and Míach. Various types of sexual union, from the formal intertribal marriage of Lug's parents to the chance encounter between the Dagda and Indech's daughter, illustrate both directly and symbolically the natural and cultural bases of social organization, including the transfer of women in marriage. Alongside these fundamental relationships — kinship and sexual union, the generation of the family — the myth examines possible relationships among larger social units: intertribal alliance as it leads to armed conflict, and warfare as a basis for a new contractual order. Various social roles are exemplified throughout the tale, with each practitioner of an art — druid and cupbearer, warrior and smith, physician and satirist — defining his unique contribution to the well-being of the tribe and its common defence. A final theme, articulated in prophecies, especially the Morrígan's closing words, is the relationship between social order and cosmic order. Although a full exploration of the tale as myth lies outside the scope of this edition, some references to the thematic and symbolic structure of the narrative will be found in the notes to the text. Further analysis may be found in the work of the scholars mentioned above, and in the series of essays by the present author beginning in *Éigse* 18.[16]

(III)

Although in many ways thematically consistent and structurally unified as mythology, the narrative clearly includes materials drawn from a variety of sources and from divergent traditions. The fundamental elements brought together to form the body of the tale appear in its full title: *Cath Maige Turedh an scél-sa sís 7 genemain Bres*

---

18 (1958), 134; Tomas Ó Máille, 'Medb Cruachna,' *ZCP* 17 (1927), 129-146; T. F. O'Rahilly, 'On the Origin of the Names *Érainn* and *Ériu*,' *Ériu* 14, pt. I (1943), 7-28. For her three requirements, see *Táin* 1. 28, where they are given, in order, as to be *cen néoit, cen ét, cen omon*.

[16] The series begins with 'Cath Maige Tuired: Myth and Structure (1-24),' *Éigse* 18 (1981), pt. 2.

meic Elathain 7 a ríghe: 'This tale below is the Battle of Mag Tuired and the birth of Bres son of Elatha and his reign.' An examination of both the language of the text and the plot suggests that an early account of the conception of Bres has been joined to a fairly early description of his reign, including his personal failure as a sovereign and his flight to his Fomorian kinsmen, followed by the battle at Mag Tuired. A third major element of the narrative deals with the battle itself and the preparations made by the Túatha Dé Danann under Lug's direction; it may be compared with the Early Modern Irish version, which begins with Lug's first review of the intended contribution to the battle by various members of the Túatha Dé Danann.[17]

Interspersed throughout the tale are items from *Lebor Gabála Érenn*, along with passages found in other branches of the learned tradition: the dindshenchus, and glossaries such as *Cormac's Glossary* and *Cóir Anmann*. Parallels from story-telling tradition link *The Second Battle of Mag Tuired* to many other Old and Middle Irish tales, notably to the older version of *Cath Maige Rath* and *Togail Bruidne Da Derga*.[18] Apart from a few direct borrowings from *Lebor Gabála Érenn*, it is often difficult to determine whether these various parallels represent sources, since the language of *The Second Battle of Mag Tuired* is often earlier than that of the corresponding passages, and the possible influence of oral tradition on any of the written works must in any case be considered, although its effect is difficult to weigh. The notes to the text include citations of these correspondences, both major and minor, emphasizing the relationship between the earlier and later versions of the tale, and the shared motifs of narrative tradition. What follows is a survey of the more important parallels and possible sources in the earlier literature. Further references to the mythic and narrative development of the material of *The Second Battle of Mag Tuired* — from *Oidheadh Chloinne Tuireann,* Fenian prose and poetry, and the Early Modern Irish version of the tale itself, to folk versions of Lug's birth and career — will be found in Ó Cuív's extensive introduction and notes; in Gerard Murphy's 'Notes on Cath Maige Tuired,' and his thorough discussion of Fenian tradition in *Duanaire Finn* III; and in Máire MacNeill's excellent study of the narrative and ritual folklore of Lugnasa.[19]

The learned tradition represented by *Lebor Gabála Érenn* is reflected in several passages in the tale, beginning with the account of

---

[17] See Ó Cuív, *Cath Muighe Tuireadh,* 11. 1-66.

[18] Carl Marstrander, 'A New Version of the Battle of Mag Rath,' *Ériu* 5 (1911), 227ff. The battle description itself begins on 236.
See E. Knott, *Togail Bruidne Da Derga* (Dublin: Dublin Institute, 1936), xi, xii. Other parallels are mentioned in the notes to the present text.

[19] Ó Cuív, esp. pp. 4-9; Murphy, 'Notes on Cath Maige Tuired,' *Éigse* 7 (1954), 191-198, including a careful discussion of the evidence from Irish literature relevant to the question of the existence of two battles of Mag Tuired in Irish tradition; and Murphy, *Duanaire Finn* III, 1953, esp. references given s.v. Lugh, Index of Heroes ... Etc.; and MacNeill, *The Festival of Lugnasa,* 1962.

the study of the occult arts by the Túatha Dé Danann in the northern islands of the world, from which they bring four talismans, the Lia Fáil, the spear of Lug, the sword of Núadu, the cauldron of the Dagda (§§ 1-7).

A second passage indebted to *Lebor Gabála Érenn* is the brief account of the arrival of the Túatha Dé Danann in Ireland, summarizing the first battle of Mag Tuired and noting the death of the Fir Bolg king Eochaid mac Eirc, Núadu's injury in combat with Sreng, and the cure devised by Dían Cécht, who replaced the missing arm with one of silver (§§ 9-13). A separate anecdote presenting the material of §§ 1-7 and 9, clearly drawn from the same tradition, has been edited by Vernam Hull from The Yellow Book of Lecan (*YBL*), The Book of Ballymote (*BB*), and Egerton 105.[20] Míach's dissatisfaction with Dían Cécht's treatment of Núadu's injury (§§ 33-35) also appears in some versions of *Lebor Gabála Érenn*, without reference to Míach's death by his father's hand, although O'Clery comments expressly on Dían Cécht's jealousy — a significant mythological detail.

The belief that Coirpre's satire against Bres was the first satire made in Ireland (§ 39) is well-known, and is cited, for example, in Cormac's *Glossary*, in the glosses to the *Amra Choluimb Chille*, and obliquely in one of the *Lebor Gabála Érenn* poems, LIV, attributed to Tanaide Ua Maoil Chonaire.[21] The satire also exists in a separate anecdote, edited by Hull from *YBL* and H. 3.17, which briefly describes the circumstances of Bres's reign, his deposition and flight, and his return to Ireland with the Fomoire to give battle for the sovereignty at Mag Tuired.[22] Bres's mistreatment of Ogma and the Dagda (§§ 24, 25, 36) are mentioned in this account of the first satire, as is Bres's extraordinary beauty, known from his father's prophecy (§ 21) and from *Cóir Anmann*, § 153. Although the Dagda's conflict with Cridenbél, leading to a false judgement by Bres, (§§ 26-29), is not included in the *YBL*, H.3.17 anecdote, reference is made to the Dagda's role in Cridenbél's death in the *Lebor Gabála Érenn* poem LVI, attributed to Flann Mainistrech, recounting the deaths of various members of the Túatha Dé Danann.

The restoration of Núadu to the kingship following his cure is noted by *Lebor Gabála Érenn*, but there is no reference to Lug's arrival at Tara nor to the other events that precede Núadu's death in battle (§§ 53-132), although many of these are treated elsewhere in Irish literature. Lug's arrival at the feast, and the restrictions on entry, for example, are described in a poem by Gofraidh Fionn Ó Dálaigh, while *Oidheadh Chloinne Tuireann* covers much of the same narrative ground, and goes on to describe Lug's preparations for battle, although reflecting a much later tradition.[23] Lug's muster of

---

[20] Vernam Hull, 'The Four Jewels of the *Tuatha Dé Danann,' ZCP* 18 (1929), 73-89.

[21] See *Cormac's Glossary* x.v. *cerníne, riss; ACC* in *RC* 20 (1899) §8, 159-161.

[22] Vernam Hull, 'Cairpre mac Edaine's Satire upon Bres mac Eladain,' *ZCP* 18 (1929), 63-69.

[23] The poem is edited by E. Knott, *Irish Syllabic Poetry* (Cork, 1934, 1957), 54-58.

his troops (§§ 95-120) includes only characters who are well-known from the Túatha Dé Danann genealogies in *Lebor Gabála Érenn*, and most of them also appear in the parallel passage that begins the Early Modern Irish version of the tale.

The mission of espionage and sabotage against the Túatha Dé Danann undertaken by the Dagda's Fomorian grandson Rúadán (§§ 122-125) seems not to be mentioned elsewhere, although the association of his mother Bríg with the practice of keening appears in *Lebor Gabála Érenn* without explanation, and the armourer's assembly-line that Rúadán would have destroyed by killing Goibniu is described in *Cormac's Glossary*, s.v. *nescóit*. The list of Fomorian leaders that precedes the description of the battle (§ 128) includes figures from the genealogical tracts edited by Ó Raithbheartaigh, many of whom also appear in the *dindshenchus* of Slíab Badbgna and in the Early Modern Irish version of the battle.[24]

The description of the actual fighting is very general (§§ 130-132), and closely matches a section of the older version of *Cath Maige Rath*, edited from *YBL* by Marstrander.[25] Some readings of the Harleian text, however, seem older than those of *YBL*, although at other points the reverse is true, and the precise relationship between the two passages is not clear. Lug's escape from custody to join the battle and his encouragement of the host, standing on one leg, using one eye (§ 129), are mentioned in the later version of the tale, where, however, Lug is left behind through Núadu's jealousy of his prowess, not for protection. The account of the confrontation between Lug and Balor in both versions includes similar, and obscure, 'rhetorical' passages; the two differ in the details of Balor's death, and in the later tale he survives the loss of an eye to be overtaken and slain at Carn Uí Néit.

Other differences in the outcome of the battle involve the Dagda and Bres. Both in the *Lebor Gabála Érenn* poem LVI and in the Early Modern Irish version of the tale, the Dagda receives an injury, which after many years proves fatal, from the Fomorian woman Ceithlenn, identified as Balor's wife in the narrative. The closest parallel in the Harleian version is the Dagda's amorous involvement with Indech's daughter (§ 93) which follows an initially hostile exchange between the two, and which leads finally to her magical assistance against her father's people. Bres, in the later tale, is killed in the course of the fighting.

Lebor Gabála Érenn material reappears in the references to the deaths of various members of the Túatha Dé Danann (§§ 133, 138), beginning with the death of Núadu and that of Ogma, who is alive again in §§ 162-164. A brief dialogue between Lug and a representative of the vanquished Fomoire appears in *Lebor Gabála Érenn*, the informant being Indech rather than the poet Lóch; both

---

[24] See especially *Genealogical Tracts* C, 201-203; *Met. Dinds.* IV 282; and Ó Cuív, 11. 353ff., also 11. 1239-1240.

[25] See note 18 above.

texts include a version of the number puzzle giving the number of the slain, as does the later version of the tale. The meeting between Lug and Bres, their dialogue in which Bres agrees to reveal secrets of agricultural prosperity, and the Dagda's retrieval of his harp and heifer seem to return to the early strata of the narrative associated with the accounts of Bres's birth and his personal failures as a king. The advice he gives as his ransom is perhaps a proverbial statement, and survives as such in Scottish Gaelic tradition, as noted by Banks.[26] The conclusion of the tale, the Morrigan's contrasted poetic prophecies of a time of prosperity followed by a return to chaos, are similar to the opposed prophecies of Néde and Ferchertne in *The Colloquy of the Two Sages*, perhaps a reflection of a native eschatological tradition.[27]

(IV)

The language of *The Second Battle of Mag Tuired* reflects the Old Irish materials upon which the text is based, although it is a compilation that has been influenced considerably by Middle Irish scribes or redactors, especially regarding its orthography. Concerning the complex character of the language, there has been general agreement. Stokes, after identifying some of the text's Middle Irish forms, notes that 'On the whole, however, the language of our story is of considerable antiquity, and this will appear more clearly if we remove, in our minds, the corruptions caused by the scribe's system of spelling.'[28] Flower, cataloguing Harleian 5280, remarks that 'the present form is apparently not older than the 11th cent. But it is probably a recension of an earlier text already existing in the 9th cent.'[29] Michael O'Brien (in fact referring only to what seem to be the earliest segments of the tale) calls it a text of the early ninth century; and Murphy, summarizing the evidence for two battles fought at Mag Tuired in literary tradition (rather than a single battle), concludes that 'it seems to be true that the story under consideration is indeed the product of an eleventh or twelfth-century redactor working mainly upon ninth-century material.'[30] There is little that appears archaic in the language, but much that is consistent with the language of the glosses. Descriptions and examples of key aspects of the language are given below, following a summary of Stokes's guide to the orthography of the text. The passages of poetic dialogue supplied by

[26] Mary M. Banks, '*Na Tri Mairt*, the Three Marts and the Man with the Withy,' *Études Celtiques* 3 (1938), 131-143.
[27] Whitley Stokes, 'The Colloquy of the Two Sages,' *RC* 26 (1905), 4-64, esp. 32-49.
[28] Whitley Stokes, *RC* 12 (1891), 53.
[29] Flower, *Catalogue*, II, 319.
[30] M. A. O'Brien, 'Varia. 5. Second Battle of Moytura § 132,' *Ériu* 12 (1938), 239-240.
Murphy, 'Notes on Cath Maige Tuired,' *Éigse* 7 (1954), 195.

Thurneysen's edition have not been included in this examination because of their obscurity. Throughout this grammatical analysis, numerical references are to sections of the text, not to lines. In both the edition and the translation, Stokes's division of the text[31] into sections has been retained, and additional material has been included at the end of preceding sections.

Orthographical variations

a for i and o; ai for a and u; ao for a and ó; au for a, á, o, and ai.

bh for mh.

c for g; cc for gh; ch for gh; chc for gh; ch for th.

d or dd for t; de or di for do; d (=dh) added; dh omitted; dh for gh; dh for th; dn for nn.

e for ai, i, ei, í, o; ei for e; ei(e) for é; eu for e; eou for e.

g (=gh) inserted or added; g (=gh) for dh; gg for ng.

i or ia for a; i for ui; ie for i and í) io for e, i, and í; iu for e and i.

ld or lld for ll.

mb for unlenited m; mh for bh.

nd for nn.

o for a, á, and e; ó for úi; oa for a; óa or oe for ó; oi for a or ai; ou for a, o, u, and ui.

p or ph for bh; p for b and f.

q for c.

t or th for dh.

u for -a, á, and ai; ua for a and ae; ua also for fo; uh for bh and f; - ui for -a and -i; uo for o, u, and ua.

ss is often used for s. Even in the abbreviation s̄, for -(a)cht, ss may be used. The n-stroke marking the abbreviation may appear over either of the two letters, but is usually placed over the second s. Both usages appear, for example, in § 133, with the first s marked in *fulucht*, (*fuluš s*), the second s in *draigechtae* (*draigessae*). Throughout the edition, the doubling of s in the abbreviation s̄, for -(a)cht, is not noted.

Archaic (or apparently archaic) features of the language:

(a) Pretonic *to-* in compound verbs (>*do-* in O.Ir.): *tolluid* 31, *togai* 32, *tos-árluid* 35, *tobert* 40, *totáed* 136, *tofoslaicc* 162.

---

[31] Stokes, *RC* 12, 53-56.

(b) Pretonic *di-* (>*do-* in O.Ir.):
dius-riubart 45; various forms of *do·gní,* compounded with *di-,* represented by *de* rather than *do*: *degníth* 86, *degníther* 89, *degéno* 97, *degén-sai* 115, *dugén-sa* 119, and *derónsud* (if reflecting an early form, to be taken as a partially-remodelled *di·rigénsat* 3 pl. perf. pret.); *derécacha* 135.

(c) Final *-th* (later *-d*):
teglomath 32; *Airmeth* 35; *anuth* 40; *druíth* n.pl. 63, 133 (MS, *druit*); *inoth, indoth,* 97, 152, 153; *cnáimreth* 99; *macraith* 164.

(d) *ó* for *úa*
slóg 43, 51, perhaps influencing *forin slóug* 93; *slógad* 51. (But see note to 51).

Forms and constructions consistent with the usage of the Old Irish glosses:

(a) The omission of the *-a-* glide before final *-e* and *-i* (*Thurn. Gramm.* § 98) occurs in several forms of *cethrae,* iä f., 31, 32, 165; *córi* 35; *lube* (a.pl.) 35.

(b) Retention of final *-ae* and *-ai.*
The change to *-a* occurs sometimes in Ml., more frequently in Sg., *Thurn. Gramm.* § 99. There is a strong scribal tendency to write *-ae* and *-ai* for original *-a,* so the value of those forms that appear to preserve old *-ae, -ai* endings is particularly hard to assess. Some possible early forms are *hadphai* (d.s.) 22, various forms of the proper name *Dagdae* 24, 26, 29, passim; *anachtae* 30; *a altai* (g.pl., for *-ae*) 35; *turui* 39; *decomlai* 42; *gobhae* 58, 97; *Rosernatai* (=*-ae*) 121.

(c) The absence of an *i*-glide at the end of a stressed syllable ending with a vowel and preceding a syllable beginning with a palatal consonant is a feature of the Old Irish glosses, where the glide is sometimes inserted, sometimes omitted, *Thurn. Gramm.* § 66. The omission is not common in the present text.
Examples include: *clodib* 16, *tene* 39, various forms of *uile* (*ule*) 67, 68, and passim.; *core* 89; *ullend* 93; *céli* 129; *tréde* 160. *Fomo(i)re,* in various plural cases, is usually written without the glide.

(d) Final unstressed vowels and therefore many declensional endings are confused, although there is a tendency for back vowels or vowel combinations beginning with them to alternate with each other, while front vowels or vowel combinations beginning with them are similarly confused.

(e) *dochom,* in O.Ir. nasalizes the initial of a following stressed syllable, *Thurn. Gramm..* § 239.4, Mid Ir. usually omits the nasalization. *doqum n-Érenn,* 51 (also 52).

ol, or, al, ar, for:

(f) A variety of forms appear in the text: *ol, al, or, ar, for, bar*. Of the roughly 100 examples, there are 38 that may be assigned to *or/ar/bar/for*; the rest are variants of *ol*. The distribution of the forms suggests that the source materials used primarily *ol*, and that the alternatives are largely scribal, since most of the *or/ar* forms cluster in extended passages of dialogue, which begin with a few interchanges using *ol*, then introduce variants of *or*. See in particular the sequences of forms in 93, and in the question and answer sequence of 97-119.

(g) A preposition followed by an anaphoric pronoun *suidiu* (*sodain*) where later the conjugated preposition and *-sium*, *-sin* became common (*Thurn. Gramm.*, § 480). Examples are *di suide* 26, *íar sudiu* 68, *im sodain* 92, *ó ssoide* 124, *le suide* 133, *di suidhiu* 147.

(h) Neuter.
The neuter article, neuter nouns (as indicated by nom. sg. nasalization), neuter dual with *dá n-*, O.Ir. neuter plural forms, and neuter pronouns all occur, although some originally neuter nouns have become masculine or feminine. The apparent uses of the neuter article include *a ngen* (or *an* for *in*?) 8, *a n-ainm* 23, *a n-arthrach* (acc.) 23, *a ndún* (acc.) 24, *a n-inchind* (acc.) 34, *a n-es n-aircit* (acc.) 42, *a ndírim* (acc.) 53, *a toichell* (acc.) (or 3 pl. poss.?) 69, *a llá* (acc.) 87, *a llátrach* (n.s.) (or 3 pl. poss.?) 93, *a llíon* (n.s.) 147, *a flettech* (acc.) 163, *a trédhi* (acc.) 164. Nasalization after nom. sg. neuter nouns is shown in *ess n-argait* 16, *delc n-óir* 16, *Dún mBrese* 24, *Loch n-Orbsen* 79, *Loch n-Echach* 79, *imforcraid n-anmo* 93, *ainm n-aild* 126, *tossach n-aipchi* 157. The dual is retained in *Dá n-ainm*, 163. An early n.pl. appears in *a-n-anmonn-sidei*, 53. Cf. *hanmanna* 143, 144, 145; *cinno* 132 also has a n. pl.nom. form. Neuter pronouns include *sodain* 92, *alaill* 122, and *n-aill* 155. Note also the agreement (or lack of it) in *ba hed an mir* 26, *as eth látrach* 93, *ní hedh mh'ainm* (2 ex.) 93, *Iss ed adn so aun líon* 147.

(i) Article: (According to Ó'Máille, *Annals*, the nom. pl. masc. *in* occurs for the last time at 999; *na* appears in 985.)
The usual form of the masculine and feminine nominative singular article is *an*. Both *in* and *na* appear in masculine nominative plural forms. Examples of the earlier plural and dual form (sometimes represented by *an*) include *an coin* 43, *i[n]d slúaig* 73, *an Fomore* 85, *iond óicc* 113, *ant slúaigh* 164; *in dá slúag-so* 94. The O. Ir. form *inna* (gen. sg. f., nom. pl. f., and n. acc. and gen. pl. of all genders) appears usually as *na*; exceptions include *ina dánu-sae* 67, *Lige ina lánomhnou* 84. According to Ó'Máille, *Annals*, the *-ib* dative pl. of the article survives until 871, but has fallen by 917. It is retained in *denaib loggaib* 9,

denaib gaíb 131, *denaib cloidbiuh* 131; it has been lost in examples appearing in 7, 38, 73, 122, and 123.

(j) Declension of adjectives.
In general, the usage is as in Old Irish, requiring agreement in number, gender, and case. For discussion of the examples from *2MT*, see Dillon, 'Nominal Predicates,' *ZCP* 16 (1927), 322 ff. In the following examples from the present text, concord in either gender or number has been lost: *ní bot scíthae* 80, *cumbat minai a cnámhae* 94, *Bati[r] slán a n-athgoíte* 123, and *Bid sírblechtach báe Érenn* 150.

(k) Comparison of adjectives.
The usage is essentially that of Old Irish, obscured slightly by orthographical changes, and with a few examples of the use of comparative forms for superlative that was already well established by the *Félire* (*Thurn. Gramm.*, § 366.3). Comparative: *mesai* 26; *móo* 32; *mó* 51; *móu* 93; *lúaithe* (=*lúaithiu*) 43; *ániu* 123; *sírie* (O.Ir. *sía*) 129 (cf. *BDD²* 1096); *feurr* 149; *luga* 159. Comparative for superlative: *ferr* 16; *socruidie* (for *socruidiu*) 43.
Superlative: *dech* 26, 27, 29; *sruitium* 29.
Equative: *méidithir* 92.
(Regarding the form *móu*, found also in Ml. 35^c31, 114^b2, Thurneysen notes that the final *-u* is there 'freshly added,' § 375). Regarding the positive form *már* (becoming *mór*, with early examples of the change found in Wb.), the most frequent form in the present text is *már* (12, 16, 2 exx. in 26, 72, 79, 147) with *móar* at 36, and *mór* in 43, 129 (rhet.), 130, 131.

(l) Infixed pronouns.
Infixed pronouns are numerous and generally reflect Old Irish usage, with the distinctions maintained among classes A, B, and C (*Thurn. Gramm.*, §§ 411-414). Exceptions include *Roborbiaa*, with Mid. Ir. 2 pl. infix, 40. There is also a group of examples with meaningless *-s-* (or *nos-*) added to passive verbs or to prototonic forms replacing deuterotonic ones: *nostaireclamat-side* 50; *nos-lintar, nos-combruithiter, nos-dórtiter* 89; *nos-tic* 93; *nís-tessaircc* 158. Another group of later infixed forms, some meaningless, are dental (see Strachan, 'Infixed Pronoun in Middle Irish,' *Ériu* 1 (1904), 171-173 for examples from this text): *níd-fríth* 44, *Níd-tallas* 45; *not-gabad* (where a plural is expected) 79. There are a few verbs with *-n-* where the infixed form seems to have no significance: *don-gníth* 24, 32; *nín-géptis* 133.

(m) Suffixed pronouns.
These are to be found in early Old Irish. See Liam Breathnach, 'The Suffixed Pronouns in Early Irish,' *Celtica* 12 (1977), 75-107, and his conclusion that they are frequent up to the mid 8th

cent., but by the early 9th cent., *no* with an infixed pronoun is predominant.

maite 10	*maidid* 3 sg. pr. ind. + *i* m. suff. pron.
faithius 50	*foidid* 3 sg. pr. ind. + *-us*, 3 pl. suff. pron.
	(Occasionally m., *Thurn. Gramm.* § 429).
slaithe 93	3 sg. pr. ind. + *i*, m. suff. pron.
lingthe 93	3 sg. pr. ind. + *i*, m. suff. pron.

(n) Stressed forms of personal pronouns.
In form and usage these conform in general to Old Irish practice. The 3 pl. form *é* is found along with *iat*, which replaces it 'very soon after the O. Ir. period,' *Dict. E* 5.58. The replacement of *sí* by *í* also occurs occasionally. An example of retained *é* occurs at 90 (Cf. 7, 9, 79, 93, 128); *sí* at 39, 74, 125, 163. The later form *(h)i* appears at 8, 11, 84, 124. (Lenition after this f. form is not shown in MS.)
Independent stressed personal pronouns do not appear as objects of verbs in O.Ir.; a few are found in *2MT*: *rophen dei hí* 11, *Agoillis an Dagdae hí* 84, *doslais tara tóin é* 93, *glanais hé* 162. There are also a few examples of independent stressed personal pronouns used as subject: 9, 44, 68, 69, 71, 79, 81, all undoubtedly late additions.

(o) Proleptic use of the possessive pronoun anticipating a following definite genitive, common in O. Ir. (*Thurn. Gramm.*, § 442). There are not many examples of this usage: *a sechtmad athseoltai ina mnáa* 23, *a mírionn an cáinte* 26; *a ainm an baile* 84. Cf. *dia deirc Baloir* 135.

(p) Use of the double article.
imon Samain an catha 84; *an dicetail na cethri lége* 123.

(q) Use of the dative without a preposition:
Bres a óenar 44; *a óenor* 68; *in lín-sin* 76; *a hóenor* 93; *leth for leth* 131; *comtuitim* 138; *a triur* 164. Dillon, 'Nominal Predicates,' *ZCP 17* (1928), 313, collects most of the above and adds *am áonur,* 81, based on an emendation (*amaon* MS.).

(r) Distinction between dative and accusative.
In general, usage seems to be that of Old Irish, although original case distinctions are often difficult to determine, being obscured by the text's orthography. The clearest evidence for dative and accusative usage is with prepositions with plural objects. *Fri,* followed by the accusative in Old Irish, is followed by the dative plural in only a few instances: *fri Fomorib* 8, *fri Loscondoib* 84, *fria a ndánoib* 120. In general *fri* (appearing at least 48 times in the text) seems to be followed by the accusative. *La,* another preposition taking the accusative in Old Irish, shows no dative plural objects at all.

(s) Forms of conjugated prepositions.
The general usage is that of Old Irish. Some exceptions follow.

a: *estib* 3 pl., earlier *essib* (Wb 12ª10); *esde* 3 sg. f. Cf. *esti PH* 197, *eisti BDD*²1405. The earlier form was *eissi, essi, esse*, *Thurn. Gramm.*, § 436.

de, di: *de* is the usual 3 sg. m. n. (*dae*, 29). Cf. Ml. 44b l; (*dei* in 5, 11, 93). *dib* is the usual 3 pl. form, with *diib* in 16, 42 (*diob(h)* in 43, 127, 132). (*dib* does not appear in Wb., but does occur in Ml.; *diib* is the earlier form.)

do: The 2 sg. forms are *deit* and *det*, once *did*. According to Thurneysen § 435, *duit* is the most common form in Wb. and Sg., with *dait* in Ml.; alongside these, Wb. and Ml. have *deit*, Wb. and Sg. *dit*. Cf. *dét-so*, Wb. 6ᶜ7.
The 3 sg. m. form *dóu* alternates with *dó*. The form *dóu* Thurneysen suggests may be the form from which *dó* developed, § 452; in the present text, it appears in 25, (as *dóo* in 28), 29, 42, 44 (2 exx.), 89 (2 exx.), 93. *dó*, on the other hand, occurs at 14, 21, 23, 24, 26, 36, 39, 42, 75, 89 (2 exx.), 93, 121, 135, 165.
For 3 pl., *dóib* is used almost exclusively, with a few exceptions, as *dóuib* 115.

eter: Note the Old Irish usage illustrated from this text in *Thurn. Gramm.*, § 247 (a), where a conjugated preposition with double object has the second co-ordinate member in the nominative case: *etorra ⁊ Fir Bolc*. 10.

fo: The 3 sg. fem. form is *fuithi* 133. Cf. *foithi Trip.* 8.10 (contrasted with the earlier *foé, Im. Br.*, § 6).

for: 3 sg. m.n. *fair* 89, 92; otherwise *foair* (with *-oa-* presumably a later scribal treatment of *-a-*), 11, 33, 39, 92, 93. The 3 sg. m.n. dative *for* does not occur.

fri: *frie* 3 sg. fem. 17, an early form, contrasts with the later *fria* 4, *ria* 19. *friu* 3 pl. 40, 43, 113 contrasts with the later *fria* 14.

iar: *ier*, found as an early spelling of the preposition, appears in certain sections of the present text. Both the preposition itself and the conjugated form *iarum* are common throughout the text, appearing as *ier* and *ierum* in 86-141, 163-4 (with a single *iarum* intervening at 93). This may represent one scribe's practice; it is noteworthy that the preposition *fri* appears as *frie* in 93-104 (while *fria* is often used for *fri* in earlier sections). The later form *iarma* does not occur, although the abbreviation *iaῤ* may well have signified *iarma* to later copyists).

la: Most conjugated forms correspond to Old Irish usage, although the 2 sg. forms are unusual (*laut* 17, *luat* 49, *luet* 93). The early form *leu* occurs twice in 44 (otherwise *léo* MS.). In the 1 pl., later orthography appears in *lionn* 61, 63 (identified as *'lochdach'*, IGT).

ó: Later forms appear in the 1 sg. form *úam-sa*, (Old Irish *úaim*) 97, and 3 sg. m. *úatha* 36 (Cf. *TBC* 2251, *PH* 841, 908).

The standard Old and Middle Irish form *úad(h)* 3 sg. m.
(n.) appears elsewhere in the text: 6, 24, 85, 93. In other
persons and numbers, usage represents that of Old Irish.

oc: The accusative appears for the dative pl. at 43, *ocu*. Cf.
LU 8874 which also occurs alongside dative forms.

re,ri: The 3 pl. form *rempuo* 43, representing early Middle Irish
rempu, replaces O. Ir. *remib*. For 3 sg. forms see 42, note.

(t)   Deponent.
The deponent verbs that appear in the text for the most part
retain deponent forms, although *ad·gladathar* is sometimes
modernized (*agoillis* 84, *Ruaicill, rus-aicill* 120), and
nemthigidir, (MS. *fora nemithir*) 164 is passive and apparently
intended as non-deponent. Retained deponent forms (not
including verbs with only partial deponent flexion in Old Irish)
include:
nát arthraigestar 16, *nát fetar* 20, *deménair-side* 32,
rotonigestar 33, *imma-cesnaidther* 52, *ducorustar, docorustar*
72 (2 exx.), *imma-n-árladair* 75, *imus-n-agallatar* 77, *nos-
égnither* 93, *arfolmotar* 94, *Tothloigestar* 124, *ní [f]edar* 146,
cona-rofhograid-setor 163.

(u)   Relative sentences where the antecedent would logically be in the
genitive. This usage occurs in *frisintí an bidh i lláimh* 4 (See
note); *duine ba ferr delph* 16.

(v)   Lenition of object of verb, occurring in Ml. and Sg., although not
in Wb. except where object is *cach*, does not appear at all in this
text.

(w)   Lenition of adverbial expressions, for the most part conjugated
prepositions, begins in the later Old Irish glosses. In this text it is
not very frequent. The few exx. include *chenu* 61, *cheno* 63,
chena 148 (contrasted with unlenited forms 57, 58, 59, 60, 62,
65, 66); *thrá* 70.

(x)   Independent construction after *as·beir*. In Wb. *as·beir*. In Wb.
as·beir is followed by independent construction, and this usage is
the more common in Ml., although Ml. does include some
examples of dependent construction. In the present text,
independent construction is much more common than dependent,
although some exx. are ambiguous. Examples of dependent
construction after *as·beir* include:
aspert . . . ná tésied 19; *co n-epérthar as* 21; *atbert . . . nach n-
ícfad* 34; *Atbertatar . . . ara n-indiset* 54; *atbert . . . go rocurit*
69; *Atbert . . . ari n-imreth* 93; *Asbert . . . ara n-ainmniged* 142.

(y)   Other Old Irish forms and usages.

Nouns
The old dative form *a n-Éri* 126 is last used in the *Annals of
Ulster* at 907, according to Ó Máille § 13. The acc. sg. form

Temair 72 is also early, see Ó Máille, *Annals,* § 164, p. 151: the guttural declension appears at 914.

Verbs
The character of the verbal system generally reflects the use of Old Irish materials, despite the presence of many Middle Irish forms, and the influence of later orthography. Some of the more noteworthy Old Irish verb forms include preterites (other than the s- preterite) and futures (apart from the f- future). Preterites: *Cúich* 18; *Deménair* 32; *decechlaid* 35; *Focres* 43; *co n-éicid* 68; *síasur* 71; *sephainn* 73; *atréracht* 74; *Imma-n-árladair* 75; *gonánacair* 78; *rot-lil* 81; *docachnotar* 86; *geogoin* 125; *roclos* 125; *co sescaind* 135; *romebhaid* (= *-memaid*) 138; *ara nenaisc* 163; *co ndegart* 163; *rogeltatar* 165; *forcóemnochair* 166; *rocachain* 167.

Futures: *Didigestar* 19; *dobiter* 21; *co n-epili* (= *-epéla*) 29; *dogegadh* 32; *méraidh* 35; *focichred* 78; *Aross·cich(er)sit* 79; *arnenas* 80; *memais* 97; *géntor* 99; *An [n-]anustar* 151; *bibsiutt* 155; *cocon ebrad* 160; *co chobibsad* 160.

Use of *nem-* compounded with verbal noun where later language would use *cen* + verbal noun: *nemét* 18; *nemlégodh* 95; *nemfhogbáil* 111.

Adjectives: Numerals
The usage is generally that of Old Irish. Exceptions to Old Irish usage include: *Dí*, 'two,' f., appears for *dá* in *Día gelgáe, dí semcradn* 16; *a dí ullend* (f., but gen., so *dá* is to be expected); *a dí mac* 123 (almost certainly simply scribal inadvertence). *Dá* replaces *dí* in *dá broicc* 93; *dá bantúathaid* 116 may represent maintenance of the original gender of the second element of the compound (m.?) (*Thurn. Gramm.*, § 254, 267).

Masculine and feminine forms of 'three,' some twenty-odd exx., are distinguished with the exception of the description of the Dagda's gold pieces (*trí* with *scildei* 28, *scitle* 29. Cf. *téorai scillice* 29, *téorai scilte* 30); and *fri téora snasau* 122 treats the noun as f. rather than m.

'Four,' *ce(i)t(h)ri*, nominative, appears for *cethir* (n., m.) or *cethéoir* (f.) in 2 (f.), 7 (m.); *cetri* for d. pl. f. in 7 is another departure from Old Irish usage.

The use of perfective for simple preterite forms:
Many sections of the tale are almost entirely free from perfective forms used where a preterite would be expected. These include 15-24, Bres's conception; 26-32 The Dagda's labour for Bres; 36-37 Ogma's labour, Bres's conditional sovereignty and flight; 75-83 Lug's first review of Túatha Dé Danann contributions to battle; 84-87 The Dagda's meeting with the Morrígan; 97-119 Lug's second muster; 149-160 Bres's ransoming of his life; 163-165 recovery of the Dagda's harp and cattle tribute; 166-167 The Morrígan's proclamation of victory.

Other sections of the tale are not necessarily later in origin, although some are almost certainly added from later sources; they do however, at least represent later rewording of earlier material.

Middle Irish forms and constructions:
(a) The verbal system. Middle Irish characteristics include the frequent replacement of deuterotonic forms by prototonic, often representing scribal modernization; the use of perfective forms where Old Irish would use the simple preterite; verbal forms that are based on Mid. Ir. stems or represent the spread of the s-preterite at the expense of other formations; and the occasional replacement of *ro* by *do*. Some examples of various alterations in the verbal system are given below.

Replacement of other preterite formations by the s-preterite: *ocar'foglaindsit* 7; *Gnísit* 8; *robenad, rophen* 11; *ronaisceatar* 25; *rocladh* 25; *Gádhuis* 40; *rofíoarfaig* 56; *Agoillis* 84; *rus-meil* 124; *roairich* 125; *roindis* 162.

Replacement of *ro* by *do*: *dofácbhud* 42; *dofágaibsid* 129.

New stems (various tenses): *tidnaic* (to *do·indnaig*) 29; *nos·taireclamat* (to *do·ecmalla*) 50; *rofíoarfaig* (O.Ir. *íarmi·foich*, Mid. Ir. *íarfaigid*) 56; *imcomaircidh* (O.Ir. *imm·comairc*) 79; *Agoillis* (*ad·gladathar*, later as simple verb *acallaid*) 84; *rag-* for *reg-* future of *téit* 93; *gonar'fétad* (O.Ir. *ad·cota*, later *fétaid*) 113; *roairich* (*ar·icc*, later as simple verb *airicid*) 125; *derónsud* (*do·gní*, O.Ir. *do·rigénsat*, 3 pl. perf. pret.) 127; *dodecaid* (*do·téit*, O.Ir. *dochuid*, 3 sg. perf. pret.) 133; *ro·indis* (*in(d)·fét*, later *indisid;* O.Ir. 3 sg. perf. pret. *in·cúaid*) 162.

Future forms: *pérut* (1 sg.) 80; *docachnopad* (*do·cáin*, O.Ir. *do·cechnad*, 3 sg. sec. fut.) 93; *dolbfamid-ne* (1 pl.) 117; *dingébat-sa* (1 sg.) 140.

Mid. Ir. passives: *robenad* 11; *níd-tallas* 45; *rohairged* 69; *roslech[t]ait* 138.

(b) The noun. Declension is often obscured by orthography, and there are many forms that represent Mid. Ir. usage such as the loss of neuter gender, and shifts from one declensional class to another. Examples of the loss of neuter gender, indicated by the loss of the neuter article, include *an ferodn* 9, *an ríge* 14, *an muir* 16, *an mír* 26, *an muir* 37, *an scél* 44, *in tír* 47, *inn nem* 133. Regarding declensional change, note the variation in the treatment of *Temair* and *Ériu* (Index of Places).

(c) The pronoun. There are a few examples of independent subject and object pronouns, all probably later intrusions. For examples, and for illustrations of the changing usage of infixed and suffixed pronouns, see §§ 1, m, and n, above.

(d) The adjective. A few examples that do not follow O.Ir. practice are noted in § j, above.

Edition and Translation

The following editorial conventions have been used in the preparation of this edition:

(1) All proper names are capitalized. In the MS. capitalization occurs only when the name begins a sentence.

(2) Where necessary, full stops are supplied before capitals which begin sentences, and capitals after full stops. The sentence division of the MS. is usually clear, but often uses only one indicator.

(3) Commas, colons, and semi-colons are supplied for clarity, as sparingly as possible. Dialogue is punctuated and capitalized according to ordinary English usage. Occasionally a full stop and capitalization have been introduced into a passage that is undivided in the MS.

(4) Ligatures are printed as separate letters.

(5) Single letter strokes are expanded silently (n, m, h). Where the m-stroke represents a syllable, the whole syllable is italicized; but where *r* is indicated by the following letter superscript, only the *r* is italicized. *n'* is occasionally used for *nn*, and is expanded silently.

Editorial [*h*] has been added to final *c* (for *ch*) and *t* (for *th*) where these were unambiguous (verbal forms excluded). In the interior of words, editorial [*h*] appears only in proper names.

(6) The symbols for *con, ur, us,* and *ra,* are italicized, as are suspended *er, en ar, or* (and their palatalized forms). Where *con, ur, us* represent inflected forms, the correct value is given to the vowel.

(7) The symbol 7 (Latin *et,* Irish *ocus*—'and') is often left without expansion. *Dn* serves as an abbreviation for *da*no, and is so expanded rather than as *dn*o).

(8) The mark of length is supplied where necessary. In the case of diphthongs, the usage is that of Thurneysen in *A Grammar of Old Irish* § 26. Where the mark of length is given in the MS. but misses its mark, it has been silently moved to its proper place.

(9) Enclitic pronouns and demonstratives are separated from nouns and verbs by a dash. Nasalization before vowels is separated from them by a dash; the same mark is used to separate infixed pronouns from verbs.

(10) In general, proclitics are separated from verbs (other than the copula), except for *no* and *ro* (without infixed pronouns), and for the first element of compound verbs.

(11) Where a word begins with two capital letters in the MS., only the first is retained.

(12) Where the correct expansion of a contraction is in doubt, the contraction is left unexpanded. An n-stroke in the MS. is represented by -, an m-stroke by —.

(13) The passages of obscure dialogue edited by Thurneysen present many problems to the editor and translator. In the edition of

these passages, even those partially translated, marks of length have not been supplied although the identity of a given word may seem clear; the usage of the MS. alone has been followed. These passages are therefore very close to Thurneysen's edition in *ZCP* 12 (1918), although a few more expansions have been interpreted; capitalization and punctuation have been introduced; and an enlarged photographic print of the MS. has suggested a few more marks of length than were noted by Thurneysen. Omissions in the translation are indicated by . . . (where less than a sentence has been omitted) and by . . . . (where a sentence or more than a sentence has been left out).

(14) The practice of concluding a poetic passage with one or more words that echo the first words of the passage (*dúnad*) occurs in some of the passages edited by Thurneysen. The repeated word or words are sometimes followed by their initial letters, separated by periods. This abbreviation, which serves only to signal the end of the passage, is not expanded.

(15) In general, the punctuation of the translation is identical with that of the edition, although a few discrepancies have been tolerated in the interest of English syntax.

The translation is fairly literal, but attempts to convey the changing style of the original — which is by and large the spare, direct, and sometimes choppy narrative style of the Old Irish period, with occasional passages of a more florid Middle Irish style. The language of all but these Middle Irish passages would have seemed to its composers contemporary, perhaps slightly formal, but not elevated or archaic. In order to reproduce these qualities, the translation generally avoids the subjunctive, which is moribund in English. Other changes sometimes occur: passive forms become active, because the English passive is weaker than the Irish; emphatic constructions with the copula are suppressed as too emphatic for regular use in English; and the heavy use of adverbial conjunctions, which in English seem unnecessarily repetitive, has been thinned out. A few words, usually prepositions, have been supplied where English syntax required them. Changes other than those of the types listed above are mentioned in the notes.

I would like to thank Professor Charles W. Dunn and Professor John V. Kelleher, who have generously shared their scholarship with me over many years; Dr. Bruce D. Boling, who introduced me to Old Irish and the structure of mythology; Dr. Alan Mac an Bhaird of the Ordnance Survey of Ireland, who kindly provided expert assistance with the place name index; and Professor Pádraig Ó Riain, whose sound suggestions and careful attention to this work in its final stages have been invaluable.

Abbreviations

These are as in RIA CONTRIBB. A, with the addition of the following:

IMT:	'The First Battle of Moytura' (Fraser, *Ériu 8*).
2MT:	*Cath Maige Turedh* (Harleian MS. 5280), 'The Second Battle of Moytura'; also the edition by Stokes, *RC* 12.
$2MT^2$:	*Cath Muighe Tuireadh: The Second Battle of Magh Tuireadh* (Ó Cuív, 1945).
Annals:	*The Language of the Annals of Ulster* (Ó Máille, 1910).
ATDM:	*Altram Tige dá Medar* (Duncan, *Ériu* 11).
BDCh.:	*Bruiden Da Chocae* (Stokes, *RC* 21).
CMM:	*Cath Maige Mucrama* (O Daly, ITS L).
Contribb.:	RIA, *Contributions to a Dictionary of the Irish Language.*
CRR^1:	*Cath Ruis na Ríg for Bóinn* (Hogan, 1892).
Dict.:	RIA, *Dictionary of the Irish Language.*
IDPP:	*Irish Dialects Past and Present* (O'Rahilly, 1932).
IHKS:	*Heldensage* (Thurneysen, 1921).
Im. Dá T.:	*Immacallam in dá Thuarad,* 'The Colloquy of the Two Sages' (Stokes, *RC* 26).
Keat.:	For vol. I, references include book, section, and page numbers for text and translation.
LG:	*Lebor Gabála Érenn* (ed. Macalister, ITS XXXIV, XXXV, XXXIX, XLI, XLIV).
Motif-Index:	*Motif-Index of Early Irish Literature* (Cross, 1952).
MR^2:	*Cath Maige Ráth* (ed. Marstrander, *Ériu* 5).
TMM:	*Tochomlod mac Miledh a hEspain* (ed. Dobbs, *ÉC 2*).

63a CATH MAIGE TUR*EDH* AN SC*ÉL*-SA SÍS 7 GENEMAIN
BRES M*EIC* ELA*T*HAIN 7 A RÍGHE

1. [B]át*ar* Túathai Dé Danonn i n-indsib túasc*er*tachaib an dom*uin*, aig foglaim fesa 7 fithnas*ach*ta 7 druíd*ech*tai 7 amaid*ech*tai 7 amains*ech*ta, combtar fo*r*tilde fo*r* súthib ce*r*d ngenntli*ch*tae.

2. Ceit*ri* cat*r*achai i rrabatar og fochlaim fhesai 7 éol*ais* 7
5 díabuldán*ach*tai .i. Falias 7 Goirias, Murias 7 Findias.

3. A Falias tuc*ad* an Lía Fáil buí a Temr*aig*. Nogés*ed* fo cech ríg nogéb*ad* Érinn.

4. A Gorias tuc*ad* ant sleg boí ac Lug. Ní gebtea cath fria nó f*r*isintí an bídh i lláimh.

10 5. A Findias tuc*ad* claidiub Núadot. Ní t*ér*ná*d*h ne*ch* dei ó dobirthe asa idnt*iu*ch boduha, 7 ní gebtai f*r*is.

6. A Murias tuc*ad* coiri an Dagdai. Ní tég*ed*h dám dimd*ach* úadh.

7. Cet*ri* druíd isna cet*ri* cathr*achaib*-sin. Mórfesae baí a Fal*ias*; Es*r*as boí hi nGorias; Uiscias boí a Findias; Semias baí a Murias. It
15 íad-sin na cet*ri* filid ocar' foglaindsit Túata Dé fios 7 éol*as*.

8. Gnísit iar*um* Túadh Dé caratr*ad* f*ri* Fomorib 7 deb*er*t[1] Balar úa Néit a ing*in* .i. Ethne, de Cén m*ac* Dien Cé*ch*t. Gonad í-side ruc a ngen mbúadha .i. Lucc.

9. Tángat*ar* Túad Dé i morloinges mór d'indsaig*id* Érionn dia gab*áil*
20 ar écin fo*r* Fer*aib* Bolc. Roloisc[s]et a mbaraca fo cétóir íar torr*ach*tain c*r*íce Corcu Belgatan (.i. Co*n*maicne mara andíu éat-sen), co*n*a pe*d*h a n-aire fo*r* teich*ed* cucu. Gu *rr*olíon an déi 7 an céu tán*ic* denaib logg*aib* an ferodn 7 an áer robo co*m*focus dóib. Co*n*id as sin rogab*ad* a tí*ch*tain a nélaip cíach.

25 10. Fectha cath Muighe Tuir*ed* etorra 7 Fir Bolc. *Ocus* maite fo*r* Fer*aib* Bolc, 7 marbt*air* cét míle díib am Eoch*daig* m*ac* n-*Eir*c immon rígh.

11. Isen cath-sin d*ano* robenad a lámh de Núadad .i. Sregg m*ac* Sengaidn roph*en* dei hí. Go tarad Díen Cé*ch*t an liaigh láim airgid
30 foair co lúth cecai láma 7 Cré*d*hne in cerd ag cungn*am* fris.

---

1 MS. deb*r̄*.

THIS TALE BELOW IS THE BATTLE OF MAG TUIRED AND THE BIRTH OF BRES SON OF ELATHA AND HIS REIGN

1.   The Túatha Dé Danann were in the northern islands of the world, studying occult lore and sorcery, druidic arts and witchcraft and magical skill, until they surpassed the sages of the pagan arts.

2.   They studied occult lore and secret knowledge and diabolic arts in four cities: Falias, Gorias, Murias, and Findias.

3. From Falias was brought the Stone of Fál which was located in Tara. It used to cry out beneath every king that would take Ireland.

4. From Gorias was brought the spear which Lug had. No battle was ever sustained against it, or against the man who held it in his hand.

5. From Findias was brought the sword of Núadu. No one ever escaped from it once it was drawn from its deadly sheath, and no one could resist it.

6. From Murias was brought the Dagda's cauldron. No company ever went away from it unsatisfied.

7. There were four wizards in those four cities. Morfesa was in Falias; Esras was in Gorias; Uiscias was in Findias; Semias was in Murias. Those are the four poets from whom the Túatha Dé learned occult lore and secret knowledge.

8. The Túatha Dé then made an alliance with the Fomoire, and Balor the grandson of Nét gave his daughter Ethne to Cían the son of Dian Cécht. And she bore the glorious child, Lug.

9. The Túatha Dé came with a great fleet to Ireland to take it by force from the Fir Bolg. Upon reaching the territory of Corcu Belgatan (which is Conmaicne Mara today), they at once burned their boats so that they would not think of fleeing to them. The smoke and the mist which came from the ships filled the land and the air which was near them. For that reason it has been thought that they arrived in clouds of mist.

10. The battle of Mag Tuired was fought between them and the Fir Bolg. The Fir Bolg were defeated, and 100,000 of them were killed including the king, Eochaid mac Eirc.

11. Núadu's hand was cut off in that battle—Sreng mac Sengainn struck it from him. So with Crédne the brazier helping him, Dían Cécht the physician put on him a silver hand that moved as well as any other hand.

12. Cid Túath Déi Dononn d*ano* deroc*ra*tar go már isin cath, im Edleo m*ac* n-Allai 7 am Ernm*as*, am Fhíoach*ai*g 7 im Turild Bicreo.

13. Do ne*och immorro* térn*á* de Feraib Bolc asin cath, lot*ar* ar tech*ed* de saig*id* na Fomo*re* gor gabsad a n-Árainn 7 a nd-Íle 7 a
35 Manaidn 7 a Rachraind.

14. Bai imcosn*am* flat*h*ae fher n-Érenn it*er* Túad Dé 7 a mná, ar nirb' inríghae Núadoo íar mbéim a láime de. Adp*er*tut*ar* ba c*um*digh dóip ríge do Pres m*ac* El*ath*an, díe ngorm*ac* fesin, 7 *co*
63b sn[a]idh[m]f*ed* caratr*ad* Fomu*re* f*ri*a an ríge de tab*air*t dó-sin, ar ba rí
40 Fomore a ath*air*, ed ón Elotha m*ac* Delbáeth.

15. Is amla*id*-so íar*um* arrích*t* compert Bresi.

16. Bai di*diu* ben díib láu n-adn oc déicsin an marai 7 an tíri do tichc Máoth Scéni .i. Éri ingen Delba*ith*; go n-acui an muir fo lánféth am*al ba* clár com*r*édh. A mbuí and íar sin, *co n*-facai [ní]: d*us*-n-árfas ess n-
45 arg*ait* isin fairce. Ba már lee a méd, *acht* nát arthr*ai*gest*ar* a delp díi; 7 dob*er*t srut[h] na tuinde riam dec*um* tírei.

Co n-acqu íar*um* pa duine ba ferr delph. Mogg órbuide foir goa díb gúaill*ib*. Brat go sreth*aib* di órsnáth imbe. A léne go nd-indledhaib de órsn*áth*. Delc n-óir ara bruinde go f*or*sann*ud* de líic lóghm*air* adn.
50 Dia gelgáe airgide 7 dí semcr*adn* snas[t]ai indib de crédumae. Cóicroith óir uara muin. Clodib órduirn go féthaidib airget 7 go cichib óir.

17. Isp*er*t an fer f*ri*e, "Inn*um*-bioa-ssae[1] úar coblide laut?"
"Ní rud-dál*us* ém," ol in phen.
55 "Tic frisna dáult*a*," ol é-si*um*.

18. *Co*nse*r*nad dóib íar*um*. Cíich an pen íar*um* an tan as-n-ér*acht* an uher.
"Cid cíi?" ol é-si*um*.
"Tátham déde rocoíner," ol in bean. "Scarad*h* f*ri*ut-sa q*ui*bindes a
60 *co*mairnecm*ar*. Maccáema Túath(a) nDéa dom nem*é*t íar mo cáenghuide 7 mo ét did-siu am*al* at*om*-cota-siu."

19. "Didigest*ar* do broc din déde-si," ol séi. Tísc*ais* a ór(s)nasc n-óir dia méor medhóin 7 deb*er*t ina láim, 7 asp*er*t ria ná tésied úaide i c*re*ic iná i n-aisc*id*, *acht* de ne*och* diamb*ad* coimsie die méor sin.

1 MS. *-bíoa* or *bíóa*.

12. Now the Túatha Dé Danann lost many men in the battle, including Edleo mac Allai, and Ernmas, and Fíacha, and Tuirill Bicreo.

13. Then those of the Fir Bolg who escaped from the battle fled to the Fomoire, and they settled in Arran and in Islay and in Man and in Rathlin.

14. There was contention regarding the sovereignty of the men of Ireland between the Túatha Dé and their wives, since Núadu was not eligible for kingship after his hand had been cut off. They said that it would be appropriate for them to give the kingship to Bres the son of Elatha, to their own adopted son, and that giving him the kingship would knit the Fomorians' alliance with them, since his father Elatha mac Delbaíth was king of the Fomoire.

15. Now the conception of Bres came about in this way.

16. One day one of their women, Ériu the daughter of Delbáeth, was looking at the sea and the land from the house of Máeth Scéni; and she saw the sea as perfectly calm as if it were a level board. After that, while she was there, she saw something: a vessel of silver appeared to her on the sea. Its size seemed great to her, but its shape did not appear clearly to her; and the current of the sea carried it to the land.

Then she saw that it was a man of fairest appearance. He had golden-yellow hair down to his shoulders, and a cloak with bands of gold thread around it. His shirt had embroidery of gold thread. On his breast was a brooch of gold with the lustre of a precious stone in it. Two shining silver spears and in them two smooth riveted shafts of bronze. Five circlets of gold around his neck. A gold-hilted sword with inlayings of silver and studs of gold.

17. The man said to her, "Shall I have an hour of lovemaking with you?"

"I certainly have not made a tryst with you," she said.

"Come without the trysting!" said he.

18. Then they stretched themselves out together. The woman wept when the man got up again.

"Why are you crying?" he asked.

"I have two things that I should lament," said the woman, "separating from you, however we have met. The young men of the Túatha Dé Danann have been entreating me in vain—and you possess me as you do."

19. "Your anxiety about those two things will be removed," he said. He drew his gold ring from his middle finger and put it into her hand, and told her that she should not part with it, either by sale or by gift, except to someone whose finger it would fit.

65   20. "Is deitheden eli d*om*-sae," ol in pen. "Nát fetar cía dom-
fáinec."

21. "Níbo hainfes det andísin," ol séie. "Dit-án*ic* Elothae m*ac*
Delp*aith* rí Fomore. Bé*ra* m*ac* diar com*r*uc, 7 ní tart*ar* ainm dó *acht*
Eoch*a* Br*es* (ed ón Eoch*a* Cruth*ach*), ar cech cruth*ach* atcícher a n-
70   Ér*inn*—eter mag 7 dún 7 cuirm 7 coindeil 7 ben 7 fer 7 ech—is risin
m*ac*-sin dobit*er*, *co* n-ep*ér*th*ar* as Br*es* dó ann sin."

22. Is íar sin luidh an fer doridisi ina fr*i*theng, 7 doluid an ph*en* dia
hadphai, 7 depreth de an *com*p*er*t aird*er*c.

23. B*er*t in m*ac* íar*um*, 7 debreth dó a n-ainm atb*er*t Ela*th*a .i. Eocha
75   Pr*es*. In tan ba láun a s*ech*t*mad* athséoltai ina mnáa, buí f*or*p*ar*t
cáeictigesi fo*r*in m*ac*; 7 rofuc a n-arthrach-sin go cend a s*ech*t
mbl*í*adan, go rou*ch*t f*or*p*ar*t .xiííí. mbl*í*ad*an*.

24. Is den cosn*am*-sin boí et*er* Túaith Déu, dobr*eth* fla*ith* flaith Ér*enn* don
m*ac*-sin; 7 dob*er*t .víí. n-aidirie di tr*é*nferuib Ér*enn* (.i. a mát*rí*) fr*i*
80   hasic na fla*th*ae úad má fofertis[1] a mífholtae fesin. Dib*er*t a m*á*thair
tír dó íar sin, 7 don-gnít dún les uaran tír .i. Dún mBr*es*e. *Ocus* ba hé
an Dagdhae dogéne a ndún-sen.

25. Ó rogeb íar*um* Br*es* ríghe, ronaisceat*ar* Fomor*aig* (.i. Indech
m*ac* Déi Domnann 7 Elath*u* m*ac* Delb*aith* 7 Tethr*a*, tr*í* ríg
85   Fomor*ach*), a cíos for Ér*inn*—con*a* boí déi do clé*th*e a n-Ér*inn* fo*r*sna
béth cíos dóib. Dobr*eth*a d*an*o na tr*é*nfirae a foghn*am* dóu .i.
Oghmae fou cúalae *con*naid*h* 7 an Daghdo 'na ráthbhuide, gon*ad*h sé
rocladh ráth mBr*es*e.

26. Ba t*oir*sich d*an*o an Dagdo ocund obair, 7 atcliched daul esba
90   isin tech, C*r*idenbél a ainm, a béolae di suide asa brundie. Ba pec la
64a C*r*ichinphél a cuid fesin 7 ba[2] már cuid an Dagdae. As inn atb*er*t, "A
Dagdae, dot inch*aib* na trí mírionn bes dech dot[chuid tap*ra*ither
d*om*-sae!" Dober*edh* íar*um* an Dagdae dó cech n-oidhche. Máru
im*morro* a mírionn an cáinte .i. mét degmuce ba h*ed* an mír. Ba tr*i*an
95   im*morro* de cuid an Dagdhua na tr*í* mírenn-sen. Mesai de bl*áth* an
Dagdhae dinnísin.

1   MS. *ma fofertís*.
1   MS. *bá*.

20. "Another matter troubles me," said the woman, "that I do not know who has come to me."

21. "You will not remain ignorant of that," he said. "Elatha mac Delbaith, king of the Fomoire, has come to you. You will bear a son as a result of our meeting, and let no name be given to him but Eochu Bres (that is, Eochu the Beautiful), because every beautiful thing that is seen in Ireland—both plain and fortress, ale and candle, woman and man and horse—will be judged in relation to that boy, so that people will then say of it, 'It is a Bres.' "

22. Then the man went back again, and the woman returned to her home, and the famous conception was given to her.

23. Then she gave birth to the boy, and the name Eochu Bres was given to him as Elatha had said. A week after the woman's lying-in was completed, the boy had two weeks' growth; and he maintained that increase for seven years, until he had reached the growth of fourteen years.

24. As a result of that contention which took place among the Túatha Dé, the sovereignty of Ireland was given to that youth; and he gave seven guarantors from the warriors of Ireland (his maternal kinsmen) for his restitution of the sovereignty if his own misdeeds should give cause. Then his mother gave him land, and he had a fortress built on the land, Dún mBrese. And it was the Dagda who built that fortress.

25. But after Bres had assumed the sovereignty, three Fomorian kings (Indech mac Dé Domnann, Elatha mac Delbaith, and Tethra) imposed their tribute upon Ireland—and there was not a smoke from a house in Ireland which was not under their tribute. In addition, the warriors of Ireland were reduced to serving him: Ogma beneath a bundle of firewood and the Dagda as a rampart-builder, and he constructed the earthwork around Bres's fort.

26. Now the Dagda was unhappy at the work, and in the house he used to meet an idle blind man named Cridenbél, whose mouth grew out of his chest. Cridenbél considered his own meal small and the Dagda's large, so he said, "Dagda, for the sake of your honor let the three best bits of your serving be given to me!" and the Dagda used to give them to him every night. But the satirist's bits were large: each bit was the size of a good pig. Furthermore those three bits were a third of the Dagda's serving. The Dagda's appearance was the worse for that.

27. Láu n-ann di*diu* baí an Dagdai isin cl*ad* co n-acai an M*a*c n-Óc cuige.

"Maith sin, a Dag*dai*," or in M*a*c Óc.

100 "Amin," ol in Dag*dae*.

"Cid deghníe drochféthol?" ol *sé*.

"Táthum a damhnai," ol é-si*um*. "C*r*idenbél cáinte gaph*as* álgas dim gacae n*ó*nae imna trí mírionn as dech dim cuibrind."

28. "Tátham airlei deit," ol in M*a*c Óc. Dob*eir* láim ina bossán 7
105 gadaig t*r*i scildei óir ass 7 dob*eir* dóo.

29. "Tap*air*-si," ol sé, "na t*r*í scitle-si isna trí mírinn deog láei do C*r*idenbél. Is *ed* íar*um*[1] is sruitium bioas f*or*t més, 7 asdofe[2] ant ór ina broinn *co n*-epili de; 7 níba maith a c*er*t do Bres íar*um*.

Atbér*tar* frisin rígh, 'Romarb an Daghdae C*r*idenbél tre luib
110 éccinéol derat dóu.' Ispérae íar*um* an rí de marb*ad*. Isbér*ae*-sa f*r*is, 'Ní fíor flat*h*u deit, a rí óc Fénei, a n-udb*ere*. Ar dom-ringarta ó gabass mo uop*air*, 7 asper*ed* frim, "Tidnaic d*o*m, a Dag*dai*, na trí mírinn ata dech dot cuibrionn. Is olc mo treb*ad* an*nocht*." Docoat-sai d*ano* de sin, minam-cobradis[3] na téorai scillice [f]úar andíu. Dus-
115 radas f*orm* cuid. Doraut*us* íar*um* do C*r*idinbél, ar is *ed*h is dech bhuí ar mo bél*aib*, and ór. As dae íar*um* ind ór a C*r*idenbél, *co n*-erbailt de.' "

"Is me*n*ann," ar an rí. "Tiscaith*er* a tarr fon cáinte d*ús* in f*u*ir*estar* ind ór ann. M*a*ni f*u*ir*estar* *con* bebau-sa. Di[a] f*u*ir*estar*, im*morro*,
120 b*ieid* pethai did."

30. Íar sin tallaid a tarr fon cáinte go f*u*ir*es*ta na téorai sci*lt*e óir adna brú, 7 an*ach*tae an Dag*dae*.

31. Tolluid an Dag*dae* ina obair íar*um* arauhárach, 7 tán*i*c an M*a*c Óg cucai 7 atb*er*t-side, "As gar go rois ch'ob*air*; 7 ni cu*n*ghis fochrec
125 go tucaith*er* det cethr*i* Ér*enn*. *Ocus* togai díib dairt mongduib nduib ndénta aicen*taig* leo."

32. Is íar sin dogéniu an Dag*dae* a oup*air* go f*or*cend, 7 asb*er*t fris Bre*s* cid nogeb*ad* i llóg a sáethair. Frisg*art* an Dag*dae*, "At(g)na-sa f*or*t cethre Ér*enn*," al sé, "de teglomath a n-óenmaighin." Don-gníth
130 an rí anndísin am*al* asp*er*t, 7 togai díb an dairt asp*er*t an M*a*c Óc fris. Ba héccomhnart la Bres annísin. Deménair-s*id*e ba ní pudh móo dogegadh.

---

1 MS. includes an extra suspension stroke, curved up at both ends, between the two lines, just after *íarum* and crossing the r in *minam-cobradís* of the line above.
2 MS. gloss: *no adsuife*.
3 MS. *minam-cobradís*.

27. Then one day the Dagda was in the trench and he saw the Mac Óc coming toward him.

"Greetings to you, Dagda!" said the Mac Óc.

"And to you," said the Dagda.

"What makes you look so bad?" he asked.

"I have good cause," he said. "Every night Cridenbél the satirist demands from me the three best bits of my serving."

28. "I have advice for you," said the Mac Óc. He puts his hand into his purse, and takes from it three coins of gold, and gives them to him.

29. "Put," he said, "these three gold coins into the three bits for Cridenbél in the evening. Then these will be the best on your dish, and the gold will stick in his belly so that he will die of it; and Bres's judgement afterwards will not be right. Men will say to the king, 'The Dagda has killed Cridenbél with a deadly herb which he gave him.' Then the king will order you to be killed, and you will say to him, 'What you say, king of the warriors of the Féni, is not a prince's truth. For he kept importuning me since I began my work, saying to me, "Give me the three best bits of your serving, Dagda. My house-keeping is bad tonight." Indeed, I would have died from that, had not the three gold coins which I found today helped me. I put them into my serving. Then I gave it to Cridenbél, because the gold was the best thing that was before me. So the gold is now in Cridenbél, and he died of it.' "

"It is clear," said the king. "Let the satirist's stomach be cut out to see whether the gold will be found in it. If it is not found, you will die. If it is found, however, you will live."

30. Then they cut out the satirist's stomach to find the three gold coins in his belly, and the Dagda was saved.

31. Then the Dagda went to his work the next morning, and the Mac Óc came to him and said, "Soon you will finish your work, but do not seek payment until the cattle of Ireland are brought to you. Choose from among them the dark, black-maned, trained, spirited heifer.

32. Then the Dagda brought his work to an end, and Bres asked him what he would take as wages for his labour. The Dagda answered, "I require that you gather the cattle of Ireland in one place." The king did that as he asked, and he chose the heifer from among them as the Mac Óc had told him. That seemed foolish to Bres. He had thought that he would have chosen something more.

33. Boí dano Núadae oga uothras, 7 dobreth láim n-argait foair lioa
Dien Cécht go lúth cecha lámha indte. Nír'uo maith dano liaa mac-
135 siu*m* sen .i. le Míach. Atréracht-sim don láim 7 atbert, ault frí halt dí
7 féith frí féth; 7 icuis frí téorai nómaidhe. In cétna nómaid immus-
curid comair a táeib, 7 rotonigestar. An dómaid tánisde immas-cuirid
aro brundib. An tres nómaid dobidced gelsgothai di bocsibnibh
dubhoib ó rodubtis a ten.

140 34. Ba holc lia Dien Cécht an freapaid-sin. Duleicc claidimh a
mullach a meic go rotend a tuidn frí féoil a cinn. Ícais an gillai tre
inndeld a eladon. Atcomaic aithurrach go roteind a féoil co rrodic
cnáim. Ícais an gilde den indel cétnae. Bissis an tres bém co ránic
srebonn a inchinde. Ícais dano an gille don indell cétnae. Bisius dano
145 an cethramad mbém co nderba a n-inchind conid apu[d] Míoach 7
64b atbert Dien Cécht nach-n-icfad lieig badesin o[n]t [s]laithie-sin. [

35. Íar sin roadhnocht lia Dien Cécht Míoach 7 ásaid cóic lube
sescut ar trí cétuib tresin athnocul fo líon a altai 7 féthe. Is íar sen
scarais Airmedh a prat 7 decechlaid na lube-sin íarna téchtai. Tos-
150 árluid Dien Céc[h]t 7 conmesc-side na lube cona fesai a frep[th]ai
córi manis-tecaisceth an Spirut íar tain. Ocus atbert Dén Cécht,
"Mane pé Míoach, méraidh Airmeth."

36. Gapuis trá Bres an flaith feib do-n-i[n]d[n]acht dó. Buí fodhord
móar imbe lie máthrui la Túaith Déi, ar níbtar béoluide a scénai
155 úatha. Cid menic notístais, níptar cormaide a n-anáulai. Ní fhacutar
dano a filidh iná a mbardai nó a cáinte nó i cruitire nó i cuslendaib nó
a cornairie nó i clesomhnaig nó a n-ónmide oga n-airfide aru cinn isin
techlug. Níco lotar dano a comramai a ségonn. Ní facutar a
trénfiorai do fromadh fri eggnamh liesin rígh acht óenfer nammá .i.
160 Oghmai mac Étnae.

37. Ba hé ord frís mboí, tobairt connaid don dún. Doberidh cúoail
cech lái a hIndsib Mod. Noberiud an muir dá trien a cóile airi fó uhíth
ba hénirt cen bieadh. Ní taprad acht éntrian, 7 nofiuradh an slúaigh
ón tráth co 'role.

165 38. Ní roan trá fochnom nó éraic dona túathaib; 7 ní tapradis séoit
na túaithe a foicidh na túaithe oli.

33. Now Núadu was being treated, and Dían Cécht put a silver hand on him which had the movement of any other hand. But his son Míach did not like that. He went to the hand and said "joint to joint of it, and sinew to sinew"; and he healed it in nine days and nights. The first three days he carried it against his side, and it became covered with skin. The second three days he carried it against his chest. The third three days he would cast white wisps of black bulrushes after they had been blackened in a fire.

34. Dían Cécht did not like that cure. He hurled a sword at the crown of his son's head and cut his skin to the flesh. The young man healed it by means of his skill. He struck him again and cut his flesh until he reached the bone. The young man healed it by the same means. He struck the third blow and reached the membrane of his brain. The young man healed this too by the same means. Then he struck the fourth blow and cut out the brain, so that Míach died; and Dían Cécht said that no physician could heal him of that blow.

35. After that, Míach was buried by Dían Cécht, and three hundred and sixty-five herbs grew through the grave, corresponding to the number of his joints and sinews. Then Airmed spread her cloak and uprooted those herbs according to their properties. Dían Cécht came to her and mixed the herbs, so that no one knows their proper healing qualities unless the Holy Spirit taught them afterwards. And Dían Cécht said, "Though Míach no longer lives, Airmed shall remain."

36. At that time, Bres held the sovereignty as it had been granted to him. There was great murmuring against him among his maternal kinsmen the Túatha Dé, for their knives were not greased by him. However frequently they might come, their breaths did not smell of ale; and they did not see their poets nor their bards nor their satirists nor their harpers nor their pipers nor their horn-blowers nor their jugglers nor their fools entertaining them in the household. They did not go to contests of those pre-eminent in the arts, nor did they see their warriors proving their skill at arms before the king, except for one man, Ogma the son of Étaín.

37. This was the duty which he had, to bring firewood to the fortress. He would bring a bundle every day from the islands of Clew Bay. The sea would carry off two-thirds of his bundle because he was weak for lack of food. He used to bring back only one third, and he supplied the host from day to day.

38. But neither service nor payment from the tribes continued; and the treasures of the tribe were not being given by the act of the whole tribe.

39. Tánic an file fecht ann for óighidect do tichc Bres[e], (edh óen Corpre mac Étoíne, file Túaithe Déi). Ránic a tech mbic cumang ndub ndorchai; sech ní raibe tene nó indel nó dérghau[d] ann.
170 Tucthae téorai bargenui becai dó atéi turui for més muhic. Atráracht iarum arnauháruch, 7 nírbo pudech. Oc techt taran les dó as ind itbert: "Cen colt for crib 7 reliqua."
      ["Cen cholt for crib cernene;
      Cín gert ferbu foro-n·assad aithrinde;
175   Cen adhbai fhir ara drúbai dísoirchi;
      Cin díl daime reisse, (m)ropsen Breisse!]¹
      "Ní fil a main trá Bresi," ol sé. Ba fír ón dano. Ní boi acht meth foair-sim ónd úair-sin. Conad sí sin cétnae hóer dorónadh a n-Érinn.

40. Íar sin trá dollotar Túath Déa a hóentai do agallaim a ngairmic
180 .i. Bres mac Eladna, 7 condioachtutar cucae die n-áraighib. Tobert dóib tasiuc na flathae, 7 níbo sofoltach friu di sin. Gádhuis im anuth fris co cend .vií. mblíadnae. "Rut-bioa," ol iont oirecht cétnai a hóentai, "acht docuí forsan ráthai cétnu comge² cech toraid tairfénat frit láimh eter treb 7 tír 7 ór 7 argat, búar 7 biad 7 díolmaine do cíos
185 7 éruic conice sin."
      "Robor-biaa," ol Pres, "amail atberthei."

41. Is airi gesu dóib an dául: co tarcomlat-sim trénfiru ant sidho .i. na Fomore fri gapáil na Túath ar écin acht go tairsed les doqhloite.³ Fa scíth lais a ionnarbad asa ríge.

190 42. Decomlai iarum dechum a máthar 7 imcomairctair dí cía bo can a cinél. "Is derb lium," ol síe, 7 luidh riam docum na tilchu dia n-acu a n-es n-aircit asin muoir. Luid remhi docum na tráchta. Ocus dobert a máthair ind órnasc dofácbhud lei dó, 7 dobert-sium imma méor medónuch, 7 ba fomhais dóu. Ar nach duine dotarfert-sí eter crec 7
195 aiscid. Ní raibe díib diambad imairgide cusan laithe-sin.

---

1   The satire is supplied from the edition by Vernam Hull, ZCP 18
    (1929), 67.
2   MS. coinge or comge.
3   MS. doqhlte or doqhl-te.

39. On one occasion the poet came to the house of Bres seeking hospitality (that is, Coirpre son of Étaín, the poet of the Túatha Dé). He entered a narrow, black, dark little house; and there was neither fire nor furniture nor bedding in it. Three small cakes were brought to him on a little dish —and they were dry. The next day he arose, and he was not thankful. As he went across the yard he said,

"Without food quickly on a dish,
Without cow's milk on which a calf grows,
Without a man's habitation after darkness remains,
Without paying a company of storytellers—let that be Bres's condition."

"Bres's prosperity no longer exists," he said, and that was true. There was only blight on him from that hour; and that is the first satire that was made in Ireland.

40. Now after that the Túatha Dé went together to talk with their adopted son Bres mac Elathan, and they asked him for their sureties. He gave them restoration of the kingship, and they did not regard him as properly qualified to rule from that time on. He asked to remain for seven years. "You will have that," the same assembly agreed, "provided that the safeguarding of every payment that has been assigned to you —including house and land, gold and silver, cattle and food –is supported by the same securities, and that we have freedom of tribute and payment until then."

"You will have what you ask," Bres said.

41. This is why they were asked for the delay: that he might gather the warriors of the *síd*, the Fomoire, to take possession of the Túatha by force provided he might gain an overwhelming advantage. He was unwilling to be driven from his kingship.

42. Then he went to his mother and asked her where his family was. "I am certain about that," she said, and went onto the hill from which she had seen the silver vessel in the sea. She then went onto the shore. His mother gave him the ring which had been left with her, and he put it around his middle finger, and it fitted him. She had not given it up for anyone, either by sale or gift. Until that day, there was none of them whom it would fit.

43. Lot*ar* re*m*puo ioair*um* con ráncut*ar* tír na Fóm*ore*. Ráncut*ar* mag mór *co n*-airecht*aib* iomd*aib*. Ant oir*echt* ba socr*uid*ie díobh dollot*ar* cucau. Immafou*cht* scélu díb isin oir*echt*. Atpert*utar* ba[1] de fh*erraib* Ér*enn*. Itb*ert* fr*iu* íar*um* an rabhut*ar* coin ocu, ar iss edh ba

65a 200   bés isin aims*ir*-sin slóg téged a n-oir*echt* alale, co*m*clu*iche*[2] do tócbháuil.] "Atát coin lenn," al Pr*es*. Fochartat*ar* íar*um* an coin co*cl*u*iche*, 7 bát*ar* lúaithe coin Túath nDéa oldáte coin na Fom*ore*. Focres forrai d*a*no dús a mbí leo eich ri comrith. Atb*er*tat*ar*-sam, "Atád," 7 bát*ar* lúaithe aldát eich na Fom*ore*.

205 44. Focres forra d*a*no dús a mbí leu nech p*a*dh calmai fr*i* láim imb*er*tai cloid*ib*, níd-fr*í*th leu *acht* Bres a óenar. An tan denu argaib-si*um* a láim cosin cloid*iub*, aithgin a ath*air* and órnasc imma méor 7 fr*i*scomhairc cíoa bo cúich en láech. Friscart a m*áthai*r daru cenn 7 atb*er*t risin ríg ba m*a*c dóu hé. Atcuad dóu an sc*él* n-uili am*al*

210 derurmes*am*.

45. Fa brón*a*ch a ath*air* fris. Atb*er*t ant ath*air*, "Cisí écin det-b*er*t asin tír hi f*or*gab*ais*?"
Frisg*ar*t Br*es*, "Ním-tucc *acht* m'anfh*i*r 7 m'anúabhar fesin. Dius-riubart die sétaib 7 maíneib 7 a mbiadh fesin. Níd-tallas cíos no éric

215 díb cosindíu."

46. "Dúaig sin," al o ath*air*. "Pa ferr a rrath oldás a rríghe. Ba ferr a nguide oldás a n-éguidhi. Cid dia tutch*a*d diu?" ol a ath*air*.

47. "Dadechad[3] do cuindch*id* tr*é*nf*er* cugaib-si," ar sé. "Nogéb*ainn* in tír-sin ar éigin."

220 48. "Ni rogaba la hainbf*í*r im*morro* ma*n*i gaba la f*í*r," ol sé.

49. "C*eist* diu: caidhe mo airrle-si luat?" ol Bres.

50. Faíthi*us* íar sin c*u*san tr*é*nf*er*, co Bal*or* húa Néitt, co r*í*gh na n-Inn*s*i, 7 co hInd*e*ch mac Dé Domnand, co ríg Fomoire; 7 nos-taireclamat-s*id*e do neoch buí ó Lochl*ainn* síar do sl*úa*g doq*um* n-

225 Ér*enn*, do astad a císa 7 a rígi ar éigin foruib, gur'ba háondroichet long ó Indsib Gallad co hÉr*inn* leo.[4]

---

1   MS. *bá*.
2   MS. gloss: *no cocluiche* (or read *concluiche*).
3   MS. *Dadechus*.
4   MS. *leó*.

43. Then they went forward until they reached the land of the Fomoire. They came to a great plain with many assemblies upon it, and they reached the finest of these assemblies. Inside, people sought information from them. They answered that they were of the men of Ireland. Then they were asked whether they had dogs, for at that time it was the custom, when a group of men visited another assembly, to challenge them to a friendly contest. "We have dogs," said Bres. Then the dogs raced, and those of the Túatha Dé were faster than those of the Fomoire. Then they were asked whether they had horses to race. They answered, "We have," and they were faster than the horses of the Fomoire.

44. Then they were asked whether they had anyone who was good at sword-play, and no one was found among them except Bres. But when he lifted the hand with the sword, his father recognized the ring on his finger and asked who the warrior was. His mother answered on his behalf and told the king that Bres was his son. She related to him the whole story as we have recounted it.

45. His father was sad about him, and asked, "What force brought you out of the land you ruled?"
    Bres answered, "Nothing brought me except my own injustice and arrogance. I deprived them of their valuables and possessions and their own food. Neither tribute nor payment was ever taken from them until now."

46. "That is bad," said his father. "Better their prosperity than their kingship. Better their requests than their curses. Why then have you come?" asked his father.

47. "I have come to ask you for warriors," he said. "I intend to take that land by force."

48. "You ought not to gain it by injustice if you do not gain it by justice," he said.

49. "I have a question then: what advice do you have for me?" said Bres.

50. After that he sent him to the champion Balor, grandson of Nét, the king of the Hebrides, and to Indech mac Dé Domnann, the king of the Fomoire; and these gathered all the forces from Lochlainn westwards to Ireland, to impose their tribute and their rule upon them by force, and they made a single bridge of ships from the Hebrides to Ireland.

51. Ní tánic doqum n-Érenn drem bud mó gráin nó adhúath indá in slóg-sin na Fomoiridhi. Ba combág ogond fir o Sgiathia Lochlaindi 7 a hInnsib Gall immon slógad-sin.

230   52. Imtúsa immorro Túaithi Dé is ed imma cesnaidther sund.

53. Buí Núadhae doridesi tar éis Brese a ríge for Túaith Déu. Buí mórfleg ocu-side di Túaith Déi a Temraig a n-inbaid-sin. Boí dano oruli ógláech og saighid de Temraid, Samhildánach a ainm-side. Bótar dorrsaidi for Temraig a n-inbuid-sin, Gamal mac Figail 7
235   Camald mac Ríaghaild a n-anmonn-sidei. A mboí-side and, adcí a ndírim n-anetarcnaidh na docum. Ógláech cóem cruthach co n-imscigg ríog a n-airenuch na buidne-sin.

54. Atbertatar risin dorrsaid ara n-indiset a Temruich a tíachtai. Atbert in dorsaid, "Cía fil and?"

240   55. "Fil sunn Luch Lonnandsclech mac Cíein meic Dien Cécht 7 Ethne ingine Baloir. Dalta siden Taill[ti]ne ingine Magmóir rí Espáine 7 Echtach Gairuh meic Dúach.

56. Rofíoarfaig ion dorsaid do tSamhilldánuch, "Cía dán frisa ng[n]éie?" al séi, "ar ní téid nech cin dán i Temruid."

245   57. "Déne mo athcomarc," ol sé. "Am sáer."
        Friscort an dorsaid, "Nít-regaim i leas. Atá sáer lenn cenu .i. Luchtai mac Lúachadhae."

58. Atpert-sum, "Atum-athcomairc a dorrsoid: am gobhae."
        Frisgart ion dorsaid dóu, "Atá gobae liond cenai .i. Colum
250   Cúaolléinech téorae núagrés."

59. Atpert-som, "Atom-athcomairc: am trénfer."
        Friscart in dorsaid, "Níd-regoim a les. Atá trênfer lend cenu .i. Oghmae mac Ethlend."

60. Atbert-sum diridesi. "Atom-athcomairc," ar sé. "Am crutiri."
65b 255   "Nít-regaim] a les. Atá crutiri lenn cenai .i. Auhcán mac Bicelmois, ara-n-utgatar fir trí ndéa i sídoib."

61. Atpert-sum, "Atom-athcomairc: am níadh."
        Friscart an dorrsoidh, "Nít-regam e les. Atá níad lionn chenu .i. Bresal Echarlam mac Echdach Báethláim."

51. No host ever came to Ireland which was more terrifying or dreadful than that host of the Fomoire. There was rivalry between the men from Scythia of Lochlainn and the men out of the Hebrides concerning that expedition.

52. As for the Túatha Dé, however, that is discussed here.

53. After Bres, Núadu was once more in the kingship over the Túatha Dé; and at that time he held a great feast for the Túatha Dé in Tara. Now there was a certain warrior whose name was Samildánach on his way to Tara. At that time there were doorkeepers at Tara named Gamal mac Figail and Camall mac Ríagail. While the latter was on duty, he saw the strange company coming toward him. A handsome, well-built young warrior with a king's diadem was at the front of the band.

54. They told the doorkeeper to announce their arrival in Tara. The doorkeeper asked, "Who is there?"

55. "Lug Lonnansclech is here, the son of Cían son of Dian Cécht and of Ethne daughter of Balor. He is the foster son of Tailtiu the daughter of Magmór, the king of Spain, and of Eochaid Garb mac Dúach."

56. The doorkeeper then asked of Samildánach, "What art do you practice? For no one without an art enters Tara."

57. "Question me," he said. "I am a builder."
   The doorkeeper answered, "We do not need you. We have a builder already, Luchta mac Lúachada."

58. He said, "Question me, doorkeeper: I am a smith."
   The doorkeeper answered him, "We have a smith already, Colum Cúaléinech of the three new techniques."

59. He said, "Question me: I am a champion."
   The doorkeeper answered, "We do not need you. We have a champion already, Ogma mac Ethlend."

60. He said again, "Question me." "I am a harper," he said.
   "We do not need you. We have a harper already, Abcán mac Bicelmois, whom the men of the three gods chose in the síd-mounds."

61. He said, "Question me: I am a warrior."
   The doorkeeper answered, "We do not need you. We have a warrior already, Bresal Etarlam mac Echdach Báethláim."

260 62. Atbert-sum iarum, "Adum-athcomairc, a dorsaid. Am file 7 am senchaid."
"Nid-regam i les. Atá file 7 senchaid cenai lenn .i. Én mac Ethomain."

63. Atbert-sum, "Atom-athcomairc," ol sé, "Im corrguinech."
265 "Nit-recom e les. Atáut corrguinidh lionn cheno. At imdou ar ndruíth 7 ar lucht cumhachtai."

64. Atbert-som, "Atom-athcomairc. Am liaich."
"Nit-regam a les. Atá Dien Cécht do liaigh lenn."

65. "Atom-athcomairc," al sé. "Am deogbore."
270 "Nit-regom a les. Atá deogbaire linn cenau .i. Delt 7 Drúcht 7 Daithe, Taei 7 Talom 7 Trog, Gléi 7 Glan 7 Glési."

66. Atbert, "Atom-athcomairc: am cert maith."
"Nit-regom e les. Atá cert lind cenu .i. Crédne Cerd."

67. Atbert-som aitherrach, "Abair frisind rig," al sé, "an fil les
275 óeinfer codo-gabai ina dánu-sae ule 7 má atá les ní tocus-sa i Temraig."

68. Luid in dorsaid isin rígtech iar sudiu co n-éicid dond ríogh ulei. "Tánic ócláech io ndoras lis," al sé, "Samilldánach a ainm; 7 na huili dáno arufognot det muntir-si, atát les ule a óenor, conedh fer cecha
280 dánai ule éi."

69. As ed atbert-som go rocurit fidhcelda na Temrach dia saigidh-sium ann sin, 7 gou rug-som a toichell, conad and sin dorigne an cró Logo. (Acht masa i n-uamas an catha Troíanna rohairged in fi[d]ceall ní torracht hÉrinn and sin í. Úair is a n-áonaimsir rogniadh cath Muigi
285 Tuired 7 togail Traoi.)

70. Rohinnised iar sin thrá do Núa[d]aitt annísin. "Tuléic isin les," ar Núadha, "ar ní tánic riam fer a samail-sin isin dún-sa."

71. Dolléig iarum an dorrsaidh seca, 7 luid isin dún, 7 síasur a suide súad, ar bo suí cacha dáno é.

290 72. Focairtt iarum Ogma an márlícc, a rabatar feidm cetri .xx. cuinge, trésan tech co mbuí fri Temair anechtair. Do cor álgusa for Lucc ón. Ducorustar Lucc for cúla co mmbuí for lár an ríghthighi; 7 docorustar an mbloig bert riam amach a táob an rígtigi combo slán.

62. Then he said, "Question me, doorkeeper. I am a poet and a historian."

"We do not need you. We already have a poet and historian, Én mac Ethamain."

63. He said, "Question me. I am a sorcerer."

"We do not need you. We have sorcerers already. Our druids and our people of power are numerous."

64. He said, "Question me. I am a physician."

"We do not need you. We have Dían Cécht as a physician."

65. "Question me," he said. "I am a cupbearer."

"We do not need you. We have cupbearers already: Delt and Drúcht and Daithe, Tae and Talom and Trog, Glé and Glan and Glésse."

66. He said, "Question me: I am a good brazier."

"We do not need you. We have a brazier already, Crédne Cerd."

67. He said, "Ask the king whether he has one man who possesses all these arts: if he has I will not be able to enter Tara."

68. Then the doorkeeper went into the royal hall and told everything to the king. "A warrior has come before the court," he said, "named Samildánach; and all the arts which help your people, he practices them all, so that he is the man of each and every art."

69. Then he said that they should bring him the *fidchell*-boards of Tara, and he won all the stakes, so that he made the *cró* of Lug. (But if *fidchell* was invented at the time of the Trojan war, it had not reached Ireland yet, for the battle of Mag Tuired and the destruction of Troy occurred at the same time.)

70. Then that was related to Núadu. "Let him into the court," said Núadu, "for a man like that has never before come into this fortress."

71. Then the doorkeeper let him past, and he went into the fortress, and he sat in the seat of the sage, because he was a sage in every art.

72. Then Ogma threw the flagstone, which required fourscore yoke of oxen to move it, through the side of the hall so that it lay outside against Tara. That was to challenge Lug, who tossed the stone back so that it lay in the centre of the royal hall; and he threw the piece which it had carried away back into the side of the royal hall so that it was whole again.

73. "Seindt*er* cruitt dúin," al i[n]d sl*ú*aig. Sephaind *í*ar*um* ant
295 ógl*á*ech s*ú*antr*a*ige dona sl*ú*agaib 7 don rígh an c*é*t oidq*u*i. Focairtt a
s*ú*an ón tráth co 'raili. Sephainn golltr*a*igis co mbát*ar* oc ca*e*í 7 ac
dog*r*a. Sephainn gendtr*a*igi co mbát*ar* hi subai 7 a fo*r*bfáilti.

74. Imrordaid íaram Núadai, ó't *con*nuirc ilq*u*mach*t*a ina óclagi, dús
an cáomnacair dingbáil na dairi díb fo mbát*ar* lasna Fomoiri. Gnis*i*t
300 íar*um* com*ui*r*l*e im dálai and ógl*a*ích. Is si com*ui*r*l*e arriacht Núadha:
cáemclodh suidi f*r*isin n-óccláech. Luid Samill[d]ánd*ach* a suide ríg, 7
atréra*ch*t an rí riam co cend. .xíií. lá.

75. Imma-n-árladair dó íar*um* f*r*ia dá bráth*air* .i. Dagdo 7 Ogma fo*r*
Greall*a*ig Doll*a*id íarnamár*ach*; co *n*-[a]ccartha cucu a br*á*thair .íi. .i.
305 Goib*n*iu 7 Dían Céc[h]t.

76. Blí*ad*h*ain* lán dóib immon rún-sin in lín-sin, *con*adh de sin
66a dogar*ar*] Amhrún Fer nDéa f*r*i Grellaid nDoll*a*id.

77. Co *n*-ocarthai cucau íar sin dr*u*íd Ér*enn* 7 a lege 7 a n-aruid 7 a
ngoboinn 7 a nbriug*a*id 7 a mbrethem*a*in. Im*us*-n-agallat*ar* dóib a
310 ndíclet[h].

78. Rofíarf*a*ig íar*um* don corrguru .i. Mat[h]gen a ainm d*ú*s cía
*cu*mang gonánacair. Atbe*r*t-side focichr*e*d [slébe] Ér*enn* tri g*r*itai
fona Fomor*i* go tocr*a*d i mmulloch f*r*i talmain. *Ocus* doadbast*a*e dóib
dá príomsl*í*ab décc tíri Ér*enn* do bith fo Túat*h*a Dé D*a*nann og
315 imbúal*a*d díb .i. Sl*í*ab Líag, 7 Denda Ul*a*d, 7 Be*n*nai Boirche, 7 Brí
Ruri 7 Sl*í*ab Bládmai 7 Sl*í*ab Snech*t*ae, Sl*í*ab Mis 7 Blaís[h]líab 7
Nemthenn 7 Sl*í*ab M*a*ccu Belgodon 7 Segois 7 Crúachán Aigle.

79. Imcomaircidh d*a*no den deogbori cía *cu*magg conánocair.
Atbe*r*t-side dob*é*radh dá p*r*ímloch d*é*c na hÉr*enn* ina fíadnoisi 7 ní
320 fugbidis *ui*sce indtib, cid íotae not-gab*a*d. At íad-sou éat-side .i.
D*e*rcloch, Loch Lumn*i*g, Loch n-Orbsen, L*o*ch Rí, L*o*ch Mescdhae,
L*o*ch Cúan, L*o*ch Láeig, L*o*ch nEchach, L*o*ch Feb*a*il, L*o*ch Dechet,
L*o*ch Ríoach, Márloch. Aross-cich(er)sit do díb p*r*ímaibn*i*b déc ina
hÉr*enn* .i. B*ú*as, Bóann, Banna, Nem, Laí, Sinond, Múaid, Sligech,
325 Samaír, Fionn, Ruirt[h]ech, Siúir, 7 decélaigt*er* ar Fomor*i*b ulie cona
foighbid bando indtib. Targébu deogh firu Ér*enn* ce bet go cenn se*ch*t
mblí*ad*nae isin cath.

73. "Let a harp be played for us," said the hosts. Then the warrior played sleep music for the hosts and for the king on the first night, putting them to sleep from that hour to the same time the next day. He played sorrowful music so that they were crying and lamenting. He played joyful music so that they were merry and rejoicing.

74. Then Núadu, when he had seen the warrior's many powers, considered whether he could release them from the bondage they suffered at the hands of the Fomoire. So they held a council concerning the warrior, and the decision which Núadu reached was to exchange seats with the warrior. So Samildánach went to the king's seat, and the king arose before him until thirteen days had passed.

75. The next day he and the two brothers, Dagda and Ogma, conversed together on Grellach Dollaid; and his two kinsmen Goibniu and Dían Cécht were summoned to them.

76. They spent a full year in that secret conference, so that Grellach Dollaid is called the *Amrún* of the Men of the Goddess.

77. Then the druids of Ireland were summoned to them, together with their physicians and their charioteers and their smiths and their wealthy landowners and their lawyers. They conversed together secretly.

78. Then he asked the sorcerer, whose name was Mathgen, what power he wielded. He answered that he would shake the mountains of Ireland beneath the Fomoire so that their summits would fall to the ground. And it would seem to them that the twelve chief mountains of the land of Ireland would be fighting on behalf of the Túatha Dé Danann: Slieve League, and Denda Ulad, and the Mourne Mountains, and Brí Erigi and Slieve Bloom and Slieve Snaght, Slemish and Blaíslíab and Nephin Mountain and Slíab Maccu Belgodon and the Curlieu hills and Croagh Patrick.

79. Then he asked the cupbearer what power he wielded. He answered that he would bring the twelve chief lochs of Ireland into the presence of the Fomoire and they would not find water in them, however thirsty they were. These are the lochs: Lough Derg, Lough Luimnig, Lough Corrib, Lough Ree, Lough Mask, Strangford Lough, Belfast Lough, Lough Neagh, Lough Foyle, Lough Gara, Loughrea, Márloch. They would proceed to the twelve chief rivers of Ireland—the Bush, the Boyne, the Bann, the Blackwater, the Lee, the Shannon, the Moy, the Sligo, the Erne, the Finn, the Liffey, the Suir—and they would all be hidden from the Fomoire so they would not find a drop in them. But drink will be provided for the men of Ireland even if they remain in battle for seven years.

80. Atbert dano Figol mac Mámois a ndruí, "Firfit téorai frasae
tened liom-sou a n-enech slúaig na Fomhore, 7 pérut dá trian a ngaili
330 7 a ngascid 7 a neirt estib, 7 arnenas a fúal ina corpoib fodesin 7 a
corpaib a n-ech. Nach anúl dot-légfet fir(u) Érenn bod formach golie
7 gaisgid 7 nirt dóib. Quia bed isin cath go cenn secht mblíadnae,
níbot scíthae a cách."

81. Atbert an Daogdae, "An cumang arbágaid-si, dogén-sou ule am
335 áon[ur]."
    "Is tusai an Dagdae!" or cách; gonad [d]e rot-lil "Dagdae" ó sin
é.

82. Scaraid iarum asin comairlie go comairsidis die téoru mblíadan.

83. Ó roindlid iarum airicill an catha amlaid sin, luid Lucc 7 Dagdae
340 7 Ogma go trí déo Danonn, 7 doberot-side grésa an cathae do Lugh;
7 roboth sect mblíadnai oca foichill 7 ag dénom a [n-]arm.
    Is dei aspert fris, "Arfolmais cath mbrisi." Conid dei atpert an
Morrígan fri Lug, "Diuchtrai cein cuild ansaim[1] slaidither truasfidir
troich tarret brothlach mbodhmhou indraither túatha do- agath-
345 diuchtra cein .d. c."
    Boí Figol mac Mámais an draí og taircetal an catha 7 oc nertodh
Túath nDéa, gonad and atbert, "Firfidhir nith na boto tria agh tithris
muir ninglas nemnadbeo brogoll brofidh airideu doifid Lug
Lamfhadae. Brisfid bemionna uathmara Ogmae orruderc dó iar- beo
350 rig. Soifider cisai, nófither bethai, ticfithir airim ethae, maigfithir
blicht túatha. Bithsaer cach ina flaithmaigh. Cenmair tairgebai bith
bioas bithsaer cách niba daer nech; a núadha focichart- de rind nith,
7 firfider nith. f. n."

84. Boí tegdas den Dagdae a nGlionn Edin antúaith. Baí dano
66b 355 bandál forsin Dagdae dia blíadhnae[imon Samain an catha oc Glind
Edind. Gongair an Unius la Connachta frioa andes.
    Co n-acu an mnaí a n-Unnes a Corand og nide, indarna cos dí fri
Allod Echae (.i. Echuinech) fri husci andes alole fri Loscondoib fri
husce antúaith. Noí trillsi taitbechtai fora ciond. Agoillis an Dagdae
360 hí 7 dogníad óentaich. Lige ina Lánomhnou a ainm an baile ó sin. Is
hí an Morrígan an uhen-sin isberur sunn.

85. Itbert-si iarum frisin Dagdae deraghdis an Fomore a tír .i. a
Maug (S)cé[t]ne, 7 ara garudh an Dagdae óes ndánu Érionn aro
cend-si for Ádh Unsen; 7 noragad-si hi Scétne do admillid [ríg] na
365 Fomore .i. Indech mac Déi Domnann a ainm, 7 dohérudh-si crú a
cride 7 áirned a gailie úadh. Dobert-si didiu a dí bois den crú-sin deno
slúagaib bátar ocon indnaidhe for Ádh Unsen. Baí "Áth Admillte"
iarum a ainm ónd admillid-sin an ríog.

1   MS. *ba* appears over the *sa* in *ansaim*.

80. Then Figol mac Mámois, their druid, said, "Three showers of fire will be rained upon the faces of the Fomorian host, and I will take out of them two-thirds of their courage and their skill at arms and their strength, and I will bind their urine in their own bodies and in the bodies of their horses. Every breath that the men of Ireland will exhale will increase their courage and skill at arms and strength. Even if they remain in battle for seven years, they will not be weary at all.

81. The Dagda said, "The power which you boast, I will wield it all myself."
"You are the Dagda ['the Good God']!" said everyone; and "Dagda" stuck to him from that time on.

82. Then they disbanded the council to meet that day three years later.

83. Then after the preparation for the battle had been settled, Lug and the Dagda and Ogma went to the three gods of Danu, and they gave Lug equipment for the battle; and for seven years they had been preparing for them and making their weapons.
Then she said to him, "Undertake a battle of overthrowing." The Morrígan said to Lug,
"Awake. . . ."
Then Figol mac Mámois, the druid, was prophesying the battle and strengthening the Túatha Dé, saying,
"Battle will be waged. . . ."

84. The Dagda had a house in Glen Edin in the north, and he had arranged to meet a woman in Glen Edin a year from that day, near the All Hallows of the battle. The Unshin of Connacht roars to the south of it.
He saw the woman at the Unshin in Corann, washing, with one of her feet at Allod Echae (that is, Aghanagh) south of the water and the other at Lisconny north of the water. There were nine loosened tresses on her head. The Dagda spoke with her, and they united. "The Bed of the Couple" was the name of that place from that time on. (The woman mentioned here is the Morrígan.)

85. Then she told the Dagda that the Fomoire would land at Mag Céidne, and that he should summon the *áes dána* of Ireland to meet her at the Ford of the Unshin, and she would go into Scétne to destroy Indech mac Dé Domnann, the king of the Fomoire, and would take from him the blood of his heart and the kidneys of his valor. Later she gave two handfuls of that blood to the hosts that were waiting at the Ford of the Unshin. Its name became "The Ford of Destruction" because of that destruction of the king.

86. Degníth íer*um* lesin óes ndánou ind sen, 7 docachnot*ar* brechtau
370 f*or* slúag*aib* na Fomor*e*.

87. S*echt*m*ad* rie Samain sen, 7 scaruis cách oroile dóib go
comairnect*ar* fir Ér*enn* uili a llá rie Samain. S*é* t*rí*chaid *cét* a llíon .i.
dá t*rí*chad [*cét*] gech t*ri*n.

88. Foídes íer*um* Lug an Dag*dae* de tascél*ad* forsna Fomhor*aib* 7
375 dia fuirech go tíostaeis fir Ér*enn* den cath.

89. Luid íer*um* an Dag*dae* go loggfort na Fomor*e* 7 cunges cairde
cathai forrai. Dobreth dó am*al* c*o*nanoic. Degníther lite dó lasna
Fomori, 7 ba dia cudb*iu*d ón, oir ba mór s*er*c liten la[is]-sium. Nos-
líntar core cóecduirn an ríog dóu a ndechot*ar* cet*ri* ficet sesrai do
380 lemla*cht* 7 a cubat *cét*nai de men 7 béoil. Dob*er*thar gabair 7 cóerig 7
mucau indtie, 7 nos-combruithit*er* lei. Nosdórtit*er* a nd*er*c talm*an*
dóu, 7 atb*er*t fris noimbérthau fair bás mono tomledh ule; ar dáig ná
berud écna*ch* Fomor*e* co rocaith*e*d a sáidh.

90. Gabois íer sin a léig, 7 ba himaircithe go tallf*ad* lánom*ain* ina
385 lige f*or*o láur na léghie. It é di*diu* m[*ír*]ionn fordu-rauhot*ar* inde:
lethau tindei 7 cethrom*thu* bloinge.

91. Is ann adb*er*t in Dag*dae*, "Fó bioath ind so má rosaigh a broth
an rosaig a blas." An tan im*morro* noberid an lég láun ina béolu, is
adn adb*er*edh, " 'Nís-collet a mícuirne,' ol in sruith."

390 92. Dob*er*t-sium im*morro* a mér cr*o*mm tar domain an d*er*cu fo
derid it*er* úr 7 g*ri*oan. Dolluid cotl*ud* foair íer*um* ar caitem a liten. Ba
méidit*hir* scabol tige a bolc fair, gon tibsid im sodain na Fomore.

93. Luid úaidib íer*um* co Trácht Aebae. Níruho herosai t*rá* den
láec[h] imd*echt* lie m*éit* a bronn. Ba drochruid a cong*ra*im: cochlíne
395 go bac a dí ullend. Inor aodhar imbe go foph a tónai. Gabol gicca
roth*ach* feidm o*cht*air ina diaid, go mba lór do clod coic*rí*ce a sli*cht*
'na degaidh. Gonad dei dogaror Sli*cht* Loirge an Dag*dai*. Is ed
d*e*nu*cht* leb*ar* p*e*nntol. Dá bróicc imbe di croicinn capoild 7 a find
s*echt*oir.

400   A mboí íer*um* og imdect *co n*-acu an n-ingen foro cind go ndeilb
nd*er*scoighte. Sí cáemt*ri*lsich. Luid m*e*nmo an Dag*dai* díi, *acht*
náruho túaloigg lia a p*ro*inn. Gabois an ingen fora cáin*ed*h, gab*ais*
an ing*en* f*or* imt*ra*scr*ad* f*ri*s. Fucerd cor de go ráinec go bac a tónai hi
tolamh. Dos-n-éco go handíaraid 7 atb*er*t, "Q*ui*d ro-mba dam, a
405 *i*ng*in*," ol sé, "dom cor dom conair cáir?"

86. So the *áes dána* did that, and they chanted spells against the Fomorian hosts.

87. This was a week before All Hallows, and they all dispersed until all the men of Ireland came together the day before All Hallows. Their number was six times thirty hundred, that is, each third consisted of twice thirty hundred.

88. Then Lug sent the Dagda to spy on the Fomoire and to delay them until the men of Ireland came to the battle.

89. Then the Dagda went to the Fomorian camp and asked them for a truce of battle. This was granted to him as he asked. The Fomoire made porridge for him to mock him, because his love of porridge was great. They filled for him the king's cauldron, which was five fists deep, and poured four score gallons of new milk and the same quantity of meal and fat into it. They put goats and sheep and swine into it, and boiled them all together with the porridge. Then they poured it into a hole in the ground, and Indech said to him that he would be killed unless he consumed it all; he should eat his fill so that he might not satirize the Fomoire.

90. Then the Dagda took his ladle, and it was big enough for a man and a woman to lie in the middle of it. These are the bits that were in it: halves of salted swine and a quarter of lard.

91. Then the Dagda said, "This is good food if its broth is equal to its taste." But when he would put the full ladle into his mouth he said, " 'Its poor bits do not spoil it,' says the wise old man."

92. Then at the end he scraped his bent finger over the bottom of the hole among mould and gravel. He fell asleep then after eating his porridge. His belly was as big as a house cauldron, and the Fomoire laughed at it.

93. Then he went away from them to Tráigh Eabha. It was not easy for the warrior to move along on account of the size of his belly. His appearance was unsightly: he had a cape to the hollow of his elbows, and a gray-brown tunic around him as far as the swelling of his rump. He trailed behind him a wheeled fork which was the work of eight men to move, and its track was enough for the boundary ditch of a province. It is called "The Track of the Dagda's Club" for that reason. His long penis was uncovered. He had on two shoes of horse-hide with the hair outside.

As he went along he saw a girl in front of him, a good-looking young woman with an excellent figure, her hair in beautiful tresses. The Dagda desired her, but he was impotent on account of his belly. The girl began to mock him, then she began wrestling with him. She hurled him so that he sank to the hollow of his rump in the ground.

"Is airi ro-mba det: gon*um*-rugae ford' muin luet cona*m*-rabor a ticc mo ath*ar*."

"Cúich ath*air*?" ol sé.

"Ingen-su ém," ol sí, "d'Indech m*ac* Dé Do*mnann*."

410 Duscaru aitherr*ach* 7 slaithe go léir, gorolín na futhorbe imbe do caindiubur a p*ro*nn; 7 nos-égnith*er* gondo-ruccoud fo*ra* muin fo th*rí*. Atb*er*t-s*um* ba ges dóu breth neich lais nád ebér*ad* a ainm f*r*is. "Cía hainm-si di*diu*?" ar sise.

"Fer B*enn*," ar é-si*um*.

415 "Imfo*r*cra*i*d n-anmo son!" ar sise. "At*ra*í, nom-ber for mhuin, a Fir Benn."

"Ní hedh mh'ainm ámh," bar é-si*um*.

"C*eist*?" ar sí. [

67a "Fer Pe*nn* Brúach," ar é-sim.

420 "At*ra*oí nom-bir fo*r*d' muin, a Fir Be*nn* Brúach," ar sise.

"Ní hedh mh'ainm," ar é-sim.

"C*eist*?" ol sise. Nos-tic díi ule taris. Tic-sí di*diu* for slio*cht*-seom and *co* n-epe*r*t, "At*ra*í nom-ber ford' muin, a Fir Be*nn* Bruaic[h] Brogaill Brou*m*ide Cerb*ad* Caic Rolaig Builc Labair Cerrce Di Brig

425 Oldath*air* Boith Athge*n* mBethai Bright*ere* T*r*i Carboid Roth Rimairie Riog Scotbe Obthe Olaithbe. Dren*n*ar rig d-dar f*r*ingar fegar fre*n*dirie. At*ra*oí, nom-ber di sunnae!"

"Ná himber cuitb*iud* form ní bos móu, a ingen," al *sé*.

"Bid atégen tacuo," al sie.

430 Is íar*um* gonglóisie asin d*er*c íar telcodh a p*ro*nd. Sech ba hairi sin boí furech na hingene dó-som go cíoan móir. At*ra*oí-sium ier*um*, 7 gabaid an ingen fo*ro* muin; 7 dobe*r*t téorae clochau ina cris. Oc*us* dofuit cech cloch ar úair aire—oc*us* atberud bat*ar* íat a ferdai dero*c*r*atar* úad. Lingthe an inge*n* foair 7 doslais t*ara* tóin é, 7

435 lomort*ar* a caither frithrosc. Gond*r*ic ier*um* ion Dagd*ae* frie a bancharoid, 7 dogníead cairdene ier*um*. Atá a llátr*ach* for T*rá*cht Eoboile áit a comarnacht*ar*.

Is and sen atbe*r*t an inge*n* fri[s]-siem, "Ní ragae ám den cath cipé tou*cht*," al in phen.

440 "Rag*at* écin," ol in Dagd*ae*.

"Ní rogae," ol en ben, "ar boam cloch-sou a mbéulai gech áthau nod-ragau."

"Bid fír," or ion Dagd*ae*, "*acht* ním-gébou dei. Ragat-so go trén t*ar* cech n-alich, 7 biaid látr*ao*ch mo sául*u*-sau i ngech ailic go

445 bráth."

"Bid fír, *acht* bud sios co*n*súfit*er* co*n*a aicith*er*. Ní rago torm-sai gom *m*-árail ma*cc*u Tethra hi sídaib. Ar bon rail-sie daruch i ncech áth 7 i ngech bel*aig* not-ragai."

"Rag*at* écin," al in Dagd*ae*, "*ocus* bieid[1] látr*ach* mo bélo-sai io

_____

1 MS. *biéid.*

He looked at her angrily and asked, "What business did you have, girl, heaving me out of my right way?"

"This business: to get you to carry me on your back to my father's house."

"Who is your father?" he asked.

"I am the daughter of Indech, son of Dé Domnann," she said.

She fell upon him again and beat him hard, so that the furrow around him filled with the excrement from his belly; and she satirized him three times so that he would carry her upon his back.

He said that it was a *ges* for him to carry anyone who would not call him by his name.

"What is your name?" she asked.

"Fer Benn," he said.

"That name is too much!" she said. "Get up, carry me on your back, Fer Benn."

"That is indeed not my name," he said.

"What is?" she asked.

"Fer Benn Brúach," he answered.

"Get up, carry me on your back, Fer Benn Brúach," she said.

"That is not my name," he said.

"What is?" she asked. Then he told her the whole thing. She replied immediately and said, "Get up, carry me on your back, Fer Benn Brúach Brogaill Broumide Cerbad Caic Rolaig Builc Labair Cerrce Di Brig Oldathair Boith Athgen mBethai Brightere Tri Carboid Roth Rimaire Riog Scotbe Obthe Olaithbe. . . . Get up, carry me away from here!"

"Do not mock me any more, girl," he said.

"It will certainly be hard," she said.

Then he moved out of the hole, after letting go the contents of his belly, and the girl had waited for that for a long time. He got up then, and took the girl on his back; and he put three stones in his belt. Each stone fell from it in turn—and it has been said that they were his testicles which fell from it. The girl jumped on him and struck him across the rump, and her curly pubic hair was revealed. Then the Dagda gained a mistress, and they made love. The mark remains at Beltraw Strand where they came together.

Then the girl said to him, "You will not go to the battle by any means."

"Certainly I will go," said the Dagda.

"You will not go," said the woman, "because I will be a stone at the mouth of every ford you will cross."

"That will be true," said the Dagda, "but you will not keep me from it. I will tread heavily on every stone, and the trace of my heel will remain on every stone forever."

"That will be true, but they will be turned over so that you may not see them. You will not go past me until I summon the sons of Tethra from the *síd*-mounds, because I will be a giant oak in every ford and in every pass you will cross."

"I will indeed go past," said the Dagda, "and the mark of my axe

450 ncech dair go bráth." (*Co n-*epert as eth lá*tr*ach béluo an Dag*dai*.)
Atbe*rt*-si ier*um*, "Légait*ir* na Fomo*re* a tír," ol síe, "ar táncot*ar* fir(u)
Ér*enn* ulie go háeninodh." Atbe*rt*-si d*a*no noríast*r*abadh-si no
Fomo*re*, 7 docachnop*ad* forrai, 7 arin-imreth-somh ce*ir*d marbth*a*ig
na gíce forro—*ocus* nogéb*ad*-si a hóenor nóm*ad* rann forin slóug.

455 94. Tecoid ier*um* na Fomo*re* co mbát*ar* a ndichmaid a Scétne. Bát*ar*
fir(u) Ér*enn* im*morro* i mMoigh Aurfhol*a*igh. Bát*ar* ier*um* ag imnesie
cathai in d*á* slúag-so.
"An cauth arfolmot*ar* fir Ér*enn* de tab*air*t dúdn?" al Pres m*a*c
Elathan[1] f*r*i hIndech m*a*c Dé Do*mn*ann.
460 "Dobiur-so inoen," ol Indech, "cumbat minai a cnámhae mina
érnet a cáno."

95. Buí comairli lia firu Ér*enn* im nemlégodh Logai isin cath, ara
coime. Go nderoch*t*or a noí [n-]oide die comét .i. Toll*us*dam 7
Echdam 7 Eru, Re*ch*t*a*id Fionn 7 Fosadh 7 Fedlim*id*h, Iubor 7
465 Scib*ar* 7 Minn. Ecol leo ier*um* mochscélie den óclaích ar imot a dán.
As airie nár'télgsit din cath.

96. Rotinálid tr*á* maithe T*ú*ath *n*Dé D*a*nann go Luch.
Roimcomhoirc a gaboinn .i. Gaibne, cía cumong c*o*nánoc*uir* dóib.

97. "Ní *anse*," al sé. "Gé bet fir Ér*enn* isin cath go cenn s*ech*t
470 *m*blíat*an*, gai detáet dia crunn ann nó cl*a*id*e*m memais ann, tarcéba
arm núa úam-sai ina inoth. Nach rind degéno mo lám-so," ol sé, "ní
focert*ar* imrold de. Nach cnes i ragae no*co* blasfe beth*a*id de íer sin.
Níbo[2] gníthe do Dulb gobhae na Fomo*re* annisin. Atú dom cor do
67b cath Muige T*ur*e*d*h anosa." [

475 98. "Os tusai, a Dien C*é*cht," or Lug, "cía cumogg c*o*nicid-si ém?"

99. "Ní *anse*," ol síe. "Nach fer géntor ann, *acht* mona bentor a
cedn de, n*ó* m*a*ni tesct*ar* srebonn a inchinde nó a smir s[m]entuinde,
bodh ógsláun lim-su 'sin cath arabhároch."

100. "Os tusai, a Crédne," or Lugh frie cerd, "caide do cumong isin
480 cath?"

101. "Ní *anse*," ar Crédne. "Semonn a ngaí 7 dornclai a cloidim 7
cobr*a*id a scíath 7 a mbile rusia lim-sai dóip ule."

1 MS. *Elier.*
2 MS. *-bó.*

will remain in every oak forever." (And people have remarked upon
the mark of the Dagda's axe.)

Then however she said, "Allow the Fomoire to enter the land,
because the men of Ireland have all come together in one place." She
said that she would hinder the Fomoire, and she would sing spells
against them, and she would practice the deadly art of the wand
against them—and she alone would take on a ninth part of the host.

94. The Fomoire advanced until their tenths were in Scétne. The
men of Ireland were in Mag Aurfolaig. At this point these two hosts
were threatening battle.

"Do the men of Ireland undertake to give battle to us?" said Bres
mac Elathan to Indech mac Dé Domnann.

"I will give the same," said Indech, "so that their bones will be
small if they do not pay their tribute."

95. In order to protect him, the men of Ireland had agreed to keep
Lug from the battle. His nine foster fathers came to guard him:
Tollusdam and Echdam and Eru, Rechtaid Finn and Fosad and
Feidlimid, Ibar and Scibar and Minn. They feared an early death for
the warrior because of the great number of his arts. For that reason
they did not let him go to the battle.

96. Then the men of rank among the Túatha Dé were assembled
around Lug. He asked his smith, Goibniu, what power he wielded for
them.

97. "Not hard to say," he said. "Even if the men of Ireland continue
the battle for seven years, for every spear that separates from its shaft
or sword that will break in battle, I will provide a new weapon in its
place. No spearpoint which my hand forges will make a missing cast.
No skin which it pierces will taste life afterward. Dolb, the Fomorian
smith, cannot do that. I am now concerned with my preparation for
the battle of Mag Tuired."

98. "And you, Dían Cécht," said Lug, "what power do you wield?"

99. "Not hard to say," he said. "Any man who will be wounded
there, unless his head is cut off, or the membrane of his brain or his
spinal cord is severed, I will make him perfectly whole in the battle on
the next day."

100. "And you, Crédne," Lug said to his brazier, "what is your
power in the battle?"

101. "Not hard to answer," said Crédne. "I will supply them all
with rivets for their spears and hilts for their swords and bosses and
rims for their shields."

102. "Os tusa, a Lu*cht*a," or Luog frie a sóer, "cía cumong rosta 'sin cat[h]?"

485 103. "Ní *anse*," or Luchtai. "A ndóethain scíath 7 crand sleg rosiae lem-sai dóib ule."

104. ".Os tu*ss*a, a Oghmau," ol Lug frie a trénfher, "caide do cumong isin cath?"

105. "Ní *anse*," ol síe. "Digguháil and ríog lia dingb*áil* trí nónuhar 490 dia cairdib, la gab*áil* in catha go trian la firu *Érenn*."

106. "Os tu*ss*a, a Morríghan," ol Lug, "cía cu*m*ang?"

107. "Ní *anse*," ol sí, "ar-rosisor; dosifius do-sseladh; ar-rosel*us*, aros-dibu nos-ríast*ais*."

108. "Os sib-sie, a corrgunechai," al Lugh, "cía cumang?"

495 109. "Ní *anse*," ar na corrguinidhgh. "A mbuind bánai forra íarn' tra*scr*a*d* trienar ce*rd*-ne, go romarbtar a n-aisc*id*; *ocus* dá trian a n*eirt* do gaid foraib, lie f*or*gab*áil* aru fúal."

110. "Os sib-sie, a deoguhairi," or Lug, "cía *cumo*ng?"

111. "Ní *anse*," ar na deogbore. "Dobéraim-ne robhar ítadh f*or*aib, 500 7 ne*m*fhogb*áil* dige dia *c*u*s*c dóib."

112. "Os sib-sie, a druíde," ol Luog, "cía cumong?"

113. "Ní *anse*," ar na druíde. "Doberom-ne cetha tened fo gnúisib no Fomor*e* gonar'fétad fégodh a n-ardou, cor*us*-gonot fou cumas iond óicc b*et* ag imgoin friu."

505 114. "Os tusai, a Corpri m*eic* Étnai," or Luog frie a filid, "cía [cumang] condoid isin cath?"

115. "Ní [anse]," ol Corpri. "Degén-sai gláim ndícind dóuib, 7 n*us*-óerub 7 n*us*-anfíalub *c*ona gébat frie hócu trie bri*ch*t mo dán*a*-sa."

116. "Os siuh-sie, a Uhé Culde 7 a Dinand," or Lug fria dá 510 bantúa[thaid], "cía [cumang] connai isin c*a*th?"

102. "And you, Luchta," Lug said to his carpenter, "what power would you attain in the battle?"

103. "Not hard to answer," said Luchta. "I will supply them all with whatever shields and spearshafts they need."

104. "And you, Ogma," said Lug to his champion, "what is your power in the battle?"

105. "Not hard to say," he said. "Being a match for the king and holding my own against twenty-seven of his friends, while winning a third of the battle for the men of Ireland."

106. "And you, Morrígan," said Lug, "what power?"

107. "Not hard to say," she said. "I have stood fast; I shall pursue what was watched; I will be able to kill; I will be able to destroy those who might be subdued."

108. "And you, sorcerers," said Lug, "what power?"

109. "Not hard to say," said the sorcerers. "Their white soles will be visible after they have been overthrown by our craft, so that they can easily be killed; and we will take two-thirds of their strength from them, and prevent them from urinating."

110. "And you, cupbearers," said Lug, "what power?"

111. "Not hard to say," said the cupbearers. "We will bring a great thirst upon them, and they will not find drink to quench it."

112. "And you, druids," said Lug, "what power?"

113. "Not hard to say," said the druids. "We will bring showers of fire upon the faces of the Fomoire so that they cannot look up, and the warriors contending with them can use their force to kill them."

114. "And you, Coirpre mac Étaíne," said Lug to his poet, "what can you do in the battle?"

115. "Not hard to say," said Coirpre. "I will make a *glám dícenn* against them, and I will satirize them and shame them so that through the spell of my art they will offer no resistance to warriors."

116. "And you, Bé Chuille and Díanann," said Lug to his two witches, "what can you do in the battle?"

54 CATH MAIGE TUIRED

117. "Ní *anse*," ol síed. "Dolbfamid-ne na c*r*adnai 7 na clochai 7 fódai an talmon gommod sl*úag* fon airmgaisc*iud* dóib; *co* rainfed hí techedh f*r*ie húatbás 7 c*r*aidenus."

118. "Os tussa, a Dag*dai*," ol Lug, "cía cumang connic for sl*úag* na
515 Fomhor*e* isin cath?"

119. "Ní *anse*," ol in Dag*dae*. "Dugén-sa leath fria fer*u* Ér*enn* et*er* cáemslec*h*t 7 admill*iud* 7 amaidic*h*tai. Bud lir bomonn egai fua cosaib g*r*egai a cnáimreth fum luirg an fec*h*t-sie, áit a comr*a*icid[1] diab*ul*námod f*or* raí Muige Tuired."

520 120. Ruaicill t*r*á Luch cách ar úair díb f*r*ia a ndánoib ón mud-sin, 7 r*us*-ne*r*t 7 r*us*-aicill a sl*úag* combo me*n*manr*a*d rígh nó rofl*a*t*h*ua la cech fer díb fon c*r*uth-sin.

121. Rose*r*natai t*r*á an cath cech láei et*er* fine Fom*r*a 7 Th*úath*a Déa, *acht* namaá ní bót*a*r rígh nó ruir*ig* oga taba*irt*, *acht* óes féigh
525 forúall*ach* namá.

122. Ba ingn*a*d t*r*á liasna Fomore alaill tárfas dóib isin cath. Bot*a*r clóite a n-airm-sie .i. a ngaoí 7 a cloidme; *ocus* an romarbad dia feruib-si*um* ní ticdis íernabháruch. Níb*a* edh im*m*orro de Túath*a*ib Déa: ar cía noclodis a n-airm-si*um* andíu, atgainidis amuhár*ach* fo
530 bíth roboí Goibnenn goba isin ce*r*dchai ag dénam calc 7 gaí 7 sleg. Ar dogníth-si*d*e na harma-sin fria téorai g*r*ésai. Dogníth[1] d*ano*
68a Luc*h*taine sóer na crondo f*r*i téora] snasau, 7 ba féith an tres snas 7 ata-ind[s]mad hi cró an gaí. Ó robídis arm de isin le*th* ina ce*r*dchai dobidcet-som na cróu c*us*na c*r*andoib, 7 níbo hécin aither*r*ach
535 indsma dóib. Dugníth d*ano* Crédne ce*r*d na semonn f*r*i téorai g*r*éssai, 7 dobidged cró na ngáu díb, 7 níbo écen tairbir remib; 7 noglentais saml*aid*.

123. Is edh d*ano* doberiud bruth isna hógaib nogontais ann, comtar ániu íarnauhár*ach*: fo bíth roboí Díen Céc*h*t 7 a dí m*a*c 7 a ingen .i.
540 Oc*h*tt*r*íuil 7 Airmedh 7 Míach oc dícet*ul* f*or*an tibr*ait* .i. Sláine a hainm. Foce*r*tdidis a n-athgóite indte im*m*airlestis; bot*a*r bí notégdis esde. Bati[r] slán a n-athgóite tre ne*r*t an dícet*ail* na ceth*r*i lege robát*a*r imon tibr*ait*.

1 MS. *comraícid*.

117. "Not hard to say," they said. "We will enchant the trees and the stones and the sods of the earth so that they will be a host under arms against them; and they will scatter in flight terrified and trembling."

118. "And you, Dagda," said Lug, "what power can you wield against the Fomorian host in the battle?"

119. "Not hard to say," said the Dagda. "I will fight for the men of Ireland with mutual smiting and destruction and wizardry. Their bones under my club will soon be as many as hailstones under the feet of herds of horses, where the double enemy meets on the battlefield of Mag Tuired."

120. Then in this way Lug addressed each of them in turn concerning their arts, strengthening them and addressing them in such a way that every man had the courage of a king or great lord.

121. Now every day the battle was drawn up between the race of the Fomoire and the Túatha Dé Danann, but there were no kings or princes waging it, only fierce and arrogant men.

122. One thing which became evident to the Fomoire in the battle seemed remarkable to them. Their weapons, their spears and their swords, were blunted; and those of their men who were killed did not come back the next day. That was not the case with the Túatha Dé Danann: although their weapons were blunted one day, they were restored the next because Goibniu the smith was in the smithy making swords and spears and javelins. He would make those weapons with three strokes. Then Luchta the carpenter would make the spearshafts in three chippings, and the third chipping was a finish and would set them in the socket of the spear. After the spearheads were in the side of the forge he would throw the sockets with the shafts, and it was not necessary to set them again. Then Crédne the brazier would make the rivets with three strokes, and he would throw the sockets of the spears at them, and it was not necessary to drill holes for them; and they stayed together this way.

123. Now this is what used to kindle the warriors who were wounded there so that they were more fiery the next day: Dían Cécht, his two sons Octriuil and Míach, and his daughter Airmed were chanting spells over the well named Sláine. They would cast their mortally-wounded men into it as they were struck down; and they were alive when they came out. Their mortally-wounded were healed through the power of the incantation made by the four physicians who were around the well.

124. Tánic didiu frisna Fomore annísin, go tudciset-som fer n-
545 úadaibh de déscin cathai 7 cosdotha Túath nDéa .i. Rúadán mac
Bresi 7 Bríghi ingene in Dagdai. Ar ba mac-side 7 ba úa do Thúaith
Déa. Atcuaid ierum gním an gaphonn 7 ant sáeir 7 an cerdou 7 na
cetri lége rouhátar imon tibrait do Fomoraib. Rofaided-som afridisie
fri marbod neich den óes dána .i. Gaibniu. Tothloigestar gaí ó ssoide,
550 a semonn ón cerdai, 7 a crand ónt sóer. Debreth ierum amal asbert.
Baí dano ben and fri bleth arm .i. Crón máthair Fíanluig; is í rus-meil
gaí Rúadáin. Dobreth di Rúadán didiu an gaí ó máthri, conud [d]e
sin doberar "gaí máthri" de garmnaib beus a n-Érinn.

125. Immesoi didiu Rúadán íer tabairt in gaí dó, 7 geogoin
555 Goibninn. Tiscais-side an gaí as 7 fochaird for Rúadán co lluid trít; 7
co n-érbailt ar bélaib a athar a n-oirecht na Fomore. Tic Bríc 7 cáines
a mac. Éghis ar tós, goilis fo deog. Conud and sin roclos gol 7 égem
ar tós a n-Érinn. (Is sí didiu an Prích-sin roairich feit do caismeirt a n-
oidci.)

560 126. Luid trá Gaibniu fon tibrait 7 ba slán-side. Baí óclaech lasno
Fomore .i. Octriallach mac Indich meic Déi Domnann, mac ríg
Fomore. Atbert-side frisna Fomore aro tabroidis cloich cech áinfir
leo de clochaib Drobésa do cor ar tibrait Sláine a n-Achad Abla fri
Magh Tuired andíar, fri Loch n-Arboch antúaid. Lotar didiu, 7
565 doberod cloich cech fir forin tiprait. Gonud [d]e atá Carn
Ochtrialdaig foran carn. Ainm n-aild dano din tibroid-sin Loch
Luibe, ar dobered Dien Cécht ind cech losa rouhótar a n-Éri.

'127. Ó tánic trá airis an cathai móir, atrárochtor na Fomore asa
scoraibh sechtair 7 derónsud catha daiggne dítogladai díb. Ní rabhu
570 trá airich nó fer egnnamae díob cen lúirig friae chnes, cen catbarr
fo[r]a cend, cin manaís muirnig 'na deis, gen cloidim tromgér fora
cris, gen scieth daiggen fora formnai. Ba "bém cinn fri hald," ba
"lárum a net natrach," ba "haigedh go tenid" cor fri slúag na Fomore
isin ló-sin.

575 128. Robtar íet-so ríg 7 toísich rouhátar og nertadh slúaig na
Fomore .i. Balor mac Doit meic Néid, Bres mac Elathon, Tuirie
Tortbuillech mac Lobois, Goll 7 Irgold, Loscennlom mac
Lomglúinigh, Indeach mac Dé Domnann rí na Fomore, Octrial[lach]
68b mac Indich,] Omna 7 Bagnai, Elotha mac Delbáet[h].

124. Now that was damaging to the Fomoire, and they picked a man to reconnoitre the battle and the practices of the Túatha Dé—Rúadán, the son of Bres and of Bríg, the daughter of the Dagda—because he was a son and a grandson of the Túatha Dé. Then he described to the Fomoire the work of the smith and the carpenter and the brazier and the four physicians who were around the well. They sent him back to kill one of the *áes dána*, Goibniu. He requested a spearpoint from him, its rivets from the brazier, and its shaft from the carpenter; and everything was given to him as he asked. Now there was a woman there grinding weapons, Crón the mother of Fíanlach; and she ground Rúadán's spear. So the spear was given to Rúadán by his maternal kin, and for that reason a weaver's beam is still called "the spear of the maternal kin" in Ireland.

125. But after the spear had been given to him, Rúadán turned and wounded Goibniu. He pulled out the spear and hurled it at Rúadán so that it went through him; and he died in his father's presence in the Fomorian assembly. Bríg came and keened for her son. At first she shrieked, in the end she wept. Then for the first time weeping and shrieking were heard in Ireland. (Now she is the Bríg who invented a whistle for signalling at night.)

126. Then Goibniu went into the well and he became whole. The Fomoire had a warrior named Ochtríallach, the son of the Fomorian king Indech mac Dé Domnann. He suggested that every single man they had should bring a stone from the stones of the river Drowes to cast into the well Sláine in Achad Abla to the west of Mag Tuired, to the east of Lough Arrow. They went, and every man put a stone into the well. For that reason the cairn is called Ochtríallach's Cairn. But another name for that well is Loch Luibe, because Dían Cécht put into it every herb that grew in Ireland.

127. Now when the time came for the great battle, the Fomoire marched out of their encampment and formed themselves into strong indestructible battalions. There was not a chief nor a skilled warrior among them without armor against his skin, a helmet on his head, a broad . . . spear in his right hand, a heavy sharp sword on his belt, a strong shield on his shoulder. To attack the Fomorian host that day was "striking a head against a cliff," was "a hand in a serpent's nest," was "a face brought close to fire."

128. These were the kings and leaders who were encouraging the Fomorian host: Balor son of Dot son of Nét, Bres mac Elathan, Tuire Tortbuillech mac Lobois, Goll and Irgoll, Loscennlomm mac Lommglúinigh, Indech mac Dé Domnann, king of the Fomoire, Ochtríallach mac Indich, Omna and Bagna, Elatha mac Delbaíth.

580 129. Atrachtotar Túatha Dé Danann don le*th* eli, 7 dofágaibsid a naie céli ag comét Logai, 7 lotar do oiris an catha. In tan ierum segar an cath, conselu Lug asa coimét a mboí ina cairptech, gombo hé baí ar inchaib catha Túath nDéa. Roferud trá imairec áith amnas and so eter fine Fomra 7 firu Érenn. Boí Lug og nertad fer n-Érenn co
585 roferdais go dícra an cath fo dégh ná beidis a ndoíri ní bod sírie. Ar ba ferr dúoib bás d'fhogáil oc diden a n-athardho indás beith fo doíri 7 fou cís amal rouhátar. Conid and rocan Lug an cétal-so síos, for lethcois 7 letsúil timchell fer n-Érenn.

"Arotroi cat comartan! Isin cathirgal robris comlondo forslecht-
590 slúaig silsiter ria sluagaib sioabrai iath fer fomnai. Cuifecithai fir gen rogain[1] lentor gala. Fordomaisit, fordomcloisid, forandechraiged, fir duib: becc find nomtam-.[2] Fó! Fó! Fé! Fé! Clé! Amainsi! Noefit-man-n ier nelscoth- trie trencerdaib druag. Nimcredbod catha fri cricha; nesit- mede midege fornemairces forlúachoir loisces martal-
595 tśuides martorainn trogais. Incomairsid fri cech naie, go comair Ogma sachu go comair nem 7 talom, go comair grioan 7 esqu. Drem niadh mo drem-sie duib. Mo sluag so sluag mor murnech mochtsailech bruithe nertoirech rogenoir et- dacri ataforroi cath comortai. Arotrai."

600 130. Ros-láisiud na slúaig gáir mór oc[1] dol isin cath. Conráncotar ier sin, 7 rogab cách for trúasdrad a céile díbbh.

131. Mór do cóemaib derochrotar ann a mbúailie báis. Mór ant ár 7 an lechtloide roboí ann. Roboí úall 7 imnáire and leth for leth. Buí ferg 7 borrfad. Ba himgae réun folu tar gelcnius móethócláech ann
605 ierna léudh do lámaiuh létmiuch oc teicht a ngáuhad ar imbnárie. Ba hamnas muirn 7 saitoi na curud 7 na láth ngali ic immdítin a ngáe 7 a scíath 7 a courp ind taun nus-bítis a céli ica trúastrud denaib gaíb 7 denaib cloidbiuh. Amnas dano an tarneuch ruboí and sechnón an cathae .i. gáir na láechraidi 7 presimb na scíath, loindreuch 7 fedgairi
610 na cloidhim 7 na calc ndéd, cairchiu 7 grindegur na saicidbolc, sían 7 etigud na foghaid 7 na ngabluch, 7 priscbémniuch na n-armb.

132. Es bec trá ná comráncatar inn a mméur ocus a coss ocin imtúarcain; co tuislitis assa sessam lie slimreth na foluo fou cossaib na míliodh, co mmbentaeis a cinno díob ana suidip. Conúargabud
615 cath crótdae, créchtocch, bróineuch, fuilech, ocus rurássa unnsenn hi crobaiph bídbad ann-side.

1 MS. *gen rogam* is also a possible reading.
2 MS. *nointam-* is also a possible reading.

129. On the other side, the Túatha Dé Danann arose and left his nine companions guarding Lug, and went to join the battle. But when the battle ensued, Lug escaped from the guard set over him, as a chariot-fighter, and it was he who was in front of the battalion of the Túatha Dé. Then a keen and cruel battle was fought between the race of the Fomoire and the men of Ireland.

Lug was urging the men of Ireland to fight the battle fiercely so they should not be in bondage any longer, because it was better for them to find death while protecting their fatherland than to be in bondage and under tribute as they had been. Then Lug chanted the spell which follows, going around the men of Ireland on one foot and with one eye closed. . . .

130. The hosts gave a great shout as they went into battle. Then they came together, and each of them began to strike the other.

131. Many beautiful men fell there in the stall of death. Great was the slaughter and the grave-lying which took place there. Pride and shame were there side by side. There was anger and indignation. Abundant was the stream of blood over the white skin of young warriors mangled by the hands of bold men while rushing into danger for shame. Harsh was the noise made by the multitude of warriors and champions protecting their swords and shields and bodies while others were striking them with spears and swords. Harsh too the tumult all over the battlefield—the shouting of the warriors and the clashing of bright shields, the swish of swords and ivory-hilted blades, the clatter and rattling of the quivers, the hum and whirr of spears and javelins, the crashing strokes of weapons.

132. As they hacked at each other their fingertips and their feet almost met; and because of the slipperiness of the blood under the warriors' feet, they kept falling down, and their heads were cut off them as they sat. A gory, wound-inflicting, sharp, bloody battle was upheaved, and spearshafts were reddened in the hands of foes.

133. Derocair dano Núodai Aircetláum ocus Maucha ingen Ernmoiss lie Balur uí Nét. Duceur Cassmóel lie hOgtríallug mac n-Indich. Imma-comairnic de Luc 7 di Bolur Birugderc esin cat[h]. Súil milldagach le suide. Ní ho(r)scailtie inn sóul acht i rroí catae nammá. Cetrar turcbaud a malaig die shól conu drolum omlithi triena malaig. Slúoac[h] do-n-éceud darsan sól, nín-géptis fri hócco, cíe pidis lir ilmíli. Es de boí inn nem-sin fuirri(r) .i. druít[h] a adhar bótar oc fulucht draígechtae. Tánic-seum 7 ruderc tarsan fundéoic, co ndechaid dé en foulachtae fuithi gonid forsan súil dodecaid nem an foulachta íer sin. Condrecat ierum Luc. Is (n)ann isbert Lucc: "Odeo cietoi fir bic ciabith imbá inlá biu fo ló marbu duit."[1]

Balor dixit, "Foriathmaigi alfois fíliu fon' fola immusriad riadha ío comrac sil silme amsil amnus fen."

630   Lug- dixit, "Is tu torat- Lughdech lisbertac totsili dotoirrse pu mo cloidim dotgart mo tuili mo cerdae cles tuatha. Bid olc de cuanaib fal Fomoiri fo tuili fo trethan duib fo tonnae lia ciptuccai conaib dinn. Niberaid mes na blicht. Niberaid arith ith niberaid eraig aigthe. Aic! Aic! Fe! Fe! Ni focen tis-sta naithech nes bretach bithmaru inarbraind beg antetru tromma fortaibsin troga forlica lim. Os me Lug namfadbid oldam dilaim denaith duilem fordiacimdes gene os-gene[3] nomnasaid mo carp- nitaidlibthi tres ceptucas atbrothru fo tonnaib lirdib. Linaid tethru trestuath commilae mara melli cr-i cruaid. Caramain bith aithis for farmnaib dea. Tetrais tuli maru luadaib. Cloidem cosst- druad menmaind logha luaithe gaithe donal druag frasaib tenid ten'al leom- laindr- greine gili escie."

134. "Tócaib mo malaig, a gille," al Balor, "co ndoécius an fer rescach fil ocom acallaim."

135. Tócauhar a malae dia deirc Baloir. Fucaird Luc íer sin líic talma dó, co ndechaid an súil triena cend. Conid a slúag bodessin derécacha. Co torcair four slúag na Fomore conda-apatar trí nónuhair díb foua tóeb; co mboí a mullach frie bruinni n-Indig meic Dé Domnann co sescaind a loim foulae tara béola-side.

---

1   The words following biu are very unclear.

133. Then Núadu Silverhand and Macha the daughter of Ernmas fell at the hands of Balor grandson of Nét. Casmáel fell at the hands of Ochtríallach son of Indech. Lug and Balor of the piercing eye met in the battle. The latter had a destructive eye which was never opened except on a battlefield. Four men would raise the lid of the eye by a polished ring in its lid. The host which looked at that eye, even if they were many thousands in number, would offer no resistance to warriors. It had that poisonous power for this reason: once his father's druids were brewing magic. He came and looked over the window, and the fumes of the concoction affected the eye and the venomous power of the brew settled in it. Then he and Lug met. . . .

134. "Lift up my eyelid, lad," said Balor, "so I may see the talkative fellow who is conversing with me."

135. The lid was raised from Balor's eye. Then Lug cast a sling stone at him which carried the eye through his head, and it was his own host that looked at it. He fell on top of the Fomorian host so that twenty-seven of them died under his side; and the crown of his head struck against the breast of Indech mac Dé Domnann so that a gush of blood spouted over his lips.

136. "*Con*garar dam-sae," ar Indiuch, "Lúoch Lethglass .i. mo
650 fhili." (.i. lethglass é ó talm*ain* go mulluch a cinn.) Totáed 'na doc*um*.
"Finnta dam-sa," ol Indeach, "cía rotollae fo*rm*-sa in n-orchur-sai."

"Cia erna isan cath *conn co*nacherna cid riun- ramid aratoruad
ann rie cach gid fo*rm* memais aratorad (.i. ara tuate)[1] afrecol."

Is ann isbe*rt* Lúog Le*t*[h]gl*as*, "Aisnes cie f*er*, snedcuruch, se*r*ig,
655 sle*ch*t*ach,[2] lathcorauch latr*as* ailig neso*main* a tailm tatbem bag
briss*ius* de*rc*, toraich drech dorig buadgalaigh Baluir tnuthgal-
ti*nn*f*h*ir."

Is ann isbe*rt* Lug na bríatr*a*-sa sís, aga f*reg*r*ae*: "Rola f*er*
nachadais nachadcaru nandidceil nachidceala cerdaib errad. Is me,
660 Lug lon*n*be*m*nech, m*ac* Qind m*ac* E*t*hlend is mo brighfas[3] firgal-[4]
de*rc*aib dam*us* cath co fergaib mor- memais foirb Fom-ib maraib
coraid míad*ach* ciptuctai tuath es mratach ealluch. Is lidh troig
dodob- comci corud cathminn-*n* ar roi, roínfimni n*er*t t*rae*tf-er f- fercc
fesaib dea nid*ur* fulriudai f- ar fodb fesmai dorngal*aib* a cath."

665 Is ann ispe*rt* Lóch, "Cengmai cichsimiu cetaib Fomo*iri* ferdae
nihinnist- imon fose*m* feoc*raib* drongaluib drongaib catbuiden
bairn*n*ech cethern cengmai duibh dobortig dounith nimtorbae rind
nimairic nimthimomna teitbe lorae loghae línn uaib Fomo*iri* fri
hEalg."

670 F*ri*sca*rt* Luch, "Bid go dait," ar Lug, "ar bid doi uaig do
69b fo*rn*diuire ragad e-ad doncath irach atogena-[5] galeng abar rae rig
Fomo*iri* trentuich f- Neíd."

Is ann ispe*rt* Lúoch, ["Bid go det, a Lugh lethsuanaigh[6] fonel nithed
moenrain-ib[7] f*ri*a far tiachta f*ri* taig intretresa tet martaib f*ri*lerg
675 intatlia lethcruidh slogaib srothaib saothnu allaib maraib níthuib. Ni
tadhna len luaith tum*m*e ferc f- neocroide iar nár sirslanaib echaib
nitadled armuriu laigniu f*ri* uaraib oldama nidad tu-s buadaich f*ri*
foep*ra* fichid cath ceol- cufil sudighud f*ri*a. Nach doich duo iariaich
dianath doncath irriaich sudf- luachair de*rc*maighi fulriutha d- magh
680 médiu."

---

1 *.i. ara tuate* is a gloss above *torad*.
2 MS. *sless-ach*.
3 A dot appears over the *a* in *fas*.
4 Over the *f* appears 1 .
5 Over the *o* appears b.
6 Over *lethsuanaigh* appears the gloss *.i. dath derc nobid fair o fuine
   greni co maidin*.
7 Or *moenirainpib*.

136. "Let Lóch Lethglas ["Halfgreen"], my poet, be summoned to me," said Indech. (He was half green from the ground to the crown of his head.) He came to him. "Find out for me," said Indech, "who hurled this cast at me." . . . Then Lóch Lethglas said,

"Declare, who is the man? . . ."

Then Lug said these words in answer to him,

"A man cast

Who does not fear you. . . ."

137. Tánic in Morrígan ingen Ernmusa anduidhe 7 boí *oc* nertad Túath nDéa co fertois[1] an cath co dúr 7 co dícrai. *Con*id ann rocachain in laíd-se sís: "Afraigid rig don cath! rucat- gruaide aisnethir rossa ronnat- feola, fennát- enech, ethát- catha -rruba[2]
685 segatar ratha radatar fleda fechatar catha, canát- natha, noat- druith denait- cuaird cui*m*nit-. Arca alat- side sennat- deda tennat- braig*it* blathnuight- tufer[3] cluinet*har* eghme ailit- cuaird cathit- lo*ch*tai lúet-ethair snaat- arma scothait- sronai. Atci cach rogenair ruadcath de*r*gbandach dremnad fiachlergai foebu*r*lai. F*r*i uab- *ru*smeb-
690 renarmársrotaib sinne f*r*i *fur* foab- líni Fom*ói*re i *m*argnaich incanaigh cop*r*aich aigid fiach dorar f*r*iarsolga garu*h* dálaig fo*rm*des-rodbadh samlaidh de*r*gbandaib dam aimc*r*itaighid *con*naechta sameth don*n*curidh dib*ur* fercurib f*r*istongarar."

138. Romebhaid íer*um* in cauth íer sin, 7 roslech[t]ait na Fomore co
695 muir. Dorochratar comtuitim Ogmae m*a*c Ealauth*an* an tré*n*fer 7 Indeouch m*a*c Dé Domnaund rí na Fomore.

139. Áilis Lóch Leut[h]gl*a*s for Lucch a anac*ul*. "Mo t*r*í d*r*innroisc daum!" *for* Luch.

140. "Rod-bie," our Lóch. "Dingébat-sa fochail Fomor*e* d'É*r*inn co
700 prauth; 7 a ngébas di teungae, íocfaid f*r*i diaid mbeuthaud ar ca*ch* n-aingceus."

141. Aunauchta Lóch íer*um*. Is ann cach*ain* "In Dáil n-Asdadha" do Gaidel*aib*.
"Gébai*d* foss findgrinde, descca doi*ne* doma*n* tuircebat ceth- torel
705 aurblathaib ticfait ioth sceo mbli*cht*, morad indber, armesaib marcainib dossuib d*r*ongaib darach oc*r*id*h*iu icribced*h*aib celar bro*n* berar failti fira fomcichet g*r*ian glessaib saorcaomaib. Sinaib serntar f*ir* fletigib ailtiu astath- f- comfercca c*r*idhiu. Celid Fom*oi*re fairrcce, findcasrao, sitt[4] bitha banba echtguidi echt*rann*, 7 suthaine f*er*aib
710 fin*n*cluiche fo*r*barsed ondiu, cobrath, bid sid ar Fom*oi*re ind Ere."

142. Asbert Lóch da*no* dobé*r*adh ainm di naí cairptip Lochca ara anac*ul*. Asbert dano Lucc ara n-ainmnig*ed*. F*r*iscart Loch cond-ep*ert*, "Luachta, Anagat, Achad, Feoch*air*, F*er*, Golla, Fosad, C*ráe*b, Carp*at*."

715 143. "C*eist*: c*íe* hanmanna na n-aradh robát*ar* inn im*morro*?"
"Medol, Medón, Moth, Mothach, Foi*m*tin*ne*, Tenda, T*r*es, Morb."

---

1 MS. *fertoís*.
2 The beginning of the word is cut off.
3 In the margin after *tufer* appears .c.
4 MS. *sitt, bitha*.

137. Then the Morrígan the daughter of Ernmas came, and she was strengthening the Túatha Dé to fight the battle resolutely and fiercely. She then chanted the following poem:
"Kings arise to the battle! . . ."

138. Immediately afterwards the battle broke, and the Fomoire were driven to the sea. The champion Ogma son of Elatha and Indech mac Dé Domnann fell together in single combat.

139. Lóch Lethglas asked Lug for quarter. "Grant my three requests," said Lug.

140. "You will have them," said Lóch. "I will remove the need to guard against the Fomoire from Ireland forever; and whatever judgement your tongue will deliver in any difficult case, it will resolve the matter until the end of life."

141. So Lóch was spared. Then he chanted "The Decree of Fastening" to the Gaels. . . .

142. Then Lóch said that he would give names to Lug's nine chariots because he had been spared. So Lug said that he should name them. Lóch answered and said, "Luachta, Anagat, Achad, Feochair, Fer, Golla, Fosad, Cráeb, Carpat."

143. "A question then: what are the names of the charioteers who were in them?"
"Medol, Medón, Moth, Mothach, Foimtinne, Tenda, Tres, Morb."

144. "Cíe hanmanna na ndeled bát*ar* 'na lámaib?"
"Ní *anse.* Fes, Res, Roches, Anagar, Ilach, Can*na,* Ríadha,
720 Búaid."

145. "Cíe hanmanna na n-ech?"
"Can, Doríadha, Romuir, Laisad, F*er* Fo*r*said, Sroba*n,*
Airchedal, Ruagar, Illan*n,* Allríadha, Rocedal."

146. "*Ceist:* cie líon ind áir?" *for* Lucc f*ri* Lóch.
725   "Ní [f]edar cía líon do aithech*aib* 7 do d*ra*barslúag. Mad an líon
d'óictiche*r*naib 7 d'airech*aib* 7 do ánr*a*daib 7 do m*a*ccuib r*í*gh 7 do
airdr*í*gaib Fom*o*re rofetar .i. t*ri*ar t*rí* fich*i*t .l. cét f*er,* .xx. cét t*ri* cóicait
.ix. cúicir cet*ri* .xx. m*í*le, ochtar ocht *fich*it móirses*er* cet*ri* .xx. seis*er*
cet*ri* .xx. cóic*er* ocht *fich*it, dias cethrachat im [húa N*é*t nóicait. Is hé
70a 730 sin líon ind áir doroch*air* di airdr*í*g*aib* 7 do airdtice*r*naib na Fom*o*re
isin cath.

147. "Mad a llíon im*morro* di aithech*aib* 7 di d*ro*chdoiniu 7 di
dáosc*a*rslúag 7 d'áos cec*ha* dánae olche*n*ae dilout*ar* a comoide*cht* an
márslu*aig*—aur dideoch*aid* cec*h* ánr*a*d 7 cec*h* ardtoíse*ch* 7 cec*h*
735 airdr*í* de Fomorch*aib* con*a* sochr*aid*e din chauth, co torc*ra*daur adn
uili, a soír 7 a ndaoir—nís-n-áirmium *acht* úoth*a*d di modhag*aib* na
n-airdr*í*gh namáu. Iss *ed* adn so aun líon roáirmios di suidhiu am*al*
attc*on*naurc: s*echt* fir s*echt* fich*i*t s*e*ch*t* cét s*e*ch*t* cáocae .l. di c*é*taib
c*é*t .xx. fichi c*é*t c*é*t .xl. immon Saub n-Úanc[h]endach m*a*c Carp*ri*
740 Cuilc, m*a*c-sidhe mog*a* di Indeuch m*a*c Dé Domnadn (.i. m*a*c [moga]
rich Fom*o*re)."

148. "Mad a ndoch*air* adn che*n*a de le*th*doínib 7 di c*ra*ndasc*tib*
fianlaic[h], di neoch nád roacht c*ri*diu cathae—co roháirmithe*r*
renda[1] nime, 7 gainem maurae, 7 lóae sn*ech*tae, 7 d*rú*cht *for* faichthi,
745 7 bommadn eghae, 7 féur fo coss*aib* g*re*ghae, 7 g*ro*igh me*ic* Lir la
máurainfini—ni háirmidt*er*-side it*er.*"

149. Íar sin don*o* f*ri*th báocc*ul* B*re*si me*ic* Elath*an* dóip. Atb*er*t-
sidhe, "Is feurr m'anac*ul,*" ol sé, "oldáss m*o* guin."

150. "Cid ann-si*de* biass de?" aur Lucc.
750   "Bid sírb*lech*tach báe Ér*enn,*" ol P*re*s, "díaen*om*-aunast*ar*-sa."
"Comarf*as*-sa diar ngáothuib," or Lug.

151. Is de sin luid Lug co Maoíltne Mórbret[h]ach co *n*-ep*er*t p*ri*s,
"An [n-]an*ust*ar B*re*s ar bithblic*ht* do búa*ib*h Ér*enn?*"

152. "Nach an*ust*air," [ar] Móeltne. "Nád cumhaicc a [n-]óes nach
755 a n-indoth, ce choni a mblic*ht* airet beat bí."

144. "What are the names of the goads which were in their hands?"
"Fes, Res, Roches, Anagar, Ilach, Canna, Ríadha, Búaid."

145. "What are the names of the horses?"
"Can, Doríadha, Romuir, Laisad, Fer Forsaid, Sroban, Airchedal, Ruagar, Ilann, Allríadha, Rocedal."

146. "A question: what is the number of the slain?" Lug said to Lóch.
"I do not know the number of peasants and rabble. As to the number of Fomorian lords and nobles and champions and over-kings, I do know: $3 + 3 \times 20 + 50 \times 100$ men $+ 20 \times 100 + 3 \times 50 + 9 \times 5 + 4 \times 20 \times 1000 + 8 + 8 \times 20 + 7 + 4 \times 20 + 6 + 4 \times 20 + 5 + 8 \times 20 + 2 + 40$, including the grandson of Nét with 90 men. That is the number of the slain of the Fomorian over-kings and high nobles who fell in the battle.

147. "But regarding the number of peasants and common people and rabble and people of every art who came in company with the great host—for every warrior and every high noble and every over-king of the Fomoire came to the battle with his personal followers, so that all fell there, both their free men and their unfree servants—I count only a few of the over-kings' servants. This then is the number of those I counted as I watched: $7 + 7 \times 20 \times 20 \times 100 \times 100 + 90$ including Sab Úanchennach son of Coirpre Colc, the son of a servant of Indech mac Dé Domnann (that is, the son of a servant of the Fomorian king).

148. "As for the men who fought in pairs and the spearmen, warriors who did not reach the heart of the battle who also fell there—until the stars of heaven can be counted, and the sands of the sea, and flakes of snow, and dew on a lawn, and hailstones, and grass beneath the feet of horses, and the horses of the son of Lir in a sea storm—they will not be counted at all."

149. Immediately afterward they found an opportunity to kill Bres mac Elathan. He said, "It is better to spare me than to kill me."

150. "What then will follow from that?" said Lug.
"The cows of Ireland will always be in milk," said Bres, "if I am spared."
"I will tell that to our wise men," said Lug.

151. So Lug went to Máeltne Mórbrethach and said to him, "Shall Bres be spared for giving constant milk to the cows of Ireland?"

152. "He shall not be spared," said Máeltne. "He has no power over their age or their calving, even if he controls their milk as long as they are alive."

153. Atpert Lug fria Bres, "Ní ed annísin not-anuig; nád cuimgi a n-óes nach a n-inddoth, ce chonis a mblicht."

154. Atpert Bres, "Forbotha rúada roicht Maíltne."

155. "An fil n-aill nut-ain, a Bres?" ar Lug.
760   "Fil écin. Abair fri bar mbrethiomain bibsiutt búain cech ráithi ar m'anocol-sa."

156. Atbert Lug fria Móeltne, "An [n-]anustar Bres ar búain n-eta cech ráithi di feruib Érenn?"

157. "Is ed imma-n-airnicc lind," or Maoíltne. "Errach fria har 7
765   silad, 7 tosach samraid fri foircend 7¹ sonairti n-etha, 7 tossach n-aipchi² foghamair fri forcend aipchi n-etha, 7 fria búain. Gaimred fria tomalta."

158. "Nís-tessaircc annísin," or Lug fria Bres.
"Forbotha rúada roicht Maíltni," or sé.

770 159. "Is luga dot-essaircc," or Lug.
"Cid?" ol Bres.

160. "Cocon ebrad, co sílfad, co chobibsad fir Érenn? Is íar fis an tréde-siu, manad-anustar."
"Abair friu, 'Mairt a n-ar; Mairt hi corad síl a ngurt; Mairt a n-
775 imbochdt.' "

161. Roléccad ass didiu Bres triasan celg-sin.

162. Isan cath-sin didiu fúair Oghma trénfer Ornai, claidiomh Tet[h]ra rí Fomore. Tofoslaicc Ogma in claideb 7 glanais hé. Is and sin roindis an claideb nach ndernad de, ar [ba] béss do claidbib an
780 tan-sin dotorsilcitis doadhbadis na gnímha dogníthea díb in tan-sin. Conid de sin dlegaid claidme cíos a nglantai íarna tosluccad. Is de dano forcométar brechda hi cloidbib ó sin amach. Is aire immorro nolabraidis demna d'armaib isan aimsir-sin ar noadraddis airm ó dainib isin ré-sin 7 ba do comaircib na haimsire-sin na hairm. Is don
785 cloidibh-sin rochacain Lóch Let[h]glas in láid-si: "Admell ma Orna, uath cath, cule leccla, fristethaind tuind formna f-roir is ress ningalne amtri locha lochaurbe imlias luch loeg trimchim am trichtaigh tighi fuaibne mifualang tighe tethrae toetrau dobert mor fodriru Fal Fomhoire foenda for Balur benn bas- alan Fomhor- lelgi mac Ethne
790 uili aoinfecht ferse colom cathram-³ ransi fodb fersamhle fersi cetharslichd fhid serbh armarmíadh.⁴ Ainm aili fes- fuil tethr- hitus faidter fuirtbe mong diafurbidh f-ruiris ilur fuil- Oghme."

1   7 seems wrongly inserted.
2   n-aipchi also seems wrongly inserted.
3   Or read cathrain-,
4   Or read armarnúsadh.

153. Lug said to Bres, "That does not save you; you have no power over their age or their calving, even if you control their milk."

154. Bres said, "Máeltne has given bitter alarms!"

155. "Is there anything else which will save you, Bres?" said Lug.
"There is indeed. Tell your lawyer they will reap a harvest every quarter in return for sparing me."

156. Lug said to Máeltne, "Shall Bres be spared for giving the men of Ireland a harvest of grain every quarter?"

157. "This has suited us," said Máeltne. "Spring for plowing and sowing, and the beginning of summer for maturing the strength of the grain, and the beginning of autumn for the full ripeness of the grain, and for reaping it. Winter for consuming it."

158. "That does not save you," said Lug to Bres.
"Máeltne has given bitter alarms," said he.

159. "Less rescues you," said Lug.
"What?" asked Bres.

160. "How shall the men of Ireland plow? How shall they sow? How shall they reap? If you make known these things, you will be saved."
"Say to them, on Tuesday their plowing; on Tuesday their sowing seed in the field; on Tuesday their reaping."

161. So through that device Bres was released.

162. Now in that battle Ogma the champion found Orna, the sword of Tethra, king of the Fomoire. Ogma unsheathed the sword and cleaned it. Then the sword told what had been done by it, because it was the habit of swords at that time to recount the deeds that had been done by them whenever they were unsheathed. And for that reason swords are entitled to the tribute of cleaning after they have been unsheathed. Moreover spells have been kept in swords from that time on. Now the reason why demons used to speak from weapons then is that weapons used to be worshipped by men and were among the sureties of that time. Lóch Lethglas chanted the following poem about that sword. . . .

163. Loutar a ndiaid na Fomore dano Lug 7 an Daghdou 7 Ogma, ar cruitire an Dagda ro-n-ucsad leo, Úaitniu a ainm. [Rosaghad ierum a flettech a mboí Bres mac Elathan 7 Elathan mac Delbaíth. Is ann boí in crot forin fraighid. Is sí in cruit sin ara nenaisc na céola conarofhograidhsetor tria gairm co ndegart in Dagda in tan atbert ann so sís,

"Tair Daur Dá Bláo,
Tair Cóir Cethairchuir,
Tair sam, tair gam,
Béola crot 7 bolg 7 buinne!"

(Dá n-ainm dano bátar foran cruit-sin .i. Dur Dá Blá 7 Cóir Cethairchuir.)

164. Doluid an crot assan froig ierum, 7 marbais nonbór 7 tánuicc docum an Daghda; 7 sepainn-sie a trédhi fora nem[th]i[g]thir cruitiri dóib .i. súantraigi 7 genntraigi 7 golltraigi. Sephainn golltraigi dóib co ngolsad a mná déracha. Sephainn genntraigi dóib co tibsiot a mná 7 a macraith. Sephainn súantraigi dóib contuilset ant slúaigh. Is de sen[1] diérlátar a triur slán úaidib—cíamadh áil a ngoin.

165. Dobert an Dagda diu laiss tria gém na dairti dobreth dó ara sóethar; ar in tan rogéssi a gaimmain rogeltatar cetri Érinn uili do neoch bertatar Fomore díp ina cíos.

166. Íar mbrisiud ierum an catha 7 íar nglanad ind áir, fochard an Morrígan ingen Ernmais do táscc an catha-sin 7 an coscair móair forcóemnochair ann do rídingnaib Érenn 7 dia sídhcairib, 7 dia arduscib 7 dia inberaiph. Conid do sin inneses Badb airdgníomha beus. "Nach scél laut?" ar cách friai-se ann suide.

"Sith co nem. Nem co doman. Doman fo nim, nert hi cach, án forlann, lan do mil, mid co saith. Sam hi ngam, gai for sciath, sciath for durnd. Dunad lonngarg; longait- tromfoíd fod di uí ross forbiur benna abu airbe imetha. Mess for crannaib, craob do scis scis do áss saith do mac mac for muin, muinel tairb tarb di arccoin odhb do crann, crann do ten. Tene a nn-ail. Ail a n-uír uích a mbuaib boinn a mbru. Brú lafefaid ossglas iaer errach, foghamar forasit etha. Iall do tir, tir co trachd lafeabrae. Bidruad rossaib síraib rithmár, 'Nach scel laut?' Sith co nemh, bidsirnae .s."

MS. sén.

163. Then Lug and the Dagda and Ogma went after the Fomoire, because they had taken the Dagda's harper, Úaithne. Eventually they reached the banqueting hall where Bres mac Elathan and Elatha mac Delbaíth were. There was the harp on the wall. That is the harp in which the Dagda had bound the melodies so that they did not make a sound until he summoned them, saying,

    "Come Daur Dá Bláo,
    Come Cóir Cetharchair,
    Come summer, come winter,
    Mouths of harps and bags and pipes!"

(Now that harp had two names, Daur Dá Bláo and Cóir Cetharchair.)

164. Then the harp came away from the wall, and it killed nine men and came to the Dagda; and he played for them the three things by which a harper is known: sleep music, joyful music, and sorrowful music. He played sorrowful music for them so that their tearful women wept. He played joyful music for them so that their women and boys laughed. He played sleep music for them so that the hosts slept. So the three of them escaped from them unharmed—although they wanted to kill them.

165. The Dagda brought with him the cattle taken by the Fomoire through the lowing of the heifer which had been given him for his work; because when she called her calf, all the cattle of Ireland which the Fomoire had taken as their tribute began to graze.

166. Then after the battle was won and the slaughter had been cleaned away, the Morrígan, the daughter of Ernmas, proceeded to announce the battle and the great victory which had occurred there to the royal heights of Ireland and to its *síd*-hosts, to its chief waters and to its rivermouths. And that is the reason Badb still relates great deeds. "Have you any news?" everyone asked her then.

    "Peace up to heaven.
    Heaven down to earth.
    Earth beneath heaven,
    Strength in each,
    A cup very full,
    Full of honey;
    Mead in abundance.
    Summer in winter. . . .
    Peace up to heaven . . ."

167. Boí-si íar*um* oc taircet*ul* deridh an be*t*ha ann be*us*, 7 *oc* tairngire cech uilc nobíad ann, 7 cech teadma 7 gac[h] díglau; *con*id
830 ann rocachain an laíd-se sís:

"Ni accus bith nombeo baid: sam cin blatha, beti bai cin blichda, mna can feli, fir gan gail. Gabala can righ ri*n*na ulcha ilmoigi beola bron, feda cin mes. Muir ca*n* toradh. Tuir bainbthine im*m*at moel rátha, fás a f*o*rgna*m* locha diersit- dinn at*r*ifit- linn lines sechilar
835 flaithie faoilti fria holc, ilach imgnath gnuse ul-. Inc*r*ada docredb-gluind ili, imairecc catha, toebh f*r*i ech delceta imda dala braith m-c flaithi forbuid bron sen saobretha. Brecfásach mbrithiom- braithiomh cech fer. Foglaid cech m*a*c. Ragaid m*a*c i lligie a ath*a*r. Ragaid ath*air* a lligi a me*i*c. Cliamain cach a brat*har*. Ni sia nech mnai assa
840 tigh. Gignit- cenmair olc aims*er* im*m*era m*a*c a ath*air*, imera inge*n* . . ."

167. She also prophesied the end of the world, foretelling every evil that would occur then, and every disease and every vengeance; and she chanted the following poem:

"I shall not see a world
Which will be dear to me:
Summer without blossoms,
Cattle will be without milk,
Women without modesty,
Men without valor.
Conquests without a king . . .
Woods without mast.
Sea without produce. . . .
False judgements of old men.
False precedents of lawyers,
Every man a betrayer.
Every son a reaver.
The son will go to the bed of his father,
The father will go to the bed of his son.
Each his brother's brother-in-law.
He will not seek any woman outside his house. . . .
An evil time,
Son will deceive his father,
Daughter will deceive . . ."

NOTES

§1. According to *Met. Dinds.* IV 300-301, 455-456, the earlier name of Mag Tuired was Mag Etrige, one of the plains cleared by Partholón.

§1:1. The space left for an ornamental initial *B* was never filled in, although ornamental, interlaced capitals do appear elsewhere in the MS. (fols. 12, 27, and 59).

§1:1. The sinister associations of the north are reflected in many sources. Macalister, *LG* IV, 292, note to §304; *Motif-Index*: A 671.0.1* 'Hell located in the North.' The references include M. E. Dobbs, 'The Battle of Findchorad,' *ZCP* 14 (1923), 398-399, where druids face north, towards Hell, to sacrifice to gods borrowed from Classical tradition, and W. Stokes, 'The Annals of Tigernach.' *RC* 17 (1896), 416-417, noting the cause of a pestilence as demons from "the northern Islands of the world." The authority for the information is no less than Óengus Óc, son of the Dagda. See also Françoise Le Roux, 'Les Isles au Nord du Monde,' *Hommages à Albert Grenier* (Brussels: Latomus, 1962), 1057-1062.

§§1-7. The account of the Tuatha Dé Danann's training in the occult arts and the list of their four talismans appears both in *Lebor Gabála Érenn* and as a separate anecdote in *YBL, BB,* and Egerton 105, edited by Hull, 'The Four Jewels of the *Tuatha Dé Danann*,' *ZCP* 18 (1929), 73-89. The language of §§1-7 is later than that of most of the rest of the narrative, although there are minor differences of wording between §§1-7 and all of the *LG* versions published by Macalister. The traditions themselves, however, may predate the earliest surviving version of *LG*.

Orthographically, these sections resemble Stowe D.4.3. (Macalister's D, a MS. belonging to Redaction 2, written by Muirges mac Páidín ua Maoil-Chonaire, the transcriber of the Book of Fenagh). Among the forms that do not appear in any of the *LG* versions printed by Macalister are the use of *druíd* (n. pl.) in §7 to describe the four teachers of the Túatha Dé Danann (other texts using *fisid* or *filid*), and the verb *foglaindsit* (itself a Mid. Ir. form, an s-pret. replacing an earlier reduplicated pret.) which is replaced by the verb *foglaimid* in the other texts. Macalister's earliest version of Redaction 1, *LL*, omits the material in §§2-7 entirely.

Besides emphasizing the Túatha Dé Danann's expertise as masters of magic, these sections introduce three major characters as possessors of talismans that symbolize aspects of their roles in the myth: Núadu, king and warrior, whose sword reflects his association with combat; Lug, the battle leader whose spear assures victory; and the Dagda, whose cauldron symbolizes his association with hospitality, and whose role requires him to combat Fomorian inhospitality.

The account of the arrival of the Túatha Dé Danann in *1MT* also emphasizes their mastery of all the arts (§§20, 23), and their journey from the northern islands of the world, but does not include the references to wizards, cities and talismans of *2MT* §§2-7.

§1:3. *combtar f*ortilde for *súthib cerd ngenntlichtae.*

fortail i (a) "having the upper hand or mastery, dominant, victorious," *Contribb.* F 364-365; examples include *LU* 1324 (*Im. Br.* ii 291), *ba f. mé for cach rét,* "I was able to do anything," and *LL* 9a 2-3, a usage close to that of the present text: *batar* ... *oc foglaim* ... *combtar fortaile for cerddaib suíthe gentliucta.*

In the present ex., *cerd*, g. pl., takes the place of *suíthe* ; but perhaps the same group of nouns is intended, hence, "until they were masters of the skills of the pagan arts," taking *súthib* as d. pl. of *suíthe* (or *suthe*), m.? orig. n.?, "learning, lore, skill, mastery," rather than as d. pl. of *suí*, t, m. "man of learning, sage, wise-man." See *Contribb. S* 411-413, s.v. *suí*, 426-427, s.v. *suíthe*.

§§2-7. On the passage describing the four cities, druids, and talismans, see Vernam Hull, 'The Four Jewels of the *Tuatha Dé Danann*,' *ZCP* 18 (1929), 73-89.

Macalister, *LG* IV, 293, discussing the parallel, associates Falias with both *fál* "hedge," and the Lia Fáil; Goirias with *gor* "fire"; Finnias or Findias with *finn* "white (or fair)"; and Muirias with *muir* "sea." He further suggests the *-ias* termination may have been borrowed from Ogham inscriptions, although later he proposes Biblical Latin models for the druids' names, Uiscias and Semias. In fact, those names can also be understood in terms of Irish roots: Mórfesae as a combination of *mór*, o, ā, "great" used substantively, and *fis*, u and o, n. later m., "wisdom," hence, "Greatness of Wisdom"; Esras, perhaps *esrais*, *esrus*, "outlet, passage; means, way, opportunity"; Uiscias, to be associated with *uisce*, io, m., "water"; and Semias, perhaps to be connected with *séim*, "slender, thin; rarified (of air)," cf. *séimide* (b) "transparent, bright, limpid."

For an interpretation of the symbolism of the druids, cities and talismans, see Françoise Le Roux, 'Les Isles au Nord du Monde,' *Hommages à Albert Grenier* (Brussels: Latomus, 1962), 1051-1062.

§3:6. For references to the Stone of Fál, see *Motif-Index*: H 171.5* "Stone of Destiny (Lia Fáil)" and cross references. Another useful collection of references appears in *Contribb. F* 36, s.v. 5 *fál*, o, m. For etymologies, see Jord Pinault, "**KRAWO-* et **WALO-*, **WALI-* dans les langues celtiques," *Ogam* 13 (1961), 599-614; Christian J. Guyonvarc'h, 'Notes d'Étymologie et Lexicographie gauloises et celtiques 21, Irlandais Lia Fáil 'Pierre de Souveraineté,'" *Ogam* 17 (1965), 436-440. Guyonvarc'h associates *fál* etymologically with *flaith* "sovereignty." *LG* §309 describes both the Stone's origin and its fate:

"It is the Túatha Dé Danann who brought with them the Great Fál ... which was in Temair, whence Ireland bears the name of 'The Plain of Fál.' He under whom it should utter a cry was King of Ireland; until Cú Chulainn smote it, for it uttered no cry under him nor under his fosterling, Lugaid son of the three Finds of Emain. And from that out the stone uttered no cry save under Conn of Temair. Then its heart flew out from it [from Temair] to Tailtiu, so that is the Heart of Fál which is there. It was no chance which caused it, but Christ's being born, which is what broke the powers of the idols."

§4:8. For the spear of Lug, see *Motif-Index* D 1653.1.2 "Unerring spear," and D 1402.8 "Magic spear always inflicts mortal wounds"; cf. D 1084 "Magic spear," and F 244.1* "The Four Jewels of the Tuatha Dé Danann."

LG §357 (M) adds, regarding Lug's spear, that he had it in the battle of Mag Tuired against the Fomoire, *.i. Ibar Conailli: Bidbad a hainm.*

*BDD*² 1242, mentions a spear called the Lúin of Celtchar meic
Uithechair, found in the Battle of Mag Tuired; cf. *RC* 23 (1902), 325.

See O'Rahilly, *EIHM*, pp. 65ff. for a theory of the symbolism of the
spear and references to the spears of Bern Buadach and Assal (the latter
obtained by Lug from the sons of Tuireann).

§4:9. *an bídh i lláimh*. See *Thurn. Gramm.* §507, d., *LG* §305, for the
idiom: *a mbid laim*. Cf. *LG* §357, *a mbí a láim*, the construction parallel to
the present example.

§5:10. For the sword of Núadu and related motifs, see *Motif-Index* D
1653.1.1 "Infallible sword," and D 1402.7.2* "Magic sword always
inflicts mortal wounds"; cf. D 1081 "Magic sword," D 1081.1 "Sword of
magic origin," and F 244.1* "The Four Jewels of the Tuatha Dé
Danann."

ní térnádh. Stokes: *Ni terládh*. The MS., however, uses the abbreviation t
(Latin *vel*, Irish *nó, no,* or *ná, na*). The verb is *do·érni*, "gets away,
escapes." Cf. the parallel passage in *LG* §§305, 325, 357.

idntiuch boduha. See *Contribb. B* 5, s.v. *badb*, ā, f. earlier *bodb*, the name
of a war goddess, and "scaldcrow," (a form in which the goddess appeared).
The attributive genitive singular is used in the sense "deadly, fatal,
dangerous, ill-fated." Cf. *badba*, explained as "evident, conspicuous,"
although it is suggested that the word is actually genitive singular of *badb*, ā,
f., for which a second meaning was inferred from examples such as those
cited. See also *badbda*, io, iā (*badb*) "appertaining to war; Badb-like, deadly,
fatal," which lists several examples with the spelling *badba*: *SR* 1904
(:ballda); *TTebe*, 3247, 2279.

§6:12. Cauldrons have many roles in Irish tradition, both practical and
magical, but references to the Dagda's cauldron seem to appear only in
sources containing some form of the text edited by Hull as 'The Four Jewels
of the *Tuatha Dé Danann*,' *ZCP* 18 (1929), 73-89.

For magic cauldrons in general, see *Motif-Index* D 1171.2 "Magic
cauldron," D 1472.1.11 "Magic cauldron supplies food," and D 1318.13
"Magic cauldron reveals guilt." On the symbolic significance of cauldrons
in Celtic tradition, see Françoise Le Roux, *"Des chaudrons Celtiques à
l'arbre d'Esus, Lucain et les Scholies Bernoises,"* *Ogam* 7 (1955), 33-58.

§8:17ff. The alliance and intermarriage between Tuatha Dé Danann and
Fomoire does not appear in the folk accounts of Lug's birth, where his
conception is the result of a secret union between Cían and Balor's
daughter. *LG* identifies Lug's parents, but does not comment on the circumstances of his birth, nor does it mention an alliance between their tribes. As
an element of the narrative, the formal marriage of Cían and Ethne
emphasizes the legitimacy of their son's association with the Tuatha Dé
Danann through paternal kinship, an important aspect of the contrast
between the career of Lug and that of Bres, son of a Fomorian king and a
woman of the Tuatha Dé Danann.

The brevity of the section makes the passage difficult to date. The form
gnisit, for example, appears in *SR* 4077; *fri* with the dative is a late usage,
but not necessarily original; *a ngen mbúadha* may represent neuter gender
or simply the absence of nasalization before g-, with *an = in*.

Folk accounts of Lug's birth are noted by Ó Cuív, *2MT*², Introduction,

8, n. 4. See also O'Sullivan, *The Folklore of Ireland*, 17-22; 167, n., and O'Sullivan and Christiansen, *The Types of the Irish Folktale*, 185, Type 934 C*, "Man will Die if he ever Sees his Daughter's son." An analysis of the Celtic mythological materials involved is given by W. J. Gruffydd, *Math vab Mathonwy* (Cardiff, 1928).

§§9-13. Returning to *LG* tradition, these sections sketch the arrival of the Tuatha Dé Danann in Ireland, the first battle of Mag Tuired, and its consequences for both Tuatha Dé Danann and Fir Bolg. Most of the details may be found in one version or another of *LG*, although they do not appear together in any single passage, and there is no clear affiliation with any particular redaction. In the context of the tale as a whole, the flight of the Fir Bolg to the Fomoire foreshadows the later breakdown of the alliance between Fomoire and Tuatha Dé Danann.

Regarding the relationship between §§9-13 and *LG*, it may be noted that Redactions 1 and 3, for example, have the Tuatha Dé Danann land at Slíab Delgaid in Conmaicne Réin, and both explain that Conmaicne Cúile is actually meant (*LL* mentions only "the mountains of Conmaicne Réin"). Redaction 2 has them land at Slíab in Iairnn, §322.

2MT identifies the landing site as in the territory of Corcu Belgatan, mislocated in Conmaicne Mara. In *1MT*, Slíab Belgadain is a site of some prominence, to which the Tuatha Dé Danann advance after landing in Conmaicne Réin; and it appears that the narrative is attempting to reconcile conflicting traditions.

§9:19. *morloinges* is taken as a compound of *muir* "sea" and *loinges* "fleet; invasion by sea," although *mór* "great" is also possible. The decision follows Macalister, *LG* §§306, 358; (there is no precise parallel in Redaction 2).

§9:20. The motif of burning one's boats to avoid the temptation of flight occurs in Aeneid V 604ff. where, however, it is the action of the women, weary of wandering and anxious to settle. Both the prose and poetry of *LG* mention the Tuatha Dé Danann's action before the first battle of Mag Tuired. Several reasons are given: to keep the Fomoire from stealing them, *LG* §§306, 322, 358; to prevent conflict between Lug and Núadu, *LG* §358; and to prevent flight, *LG* §§306, 358, see also poem LIX. Cf. *1MT* 19, §22, where, however, no reasons for the Tuatha Dé Danann's decision are given. A similar incident occurs in 'Battle of the Assembly of Macha,' edited and translated by M. E. dobbs, *ZCP* 16 (1927), 149.

§9:22-23. Regarding the belief that the Tuatha Dé Danann arrived in a magic mist, contrast the account in the *LL* version of *LG* §306, where only the clouds are mentioned.

§9:24. Regarding the creation of a magic mist, see *Motif-Index* D 902.1 "Magic mist" and D 902.1.1 "Druidic mist."

§10. Stokes notes that a tradition of two battles of Mag Tuired appears in Harleian 432 fo. 3^{b}2 (=Laws I, 46). For a thorough discussion of the evidence regarding the existence of two battles in early tradition, see Murphy, "Notes on Cath Maige Tuired," *Éigse* 7 (1954), 191-198. Among other points, he notes that the saga lists (apparently based upon a tenth-century original) include only one battle (194). See also Georges Dumézil, *Mitra-Varuna*, 2nd ed. (1948), 179-188.

LG §§281, 289-290, 297 give accounts of the first battle of Mag Tuired.

§10:26. Regarding the number of the Fir Bolg slain, there are two traditions. The dominant one, represented by *LG* §§281, 297, 307, 322, 359, and *Keat.* I: x: 212-213, gives 100,000 (*cét míle*). The other, perhaps an error, gives 1100 (*cét ar míle*): *LG* §96.

On the identification of the refuge sites, see Macalister, *LG* IV "Notes on Section VI," 80-82.

In *IMT*, the Fir Bolg do not flee Ireland, but are ceded the province of Connacht by the Tuatha Dé Danann, lest they lose their injured king Núadu in a renewed combat with the Fomorian champion Sreng; 57-59, §58.

§11:28ff. Regarding Núadu's injury and healing, see *LG* §§310, 329, 362. For references to Sreng, see §§290, 279 and the poem L. There is a full account of the single combat between Núadu and Sreng in *IMT*.

§11:29. *liaigh.* For the vowel length, see *Contribb. L* 145, s.v. *líaig,* i, m. (perhaps orig. disyll.) and *Thurn. Gramm.* pp. 63, 66, 191. The vowel is never long in the present MS.

§11:30. *co lúth cecai láma.* Lit., "with the movement of every hand."

§11:30. MS. *Credhne.* The vowel is short throughout this text, but elsewhere varies: *LG* LIII §12, Creidhne: Eithne; *LG* LVI §10 (not final), restored as Crëidne; *Met. Dinds.* I 46 14, given as Créidne.

§12:31-32. The list of slain members of the Túatha Dé Danann resembles *LG* R$_1$ §310 (Min), which includes Tuirill Piccreo among the fallen. Min, however, also includes Echtach and Etargal, as do the other *LG* redactions.

§13. The information about the Fir Bolg flight to seek the Fomoire, found in the Fir Bolg section of *LG*, does not appear in *LL*.

§14. Evidence for a partly overlapping and now lost version of *2MT* is given by some of the entries in the H.3.18 623ª glossary edited by A. I. Pearson, *Ériu* 13 (1940), 61-87. The entries §8 *Arra,* §74 *Cosnam* and §172 *Dighe* include quotations from an unknown text of *2MT*, although §74 and §172 seem close to the present text's §14 and §19 respectively. See note §19. *Arra .i. íc, ut est i cath Mhaighi Tuiredh: ni rabhadar fir Erenn ac arra in chísa géin ro mhair Lugh.*

Cosnam .i. imrisan no cogadh, ut est Mag Tuired: buí cosnam flatha fer nErinn eter Tuatha De Danann 7 a mná.

§14:36ff. The conflict between the Túatha Dé Danann and their womenfolk begins the segment of the tale concerned with the kingship of Bres. This early stratum of the narrative appears to have stressed the contrast between maternal kinship and paternal kinship as bases for tribal membership and loyalty, and to have shown Bres's election as the result of the women's overvaluing of maternal kinship. The women's argument that the election of Bres would strengthen the Fomorian alliance may be a later addition.

Bres's questioning of his mother (§42) concerning the place from which his people came, together with Elatha's apparent ignorance of his son's career (§45ff.) suggest that in an early version of the tale, Bres's election as king was not a matter of international politics, but simply the result of overvaluing maternal kinship relations, which the myth at all levels contrasts with paternal kinship as the essential and proper basis of social interdependence.

On the folly of taking the advice of women, see *Motif-Index* C 195* "Tabu: taking the advice of a woman." The classic description of the folly of choosing women as counsellors appears in "The Instructions of King Cormac mac Airt," ed. and trans. Kuno Meyer, *Royal Irish Academy Todd Lecture Series,* 15 (1909), 28-37.

§14:36-37. The prohibition against a maimed king is also illustrated in the account of the disfigurement of King Fergus of Ulster, *Laws* I, 73; see also III, 83-85.

For additional references see *Motif-Index, P 16.2* "King must resign if maimed (disfigured)," *C 563.2** "Tabu: King having physical blemish."

§15:41. Before continuing with the events of Bres's reign, the tale explains the circumstances surrounding his birth, introducing what was in all likelihood once a separate tale, the *genemain Bres meic Elathain* of the title. The language of these sections (§§16-23) is as early as any in the entire tale: see Murphy, *Éigse* 7 (1954), 195.

§16:42ff. An account of the meeting of Ériu and Elatha is not found elsewhere, although there is general agreement in early texts that Bres is their son. The dialogue between the lovers echoes that between Eochaid and Étaín in *BDD²* 48 and is one of several stylistic correspondences between the two tales.

§16:43. *Máoth Scéni.* The location of the house of Máoth Scéni is unknown. Elsewhere in the text *Scétne* is associated with the Loch Skean area in N. Roscommon. Did the territory of the Fir Scéinne extend to the coast? (See *Scétne). It might also be possible to see here a link with Inber Scéne, although that site (if the mouth of the Kenmare river) lies outside the general locale of the tale.

Since Éri is identified only as *ingen Delbaíth* it is impossible to say whether she is daughter of the Delbáeth who is father of Elatha (and half or full sister to Bres), or of some other Delbáeth. The Túatha Dé Danann genealogies of *LG* §§316, 338, 368 make her the daughter of Fíachna (Fiachu) m. Delbaíth (son of Ogma m. Elathain m. Delbaíth) and of Ernmas. *Leb. Gab.* §101 gives this tradition, but in §106 identifies her as a daughter of Dealbaoth. Perhaps Fiacha (-na, -ra) has simply been omitted, or perhaps *Leb. Gab.* §106 and *2MT* represent a distinct genealogical tradition.

§16-45. *acht nát arthraigestar.* The verb *arthraigidir,* "appears (to, *do*), makes manifest, shows clearly," with *acht* "save only that," is followed by a nasalizing relative clause in O. Ir., see *Thurn. Gramm.* §503. Stokes' edition suggests a compound form **do·arthraigedar,* otherwise unattested.

§16:42ff. The description of Elatha is formulaic in character, and may, for example, be compared with the many descriptions of the warriors identified by Fergus, *Táin* 4296ff., and by Cú Roí in *MU²* 525ff. It is somewhat unusual, however, in its extensive use of metallic and light-reflective terms, and the absence of other color references.

§16:44, 47-48. *co n-* "until" takes the acc.; *gúala* n.f. acc. dual. should be *gúalainn*. *Día gelge* may be simply orthographical — or may represent hesitation between *dá* and *dí* (O.Ir. m. *da*; *dí semcradn*, however, a compound of *crann* o.n., later m., should have *dá n-*(if neuter) or *dá*, (if masc.).

Gáe is normally masculine, but here the feminine dual numeral is used; cf. §124, where the infixed pronoun (f.) in *rus·meil* refers to *gaí Rúadáin*. Note also *Dí gáe* in a poem attributed to Cúan O'Lothchain, *Ériu* 4 (1910) 102 §43.

§16:50. MS. *snasai*, emended to read *snas[t]ai*, *snasta* "cut, trimmed, polished" fits better here than *snas*, vn. of *snaidid*, o,m., "cutting, finish, polish." The term is applied to spears in several instances, see *Contribb. S* 298-299, s.v. *snasta*.

§17:53. *-bioa*. MS. *-bíoa* or *-bióa*, cf. §40:186, *-biaa*.
"Innum bioa-ssae úar coblide laut?" This division of words reflects the parallel in *BDD²*, 48, *"Inum biasa úair coibligi lat?"*
Stokes "Is this the time that our lying with thee will be easy?" is based on a misreading of the text, taking *-a-ssae* as the adj. a*ssa(e)*, "easy."
On the parallel dialogue in *BDD²*, see Knott's introduction, xi, and text 48.

§17:55. *Tic*, 2 sg. ipv. of *do-icc*. *tair* is the usual form of the 2 sg. ipv. for both *do-icc* and *do-téit*, from *t-air-ic*, *Thurn. Gramm.* §588.

§18:56. MS. *ciich*, the double letter presumably indicating length, hence *cïich*. Cf. *cích*, *LU* 10964.
an uher. An unusual spelling for *f*; *uh* is commonly used in this text for lenited *b*.

§18:59. *rocoíner*. See *Contribb. C* 40-41, s.v. *caínid* "laments, bewails; weeps at, deplores." The verb often shows deponent forms: see *Blathm.* 138, n. 534.

§18:60. *comairnecmar*. 1 pl. pret. of *con-ricc*.
dom nemét. The MS. uses the abbreviation for *nem-* consisting of the letter *n* with a mark of suspension (n-stroke) midway down the right stroke of the letter: Cf. Stokes' transcription: *Domnonn [is] ét . . . mo ét did-siu amal atom-cota-siu*.
Do usually expresses the actor-agent in such a sentence (with possessive pronoun and verbal noun, the possessive pronoun normally indicating the object); and it is possible to translate "and you possessing me as (soon as) you can" (or "in the way that you do possess me") with *amal* as a temporal conjunction expressing simultaneousness (II c), or an explicative conjunction with adverbial force, or simply as a comparative conjunction, *atom-cota-siu* being 2 sg. present indicative of *ad-cota* "gets, obtains, procures; is able, can," with 1 sg. infixed pronoun; and *ét* as verbal noun of *ad-cota*.
On the other hand, *ét* might be taken as o, m., "jealousy, zeal," used of a woman's jealousy regarding her husband, usually with *la* (and agent), but also with the possessive pronoun. See additional notes, *Thurn. Gramm.* §103 (to p. 276, 1. 30) for possessive pronoun as subjective genitive in verbal noun constructions. Compare the construction with *étugud*, u, m.,

"zeal, jealousy" in *M1.* 32^d 10: *étugud Dáe desom*, "jealousy of God concerning him." This passage, then, might be taken as "and my possessive love for you as soon as you possess me . . ." with a play on the two meanings of *ét*.

§19:62. *Didigestar.* Cf. §172 *(Dighe)* in the glossary ed. A. I. Pearson, *Ériu* 13 (1940), 61-87: *Dighe .i. slanughadh, ut est Cath Muighe Tuiredh: do dighisi do brog donnega so.*

   a ór(s)nasc n-óir. On the gender of *ordnasc,* see *CMM* note *440,* where the possibility that the word was originally neuter is discussed.

   The motif of the ring appears also in *Scéla Éogain* §§9, 16 in *CMM*; the parallel in *2MT* is noted on p. 16. Another parallel is to be found in *Aided Óenfir Aífe And So,* ed. A. G. van Hamel in *Comp. Con C.,* §1.

   See also *Motif-Index*: T 645 "Paramour leaves token with girl to give their son," H 94 "Identification by ring."

§19:63. *ná tésied.* Perhaps scribal methathesis for *·téised?*

§19:64. *diambad coimsie die méor sin. sin* might be taken as enclitic, emphasizing the 3 sg. m. pronoun in *die,* but such a usage is uncommon in O. Ir. Instead, *sin* is here taken to be the subject of its clause.

§20:65. *Is deitheden eli dom-sae. Contribb. D* 15, s.v. *deithiden,* ā, f., this ex., "I have something else on my mind."

   Deithiden means not only "care, concern, solicitude, attention," (bestowed on a person or thing) but also, in a negative sense, "care, anxiety, trouble."

§21:67ff. The general character of Elatha's prophecy is represented by the short prose introduction to the account of the first satire made in Ireland that appears as an independent anecdote in *YBL and H. 3. 17.* Apart from the words of the satire itself, this anecdote is verbally independent of *2MT,* although it outlines the events of Bres's career, noting his beauty; his paternal kinship with the Fomoire; his election as king of his mother's people; his inhospitable behaviour and Coirpre's consequent satire; his flight to the Fomoire followed by the second battle of Mag Tuired. Bres is also mentioned as a standard of beauty in *Cóir Anm.* §153, in words reminiscent of Elatha's prophecy, both texts describing him as *cruthach*; there is, however, no mention of his kingship.

§21:69. The explanation of the meaning of the name Bres as *cruthach* "shapely, fair, beautiful," given by his father Elatha, is repeated in *Cóir Anm.* §153, in not quite the same words. Other examples of *bres* with this meaning remain to be discovered. *Contribb B* 179, s.v. 2 *bres,* i, ā, gives the primary meaning as "great, mighty"; 1 *bres,* ā, f., on the other hand, ranges in meaning from (a) "fight, blow; effort"; (b) "uproar, din"; (c) "metaphor of a hero, chief (or a substantive use of 2 *bres*) to (d) "beauty, worth."

§21:69. *atcícher.* For *ad·cíther,* 3 sg. pr. ind. pass. of *ad·cí.*

§21:71. *dobiter.* Taken by Stokes as a form of *do·midethar* "weighs, measures, estimates." This example, however, is cited in *Contribb D* 213, s.v. 2 *do-ben* (d) with *fri,* "measures by (as a standard), compares with," along with an example from Cormac's Glossary (Y 606), *dobentai.*

§22:73. *de* for *dí,* 3 sg. f.

§23:75. *Contribb. A* 275, s.v. *?aithséolta* (cf. 2 *séolta,* etc.) gives only this example, "when a week after the woman's lying-in was complete." (Stokes).

The prefix *aith-, ath-,* with nouns, may mean "second" or "further"; it is sometimes used with merely intensive force. 2 *séolta* appears in the phrase *ben shéolta,* "woman in childbed." The present example may be taken as meaning "seven days of further lying-in (after delivery)," "seven days remaining in childbed (after delivery)."

§23:75-77. Bres's precocity, if not his rapid growth, is shared by other heroic infants, notably Cú Chulainn (*Táin* 1208-1213) and Cú Chulainn's only son (*Comp. Con. C.: Aided Óenfir Aife And So,* §2) who undertake manly feats of arms at the age of seven. If Bres's growth is exactly double the normal rate, at seven he seems fourteen, the age at which fosterage (and childhood) ended, according to some legal texts, although seventeen is given by others. See Kathleen Mulchrone, 'The Rights and Duties of Women with Regard to the Education of their Children." *Studies in Early Irish Law* (Dublin, 1936), 188, esp. note 5. See also *Motif-Index:* T 615 "Supernatural growth."

§24:78ff. The account of Bres's reign emphasizes the anomaly of his dependence upon maternal kinship for his property and position, and might originally have followed §14, prior to the synthesis of the events of Bres's kingship with the account of his birth.

§24:79. The giving of guarantors or hostages was usual between a king and his over-king, or over-kings, but there is no indication that it ordinarily characterized the relation between the king of a *túath* and his people. See Francis John Byrne, *Irish Kings and High-Kings* (1973), 43-44.

The significance of seven guarantors in this context is not clear, but a parallel to the situation in which a king offers sureties for the success of his rule appears in *Dinds.* §161 (Emain Macha), 279-282. There, three kings who agree to alternating rule give twenty-one sureties that each will yield the kingship after seven years, "with safeguarding of a prince's truth, to wit, mast every year, and no failure of dyestuff (?) of every colour, and no women to die in childbed." The sureties given for Bres are not identified; in the arrangement described above, there are "seven druids, seven poets, and seven chieftains."

The comment that the Dagda built Dún mBrese may be a scribal remark inadvertently anticipating §25 and the account of the Dagda's labor that follows.

Stokes, reading *mátri* as if *maithi,* translated, "gave seven hostages to Ireland's champions, that is, to her chiefs"; *Contribb. M* 47, s.v. *máithre* suggests, "?'gave seven sureties from among Ireland's champions, i.e. of his mother's tribe.' " The passage develops the contrast between the kinship relations of Bres with the Tuatha Dé Danann and those of Lug, thereby illustrating the strength of paternal kinship in determining both a man's obligations and his loyalties.

§25:83ff. The demands for tribute made by the three Fomorian overkings seem to belong to post-Viking narrative tradition. The names of the kings themselves may be an incorporated gloss drawn from their subsequent appearances in the tale, or may reflect a separate narrative tradition now lost. The anecdotal accounts of the first satire make no reference to

Fomorian overlordship, only to Bres's misdeeds. See Hull's edition of the *YBL*, H.3.17 version of Coirpre's satire against Bres, *ZCP* 18 (1929), 63-69.

There are verbal correspondences between the *YBL*, H.3.17 passages and the references to the servitude of Ogma and the Dagda in §§25 and 37.

§25:84. *Domnann.* For a discussion of the associations of the name Domnann, including both place and population names, see O'Rahilly, *EIHM*, 92ff.

§25:85-6. *forsna béth.* Taken as equivalent to *forsna bíth,* the 3 sg. imp. ind. subst. verb denoting customary action. It could also be read as *forsna beth,* 3 sg. past subj. denoting unreality, *Thurn. Gramm.* §520 (b), used as subjunctive of secondary future. The MS. vowel is short, but missing accents are not uncommon.

§§26-30:89ff. 2MT provides a lengthy treatment of the affairs of the Dagda and Ogma during Bres's reign, with §§26-32 recounting the Dagda's adventures with the satirist Cridenbél during the construction of Dún mBrese. The *YBL* and H.3.17 account omits all but the fact of the Dagda's service; the death of Cridenbél, however, is known also from *LG* poem LVI, §25, which indicates that Cridenbél died from consuming gold, through the agency of the Dagda.

§26:89. *Ba toirsich. Contribb. T.* 229, s.v. *toirsech,* o, ā, lists basic meanings that include (a) "sorrowful, grieved," (b) "grievous, violent," and (c) "fatigued, tired." Either (a) or (c) is possible here; the former is reflected in the translation.

atcliched. A 3 sg. imp. form, the verb is not otherwise attested; Stokes suggests its basic meaning is "meet." Cf. *clichid* "stirs (?), bestirs oneself (?)" and the compounds *ar·clich* "wards off, defends," and *?fo·clich* "steps (leaps) up, advances (?), alights (?)."

daul esba. See *Dict. E* 181-182, s.v. *esba(e)* io, m. "uselessness, vanity, folly; idleness, play, wantonness," often used attributively in the genitive. Used attributively, its meanings also include "useless, idle, unoccupied."

§26:91. MS. *bá,* the mark of length perhaps misplaced from *mar,* which follows immediately.

§27:98. *cuige.* The form is feminine (=*cuicce*), although a masculine object is required, which would give *cuc(c)i.*

It is also possible that the form is an intermediate, "modernized" masculine, for Modern Irish *chuige,* "to him."

§27:99-100. *"Maith sin, a Dagdai"* . . . *"Amin."* Literally, "Well, then, Dagda," and "Indeed," but an idiomatic translation seems preferable. The forms are used in opening exchanges between individuals who meet in *LL* 284a 50 (*maith sin a chlerech arse. amin ar Moling*), and parallel examples are also cited, *Contribb. A.* 304, s.v. *amein* (b).

§28:98. *scildei.* Word of Norse extraction? cf. *scillice* in §29:114. *Contribb. S* 94 cites only the examples in this text: *"scildei, scilte, scitle,"* pl. (OE *sceld,* Bidrag 126), explaining the word as the name of a coin, apparently the same as *scilling.*

The entry for *scilling, scillic* gives the source as OE *scilling,* "shilling," and cites two other exx., *FM* V 1840.9 and *ALC* ii 354.22.

The loanwords for coins may modernize an older tradition in which the gold was simply in nugget form. The *LG*: LVI: §25 poetic account of Cridenbél's death merely indicates that he died of gold found in the Bann (with "Banbha" as a variant), and through the Dagda's agency.

§29:107. *asdofe* is glossed by *adsuife* (=*nó adsuife*). The gloss is perhaps simply a correction of scribal metathesis, since the verb may be *as-soí* with infixed pronoun, or may represent a compound**ad·soí* (Stokes, 112) with the same basic meaning, "turns."

§29:111. *a rí óc Fénei*. The phrase seems a traditional one, but precise parallels are lacking. "*A rí Féne*" occurs in *Táin* 930, and in *TBC*² 566. (Cú Chulainn to Conchobor in both cases). Cf. the use of the expression in *Hériu ard inis na rríg*, LL 14831 (127b). Presumably the present example represents an anachronistic use of the people-name Féni, the old name of the Goidelic people: see Binchy, *Críth Gabl.* 88-89 for the term's various legal meanings. It could, however, represent the genitive singular of *fían*, ā, f., as in the phrase *airiseom óc féne*, "a resting place of fían-warriors," *LU* 5089, or it could reflect the influence of such a phrase on a later scribe.

ar dom-ringarta. Perhaps for 3 sg. imp. passive, 1 sg. infixed pronoun, and *ro* used for action repeatedly completed in past time, *Thurn. Gramm.* §530. The verb itself is uncertain: *do·ingair* "calls by a name" is possible, but *Contribb. D* 317, s.v. 1 *do·ingair* suggests that this ex. represents confusion with perf. of *do·imgair* ("asks, claims; asks for, calls, summons"), and further suggests that the text be emended to *domringart-sa* (cf. *LU* 10307). See also the example and note in *CMM*, 418.

§§31-32:123ff. The significance of the Dagda's reward for his labour, a single black heifer chosen on the advice of his son, Óengus, is revealed only at the end of the tale (§165), and indicates the continuity of that passage with the account of Bres's failed kingship and its consequences.

§31:124. *ch'obair* for *th'obair*, with lenition of possessive 2 sg. as described in *Thurn. Gramm.* §439, 277.

ní cunghis. Stokes notes this as 2 sg. fut. of *cuindigim* "I request." The verb could also be taken as 2 sg. subj. with the force of advice or command: "let you not, do not."

§31:126. *ndénta aicentaig leo*. The words may be taken as *déntae*, io, iā, part. of *do·gní*, I (b), "broken in, trained," and *aicentach*, o, ā, adj., "courageous, high-spirited," with *leo*, the prep. *la* (with 3 pl. suff. pron. object, "among them").

Stokes gives *ndentaaicenn leo*, but does not translate.

§32:128. *At-(g)na-sa*. Probably for *ad·noí*, later *aithid, aithnigid*, exceptionally with *for* rather than *de* indicating a demand.

At(g)na-sa. See *Contribb. A* 64, s.v. *ad·noí* "entrusts, commends:" and 269, s.v. *aithne* "(a) act of depositing, handing over, (b) act of commanding, enforcing, command, behest"; and 271, s.v. 1 *aithnid*, esp. (c) "commends, prescribes a course of action to" (with *do*); with *de*, "orders, commands."

§32:130. *anndísin*, for *anísin* (neut. art. *an-* sg. + i + sin) (See *Thurn. Gramm.* §476). *Do(n)-gníth* may include 3 sg. m. inf. pron., Class A, not agreeing with *anndísin*. (Although given the parallel passage with unnecessary (-*n*-), §24, it seems better to delete the -*n*- than to interpret *anndísin* as a masc. acc. sg. form.)

§32:131. *héccomhnart*. Literally, "a weakness, a task or situation to which one's powers are not equal," *Contribb. E.* 18, s.v. *éccomnart*.

§§33-35:133ff. Núadu's cure by Dían Cécht, Míach's dissatisfaction with the remedy, and his restoration of Núadu's own arm are known to *LG* (excluding *LL*, which mentions only the work of Dían Cécht and Crédne). *LG* does not, however, mention Míach's death, and *Leb. Gab.* notes merely that Dían Cécht was jealous of his son, while *OCT* includes a version of the double cure without any reference to Míach's death. In *2MT*, the relationship between Dían Cécht and his ambitious and able son points up the differing character of two other father and son relationships: that between the Dagda and Óengus, on the one hand, and that between Bres and Elatha on the other.

For Núadu's cure, see *LG* R^1§310; R^2 §329; R^3 §362; *Leb. Gab.* §97, *OCT* (*GJ* 1884), 33-34.

§33:133. *dobreth láim n-argait*. The use of the accusative after a passive is noted in *CMM* (N) §23, Introduction; the verb here, however, is not impersonal, and the agent (Dían Cécht) is mentioned (following *la*, prep., expressing agency —"by, by the hands of, by direction or order of"—with a passive verb). See the discussion by Vendryes in *Celtica* 3 (1956), esp. 186.

§33:135-136. Parallels to this charm occur in several other Indo-European traditions. Cf. Atharva Veda 4.12; also the references given by J. Puhvel in *Indo-Europeans*, ed. G. Cardona *et al.* (1970), 379, 382.

See also *LG* IV:VII (Notes), 296, for a similar Scottish Gaelic charm.

§33:136. *nómad* = 3 days, á, f., (also *nómaide*, iá, f.). See *Contribb. N.* 63, s.v. 2 *nómad*: "In literature the word seems to be used rather loosely for a period of three days or somewhat more; frequently mentioned as . . . the time within which a cure is effected."

§33:138. *gelsgothai*. See *Contribb. S* 104-105, s.v. *scoth* "tress, tuft," with ex. of its use in reference to rushes. Here compounded with *gel* "fair, white, bright, shining," *Contribb. G* 58-59, s.v. *gel*.

§33:139. *ó rodubtis*. See *Contribb. D* 430, s.v. *dubaid*, (a) "grows dark, turns black or discoloured," (b) "blackens, makes or turns black." This ex. "when they had turned black," noting that the construction may in fact be passive. The third element of Míach's medical practice, casting wisps or tufts of blackened rush, remains obscure.

§34:142. *Atcomaic*. 3 sg. pr. ind. of *ad·cumaing*, an archaic form, *Thurn. Gramm.* §549.

co rrodic. Apparently with *ro* indicating ability, and with narr. pres. of *do·icc*: "until/ so that he could reach . . ."

§34:143. *Benaid*, although forming a preterite modelled upon that of *fen-* (*Thurn. Gramm.* §691a), is here treated as an s-preterite verb, although not — as later — with retained -*n* in the stem. The suffixed pronoun is feminine, apparently continuing the reference to *féoil*, f., "flesh."

§34:145. *co nderba. do·ben* "cuts away, takes away, deprives of"; this example, *Contribb. D.* 213 "cut out the brain." Another possibility, *do·rorban* "reaches" (cf. *Corm. Y* 1059, *dororba*) might be preferable but would require emendation.

conid apu[d]. Contribb. A 443 s.v. *at·bail(l)*, 3 sg. supp. pret. *ad·bath*, cf. *conid apad LU* 4916 (*TBC*); *conid abbad LL* 250 b 25.

§34:146. *badesin* (3 sg.m.) can mean either "himself" or "even," *Contribb. F.* 4-9, s.v. *fadéin*.

The sentence has a number of possible meanings, and *lieig* may refer to any physician (as translated) or, if intended as definite in the context, to the divine physician, Dian Cécht, perhaps even to his son. In any case, both meanings of *badesin* are possible.

§35:147ff. See *Motif-Index* E 631.3* "Herbs grow from grave of healer." The motif seems not to be widespread in Irish tradition, and all three references given are to Míach's grave.

§35:149. *íarna téchtai.* For *téchtu*, d. sg., after *íarna*; the idiom is parallel to *ina théchtu*, "in its proper form, arrangement." *Contribb. T*, 100-101, s.v. *téchtae* (io, n., as subst.), this ex. "according to their properties." (Or, with the same meaning, emend to *téchtai[b].*)

§35:150-1. MS. *a frepai córi*, restored as *a frep[th]ai, frepaid* i, f., is the vn. of *fris·ben*, "healing," here n. pl. with passive verb.

§35:151. *an Spirut.* "The Holy Spirit," lit. "the Spirit."

§35:152. *méraidh.* The verb, *maraid* (a), *mairid* (i), has an early *é* future, cf. *Ml.* 100 b 4, later replaced by an f-future.

§§36-38:153ff. *2MT* provides a more complex illustration of the failings of Bres's kingship than the *YBL*- H.3.17 anecdote, inserting a description of Bres's inhospitality that includes his refusal to reward the practice of the arts (§36) between the first reference to Ogma's servitude (§25) and the actual description of his plight as a supplier of firewood (§37). See §25:79 supra and Hull's edition of Coirpre's satire from *YBL* and H.3.17, *ZCP* 18 (1929), 63-69.

This inversion and disruption of the social order, coupled with the denial of reciprocity between king and people, symbolized by royal hospitality, leads first to the tribe's reluctance to meet its obligations to the king (§38) and, following Coirpre's satire, to an attempt to depose him (§40).

§36:153. *do-n-i[n]dnacht.* 3 sg. pret. pass of *do·indnaig*, "gives, bestows," with *do* of recipient, nasalizing rel. clause after *amal.*

§36:153. Bres's inhospitality contrasts sharply with his positive attributes (beauty, power over abundance and fertility of crops)—attributes that link him to Dumézil's "third function." His reign may be viewed as a cautionary example, showing the disasters that ensue from placing a "third function" figure on the throne (which is only legitimately occupied by characters such as the warrior king Núadu, or Lug, the perfect sage and master of all the arts).

On the associations of Bres with Indo-European myth, see Dumézil, "La Guerre des Sabines," chapter 5 of *Jupiter, Mars, Quirinus*, 155-198; and Jan de Vries, *Keltische Religion* (1961), 153-154.

§36:153ff. In the series of professional entertainers who did not display their arts before the king, a series of accusatives is to be expected after *Ní fhacutar*. Instead, one finds nominative plurals in most of the words spelled out by the scribe, and *cuslendaib*, perhaps to be interpreted not as a dative plural, but as an error for nominative plural *cuslendaig*. The reason for the use of the nominative case remains unclear, but *filidh* and *clesomhnaig* are expanded to conform with the series. Perhaps the influence of some passage well-known to the scribe is reflected here; a partial parallel occurs in *Críth Gabl.* 590: *cu/i/slennaig, cornairi, clesamnaig*.

§36:159. *liesin rígh. la*, prep. with acc., may express agency: "by, by the hands of, by direction or order or," or slatel proximity, "with, in the company of." See *Contribb. L* 1-9, s.v. *la* for the full range of possibilities.

§36:160. The matronymic given for Ogma and Coirpre (§§39, 114) is uncertain and variable in form. Coirpre is *mac Étoíne* (§39) and *mac Étnai* (§114); Ogma is *mac Étnae* (§36) (vs. *mac Ethlend*, §59, and *m. Ealauthan*, §138, where presumably the patronymic is intended). (In the MS. all the vowels are short). *LG* identifies Etan, the daughter of Dían Cécht, as mother of Coirpre.

mac Étnae. The independent account of Coirpre's satire against Bres (including reference to Bres's failure to treat his people with generosity) found in *YBL* and H.3.17, edited by Hull, *ZCP* 18 (1929), 63-69, mentions Ogma's role as supplier of firewood. The form of his matronymic in *YBL* (*mac Etaine*) is close to the *mac Etnae* (MS.) of §36:160. The form given in H.3.17, *mac Eladhan*, is presumably a patronymic.

§37:161. *tobairt*. The spelling may reflect a dialect variation: Mod. Ir. (Conn.) *tóirt* (O'Rahilly suggests the form is taken from Ulster Irish, *IDPP*, 178).

On the thematic relationship between the collection of firewood and madness, see Ó Riain, *Éigse* 14 (1972), 183, 200. Here, the primary theme seems to be Bres's subversion of the normal social order with the result that the warrior does not perform his proper function, but does menial labour.

§37:163. *slúaigh*. The nominative plural is used here instead of the acc.

§37:164. *ón tráth co 'role. tráth*, neuter in O. Ir., would originally have been followed by *alaill*, later *alaile, araile* (= *'role*). Cf. §73, *ón tráth co 'raili*.

§39:167ff. The tradition that Bres was subject of the first satire made in Ireland is well established. See Vernam Hull, "Cairpre mac Edaine's Satire upon Bres mac Eladain," *ZCP* 18 (1929), 63-69.

A poem and gloss in *LG*, LIV, §5, makes a reference to the satire; see also Macalister's note, 317. Glosses to the Bodleian and *LU* versions of *ACC* give author, victim, text, and identify it as Ireland's first satire: *RC* 20 (1899) §8, 159-161; *LU*, 8a, 554ff. The references in *Corm.* appear under *"Cernine"* and *"Riss,"* . The glossary from *H.*3.18 623ᵃ, *Ascolt*, substitutes Neidhe for Cairbre as the satirist: A. J. Pearson, "A Medieval Glossary," *Ériu* 13 (1940) §4, 61. Cf. the references given in the *Motif-Index* A 1464.3* "Origin of Satire."

§39:168-169. *Ránic a tech mbic cumang ndub ndorchai. mbic* and *ndorchai* are feminine forms, probably to be taken as scribal errors, since both *dub* and *cumang* are neuter (or masculine).

Cf. *tech mbecc*, H.3.17; *mbeg YBL*, the forms in the account of the first satire published by Hull. On the legal consequences for a king of tolerating a satire, see *Laws* V, 173, where such a king is listed among seven who are not entitled to honour price.

§39:169. *sech ní raibe*. 3 sg. perf. pret. of the subst. verb, a form somewhat later than those of the glosses, cf. *-roibe BDD²* 498, *-raibhe TD* 2.25. In the present text, also in §42; cf. *ní rabhu*, §127.

§39:170. *muhic*. *uh* uncharacteristically represents unlenited *b*.

§39:172. *MT* omits all but the first line of the satire, assuming the reader's familiarity with it. There are many other references to the poem in Irish tradition, including the *YBL* and *H.3.17* anecdote, Cormac's *Glossary* (s.v. *Riss, Cerníne*), and the glosses to *ACC*. An oblique reference to the entire incident appears in *LG* LIV §5; see Macalister's note, 317.

§§40-49:179ff. The negotiations between Bres and the Tuatha Dé Danann over the terms of the kingship, followed by his flight to his father's people, are not described elsewhere. The discussion between Bres and Elatha, in which Elatha seems both surprised and grieved by his son's misrule, develops the theme of Bres's personal failure as sovereign.

§40:181. *Gádhuis*. MS. *Gadhuis*, lengthened here on the assumption that it represents a partially-modernized treatment of Old Ir. *gáid*, 3 sg. pret. of *guidid*, "prays, begs."

§40:182. For seven-year kingship as a motif, see *Motif-Index* Z 71.5.4*.

iont oirecht. *airecht*, f. later also m. The latter gender is indicated here by the masculine nominative singular article *iont* (O.Ir. *int*); cf. §43, *Ant oirecht*.

a hóentai. *óentu*, d, m. f., here perhaps the shorter dative *óentu* (*Wb* 9 c 28). *a h-* agreeing with *Túath*, f., and *oirecht*, (originally f.); the usage is apparently dative of accompaniment, without the preposition *i n-*. See *Thurn. Gramm.* §§251.2.

§40:183. *acht docuí. do·cuí*, 3 sg. perf. subj. of *téit*, which in legal usage may mean "is supported by." See *Contribb.* T, 131, s.v. *téit* IV, with *ar* and *for*, (d).

forsan ráthai cétnu. The form of *cétnu*, if correct, indicates an original in which *ráth* was masculine sg. dat.; *forsan*, too, seems sg. as it stands, representing *forsind*.

comge. For *coimge*, "act of protecting, safeguarding; protection, safe keeping," see *Contribb.* C, 302-303, s.v. *coimge*. With *torad*, o.n. "produce, increase, result, profit, fruit." *Contribb.* T, 253-254, s.v. *torad*.

§41:188. *acht go tairsed*. The verb may represent *do·airicc* "find, get, come," or *do·airret* "reach, come to, attain, secure," 3 sg. secondary subj. The s-subj. of *do·airret* early fell together in both form and meaning with that of *do·airicc*. See *Contribb.* D, 193-194 s.v. *do·airret*.

doqhloíte. See *Contribb.* D 223, s.v. *dochloíte*, "invincible, impregnable," perhaps here "overwhelming."

§42:190-191. *cía bo can a cinél*. For the construction, see O'Brien, *Feil. Mhic Neill* 88; a parallel question occurs in *TBFr.* 65.

§42:191-192. Both *riam* and *remhi* appear in §42, both perhaps simply as adverbs ("forth"), although it is possible that the first, 3 sg. m., refers to Bres, while the second, 3 sg. f., refers to his mother Ériu. The feminine form, however, is generalized as an adverb in Mid. Ir., alongside the m. sg. *riam*.

§42:194. *ba fomhais dóu.* See *CMM* note 477 for another example that points to *fomais* as an i-stem adjective.

§43:200. The gloss to *comcluiche* is *nó ɔocluiche,* which might be transcribed as either *concluiche* or *cocluiche.* The ambiguity is perhaps intended as a play on words. See *Contribb. C* 283, s.v. *cocluiche* (*com+cluiche*) "playing games," this example: "a coursing match"; spelled *comcluithe* (*O'C* 2371), and *comchluicheo* (*Acall.* 1384); *con +cluiche,* on the other hand, might be translated, "hound-contest."

§44:205-6. *fri láim imbertai cloidib.* For this ex., see *Contribb. L 35-42,* s.v. *lám,* ā f. IV (e), with *fri,* and is translated "when it came to swordplay." It is also possible to interpret *láimimbertai* as a compound noun; the meaning would in any case be unchanged.

§44:206. *níd-fríth.* For the *d,* a meaningless dental infix, see Strachan, *Ériu* 1 (1904), 173.

§45:212. *hi forgabais. for·gaib* (a) "seizes forcibly," (b) "attacks" (with a pointed weapon) seems inappropriate; *ar·gaib* "seizes, captures, takes hold of; raises up, lifts, assumes," is scarcely preferable, there being, in any case, no direct object. Stokes suggests *for·gaib* with the meaning passing from "take forcibly" to "control." *Gaibid* itself, with a prepositional phrase beginning with *for,* means "rule over." The original text may have read *tír fora ngabais,* (without *hi*) "over which you ruled," prep. +rel. *a n-,* with *gaibid,* 2 sg. pret.

§45:214. *Níd-tallas.* Explained by Stokes as parallel to *fo·cres,* 3 sg. pass. pret. The verb, *do·alla,* was originally used in impers. construction with the accus., later in personal construction with the nom.; see *Contribb. D,* 199.

Níd-tallas. Regarding the *d,* an apparently meaningless infix, see Strachan, *Ériu* 1 (1904), 173.

§46:216. *Pa ferr a rrath oldás a rríghe.* The line has several possible interpretations. See *Contribb. R* 15, s.v. 1 *rath,* o, n. and m., (a) "grace," (b) "grace, virtue, gift," (c) "the granting of a favour," (d) "good luck, fortune, prosperity (usual later sense)." The other words, 2 *rath,* o, m. "goods"; 1 *ráth,* "surety, guarantor"; and 2 *ráth,* "earthen rampart," seem excluded by the sense of the passage.

For *rige,* there are again several possibilities and a broad range of meanings: *rige,* iā, f., vn. of *rigid,* "the act of distending"; (b) "binding, controlling, ruling"; (c) "putting to shame, reproach?" A second possibility is *rige,* io, n. "ruling, kingship, sovereignty." Under 1 *rath* (c), there is an example that combines several of the words of the context of the present passage: *cuma lais ... a rath ocus a ghueide,* "alike to him whether he receive favours or be asked for them," *ZCP* 7 (1910), 298; and the present passage might be translated, "Better to favour them than to put them to shame," or, with *rige,* "Better to favour them than to rule them." The combination chosen for translation, however, is 1 *rath* (d) and *rige* (or *rige*), "Better their prosperity than their sovereignty," carrying the implication that a king's position is founded on his people's well-being.

§47:218. *Dadechad,* MS. *Dadechus.* The emendation to 1 sg. perf. pret., "I have come," follows Stokes' suggestion in tense (*Dadech/ad/us,* an s-form of 1 sg., cf. *dodheochadus, BNnÉ* 302 §10), but not in form, taking *-us* as simply an error. Another possibility, however, is simply to take the vetb as 3 sg. perf. pret. passive, *dodechas, Im. Brain* i 41.3.Cf. the usage in impersonal constructions, *Contribb.* D. 382, s.v. *do·tít,* (g), *dotíagar uad do chuindchid* "he sends messengers to seek," *Trip²* 2313; see also *Im. Brain* i 41; *Dinds.* §112.

The literal translation would then be, "people (the embassy including Bres) have come to you to seek" (cf. further the example with *la, dochuas limsa chuici,* "I went to it," *Ériu 4 (1910),* 134.11).

§§50-51:222ff. The Fomorian muster, led by Balor and Indech, introduces the association of the Fomoire with Lochlainn and with Insi Gall, the Hebrides, under the influence of post-Viking tradition. While Balor (and probably Indech) belong to an early stratum of the legend, the geographical details—at least insofar as they represent Scandinavia and the Hebrides, rather than an Otherworld land over sea—reflect later tradition; and in this context, their absence from the account of Bres's flight to his father's people is noteworthy.

§50:222. *Faíthius.* The form represents 3 sg. historical present of *foídid,* i, with 3 sg. f., 3 pl. suffixed pronoun. Since Bres is travelling with his mother and other companions, a plural translation is acceptable, although Stokes (followed here) prefers the singular "him" *Thurn. Gram.* §429 notes the use of *-us* in reference to a masculine noun in *SP (Thes.* II, 294, 2).

§50:223-4. *nos-taireclamat-side. Contribb.* D. 187, s.v. *do·airecmalla,* this example only, "they assemble." 3 pl. narrative present indicative, with the same basic meaning as *do·ecmalla.*

§50:224. *do neoch buí ó Lochlainn síar do slúag.* See *Contribb.* N 19, s.v. *nech:* Mid. Ir. *de (do) neoch,* followed by relative clause, "of that which, of all that" . . . a common construction in Mid. Ir., always with a singular verb in the relative clause. For *buí,* the relative form 3 sg. preterite substantive verb, *boíe* is to be expected in O. Ir, *Thurn. Gramm.* §789; the relative *boí* appears in *Trip.²* 626, *Contribb. A* 470, s.v. *attá.* Cf. §148, *di neoch nád roacht cridiu cathae.*

Reidar T. Christiansen, *The Vikings and the Viking Wars in Irish and Gaelic Tradition* (Oslo, 1931), 417: "Lochlann Lothlin originally denoted a fabulous land far away over the sea, from whence all kinds of dangers and strange visitors might be expected to come. Later it was definitely associated with the Vikings and their home country. . . . Then in historical works and annals Lochlann was the name for Norway."

In *2MT²,* the Fomoire are also said to come from Lochlainn, 460, cf. *CML* §4, 83.

In Irish tradition the Otherworld has many locations: beneath the sea, beneath lakes, on distant islands, inside hills and mounds, and underground. The Fomoire are particularly associated with the sea, and their realm is usually located on distant islands or under water. For references, see Cross, *Motif-Index,* F. 80-109 "The Lower World" and F. 110-199

"Miscellaneous Otherworlds." See also de Vries, 'Die Vorstellungen von der Totenwelt und vom Weltende,' *Keltische Religion*, 248-261.

§50:225. *ba háondroichet.* For a similar passage, see *CMM* 159, and note.

§51:228, 229. *slóg, slógad,* although showing the undiphthongized vowel, are not necessarily early: Ó Máille cites exx. of *slóg* to 923, *slógad* to 959, *Annals* §§86-87, and *slógadh* occurs as a Modern Irish form as well.

§51:228. *o* is taken as =*a*, since there are parallel phrases, but may in fact =*ó*. Both preps. take the dative, but only *ó* lenites.

The connection made between Scythia and Lochlainn seems to be the result of an attempt to reconcile at least two different traditions: that the Tuatha Dé Danann learned their magic arts in islands in the north of the world, sometimes said to be in Lochlainn, and that they were "Greeks of Scythia" who completed their education among the Greeks before heading for Ireland. There seems also to have been considerable confusion between the "northern islands of the world" (=Lochlainn, in some sources) and the "northern islands of Greece" (=Scythia, in some sources).

For the Túatha Dé Danann acquiring the arts of magic in Lochlainn, see *LG*: LXII, §3. In *Keat.* I: x: 204-205, the Tuatha Dé Danann teach rather than learn there. *LG* §§320, 322 seem to equate studying magic in the northern islands of the world with being among the Greeks. See Macalister's comments in *LG* IV, 292, notes to §304, and Fraser, *1MT*, 7, note 1. For the connection between Scythia and Greece, *1MT*, 7, note 1 citations; *Keat.* I: xiv: 230-231.

The same association appears in a reference to Cessair "of the Greeks of Scythia," *Bod. Dinds.* (Introductory), 469.

§52:230. *is ed imma cesnaidther sund. cestnaigid,* earlier *cestnaigidir,* later also *cesnaigid,* as here; *imm + a n-,* with relative construction. Cf. *iss ed chestnigther sund colléic,* LU 7898 (*BDD* 149).

This transition may mark the end of a segment within the tale, or may indicate the union of two once-separate narratives.

§§53-74:231ff. Lug's arrival at Tara, including his dialogue with the door-keeper, the demonstration of his skill in the arts, and his exchange of places with Núadu, has no complete parallel in either prose or verse. The later tradition represented by *OCT* omits the doorkeeper's extended questioning, identifies Lug's fosterer as Manannán rather than Tailtiu, and makes no reference to the exchange of places with the king. A poetic description that includes the doorkeeper's questions, although without identifying particular members of the Tuatha Dé Danann as practitioners of the arts, appears in a poem by Gofraidh Fionn Ó Dálaigh, ed. Knott, *Irish Syllabic Poetry*, 54-58. Unlike the later *2MT* passage in which Lug reviews his troops (§§96-119), these sections include members of the Tuatha Dé Danann who are not mentioned in *LG*, although most appear at least briefly elsewhere in Irish literature: the doorkeepers themselves, Gamal and Camald (§53); Colum Cúaolléinech (§58); Bresal Echarlam (§61); Én mac Ethomain (§62); and the cupbearers (§65). Some of the names given to the cupbearers appear with other associations in *LG*: §§317, 350, 369.

§53:233. *Samhildánach.* In *LG* §§311, 363, Lug's epithet appears as *Illanach.* See *Contribb. I* 60, s.v. *il·ildánach,* "very gifted, skilled, accomplished, having many gifts or accomplishments." Often used as a substantive, and by Keating (iii 664-666) in reference to the heads of crafts appointed to preside over the industries of the country.

See also *Contribb. S.* 45, s.v. *sam-*, a prefix meaning "joint, united, together."

In the present passage, the narrative introduces the epithet before its significance is revealed by the dialogue; its insertion may represent the incorporation of a gloss or scribal interpolation.

§54:238. *tíachtai.* Cf. *tíchtain* §9, the later form.

§55:241. *Taill/ti/ne.* MS. *Taillne,* an error for the variant genitive Tailtine found also in *Dinds.* §20. Cf. Taillne in *T. Em.* §47 in *Comp. Con C.*

§56:243-244. *frisa ng/n/éie.* The form of the verb suggests that it is a compound formed of *fri* + *a n-* (rel.) + *gníid,* 2 sg. conj., rather than the compound verb *fris·gní.* The meaning is the same.

§56:243. Regarding the doorkeeper's refusal to allow Lug to enter Tara, see *Motif-Index*: P 14.7* "None permitted to enter hall of king unless he possesses an art"; C 864* "Tabus concerning entry into assembly"; cf. C 752.1.4* "Tabu: allowing person to come to feast after sunset." The restrictions on entry to Tara are mentioned in a poem by Gofraidh Fionn Ó Dálaigh, ed. and trans. O. Bergin, *Essays and Studies presented to William Ridgeway* (Cambridge, 1913), §28, 326, 329 (two men of the same art not admitted to Tara) and §44, 327, 330 (fortress not to be opened, once closed for the night, until sunrise).

§57:245, 246. *sáer.* See *Contribb. S* 11-12, s.v. 2 *sáer,* "an artificer, in older lang. apparently used in wider sense of a craftsman in general, later restricted to workers in wood, carpenters, and masons." English "builder" seems to cover these possibilities fairly well. Where the context seems to refer to a more specialized function (as in §§102, 124), "carpenter" has been used in translation.

§57:246. *Nít-regaim i leas.* Strachan, "Infixed Pronoun in Middle Irish," *Ériu* 1 (1904), 173, regards the *-t-* as meaningless, as are many other dental infixed forms in Mid. Ir. texts. See *Contribb.* R. 90-92, s.v. *ro·icc* for the idiom *ro·icc les* (with gen.), "attains to the benefit (of), needs"; later, with following nominative out of the construction. That entry also notes that in the present series of examples, the logical object is an infixed pronoun. No other examples of this use of the infixed pronoun are given.

§60:256. *ara-n-utgatar.* Stokes suggests a verb **ar-ud-gaim* "I select." Another possibility is *ar·utaing,* "builds up, restores, refreshes." Cf. *arautgatar,* 3 pl. present indicative, *Anecd.* v 26.8.

§60:256. 'Men of the three gods' is evidently another name for the Tuatha Dé Danann. The three gods, by most accounts, are the three sons of Dana and Delbáeth (also called Tuirenn, Tuirill Biccreo), son of Ogma. The three brothers' names vary; Brian, Iuchar and Iucharba represent the dominant *LG* tradition: §§316; 348; 368. O'Rahilly, *EIHM* 308 ff., has discussed the expression, suggesting that the original reference was to the three craftsman-gods, Goibniu, Crédne and Luchta. *1MT* §§48, 51 includes Brian m. Turenn Bigrenn, along with his brothers Iuchar and Iucharba, among the

Tuatha Dé Danann host. A variant tradition, perhaps originally simply an allegorical statement, in a gloss in *Im. Dá T.* §139, makes the three gods of *dána* ("art") sons of Brigit *banfili*, who was wife to Bres. *LL* 30 d 3902ff. identifies the three as sons of Bres, and gives a poetic description of their appearance. This alternative identification is also given in *LG* §§350, 369. *OCT* describes the murder of Lug's father Cian by the three sons of Tuireann, followed by their quest for the wergild imposed by Lug, a quest that ultimately destroys them. See Thurneysen, "Tuirill Bicrenn und seine Kinder," *ZCP* 12 (1918), 240ff.

§60:256. *i sídoib. síd* s,n, later u, and o,m., á.f. "a fairy hill or mound." The use here is somewhat anachronistic, since the mounds were, according to tradition, not inhabited by supernatural people until the Tuatha Dé Danann themselves were defeated and fled under the hills and mounds.

§61:257. MS. *níadh*.

§61:258. MS. *níad*. See *Contribb.* N. 43, s.v. *nia* (*niae*), d.m., "a warrior," disyll. in O. Ir. The MS. reading has been retained.

§61:259. *Bresal Echarlam*. The name is taken as *etarlam*, "opportune,"?, see *Contribb.* E 220, s.v. *etarlam*. The same name or epithet (or a homonym), although apparently a different character, appears as Etarlám in *Met. Dinds.* III 400 14 (Loch Cé).

§62:262-3. *Én mac Ethomain*. The patronymic is here taken as =*ethamain* (vn. of *ethaid*), *Contribb.* E 237, "going, moving."

§65:270-271. Some of the names of the cupbearers may be interpreted in more than one way; not all possibilities are noted, and the suggestions below emphasize related meanings.

Daithe, iā, n.pr. is given in *Dict. D* 41, as daughter of Ross Aichi, sister of Ailill, (with Drúcht), and cupbearer of Lug: *YBL* 192a 36, 37; *LU* 38 b 13-14.

Perhaps a use of 1 *daithe*, iā, f., "nimbleness, swiftness, deftness," or of 2 *daithe*, "light." *Delt* is not glossed, *Contribb.* D. 21; *drúcht*, 406, means "dew," both literally and figuratively.

Tae, *Contribb.* T. 12, s.v. 1 *tae*, "parturition, birth."

Talom ?for *talam*, *Contribb.* T. 60, "the earth, ground," or read *tolam*, 239, "ready, speedy," an appropriate name for a cupbearer.

Trog, if =1 *trog*, *Contribb.* T 314-315, again reflects the meaning of *tae*, "parturition," or "offspring." Cf. 1 *trogan*, "earth," 315.

Glé, *Contribb.* G 98, s.v. 1 *glé*, "clear, plain, evident," or 2 *glé* "clearness, brightness." The other two names continue the same theme: *glan*, 92, "clean, pure, clear," and *glésse* 104, "brightness."

§67:275. *ní tocus*. 1 sg. perfective future of *téit*, with the meaning "be able" associated with the perfective form. Strachan, *Paradigms*, 91, notes two examples of a secondary future built on a perfective stem, with the sense "it, they would be (would have been) able to go," *do·coísed*, *LU* 5919, *do·coéstis* 5370.

§69:281. *fidhcelda*. See *Contribb.* F. 128-129, s.v. *fidchell*, ā,f., "wood-intelligence, a game played for a stake with two sets of figures on a square board divided into black and white squares. The rules are largely unknown."

§69:283ff. On the game of *fidchell,* see E. MacWhite, "Early Irish Board Games," *Éigse* 5 (1945), 25-35. There seems to be no other reference to the invention of chess at the time of the Trojan War, nor to the synchronism of that conflict and the Battle of Mag Tuired. *LG* §376, on the contrary, synchronizes the reign of Sosarmus of Assyria, the rule over Ireland of the children of Cermat, and the capture of Troy by Laomedon.

Irish tradition outside *2MT* credits Lug himself with the introduction of the game, *LG* §316 (apparently only R[1]). Cf. *Motif-Index:* A. 1469.1 "Origin of Chess." *TTr.*[2] 218-219 does indicate that *fidchell* (and *brandub*) were played by Trojan warriors at the time of the Trojan war, but does not suggest that either game was a new invention.

§69:282-3. *an cró Logo.* See *Contribb. C* 536-538, s.v., *cró.* Originally probably *croë,* io, m. "A term of very wide application, the basic meaning being enclosure, enclosed space, fold, pen." Another meaning is "encircling band of weapons, persons, warriors, etc."

For the *cró* of Lug, see Christian J. Guyonvarceh, "Notes d'Etymologie et de Lexicographie Gauloises et Celtiques, XII,-*H* 45—Le *Cró Logo* ou 'enclos de Lug', enclos sacré ou parc à bétail?" *Ogam* 13 (1961), 587-592.

§71:288-9. According to both legal and saga texts, the arrangement of guests at a royal banquet was governed by elaborate rules of precedence, each social rank or profession having its particular "seat". It was a part of the king's responsibility to see that each professional was duly recognized and given his proper seat: *ZCP* 11 (1916), 82 §24, cf. 93 §24. One example of the arrangement of a king's banquet is discussed by Máirín O Daly, "*Lánellach Tigi Rīch* 7 *Ruirech,*" *Ériu* 19 (1962), 81-86.

See also *LL* 29a ff. for the seating inside the banquet hall at Tara, including a diagram of the hall, with the names and precedence of the principal guests, and the portions assigned to them.

The poet's seat (*suide filed*), also called the ollam's chair (*cathair ollaman*), is mentioned as existing within the palace at Emain Macha: *Im. Dá T,* 50-51 §273; 14-15 §x.

The seat taken by Lug, however, is called "the sage's seat," (*suide súad*). For *suí,* t, m. (later lang. also f.) the basic meanings are I(a) "man of learning, scholar, wise man, sage." The term is sometimes used as equivalent to *ollam* or *fili,* as in a reference to the poetic contention mentioned above (*Auraic.* 4644: *isan imagallaim in Da Suadh no in Da Tuarad*) and to a poetic mantle: *a stuigen suad, Corm.* 36. 17 (*Contribb. T* 358, s.v. *tuigen,* ā, f.), and II "expert, master (in various specific arts, crafts, accomplishments)": Lug is both a poet (I), and an expert in other arts (II), so the "sage's seat" is doubly appropriate.

suide súad. See also *Motif-Index: A* 1539.1* "Origin of seating arrangements in royal hall"—the main reference is to Keating I: xxxix: 250-253.

§72:291. *trésan tech co mbuí fri Temair anechtair.* Literally, "through the hall so that it was against Tara outside."

§73:295-7ff. On the three strains played by Lug (and in §164 by the Dagda) see *Motif-Index:* D 1275.1.1* "Three magical musical strains" and cross references. See also *Corm. Tr.* s.v. *Golltraigi, Gentraigi.*

§74:298ff. Núadu, by considering the possible contribution that Lug might make toward aiding the Tuatha Dé Danann in their predicament, facing certain attack by a vast Fomorian host, shows himself to be without jealousy, just as he has already demonstrated his hospitality (in contrast to the niggardly king he has replaced) by holding a feast for his people at Tara. Núadu has, in fact, all the royal virtues required by Medb's threefold demand (*Táin*, 28, perhaps a proverbial definition of true kingship), but he is symbolically linked most strongly with the martial function, demonstrating by his career the expendability of the warrior as defender of the tribe. As *LG* §370 comments: "And in the first battle of Mag Tuired his arm was hewn from Núadu, and his head in the last battle."

§74:300. *Is sí comuirle arriacht Núadha. ar·icc*, 3 sg. pret. pass. used with active meaning. Later used as a simple verb, *air(i)cid*. A variety of forms appear in the present text: *arrícht*, §15 (perhaps to be taken as passive in meaning as well as in form); *roairich*, 3 sg. perf. pret., §125; *rohairged*, 3 sg. perf. pret. pass., §69.

§74:302. MS. *xiii. la* is written over the numeral; elsewhere in the MS., the *i*'s used in forming Roman numerals have marks of length (excluding *ix* in §146:695).

The king rises in Lug's presence in acknowledgement of Lug's high rank (as master of all the arts, entitled to the honor due to each, and as temporary occupant of the king's own seat of honor). For the custom of rising to show honor (king to bishop), see *Críth Gabl.* §48, 604-605.

The significance of the thirteen days remains to be discovered. Parallel "temporary kingships" in other traditions are noted by Rees and Rees, *Celtic Heritage*, 143.

§75:303-4. *dá bráthair*, "two brothers" (translated with the definite article since the two have already been introduced).

a bráthair, "his kinsmen". The word *bráthair* can mean both "brother" and "paternal kinsman." In some genealogies, Lug's father Cían is the nephew of Goibniu; Dian Cécht is Lug's grandfather. See Index of Persons.

§75:304. *for Greallaig Dollaid*. Hogan, doubting the identification made by O'Donovan with Girley, in Kells, Co. Meath, and noting both that King Finachta was slain there by the lord of Fir Cúla Breg, and that it is associated with Athe Dá Ferta, suggests a location associated with cc. Louth, Armagh and Down, Grallagh Greenan tl., the only Grellach in the region, near Lower Iveagh.

In *Met. Dinds.* IV 302 (Grellach Dolluid) Gwynn notes that the article, in prose, is borrowed from *Tochmarc Emire* §35 and explains the older name of the site (Amrún Fer nDéa) as the place where the Tuatha Dé Danann first planned battles against the Fomoire. *TB Regamna* §2 gives the earlier name as G. Culgairi (g.s.), and offers an entirely different account of the renaming of the site (§5) based on Cú Chulainn's description of the Morrígan as "*doltach*".

a bráthair .íí. íí, for *dá'*, "two," masc., should precede, not follow, the word it modifies, and seems therefore an almost scribal afterthought.

§76:307. *Amhrún*, MS. *Amhrun*. The second syllable is taken by native glossators as *rún*, "secret, something hidden, secret intent," *Contribb. R* 120-121, s.v. 1 *rún*. See *Contribb. A* 312, s.v. *?amrun* for references.

§77-8:308ff. The first muster of the Tuatha Dé Danann emphasizes the role of the tribe's specialists in magical warfare. The list of chief rivers and the list of chief lakes closely resemble those in BDD^2, and the various motifs of magical warfare, including the imposition of intolerable thirst upon the enemy, are well-known from many other sources. The overlap between $2MT$ and $2MT^2$ begins with these sections, although there are major differences of arrangement and detail between the two narratives.

Lug's first muster of his troops occupies 11.1-66 of $2MT^2$, ending: *Gonadh é sin congnamh gach triatha ⁊ gach tréinmhĩlidh do mhaithibh T.D.D. a ccath Mhuighe Tuireadh*. In its character, however, this passage resembles the second muster of $2MT$, §§96-120.

§78:310. The sorcerer (*corrguinech*) is identified in a note above the line: *.i. Matgen a ainm*. The term itself is oddly spelled as *corrguru*.

§78:313. *i mmulloch*. *mulloch*, o, m., also treated as n., seems here to be treated as neuter o-stem, accusative plural. Perhaps there has been a scribal metathesis of **mmullcho* from an earlier version of the text.

§79:320. Thirst as an important factor in warfare: BDD^2 §§145-156, Mac Cécht seeks a drink for Conaire from the chief rivers and lakes of Ireland: the water, however, is hidden from him, and when he finally returns, Conaire has already been slain. Similar incidents occur in $1MT$ (*Ériu* 8 (1915), 52-54) and *Forbuis Droma Damghaire*, ed. Sjoestedt, *RC* 43 (1926) 51-53.

Related motifs include: D 2091.8* "Druids dry up water in enemy's camp," D 2151.2.3* "Rivers magically made dry," D 2151.2 "Magic control of rivers," and D 2151.7* "Magic control of lakes."

Only ten of the lake names in $2MT$ are given in BDD^2 §§155, 156 (Loch Dechet and Loch Ríoach are missing). The order of the names differs, but otherwise the lists represent the same tradition.

§79:323. *Aross-cich(er)sit do díb prímaibnib*. For *ar·cichset*, 3 pl. future of *ar·cing*, "steps forward, marches to the encounter"; cf. *ar·cichset*, *Sc. M.*² 15 and note. The infixed pronoun, if not a meaningless later addition, is reflexive — "They will advance (themselves) to the twelve chief rivers." Stokes simply noted the form as 3 pl. redup. future of an unknown verb.

§79:318ff. Rivers listed as *rígusci Érenn* in BDD^2 §154 are *Búas* (the Bush), *Boand* (the Boyne), *Bandai* (the Bann), *Berbai* (the Barrow), *Nem* (Blackwater, Cork), *Laí* (the Lee, Cork), *Laígdai* (the Bandon, see O'Rahilly, *Hermathena* 23 (1933), 219), *Sinand* (the Shannon), *Síuir* (the Suir), *Slicech* (the Sligo), *Samair* (the Erne), *Find* (the Finn, Donegal), and *Ruirthech* (the Liffey). The Barrow and the Bandon, found in BDD^2, do not appear in $2MT$, which does, however, include *Múaid*, the Moy.

§79:325. *decélaigter*. Apparently for *do·ceil*, "conceals," with an é future; here 3 pl. future passive (normally *do·céltar*), perhaps influenced by *do·cíallathar*, which seems also at times to mean "conceals"; cf. such a form as *dociallaigter*, *O'C* 2497 [*Eg.* 88, 40 (41ꝼ]. *Do·cíallathar* itself, however, has an f- future.

§80:328. *Firfit*. Perhaps a 3 pl. Mid. Ir. future passive (modelled on the preterite form ending -*it*) of *feraid*, "grant, supply; pour," or emend to earlier passive form; cf. *firfitir*, *LU* 10379.

§80:329. *pérut.* 1 sg. fut. of *berid.* The -t ending of the 1 sg. fut. appears in the *Tripartite Life*: *bérait-se, Trip².* 2811; see Thurneysen, *ZCP* 19 (1932), 134ff.

§80:331. *fir(u).* The form is accusative plural; either a slip of the pen for n. pl. *fir,* or representing a late, perhaps dialectal, replacement of nominative plural by accusative plural.

bod formach. bod=bud, Mid. Ir. form of 3 sg. abs. fut. copula. Cf. *bodh,* §99:478.

§81:335. *am áon[ur]* MS. *amaon.* The editorial change is suggested by Dillon, "Nominal Predicates," *ZCP* 17 (1928), 313-314. *amaon* may, on the other hand, represent *amáin* "only, alone, by oneself"—as in *gé do ríne Muire amháin* "by herself," *Dán Dé* XVII 28. For the various uses of *amáin,* see *Contribb. A* 298, s.v. *amáin,* also *CMM,* note 254, for the suggestion that it was an O. Ir. form.

§82:338. *go comairsidis,* 3 pl. sec. subj. of *con·ricc* = *-comairsitis, Ml.* *119ᵈ12.*

§83:340. The items obtained from the *trí déo Danann* are not identified, nor are the gods themselves named. Later tradition, including *LG* and *OCT,* identifies the three as the sons of Tuireann, but it is possible that in the earliest stratum of *2MT* itself, the reference was to Goibniu, Crédne, and Luchta(ine). The problem is discussed by O'Rahilly, *EIHM,* 308ff.

grésa. Two words are possible here:

(1) *grés* m.u. "handicraft, workmanship, ornamentation, artistic work, doings."

(2) *gres* ā,f. This ex., *Contribb. G* 155, "an attack, a hostile encounter, an onset; an attack on honour, an insult." A very different meaning is "an essay, attempt, amount of anything done at a time," and the example: *Colum Cuaolléinech teorae nua-gres,* translated, "Colum Cúaolléinech of the three new processes," §58 supra.

roboth. Impersonal use of the pret. passive of the substantive verb; see *Thurn. Gramm.* §514.

roboth. See J. H. Lloyd, *Ériu* 1 (1904) 49ff. for the impersonal passive use of the verb.

§§84-93:354ff. The diplomatic and amatory adventures of the Dagda, showing a good knowledge of the topography of the area around Mag Tuired and Loch Arrow, have no real parallel in *2MT².* There, the Dagda engages in a single combat with Balor's wife, but there are no amorous overtones.

In *2MT²,* the truce between Tuatha Dé Danann and Fomoire is negotiated not by the Dagda but by Lug, 196ff. In *OCT (GJ,* 1884), 38, Lug spares Bres's life after an early encounter between the opposed forces, upon Bres's promise that the two tribes will meet later for battle at Mag Tuired. The delay allows Lug to collect the items specified as his father's wergild from the sons of Tuireann.

§84-85:354ff. Here the Morrígan resembles a Washer at the Ford, *Motif-Index:* D 1812.5.1.1.7* "Appearance of a female figure (Bodb, Badb) washing bloody armor, chariot cushions or human limb (at ford) as sign of coming disaster in battle." Although she is not said to be washing spoils, she does display blood of the enemy king at the ford as a sign of his impending doom. The *Motif-Index* has an extensive collection of references to the Washer at the Ford in Irish literature. One classic example is the Badb's appearance to Cormac in *BDCh*, §§15-16.

§84:355. For references to Samain see *Motif-Index*: V 70.5* "Festival of Samhain (Hallowe'en, Tara [Temair])" and cross references given there. For a discussion of the character of the festival, see Rees and Rees, "Darkness and Light," *Celtic Heritage*, 83-94. See also Françoise Le Roux, "Études sur le Festiare Celtique *I. SAMAIN*," *Ogam* 13 (1961), 481-506; Christian J. Guyonvarc'h, "Notes d'etymologie et de lexicographie gauloises et celtiques, 11 # 43, Remarques sur *SAMAIN*, **SAMON(I)OS*, *Ogam* 13 (1961), 474-477; R. H. Buchanan, "Calendar Customs, Part 2," *Ulster Folklife* 9 (1963), 61-79; A. J. Pollock, "Hallowe'en Customs in Lecale, Co. Down," *Ulster Folklife* 6 (1960), 62-64.

§84:357. *indarna*, Middle Irish for *indala* (def. art. + *ala*), indeclinable and proclitic. Mod. Ir. *darna* (Con., U., smt. M.), *tara, tarna* (M.) *(Dinneen)*, *s.v. dara*.

§84:357-358. For giant size as a divine characteristic, see *Motif-Index* A 133 "Giant God" and cross-references.

§84:360. There is a reference in *Met. Dinds*. II 10.21-24 to the "married pair" (*lánamhain*) sleeping together at Lind Féic na Fían on the Boyne after *2MT*, but Murphy, *Éigse* 7 (1954), 193, points out that this translation goes against all the *MSS*., which place the union before the battle. This seems to be evidence of a differently localized version of the Dagda's adventures preceding the battle.

§85:362. *deraghdis an Fomore a tír .i. a Maug (S)cé[t]ne*. In Mod. Ir. *dul i dtír* means "to land."

The site of their arrival is presumably Mag Cétne, in Ahamlish parish, Carbury barony, sometimes referred to as Magh Céidne na bhFomhórach. This is traditionally the place where tribute was delivered to the Fomorians. See, for example, *LG* III, §255 (regarding the people of Nemed).

§85:363. *ara garudh*. This is almost certainly a use of *ar* prep. + rel. *a n-*, and *gairid*, "calls, invites, summons," since the basic meaning of the alternative, the compound *ar·gair* is "hinders, prevents," although it does have an extended meaning "herds." See *Contribb*. A. 397, s.v. *ar·gair*.

óes ndánu. See *Contribb*. A. 80-81, s.v. 2 *áes*, "people, folk, those who, etc." and *Dict. D*. 70-77, s.v. *dán*, "art, profession," esp. II and IV, which lists the various legal divisions of the "people of an art," a group that included poets and craftsmen, physicians and lawyers, to name only a few representative professions.

§85:367. *Bai "Áth Admillte"*. MS. *Bai*. Dillon, "Nominal Predicates," *ZCP* 17 (1928), 338 discusses this passage, suggesting it "can be read *ba é*, i.e., copula and pronoun before the proper noun. On the other hand, the text is old, and an archaism such as that suggested for the *Amra* is not out of the question." Regarding the *Amra*, where *boe* and *ba* seem confused, he suggests, 337, that both are often copula forms, "a deliberate archaism on the part of an author, who, in the sixth or seventh century, when the text was composed . . ., had still the tradition of a time when the unstressed form had not become reduced (Bergin, orally)."

§86:369. *óes ndánou.* See note §85:363.

§87:372. *go comairnectar* 3 pl. pret. of *con·ricc,* cf. *comairnechtair, BDD²* 220.

§87:372. *Sé tríchaid cét* is six times thirty hundreds, 18,000 men. The *trícha cét,* lit. "thirty hundreds," used both of a military force and of a political or territorial unit, here indicates the size of the Tuatha Dé Danann host.

§89:376ff. The position of the ambassador or messenger is not defined by the laws, but is clearly illustrated in epic. See, for example, Daire's angry response to Medb's messengers: "If it were my custom to deal treacherously with messengers or travellers or voyagers not one of you should escape alive." *Táin,* 132ff.). Later, Cú Chulainn remarks, "I do not wound charioteers or messengers or men unarmed." (1239ff.). Persons in all of these categories are by implication safe from attack by any honourable man.

§89:377. *amal conanoic.* Stokes interpreted the verb as a form of *con·dieig*; cf. *connaig, Táin* 1548, *condnaig, LL* 12908, both 3 sg. pr. ind.
    Another possibility, not requiring the deletion of a letter, would be to take the verb as 3 sg. pret. of *con·icc: con·ánic.* See *Contribb.* C 445-446, s.v. *con·icc,* 2, "with conjunctions, superlatives, etc., 'as best one can, to the best of one's ability', illustrated by *PH* 332, *amal connicfitis,* 'according to their ability'." In this context, then, the meaning would be "It was granted to him according to his ability."
    Con·anaig, Contribb. C 425 "protects" is also formally possible but the sense is unclear unless the expression has a technical meaning associated with the negotiation of a treaty. One could take *ãm* as *airisem,* u, m., *Contribb. A* 216 (a) "act of resting, remaining, stopping; delay" (b) act of desisting from, stopping," hence "was granted to him the respite that he protects (guarantees)."

§89:381. *indtie. coire* is m., so a masc. suff. pron. (*ind*) is to be expected. *indtie* and *lei,* both f., suggest that for some author or scribe, *core* (*coire*) was feminine.

§90:384. *go tallfad lánomain.* The accusative originally followed the impersonal verb *do·alla,* meaning "there is room for." Later it is used in personal construction, "fits, finds room (in), is contained (in)."

§93:393. *co Trácht Aebae.* For Tráig Eba, identified as the site of Cessair's landing, a stretch of the Sligo coast, see *Met. Dinds.* IV 292-293; 453.

§93:394. *drochruid.* For *dochruid*; see *Contribb.* D. 225-226, s.v. *dochraid,* i, "unshapely, ugly."

§93:395. *Gabol gicca.* Cf. the *tri gabulgici* of Conaire's swineherds, *LU* 7585 (BDD), tentatively given as referring to "a pronged pole," *Contribb. G.* 9, s.v. *gabul.*

§93:397. *Slicht Loirge an Dagdai.* Perhaps with double meaning: "The Track of the Dagda's Club," and "The Track of the Dagda's Penis," as *lorg* means "staff, stick; club, rod; also the membrum virile." See *Contribb. L* 56-58, s.v. 2 *lorg*.

§93:400. The nearest approach to the Dagda's adventures with Indech's daughter is his single combat with Balor's wife in *2MT²*, but the meeting is entirely a hostile one (1094ff.).

§93:401-2. *acht náruho.* In O.Ir., *acht* with the meaning "save only that, except that" is followed by a relative clause, hence *ná.*

§93:412. *ges.* See *Contribb. G.* 56-58, s.v. *ges* or *geis,* f., "a prayer or request, the refusal of which brings reproach or ill-luck; a tabu, a prohibition, the infraction of which involved disastrous consequences."

§93:412ff. On the exchange of names, cf. *BDD²* 550-560, beginning: *Cía do chomainmseo, a banscál? ol Conaire. Cailb, ol sí. Ní forcrad n-anma són ém, ol Conaire.* ...

§93:423ff. His names illustrate the Dagda's complexity, reflecting both his immediate condition and enduring aspects of his character. *Oldathair* (MS. *oldath-*, =*Ollathair*) is found elsewhere, but the other names seem to describe his distended person, his soiled state, and his on-going association with creation and regeneration.

Suggested meanings are given, but here (as with other lists of names in the text), there is much uncertainty.

§93:423ff. The Dagda's names (voc.), with suggestions regarding possible meanings follow. Vowel length reflects the MS. *Fer: fer* o, m. "man." *Benn: benn* ā, f. "horn, peak, point," g. pl. *Bruaic[h]: brúach* o, ā. "big-bellied." ?*Brogaill.* ?*Broumide.* Cf. SG *broumach* 'heavy bellied' — a Nova Scotia usage mentioned by Sr. Margaret MacDonell. *Cerb-:* perhaps *cerbad,* vn. of *cerbaid,* "act of hacking, cutting (off)." *Caic: cacc* "excrement." *Rolaig:* perhaps *ro* intens. prefix, with *láech* o, m. "warrior." *Builc: bolg* o, m., ā, f. "belly, stomach." *Labair: labar* o, ā. "talkative, arrogant, boastful." ?*Cerrce.* ?*Di Brig:* perhaps includes *bríg* ā, f. "power, strength, force, authority." *Oldathair: oll* o, ā. "great, ample," with *athair* r, m. "father." *Boith: buith* ā, f. "being, existing." *Athgen mBethai: aithgein* n. "birth, regeneration," with *bith* u, m. "world," see *Fél. Ep.* 240 *aithgin mbetha* "rebirth of the world." ?*Brightere. Tri Carboid:* perhaps *trí,* num. adj. with *carpat* o, m. "war-chariot." *Roth: roth* o, m. "wheel." ?*Rimairie. Riog:* perhaps *rí* g, m. "king." ?*Scotbe. Obthe:* perhaps *opad* o, and u, m., later *optha, obtha* "act of refusing or rejecting." *Olaithbe:* perhaps *oll* o, ā. "great, ample," with *aithbe* io, m. "ebb, decline, decay."

§93:423ff. After Brúach (=1. 423) the names are given in the translation as in the text, although expansions are not indicated.

§93:429. *Bid atégen tacuo* (MS. word division). The word division as it stands allows the line to be interpreted as *bid* (3 sg. fut. abs. of the copula) and a form of *aithéicin,* with *aith-* used intensively, and taking *éicen* ā, f. to mean "difficulty, hardship." *tacuo* may be the asseverative particle, *taccu,* and the line might be translated, "It will be a great difficulty indeed!" (to stop the mockery).

If the word division be altered, one could read *Bidat égen,* 3 sg. cop. with suff. 2 sg. pron., "you will have," sometimes used with *éicen* to mean "you must." Cf. *bidat eigen dola, Aisl. Tund.* 101.x.

It is also possible that *tacuo* represents *tacha* (?f.) (a) "want, necessity, scarcity"; (b) "hardship, distress, extremity." See *Contribb. T* 7, s.v. *tacha.*

§93:441. *boam.* 1 sg. abs. fut. copula, =*bam,* Mid. Ir. form, cf. *SR* 3187.

§93:446. *bud.* 3 sg. abs. fut. copula, Mid. Ir. form (appears also in §§99, 119).

consúfiter. Taken as a form of *con·soí* rather than *co n-* with the verb *sōid,* as one expects the subjunctive with explicative *co n-* (*Thurn. Gramm.,* §896, 2, d).

cona aicither. co n- "so that" takes the subjunctive if its meaning is final, and the indicative or the subjunctive (depending upon the character of the sentence as a whole) if consecutive, *Thurn. Gramm.* §896.

The best interpretation of *cona aicither* seems to be as 2 sg. pr. subjunctive, "so that you may not see." If this were a passive verb form, conjunct, *·accastar* would be expected for 3 sg., both present indicative and present subjunctive (pl. forms not attested). A pronoun object has been added in the translation.

§93:447. *hi sídaib.* See note §60:256.

Ar bon. 1 sg. abs. fut. copula, for *bam,* Mid. Ir. form, as above, §93:441.

§93:449. MS. *biéid* 3 sg. fut. subst. vb., cf. Wb. 4^{d}6, *bieid,* cited in *Contribb. A.* 468, s.v. *attá,* fut. forms.

§93:451. *Légaitir . . .* "Allow the Fomoire to enter the land, because the men of Ireland have all come together in one place." See *Contribb. L.* 79, s.v. *léicid* II (k) with *i,* "allows to enter."

Another possible interpretation of the text would take *ar tan* as adverbial, (=*íar tain*), "then," and would expand *cot-* as *co tístis* (*co n-* with 3 pl. secondary subj. of *do-icc*), with the meaning, "until the men of Ireland might come together in one place," as paralleled in §88:375.

The first interpretation has been preferred in the light of §94, from which it appears that the Tuatha Dé Danann have already gathered and that battle is imminent.

With either interpretation, the acc. pl. *firu* is taken as =n. pl., cf. §80, 331, §94:456.

ol síe is deleted from the translation as repetitive.

§93:452ff. The precise form and meaning of the series of verbs is not clear. The first, *no ríasttrabadh,* for *-fad,* is a 3 sg. sec. fut. of *ríastraid,* while *do·cachnopad,* is apparently a new formation (from O.Ir. *do-cechnad*) of the 3 sg. sec. fut. of *do·cain* (cf. *Contribb. C* 66, s.v. *canaid,* condit. 3 sg. *·cechnad, Caithr. Thoirdh.* 60.13, later with f-future). In regard to *ari-n-imreth,* since *ara n-* takes the subj., the form is 3 sg. sec. subj. of *imm·beir. Nogebad,* lacking any mark of length in the MS., may be taken as either 3 sg. imp. ind., or 3 sg. sec. fut. (=*no·gébad*). For purposes of translation, the group is treated as if all were conditional.

§94:455. Specific reference to sites around Mag Tuired continues in this section describing the position of the two forces prior to the battle. The dialogue between Bres and Indech does not appear in *2MT²*.

§94:456. See note §80:331 *fir(u).*

§94:460. *inoen. inunn*? or *in/unn/óen,* "one and the same, identical"? See *Contribb. I.* 205, s.v. *inunn* (II, substantival usage).

Dobiur-so, 1 sg. pr. ind. of *do·beir,* "I give," or for *do·bér,* 1 sg. fut. of the same verb (the latter being used for translation). *do·beir* has a broad range of meanings, (I, i, "utters, pronounces," being another possibility here), see *Contribb. D* 206, s.v. *do·beir.*

mina érnet. mina for *mani,* "if not," with 3 pl. pr. subj. of *as·ren,* "pays," the older prot. stem. *-éren-* here replaced by the later stem *-érn-*.

§95:462ff. Both versions of the tale agree that the Tuatha Dé Danann leave Lug behind when the battle begins, but in *2MT²* (80ff.) the motive seems to be jealousy of Lug's abilities, not concern for his well-being.

In *OCT* (*GJ* 1884) 34, Lug is accompanied by his fosterbrothers, the sons of Manannán, when he arrives among the Tuatha Dé Danann, but there is no reference to several foster-fathers, nor do Lug's fosterbrothers participate in an attempt to keep him from battle.

ara coime. Perhaps for *caíme,* iā, f. "beauty, loveliness; charity, kindness." But see also *Contribb. C.* 589, s.v. 1. *cuime,* explained as "protection" (*faosamh*) in *Met. Gl.* 14 §31, *in fer i/s/ sandach ima chuimi, O'C.* 431 (*H.*3.18 234^(ab)). The latter word seems more appropriate, given the tale's emphasis on Lug's skills and leadership, of continuing importance to his tribe.

§95:463. Regarding the number of fosterers, Kathleen Mulchrone, "The Rights and Duties of Women with Regard to the Education of their Children," *Studies in Early Irish Law,* 188, notes, "the more distinguished the child's family, the more numerous the fosterers," and cites early evidence.

The names of Lugh's fosterers seem not to occur as a group elsewhere, nor are they included individually in other references to the Tuatha Dé Danann within the sources examined. They do not figure in *2MT²* at all; the parallel passage begins at 113, and describes the means used to keep Lug from battle, but makes no reference to his fosterers.

§§96-120:467ff. Lug's second muster of the Tuatha Dé Danann includes only figures who are prominent in *LG.* His second muster in *2MT²* (222-315) involves Lug's arrangement of a series of single combats rather than a review of the contributions to be made to the battle by practitioners of the various arts; and the better comparison is in fact with Lug's *first* muster, 1-66 of *2MT²*, where the list of practitioners omits Crédne, while adding the harper Craiftine, the satirist Cridenbél, and the Dagda's son Bodb Derg. The second review in *2MT²* includes even more characters who do not appear in *2MT*, among them Tadhg Mór mac Nuadhad, his son Labraidh Lámhfhada, Cairbre Crom, his son Sioghmhall, Miodhair (identified as son of the Dagda), Dealbhaoth Dána, and Alladh Áluinn mac Ealathan.

§96:467. *Rotinálid.* 3 pl. Mid. Ir. perf. pret. pass. of *do·inóla,* "gathers, musters."

§96:468ff. Compare the promises of Goibniu and Luchtuinne regarding the provision of arms, *2MT²* 25ff.

§97:469. *Gé* represents the later usage, *ce* the earlier. MS. *Gé* is allowed to stand, but cf. §152:755, §153:757.

§97:473. *Atú dom cor* ... "I am now concerned with my preparation for the battle of Mag Tuired." *Contribb.* D 175, s.v. I *do* II 5, with the subst. verb in the idiom *atú dó,* "I am concerned with him, have to deal with him, generally with hostile significance." The significance here, however, is not hostile.

§99:476. *géntor.* 3 sg. passive relative ē-future of *gonaid,* an early form, as *gonaid,* "wounds," has a later reduplicated future; see *Thurn. Gramm.* §651(c).

acht mona bentor. For *mani* with the meaning of *má* (after *acht*), see Vendryes, *Ériu* 16 (1952), 21ff.

§99:477. *mani tesctar.* The verb is *do·esc,* almost always appearing as simple verb *tescaid,* "cuts, severs."

For the phrase *smir s[m]entuinde,* see *Contribb.* S 287, s.v. *smennta, smentain(e).*

§102:483. *rosta.* If not simply a scribal error for a second person future form, perhaps scribal metathesis of **ro-t-sa* (Cf. *LU* 4841 3 sg. subj. pr. *ró-d-sá,* = *ra-d-sia TBC²* 351, really a future). The idiom would roughly parallel the usage of *ro·saig* with the prep. *do* "comes (falls) to me (as a share, due, turn, duty, etc.)," with an infixed 2nd pers. sg. pronoun in the place of the pronominal object of *do.* Stokes suggests that the form represents a secondary s future of *roichim,* a late Mid. Ir. development of *ro·saig* (in late MSS. often written *roith-*), *Contribb.* R 99.

§107:493-4. *ar-rosisor.* Stokes suggests 1 sg. future of *sechithir,* but this verb forms an f-future. Another possibility is *ar·sissedar,* "stay, stand fast; endure, persist," 1 sg. perfect indicative preterite, without the suppression of the reduplicating syllable. Cf. 3 sg. perf. pret. *arosisir YBL* 212 b 19.

dosifius. do·seinn, "pursues, drives, hunts," 1 sg. future.

do-sselladh. Perhaps from a verb **do·sella,* meaning something like "watch, observe" and related to *sellaid* "sees, perceives." 3 sg. passive preterite, with *-ss-* indicating a nasalizing relative clause, object of the preceding verb, or with *-s-* as the generalized infixed pronoun.

ar-roselus. ar·slig "kills, smites," 1 sg. future with *ro* expressing possibility.

aros-dibu. ar·diben "cuts off, slays, destroys," 1 sg. future with *ro* expressing possibility or 1 sg. perfective preterite. *-s-* is the 3 pl. infixed pronoun.

§107:493. *nos-ríastais.* See *Contribb.* R 68, s.v. *rigid,* for this ex., expanded as *nos-riastar,* 3 sg. pass. pr. subj. The alternate possibility, preferred here, is 3 pl. pass. secondary subj., with unnecessary 3 pl. infixed pron.

§114:506. Stokes, perhaps rightly, takes *condoid* (with sg. subject) and *connai* (for *connaid*? with pl. subject, §116) as errors for forms of *con·icc.* Another possibility, however, is the verb *con·oí* (2 pl. pr. ind.). Its meaning, "protect, preserve, guard, keep" seems a possible one in the context. Perhaps the verb is used with a slightly extended meaning: "look after, maintain."

The 2 pl. pr. ind. is used for the sing. in §98 also.

§115:507. *gláim ndícind.* See *Contribb. G* 91, s.v. *glám,* ā, f., "satire," with references to the phrase *glám dícenn,* "extempore satire, a kind of metrical malediction." See also the illustration of the process included in Stokes' glossary, *RC* 12 (1891), 119-121.

§117:512ff. The transformation of trees into soldiers — at least, into an illusionary army — also appears as a piece of women's magic in *2MT²* 46-49 (*Motif-Index:* D 431.2.1*). Sín, in *Aided M.* 610-611, enchants fern or bracken, stones, and puff-balls, with similar results; see also the introduction, xvii-xviii. The children of Calitín practice similar sorcery in *Aided Con Culainn, Comp. Con C* §20, 88, as do the three women-warriors and sorceresses in *CF* 6-7.

The opposite effect, the Macbeth motif, occurs in *CRR* 37, where men cut and carry oak branches before them.

§117:513. *craidenus. Contribb. C* 507, s.v. *craidenus* lists this ex., "horror and affliction," cf. *crád, cráidid.* Perhaps to be associated rather with *cridenas,* 529 (*cride? crith?*), with many exx. given of the phrase, *úathbás* 7 *c.* (whence by-form, *cridenbás?*) "fright and terror."

§119:516. *feru,* for a.pl. *firu,* unless *fri* is here intended to take the dative; if so, the expansion should be *feraib.* In several other contexts, however, *e* appears for *i* as simply an orthographic variant, so the intent is not certain.

Ó Máille, *Annals,* §99, cites exx. of apl. *firu* spelled *feru,* beginning in 1077, 1080, 1084.

§119:516ff. The elements of the Dagda's simile are traditional. Cf. *BDD²* 860, 986 "*bit lir bomand ega . . .*"; *Táin* 4710-4711 "*combús lir bommana ega . .*" (note 4710 on parallel passages in other versions); *LL* (120b) 13952ff. mentions both *bommand ega* and *fér fo chossaib grega,* as does *TTr.²* 1162.

cáemslecht. Contribb. C 17, citing only this example, suggests *cáemślecht* (? com + imm + slecht). See also *Contribb. C.* 308, s.v. *coimślechtad,* with the ex. *Leb. Gab.* 106.3 *da ccoimslechtadh,* "to slaughter them." and *Contribb. S* 266, s.v. *slecht* "a cutting, hewing (?) . . . used also in the sense of slaughter."

§119:518. *áit a comraicid díabulnámod.* Cf. *BDD²* 733: *áit i comraicfead díabolnámaid.*

§121:523. The skirmishes before the main battle offer another contrast with the order of events in *2MT²,* where the nearest equivalent is the fighting that occurs before Lug awakes to join the battle, 126ff.

§122:529-30. *fo bíth roboí.* In the O.Ir. glosses, *fo bíth* is followed by relative *n-.* Relative *-n-* is, however, infrequently shown in the present text.

§122:529ff. The assembly line production by the craftsmen is also described in *Cormac's Glossary,* s.v. *Nescoit,* and is there expanded by an account of Goibniu's response to the news of his wife's infidelity. The two texts are verbally similar at many points, but they are by no means identical, and both could be, at least in part, reflections of oral tradition.

In *2MT²,* the assembly line is not described, but there is a description of Goibniu's work in preparing Lug's sling-stone, 580ff. (Note the promises of Goibniu and Luchtuinne regarding the preparation of arms earlier in the text, *2MT²* 25ff.)

§123:540. The Well of Sláine is mentioned in *Met. Dinds.* IV 182 (Lusmag); *Dinds.* §108 (Lusmag); *Ed. Dinds.* §71 (Lusmag). Cf. *Motif-Index*: D 1500.1.1.1 *"Magic (healing) well dug by saint," V 134 "Sacred (holy) wells" and cross references. A secular example appears in *CF* 6-7, the healing well offered by three women-warriors to Conncrither m. Brain m. Febail.

§123:541. *iṁ*, usually the abbreviation for *immorro*, is perhaps to be taken here as prefix to a compound of *slig-*, giving *imm·airlestis*, secondary future 3 pass. "who would be severely wounded," with 2 *imm* used as intensive prefix. Such a use of *imm-*, rare in O. Ir., becomes common in Early Mod. Ir.

botar bí . . . Bati[r] slán. botar bí shows agreement in number (pl.) of verb, subject, and predicate adjective *bati[r] slán,* on the other hand, shows the later use of sg. adj. with pl. verb. See Dillon, "Nominal Predicates," *ZCP* 16 (1927), 324, 329. Cf. other examples at §§26, 36, 63, 94, 122, and 150.

§§124-125:545ff. The incident of Rúadán's espionage and treachery points once again to a frequent theme of the tale as a whole, the strength of paternal kinship in determining a man's true loyalties.

§124:524. *óes dána.* See note to §85:549.

§125:557-8. Bríg's association with the first keening heard in Ireland appears in *LG*: §§317, 344, 369, but no reason for the association is given.

LG identifies the cries as *Fét 7 Gol 7 Eigem,* and the association of the three may be responsible for the added reference in *2MT* to Bríg's discovery of a *feit do caismeirt in oidci* (no doubt an incorporated gloss).

§126:567ff. Dian Cécht's healing well is also described in *dindshenchus* tradition (Lusmag), but without reference to Ochtríallach, son of Indech.

§127:569. *Ní rabhu.* 3 sg. perf. pret. of the substantive verb, Mid. Ir. form. Cf. *-roba BDD²* 251, *-raba* 1533, *-rabha TD* 8.36. Note also §§39, 42 above.

§127:572-3. A close parallel to the expression *"bém cinn fri hald"* appears in *CRR¹* §42: *"Is essarcain cind fri hallib."*

"Ba láum a net natrach" appears also in *LL* 225b 8, and *LL* 304b 20 (= *RC* 13 (1892), 94.2) (pl. form). I have not yet found another example of *"ba haigedh go tenid."* Cf. *Motif-Index:* Z 63* "Formulas signifying fruitlessness."

§128:575ff. All of the characters listed as Fomorian chiefs and leaders appear elsewhere in Irish literature, most of them in *2MT²* and in *dindshenchus* tradition, although only a few play major roles within *2MT* itself. The corresponding account of the exhortation of the Fomorian host is *2MT²* 353ff. The list of Fomorian leaders is much expanded, but omits Omna and Bagna (although Oghma mac Badhna appears at 1239-1240); Goll and Irgoll; and Tuirie Tortbuillech (Tinne Thortbhuilligh, g.s., appears as Badhna's father in 1239).

§128:576. *Doit.* This MS. and Rawl. 162 f 2 (*mac Doith*) give the vowel as short; *2MT²*, 293, on the other hand, has *mac Dóit.* See *Contribb. D* 378, s.v. *Dot,* n. pr. o, m.

§129:580ff. Lug's escape to join the battle and his words of encouragement to the Tuatha Dé Danann, together with his circuit of the host on one
foot, using one hand and one eye, recall three separate passages in *2MT²*:
126-221; 400-462; and 741-745.

§129:582. *con·selu*. To *con·slá*, "goes away," 3 sg. preterite *con·sela*,
Thurn. Gramm. §680.

ina cairptech. *cairptech*, o, m., "chariot-fighter, chariot-warrior,"
Contribb. C 49; *i n-* with dative, governing noun in apposition, with
possessive pronoun (replacing the older dative usage without a preposition).
The motif of using only one foot, one eye and one hand (*Motif-Index:* D
1273.0.4* "Spell chanted while standing on one foot with one eye shut,
etc.") is common in Irish tradition. Cf. the motifs involving persons or
groups having only one foot, hand and eye: F 525.3*, F 525.3.1*, F 531
.1.6.12* "Giant with one hand and one foot." See also F 682.0.1* "Person
(warrior) uses only one leg, one hand, one eye." See also the references
given by Rees and Rees, *Celtic Heritage,* 425, "One eye, one arm, one leg."

For discussions of Lug's action, see Jan de Vries, 'L'aspect magique de la
religion Celtique,' *Ogam* 10 (1958), 273-284, especially 280-284; Christian
J. Guyonvarc'h, 'Notes d'Etymologie et Lexicographie gauloises et
celtiques, 21, ♯82,' *Ogam* 16 (1964), 441-446, concluded in *Ogam* 17
(1965), 143-144.

When Lug arrives at Tara, he proclaims himself a *corrguinech*
("sorcerer"); Guyonvarc'h suggests that Lug's recitation in the battle is an
example of *corrguinecht,* and he cites O'Davoran's Glossary describing
corrguinecht as the process of making *glám dícenn*, a type of satire, on one
foot, with one eye open, and using only one hand.

§§130-132:600ff. The general description of the battle, shared with the
older version of the battle of Mag Rath (ed. Marstrander, *Ériu* 5, (1911)
227ff.) may be compared with the very different account in *2MT²* 746-812.

O'Brien, *Ériu* 12, 239-40, comments on the battle description found in
both *MR²* and *2MT*, noting that *MR²* sometimes has better readings than
2MT. Regarding the passage beginning at 1. 588, he concludes "*Crob* can
hardly be anything other than the ordinary word for 'hand.' *Unnsenn* (*recte
uinnsinn*) I take to be the plural of *uinnius*= 'ash tree, spear-shaft of ash,' a
meaning the word often has. *Rurassa* I take to be the plural passive perfect
of *rondaid*, 'he colours, he reddens.' I would translate the passage: 'and then
spear-shafts were reddened in the hands of enemies." In the context of *2MT*,
there is a possible play on *unnsenn*, the river Unshin mentioned earlier in the
text as the meeting-place of the Morrígan and the Tuatha Dé Danann *áes
dána* (§85). Some readings of Mag Rath, as O'Brien noted, suggest that it is
closer to the original than *2MT*, although there are early forms (retained
dative plural article, for example) that appear only in *2MT*.

§132:612. *ocin imtúarcain*. Or, read *oci n-imtúarcain*, taking *oci* as *oc* + 3
pl. poss. pron. *a n-*, rather than *oc* + def. art. See *Contribb*. O 84, s.v. *oc,* III
(f), (vn. used in pass. sense, with poss. pron. preceding). This reading follows
that of *MR²*.

§133:617ff. The death of Núadu and the subsequent victory of the Tuatha
Dé Danann seems contrary to the belief that the presence of a king was
required for victory. But by this sequence of events, the myth underscores

the kingliness of Lug who, although not inaugurated, is symbolically and potentially a ruler of the Tuatha Dé Danann, one who has sat in the king's seat, receiving honour due to the king, and one who is ready to take his place on the field when Núadu is killed. On the customs of deciding battle, by the death of the king, see D. A. Binchy, *Proceedings of the International Congress of Celtic Studies* (1962; repr. 1975), 128.

The deaths of Núadu, Macha and Casmáel are mentioned in *LG* §§312, 331, 364; poem LVI §§7-8.

Casmáel's death occurs in *2MT²*, 1009-1019, as he seeks to avenge Ogma but is instead slain by Olltríathach; Macha's death is not mentioned in *2MT²*; Núadu falls at Balor's hands, 1085-1086.

§133-135:617ff. Only a few single combats are mentioned in *2MT*, and the specific references to the fates of various members of the Tuatha Dé Danann in §133 also appear as a group in *LG*, suggesting that they may have been borrowed from that text.

The account of the origin of the malefic power of Balor's eye does not appear elsewhere, but his conversation with Lug is echoed in a difficult "rhetorical" passage of *2MT²* (668-676). Unlike *2MT*, *2MT²* separates the incident in which Lug destroys Balor's eye (668ff.) from the final combat between the two at Carn Uí Néit, where Balor is slain (1295ff.).

Although Balor is not said to be one-eyed, there is malefic power in only one of his eyes, and parallels have been suggested with various other one-eyed divine or supernatural figures.

§133:619ff. For the Indo-European tradition of a one-eyed divine figure possibly underlying various Celtic mythic and epic traditions, see Dumézil, *Mitra-Varuna*, 2nd ed., (1948), discussed by C. Scott Littleton in *The New Comparative Mythology* (1973), 86ff., 99.

For examples of figures with a single eye, with possible sun and lightning associations, see O'Rahilly, *EIHM*, ch. 3, "The Gai Bulga and its Kin," 58ff. For one-eyed opponents of heroes, see Murphy, *Duan. Finn* III, lxix ff. The international tale type is Type 1137 "The ogre blinded: Polyphemus." The savage Welsh giant Yspaddaden requires attendants to raise his eyelids by means of forks; the Irish parallel, *drolum omlithi*, seems to be "a polished handle or ring". See *Contribb. D* 404, s.v. *drolam*, "ring attached to an object serving as a handle," and *Contribb. O* 141, s.v. *?omlithe*, citing Stokes.

milldagach = *milledach*; see *Contribb. M* 138, s.v. *milledach*, "destructive, malefic."

§133:621ff. *inn sóul, die shól, darsan sól.* These forms are perhaps influenced by some glossarial tradition such as *súil quasi sol, ar is treithi atá soillsi do duine, Corm. Y* 1129.

§133:622. *Slúoac[h] do-n-éceud darsan sól.* "The host which looked at that eye," or "The host that he would see through the eye . . ." *slúag,* a collective noun, could be used with a sg. verb, and *do-n-* might be taken as *do* + *a n-*, 3 sg. m. infixed pronoun (Class A instead of C); cf. Stokes' translation, "If an army looked at that eye . . ." It might be preferable, however, to take the *n-* as indicating a nasalizing relative clause. *Tar, dar* "over, across," may be used to indicate "through, out of, (an aperture)"

(IV), and of a tear dropping from the eye. See *Contribb. T* 72ff., s.v. *tar*.

§133:622. *nín-géptis*. Perhaps with meaningless 3 sg. inf. pron.; cf. exx. in Strachan, "The Infixed Pronoun in Middle Irish," *Ériu* 1 (1904), 173.

§133:626. *Condrecat*. *Contribb. C* 457, s.v. *con·ricc*, "meets, encounters," (2) "in 'inclusive plural' construction: *conráncatar* 7 *D*. 'he and D. met,' *Thes*. ii 241.5."
The "inclusive plural" construction is to be expected here: [7] *Lug*.

§133:626. *Is nann*. The initial *n-* here is an error—perhaps influenced by the *n-* that would follow a noun denoting time, used adverbially in the accusative, *Thurn. Gramm*. §249.3.
The dialogue between Lug and Balor has definite, if obscure, parallels in *2MT²*, 668-676.

§134:642. In the marginal attribution of Lug's speech to Balor, the variant Lug*aid* is used, and Lugdech occurs within the speech itself, alternating with Lug. This variation is common in later usage, and in *2MT²* Lug*aid*h occurs at 85, although the most common form of the name in that text is Lugh. See also the poem on Lug's slingstone, edited by Meyer, *ZCP* 5 (1905), 504, where the dative singular *Lugdaig* is used.

§134:642. *co ndoécius*. *Contribb. D*. 244-245, s.v. *do·éccai* "looks at, beholds, sees," this example: 1 sg. present subjunctive? Cf. the future form 1 sg. *do-n-écucus-sa*, *LU* 1490, *Thurn. Gramm*. §655, for another sigmatic form, contrasted with the usual formations of *·cí*.

§135:644ff. Lug's destruction of Balor's evil eye with a slingstone (rather than the spear of some folk accounts) also occurs in *2MT²*, where the stone is prepared by Goibniu (578ff. and note 578).
The poem mentioned by Ó Cuiv, printed by Meyer in *ZCP* 5 (1905), 504 (Eg. 1782) indicates that the stone came from "Briuin mac Bethrach."
On the actual results of Lug's cast, causing Balor's own people to be harmed by his evil eye, see *2MT²*, 715-719. In *2MT²*, the general account of the battle proper follows the uncovering of Balor's eye; and Balor survives the injury to be slain by Lug at Carn Í Néid (1286ff.).
líic. MS. *liic*, elsewhere in the MS. with *í* (§3, §16, §72). See *Contribb. L* 142, s.v. *lía* (orig. disyll.), "stone."

§135:645. *co ndechaid an súil triena cend*. "Which carried the eye through his head ..." Literally, "and the eye went through his head."

§135:646. Three times nine men are needed to open Balor's evil eye in *2MT²* 568; in *2MT*, three times nine are killed in his fall, but *cethrar* (§133) suffice to open the eye.
conda-apatar. *at·bail(l)*, "dies," suppletive *ad·bath* in narrative tense; with *-da-* 3 pl. infixed pronoun, here agreeing with the subject in number.

§136:651. *cía rotollae form-sa*. *rotollae* seems a metathesized mixture of forms, based upon the suppletive form to *do·cuirethar* (**to·ro·la*), "cast," perfect preterite 3 sg.: *dus·rale*, *Ml*. 23c 16, *co·toralae*, *Corm. Y* 698, perhaps also influenced by *tollaid*, "pierces, penetrates."
rotollae. Stokes suggests the form represents a scribal error for *tolléci* (cf. *LU* 111ª).

§136:649ff. The dialogue between Lug and Lóch has echoes in that between Lug and Liath Leathghlas (without reference to Indech) in $2MT^2$, 720-732. In both Lug identifies himself as the warrior who has destroyed Balor's eye, but the language of both is obscure. See also $2MT$ §§139-146, and $2MT^2$ 1414, where the Fomorian addressed by Lug is Luath Lineach.

In the obscure dialogue between Lug and Lóch, after Lug has identified himself as the champion who cast the slingstone at Balor, the two exchange mutual accusations of false prophecy.

§136:665, 668. *Fomoiri* is expanded here in accordance with §133:632, *Fomoiri*, and §162:778 *Fomhoire*.

§136:665. The gloss at 665 over *lethsuanaigh* reads .*i. dath derc nobid fair o fuine greni co maidin* and is noted by Stokes, 127, who cites Rhys's emendation (to the adjective *lethsíanach*, associated with *sían*, "foxglove"). This meaning seems appropriate given the gloss, which states that a red colour used to be upon him [Lug] from sunset to morning.

§137:681. *anduidhe*. O.Ir. usage would give either *i suidiu* (*Contribb. I* 8, s.v. *i n-*, IV), "then, thereat," or *ann-side* as in §150, with stressed pronoun object and unstressed emphasizing pronoun respectively.

§137:683ff. The Morrígan's words strengthening her troops, marking a turning point in the battle, do not appear in $2MT^2$.

§138:694ff. The total victory of the Tuatha Dé Danann is acknowledged by all accounts. In $2MT^2$, both Ogma and Indech are slain, but they do not fall at each other's hands; instead, Indech kills Ogma and is himself slain by Lug. In *LG*, Ogma is killed but Indech survives. Ogma's survival may, however, represent an early tradition, since at least one of the $2MT$ sections in which he appears alive after the battle (§163) is linked by plot development to the early stratum of the tale that emphasizes Bres's misdeeds.

Ogma's death at the hands of Indech appears in $2MT^2$ 1006-1008; in 1020-1022, Indech is slain by Lug. In *LG*, Indech survives the battle, and takes the place of Lóch (*2MT*) in discussing with Lug the number of the slain (§§312, 332, 364), while Ogma's death in the battle is mentioned in §§312, 331, 364, LVI §8. The account of the Fomorian rout is much more detailed in $2MT^2$, 1187ff.

roslech[t]ait. The verb may be assigned to *slechtaid*, "cuts, cuts down, slaughters," 3 pl. Mid. Ir. perf. pret. passive, or, as in *Contribb S 273-274*, s.v. *sligid*, "cuts, strikes down; lays low, slays, defeats," to the latter verb (apparently as a Mid. Ir. pl. passive form built on the older pl. *roslechta*).

§§139-148:697ff. Lug's discussion with the Fomorian poet Lóch may be compared with $2MT^2$, 1414ff. (where Luath Lineach is addressed) and with *LG* §§312, 332, 364, where Indech provides the account of the fallen.

§140:700. *a ngébas*. 3 sg. fut. rel. of *gaibid*, with the meaning "sing, chant, recite, declare." See *Contribb. G* 19, s.v. *gaibid* IV.

§140:700-1. *ar cach n-aingceus*. See *Contribb. A* 136-137, s.v. *ainces*, form and inflection variable, "pain, ailment, difficulty, trouble, doubt; in a legal context, 'difficult case or decision.'" Cf. *is tré erchoiliud foillsighter aincesa in betha, O Dav.* 812, "It is through legal pronouncements that the difficulties of the world are made clear."

See note 561, *CMM*, where the neuter gender is suggested, based on two examples from *Blathm*.

§141:702. *In Dáil n-Asdadha. Dict. D* 43 s.v. 2 *dál*, ā, f. cites a range of meanings (Ia) "meeting," (b) "encounter"; (II) "conference, assembly"; (III) "a law case"; (IVa) "a judgment, decree," (b) "an agreement, a contract, covenant."

Contribb. A 441 defines *astud* u, m. as (a) the "act of holding back, detaining, keeping (in a place)." The present example is given, doubtfully, in association with this meaning, given that Lóch has undertaken to ward off the Fomoire, however (b) "the act of fixing or establishing"—including contractual references—might also be appropriate.

§141:708, 710. *Fomoire*, cf. §133:623; §162:778. In 680, *Ere* (for *Ére*) is another ex. of the early d.s. form, cf. §126:562.

§§142-145:711ff. The chariot names are given in the edition with length added where the meaning seems plain; in the translation, the names remain as edited, but are given without indication of expansions. These practices apply also to the lists of charioteers, goads, and horses.

§142:713-4. Some tentative suggestions regarding the names of Lug's chariots are given below.

?*Luachta*. ?*Anagat. Achad*: achad o, m. "expanse of ground; pasture, field." *Feochair*: feochair i "fierce, wild." *Fer*: fer o,m. 'man' ?*Golla*. *Fosad*: fossad o, ā, "firm, steady." *Cráeb*: cráeb ā, f. "branch, wand, rod, tree, bush." *Carpat*: carpat o, m. "war-chariot."

§143:716-7. Tentative suggestions regarding the names of Lug's charioteers follow.

?*Medol*.

Medón: medón o, m. "middle, center."

Moth: moth m. "the membrum virile."

Mothach: mothach o, ā "prolific, abounding in produce." *Foimtinne*: cf. *foimtiu* n, f., later n, s. *foimtin* "being in readiness."

Tenda: cf. *tend* o, ā "strong, hard, firm" and *tendad* u, m. "pressing, straining, tightening; encouraging, urging."

Tres: tress u, m. "contention, fight."

Morb: marb o, ā "dead; deadly."

§144:719-20. Some possible meanings of the names of the charioteers' goads are given below.

Fes for *fis* u, and o, m. "knowledge," or without mark of length for *fés* "lip" or *fés* "hair." *Res*: res ā, f. "a dream, vision."

Roches: perhaps *ro* "intensive prefix" + *ces* ā, f. "spear"; or *ces* "haunch."

Anagar: anacair "unevenness, roughness" or *an-* neg. prefix + *agar* "fear."

Ilach: ilach o, m. "a cry of exultation, a shout of victory."

?*Canna*.

Ríadha: ríata io, iā "trained for driving or racing; broken." *Búaid*: búaid i, m. "victory, triumph."

§§145:722-3. The names of Lug's horses might be rendered as follows.

?*Can*.

Doríadha: *do* "prefix with negative or pejorative meaning," this example, "hard to ride," *Contribb. D.* 358, s.v. *Doriada*.

Romuir: *romuir* i, n. "the sea, the ocean."

Laisad: *lasad* u, m. "act of burning, blazing."

Fer Forsaid: *fer* o, m. "man," *forsaid* "firm, steady, established."

Sroban: perhaps *srúb* n.? "snout, muzzle," with *-án* "diminutive prefix."

Airchedal: *airchetal* o, m. "poem; poetry."

Ruagar: *ro*, intensive prefix, with *agar* "fear."

Illann: appears as a warrior's name in *Táin* 4055.

Allríadha: *oll* o, ā "great, ample" with *ríata* io, iā "trained for driving or racing, broken."

Rocedal: *rochetal* o, m., n. "a great song; singing; chant."

§146:732ff. The pattern of this numerical string, if one was intended, remains unclear. Another reckoning appears in *LG* §§312, 332, 364; LXIV and in *2MT²* 1428-1431. Macalister discusses the *LG* version, found in *LG* IV: VII, on 322.

§147:736. *a soír* ₇ *a ndaoír* are nominatives of apposition. Regarding this passage, Dillon, "Nominal Predicates," *ZCP* 17 (1928), 345, notes: "For Early Middle Irish, the rule may be formulated that when the apposition is not complete, it is expressed by the nominative case. The nominative of apposition appears c. 900 (Dá Derga), and has taken the place of *i n-a* with the dative by the 13th century (AS and Aid. Fergh.). The example from Cath Maige Tuired will date from this later period."

§148:742. *lethdoínib*. *leth-* "half," also means "one of a pair," here, "one of a pair of men," a reference to the custom noted in *Motif-Index*: P 551.2* "Soldiers chained (tied) together to prevent flight from battle. On the custom of tying warriors together to prevent flight, see also *CMM* §48.

§148:743. *cridiu*. *cride*, io, n., later m., O. Ir. *cride* in the accusative singular.

§148:743ff. The expressions of impossibility are traditional, and often appear in groups, as here.

Cf. *ACC* §64 "*rimfed rind . . . no airmebad rétglanna nime*"; *RC* 18 (1897), 173.12, "*noco n-airimther ganim mara . . .*" and *RC* 24(1903), 381.4, "*co-n-airmestur gainemh mara . . .*"

Drúcht for faithchi (sic leg.) recalls "*drúcht cétamuin*," *RC* 3(1876-78), 177.29 and "*bit lir . . . fér for faichthi*," *BDD²* 89.

For *bommand ega*, see note §119.

For the waves as horses, *groigh mic Lir*, see motif A 1118.1*, and *Contribb. G.* 145, s.v. *graig*, i, n., for this example. Cf. *Contribb. G* 6, s.v. 2 *gabor*, for *gabra lir*, *Im. Brain* 36.

For several together, see *LL* 13952ff.: ". . .*comtar lir gainem mara* ₇ *renna nime* ₇ *drúcht cétamuin* ₇ *loa snechtai* ₇ *bommand ega*. ₇ *dulli for fidbaid* ₇ *budi for Bregmaig*. ₇ *fér fo chossaib grega . . .*' (*Brislech Mór Maige Murthemni*).

See also *Motif-Index*: Z 61, Z 61.1 "Never," for various other ways of expressing this idea.

2MT² ends with an account of the fallen, and there is nothing to correspond with §§149-166 of *2MT*.

§§149-160:747ff. The dialogue between Lug and Bres returns to the earlier focus on Bres's misrule and its consequences. *2MT²*, in contrast, describes the death of Bres at the hands of Lug, 1139-1173.

§150:750. *bid sírblechtach báe.* The nom. pl., rather than nom. sg., form is to be expected here. Cf. Dillon, "Nominal Predicates," *ZCP* 16 (1927), 324, 329.

§150:751. *Comarfas-sa.* 1 sg. fut. prototonic form of a verb **con·arfét* with the meaning of *ar·fét*, variant of *ad·fét* (see Pedersen II 519), "sets forth." The prototonic form often appears in replies to questions. For *-as*, 1 sg. fut. ending, see *Thurn. Gramm.* §666 (a).

    Cf. *BDD²* §15, 166: *Im-caemros/s/ado gaethaib* ...

§152:755. *ce.* For *ce* (*cía, cè*) see *Contribb. C* 165, s.v. *cía.*

§153:722. *ce.* See note §152:755.

§154:758. *Forbotha.* See *Contribb. F* 316, s.v. ?*forbotha* subst. pl., "alarms?" cf. *fo-botha.*

§155:759. *An fil n-aill.* Cf. the similar passage, *Trip.* 116, 18f., *Infail naill con·desta*?, concerning which *Thurn. Gramm.* §780.2 suggests that the *n* represents that in *na aill* or *a n-aill.*

§155:759. *bibsiutt.* See *Contribb. B* 136, s.v. *boingid* "reaps"; this example is 3 pl. reduplicated future.

§157:765. *foircend.* See *Contribb. F* 319-320, s.v. *forcenn* "end, final limit."

§160:772. *cocon ebrad, co sílfad, co chobibsad.* For *cocon* with the prototonic (or conjunct) form of the verb, see M. A. O'Brien, "Varia II. 4," *Ériu* 12 (1938) 239. *Ebra-*, the future stem of *airid*, "ploughs," is also discussed. Cf. *Thurn. Gramm.* §649.

    For *co chobibsad*, see *Contribb. C* 427, s.v. *con·boing*, this ex., with the meaning of *boingid* "reaps."

§161:776. *celg.* The tone of this editorial comment is ambiguous. *Contribb. C* 109, s.v. *celg* offers (a) "deceit, treachery, guile, stratagem," but gives examples of favorable usage as in *tre chealgaibh* "charms" (of Mary), *Aith. D.* 85.10; (b) "ambush, trap"; (c) "sting." Most of the usages have a negative connotation and it may be that the sentence reflects an interpretation that Bres's advice was valueless. Such an attitude was doubtless not that of the original narrator, as this advice for the best days for beginning agricultural work survives in Scottish Gaelic tradition. See M. M. Banks, "*Na Tri Mairt,* the Three Marts and the Man with the Withy," *Études Celtiques* 3 (1938), 131-143.

§162:777ff. Ogma's discovery of Tethra's sword Orna and Lóch's praise of the sword reflect the tradition that Ogma was not killed in the battle, a tradition also appearing in §163.

§162:777ff. The account of Tethra's sword includes the motifs: D 1610.9 "Speaking sword," and F 408.1* "Demon occupies sword"; cf. M 113.1* "Oath taken on arms."

    One reflection of the tradition of weapons recounting deeds done by them is Cian's remark to his murderers that the weapons used to kill him would reveal the identity of his killers, *OCT* (*GJ* 1884). A similar belief is found in *SC²* §2, where their swords turn against falsely boasting warriors, and the passage ends with lines (16-17) reminiscent of *2MT*: *ar no labraitis demna friu dia n-armaib conid de batir comarchi forro a n-airm.*

§162:779. *nach n-*, for *nech*, replacing the neuter form *ní* "anything, aught," with 3 sg. perf. pret. pass. of *do·gní*, "makes, does."

§§163-165:793ff. These sections, demonstrating again the power of music (cf. §73), reveal the consequences of the Dagda's earlier choice of payment for his construction of Dún mBrese: the eventual recovery of the cattle taken by the Fomoire as tribute (perhaps originally simply by Bres himself, as the passage evidently belongs to an early stratum of the legend).

§163:796. *ara nenaisc. ar*, prep. + *a n-* rel., + *naiscid*, "binds" (3 sg. reduplicated pret.), cf. *Contribb.* N 11, s.v. *naiscid.*

§163:796ff. Regarding the harp that can only be played by the Dagda, see *Motif-Index:* D 1651.7.1 "Magic harp plays only for owner" and D 1231 "Magic harp."

§163:799-800. *Daur Dá Bláo* and *Cóir Cethairchuir.* The two names of the Dagda's harp: "Oak of Two Meadows" with *daur* u, f. "an oak" and *blá* f. "lawn, green, level field, plain, meadow"; and *Cóir Cethairchuir*, with *cóir*, an adj. meaning "proper, fitting, just, true," here used as a noun, and *cetharchair*, an adj. meaning "four-sided, square, rectangular."

§164:806ff. The three musical strains that qualify a harper are also played by Lug (§73, note). *Triads* §122 includes them in a group defining the accomplishments of various professionals. Cf. *LL* 189b, 24916ff., *Do nemthigud filed i scélaib.*

MS. *fora nemithir*, emended to *fora nem[th]i[g]thir. neimthigid(ir)*, g. deponent and active verb, "gives status, qualifies as a professional," here with *for* + *a n-*, meaning "through which, by means of which," in a passive construction, 3 sg. present indicative (= *-neimthigther*). For non-passive usage, see for example, *Triads* 116: *tréde neimthigedar crossán.*

crutiri for n. sg. *cruitire*, or one can take the verb as plural erroneously lenited, making *crutiri* n. pl.

§165:812. *in tan ro géssi.* 3 sg. perf. pret. of *géisid*, used especially of the sounds made by cow or bull. The form may be the pret. conjunct ending in -*i*, see *Thurn. Gramm.* §678, or -*gés-si*, with 3 sg. fem. emphasizing pronoun.

§166:816. *sídhcairib.* See note §60:256.

§166:817. Badb may be taken either as the proper name of a goddess (as in the translation) or as the ordinary word for "scaldcrow," a form in which that divine figure, a wargoddess, often appeared. See Index of Persons, s.v. *Badb.*

§§166-167:819ff. The Morrígan's double prophecy graphically presents the balance between good and evil, the inevitable end of what is right and orderly—symbolized by the end of the world—through the power of chaos. Christian tradition may have reinforced a belief in the principles of pagan eschatology, but the Morrígan's words, like the competitive prophecies of Néde and Ferchertne in *The Colloquy of the Two Sages,* seem rooted in native tradition.

See Stokes's edition, RC 26 (1905), 4-64, esp. 32-49.

INDEX TO NOTES

INDEX OF PERSONS

The first form given (n.s.) is that used in translation, prefixed by an * if the n.s. does not actually occur in the text. It is followed by the actual MS. form (or forms, if there are others of interest) if different from the form of the name used in translation. Other case forms may be given, in the following order: g.s., d.s., a.s., v.s. and plurals. Not every orthographic or declensional form is listed, but an attempt is made to illustrate the range of variation for any particular name. Within the text of each entry, the prefixed asterisk indicates that the name is listed in the Index of Persons.

References to the banshenchus materials are drawn from the index compiled by M. Magrath, an unpublished thesis entitled: *An Examination of the Historical Portions of the BanShenchas* (Harvard, 1978). p. and v. stand for *prose* and *verse*. The texts are found in *LL, Lec.* (Book of Lecan), *D* (Book of Uí Maine), *BB, Edinburgh* (Kilbride VII), *BRS* (Brussels 2542), H. 3.17. The oldest banshenchus text, *LL*, mentions most of the Túatha Dé Danann women who appear in *2MT*, but omits Airmed, Bríg, Crón and Ernmas.

TÚATHA DÉ DANANN

The form Túath Déa (variously spelled) is common in the present text. By contrast, Macalister, in notes on the prose text of *LG*, section VII, 295, identifies it as unusual. The omission of Danann in the *LG* passages mentioned by Macalister is perhaps to be associated with the tradition found in *Cóir Anm.* §149, *Tuatha Dea (i. Donann)*, "The Tribes of the Goddess, that is of Dana." The passage suggests that Túatha Dé(a) was, in fact, common as an alternate form of the name, and that the fuller form could be considered "glossed," that is, as expanded by the identification of the goddess in question, with *Donann* perhaps simply a scribal error.

The fluctuation between singular and plural of Túath(a) Dé(a) (Danann) is common to many texts. *Cóir Anm.* itself is almost evenly divided (§§25, 76, 154 sg., §§150, 151 pl., also §149 as noted. *2MT*[2] however, uses only T.D.D., usually abbreviated, occasionally expanded, apparently always plural. *Airne F.* and *Táin* use only the full plural form of the name; both forms appear in *T. Emire* (*Comp. Con C.* §35, §44 pl. full; §36 sg. shorter form).

The usage in the present text is heavily weighted toward the shorter form, and almost evenly divided between the treatment of Túath(a) as singular and as plural. Some form of Túath Dé appears in §§8, 9, 14, 24, 36, 39, 40, 52; of Túatha Dé in §§18, 43, 83, 121, 122, 124, 129, 137. The fuller form, Túatha Dé Danann, appears only in §12 (sg.), and in §§1, 78, 96 (pl.).

That Túath(a) Déa is an early form of the name is suggested not only by the usage of the present text and the distribution in other major texts noted, but by a comparison of the usage in the two versions of *De Gabáil in tSída*. The older version (*LL*) Thurneysen dated to the 9th century (*IHKS*, 604; Hull, *ZCP* 19(1931), 54); it uses only Túatha Déa or Fér Déa (in dat. pl.) (three exx. in all), while D. 4.2 uses Túatha Dé Danann (various cases) exclusively, and has six examples.

For a general discussion of the name, see Thurneysen, *IHKS*, 63; *Duan. Finn*, Appendix I, "Donu and Tuatha Dé Donann," 208-210, with reasons for considering the name as meaning "Peoples of the Goddess Donu" (including absence of *n-*, expected if genitive plural). Could the usage with *Donu represent later confusion, and the earlier form, in fact, be genitive plural, correctly translated *plebes deorum* (*L. Bretnach* §12)?

Abcán mac Bicelmois (Auhcán mac Bicelmois) 60. A harper.

   LG §§316 (=339, 368) identifies *Abcan mac Bicc Felmais meic Con meic Dein Cecht* as Lug's poet; according to *LG* LVI §17, he was killed by Óengus.

The circumstances surrounding his death, and the begetting of his son Senbecc upon Etan daughter of Dían Cécht, are summarized by Thurneysen, *IHKS*, 490, from the text edited in *ZCP* 13 (1919), 130, where Abcán is identified as ua húa Ebricc.

The adventures of Senbecc with Cú Chulainn—from whom he escapes without ransom by playing harp music so that the hero falls asleep—may be found in *RC* 6 (1884), 182-185 and *Ériu* 13 (1940, 1942), 26, 222-223.

Dindsenchus tradition (Ess Rúaid) identifies Abcán *éices* as the owner of a boat in which Rúad, daughter of Maine Milscothach, elopes, although he is not himself her suitor.

Airmed (Airmedh, Airmeth) 35, 123.

Daughter of *Dían Cécht, and herself a physician, *LG* §§314; 343; 366, 368. Perhaps her name, through misreading or miscopying, generates that of the physician Ormiach in *OCT* (*GJ* 1884), 33ff, and that of Oirmed in *Acall.* 2547. Banshenchus tradition (*Lec. BB, Edin.*) identifies her as a daughter of Dían Cécht.

*Al(l)(d)a(e) 12, in the name *Edleo mac Allai.

Identified in various *LG* genealogies as son of Tat (ancestor of all the Túatha Dé Danann) and father of Indui, Ordan, and Eidleo; sometimes, however, omitted between Tat and Indui. See *LG* §§316, 335, 343, 368; *Leb. Gab.* §118; and *Keat.* I: x : 214-215.

Badb 166. Equated in this passage with the *Morrigan.

The hooded crow, scaldcrow, a shape taken by the Morrigan, goddess of war. Badb is sometimes represented as a separate person, usually a sister of the Morrigan, of Macha, and of Neman; in many texts, however, Badb and Morrigan are identified, and *badb* may refer to any of the goddesses in scaldcrow form. See the *Motif Index* A 132.6.2* Goddess in form of bird, and A 485.1. Goddess of war.

Traditions regarding her appear in *LG* §§316, 338; 368; *Keat.* I: xi, 218-219; *IMT* §§29, 39, 48; *Leb. Gab.* §103; *2MT*² 40, 298-306. According to §368, Badb is the daughter of Ernmas, daughter of Etarlám and of Delbáeth, son of Ogma, while in §338 Badb and Neman are daughters of Elcmar of the Brug by Ernmas.

See also the references collected by Hennessy, "The Ancient Irish Goddess of War," *RC* 1 (1870), 32-55. Regarding the identification of Badb with Bé Néit, as in *Corm Tr.* 25, it may be noted that Bé Néit could also be taken as a descriptive title meaning "Woman (Goddess) of Battle" rather than "Nét's wife," perhaps the source of some confusion among Túatha Dé Danann genealogies.

If *badb* is taken as a proper name, she may be identified as the wife of Tethra in a gloss, *LU* 50ª (a quatrain in the margin of *Serglige Con Culainn*): *Mian mná Tethrach (.i. badb) a tenid.*

In the banshenchus, Badb is said to be wife of the Dagda (*Lec., Edin.*) or of Indai (*D.* p., *BB*, H.3.17). For the *badb* as a bringer of tidings, see *Contribb. B* 5, s.v. *badb*, particularly the examples *LU* 8939 (giving the compound, *badbscél* "a tale of slaughter") and *TTebe* 1899, where it seems to be assumed that the *badb* brings news of death in battle.

*Bé Chuille 116 v.s. Uhé Culde. A sorceress.

Bé Chuille is identified as a sorceress or druidess in a number of sources: *LG* §§314, 345, 369 (killed by druidry *LG* LVI §12); *Leb. Gab.* §104; *Keat.* I: xi: 218-219. She is mentioned in the Banshenchus among Túatha Dé Danann women: *LL, Lec., D, BB, Edin.* She is listed among the Túatha Dé Danann host in *IMT* §48, and is one of four members of the Túatha Dé Danann who fight Carmun and her sons, *Met. Dinds.* III 6 51. Her rôle in *2MT*² 44-46, creating the illusion of armed men out of leaves and grass, resembles that in *2MT*. In *TMM* 67, with Danann, she predicts the number to be slain in the forthcoming battle between the Túatha Dé Danann and the sons of Mil.

*Bicelmos (for Becc-Felmas) 60 g.s. Bicelmois. In the name *Abcán mac Bicelmois.
Mentioned as father of the harper *Abcán and as son of Cú son of *Dian Cécht,
LG §§316, 339, 368; *Leb. Gab.* §118.

Bresal Etarlam mac Echdach Báethláim (Bresal Echarlam mac Echdach Báethláim)
61. A champion. For his epithet, see note §61.
According to *TE*² I 18, Bresal Etarlám was the fosterfather of Fúamnach, Midir's
wife, who flees to his house in Aenach Bodbgna (I 25) after turning her rival Étaín
into a pool of water.

Bríg (Bríc, Brich) 125, 124 g.s. Bríghi.
Bríg (sometimes Brigit) appears as daughter of the *Dagda, wife of *Bres, and
mother of *Rúadán. The Banshenchus tradition mentions only her father and
husband (*D, BB,* H. 3. 17, *Edin.*). *LG* §§344, 345, 369 provide a good deal of
information about her, especially linking her with certain animals (oxen, a boar, a
wether), with poetry, and with various types of outcry. She is usually identified as a
poet (*Keat.* I: xi: 218-219, *Leb. Gab.* §117); *Corm. Tr.* 23 calls her "the goddess
whom poets adored, because very great and very famous was her protecting care,"
mentioning that she has two sisters with the same name, one a smith and one a
physician. Her association with the expression of grief is recognized in *Dinds.* §159
(Loch n-Oirbsen) where she is said to have ordained wailing and keening for the dead
in response to the death of Mac Gréine. *2MT,* on the other hand, associates this
origin with the loss of her son, Rúadán. The identification of Brian, Iuchar, and Úar
as the three gods of Dána and three sons of Bres and Bríg (*Im. Dá T.* §139), and as
sons of Bres in *LG* §§350, 369, seems only to indicate the considerable confusion
regarding them.

Camall mac Ríagail (Camald mac Ríaghaild) 53. Doorkeeper at Tara.
His patronymic is appropriate to his position as doorwarden: he is the son of
"Rule," *ríagal* ā, f. (Lat. *regula*), despite the difference in declension.

Casmáel (Cassmóel) 133. Túatha Dé Danann warrior killed by *Ochtríallach.
Casmáel, identified as one of the three Túatha Dé Danann satirists, appears in
LG: §§312, 314; 331; 364; *LG* LVI §8; *Leb. Gab.* §§104, 121; and *Keat.* I: xi:
218-219. *2MT*² mentions various combats in which he takes part and his death at
the hands of *Olltriathach* (276, 1009, 1015-1016). *LG* LVI, on the deaths of the
Túatha Dé Danann, is very close to *Leb. Gab.* §121, but the latter substitutes *Dé
Domhnann d'Fomoiribh* for *Hochtrilach mac Innig,* in naming Casmáel's slayer.

*Cían 55 g.s. Ciéin; 8 d.s. Cén. Son of *Dían Cécht, husband of *Ethne and father
of *Lug.
Father of Lug, and son of Dían Cécht in *LG*: §§314; 341; 366, 368; also
husband of Ethne, daughter of Balor, *LG* §§310-311; 330; 363. A brief summary of
OCT and the circumstances of Cían's death appears in *LG* §319. In *LG* §376,
Cían's death is synchronized with the reign of Lamprides. Later sources, however,
represent Cían as a son of Cáinte: *1MT* §48, where Cían is listed among the Túatha
Dé Danann host; *OCT* (*GJ* 1884), 36, the account of Cían's murder by the sons of
Tuireann; *Acall.* 2559, simply a passing reference to Lug, son of Cían son of Cáinte.
This genealogical tradition is reflected in some folk accounts of Lug's birth. For an
example, see William Larminie, *West Irish Folk Tales and Romances* (London,
1893) 1-9. See also *Duan. Finn* XLV §4 and the references given for Cían in the
Index of Heroes.

Coirpre mac Etaíne (Corpre mac Étoíne) 39; 114 v.s. meic Étnai; 115 omits the
matronymic. A poet.
Coirpre's identity as a poet is well-established, but his genealogy fluctuates slightly
in the various recensions of *LG*. R_2 (D) §348: *mac Tuaro meic Tuirill meic Cait
Conatchinn meic Ordain meic Alduí meic Tait* is typical, cf. §§314, 316 W and Z;
333, 341; 366, 368; (the R_3 §366 M reference to Ogma as Coirpre's father is

contradicted by another passage found only in M, §368); *Leb. Gab* §104; *Keat.* I: xi: 218-219. *LG* LVI §6 adds a reference to his death of sunstroke; *LG* LIII §13 simply lists him among the Túatha Dé Danann, giving the genitive of his matronymic as Etna. Confusion between Etan and Ethne, not to mention Ethliu and Elatha, is frequent in the divine genealogies, but the identification of Etan, daughter of Dían Cécht (whatever the genitive singular or vowel lengths of her name) as Coirpre's mother is well established in *LG*. Coirpre's role outside *2MT* is limited. In *1MT* §30, he serves as envoy to the Fir Bolg king; he has a son Cerna or Cerniam (*Met. Dinds.* IV 202 7 (Cerna); *Dinds.* §115) buried in the place of that name; in *Duan. Finn XVI* 26, 28. He gains a shield meant for Finn in return for a poem, later giving the shield—itself made from a hazel poisoned by Balor's head—to the Dagda. His most famous accomplishment was the satire against Bres, the first satire made in Ireland, mentioned in *Cormac's Glossary* (*Cernine, Riss*), and in *ACC* 161.

LG §376 synchronizes his death with the reign of Lamprides.

Colum Cúaléinech (Cúaolléinech) 58. A smith.

Colum Cúaléinech is not a well-known member of the Túatha Dé Danann, and it is surprising to find a reference to him rather than to Goibniu (perhaps evidence of two strands of the narrative). Reference to him is made in *Laws* V 472.7, Commentary: *Colam Collereach gaba na tri fuar-gres*, in connection with a type of ordeal involving a vessel that breaks in the hands of a liar but is remade in the hands of one telling the truth, the Lestar Baduirn. (A different tradition regarding this particular ordeal appears in *The Irish Ordeals*).

Crédne 11, 66, 100, 101, 122. A gold, silver, and bronze smith (*cerd*).

Crédne's epithet, *cerd*, "craftsman, artisan," is used of a gold and silver smith or a worker in bronze or brass. He is mentioned as helping Dian Cécht with the creation of Núadu's silver arm and identified as a son of Esarg meic Néit meic Innai in *LG* §§310, 314; 329, 341, 343, 346; 362, 366, 368. See also *LG* LIII §12, LVI §10; *Leb. Gab.* §§97, 104; *Keat* I: xi: 218-219. In *LG* §353, LX he is called a son of Ethliu.

Crédne's death by drowning while seeking treasures from Spain is mentioned in *LG* LVI §10 and synchronized with the reign of Acrisius in §376. He is named as one of the Túatha Dé Danann host in *1MT* §48. Otherwise, he is chiefly known for his work as a metal smith.

Cormac's Glossary (*Nescōit*) includes an account of his collaboration with Goibniu and Luchta in preparing weapons for the second battle similar to that in *2MT*. Duma Créidne is named among the notable features of Tara, *Met. Dinds.* I 46 14 (Achall).

O'Dav, §679 (*Dírna*) makes reference to Judgments of Creidhine, as do *Laws* I 24 4; V 98 21.

Cridenbél (also Crichinphél) 26, 27, 29. A satirist.

Cridenbél is well-known as one of the three Túatha Dé Danann satirists, *LG* §§314, 333, 366; *Leb. Gab.* §121. *Keat.* I: xi: 218-219. *LG* LVI §25 mentions his death from the gold given him by the Dagda. In *LG* §376 his death is synchronized with the reign of Acrisius. He is named among the Túatha Dé Danann preparing for battle in *2MT*[2] 50. *Met. Dinds.* III 6 48 (Carmun) mentions him as one of the four Túatha Dé Danann chosen to fight Carmun and her sons. *Cóir Anm.* §240 includes various unsatisfactory attempts to etymologize Cridenbél, one suggesting that his heart (*cride*) was in his mouth (*bél*), another associating his name with sparks (*crithir*).

Crón 124. A grinder of weapons, mother of *Fíanlach.

Crón is otherwise unknown as a woman of the Túatha Dé Danann; her name may be associated with *cron*, o. m. "crime, blame, fault." Another possibility *crón*, an adjective meaning "brown, reddish-brown" is used as a proper name, and is the more likely choice, frequently occurring as a saint's name, masc. Crónán, fem. Crón (Cróne).

Dagda (Daghdae, Dagdai, Daghdo, Daghdou) 24, 25, 26, 27, 29, 30, 31, 32, 75, 81, 83, 84, 85, 88, 89, 91, 93 passim; 118, 119, 163, 165, 6 g.s. Dagdai, 26 variously Dagdae, Dagdhua, Dagdhae, 163, 164 Dagda; 26 v.s. Dagdae. Master of druidic arts, father of *Bríg and the *Mac Óc.

The Dagda is introduced in *2MT* in terms of the relationship between himself and his son (contrasted with that of other father-son pairs), and his ability, in conjunction with his son, to use contractual trickery to gain his ends. In addition to the usual identification as Eochaid Ollathair (*LG* §313), *Cóir Anm*. adds §152 Rúad Rofessa, while *Corm. Tr.* gives Cera and Ruad Rofhessa. The *YBL* 176 tract on the Dagda's magic staff adds Áed Abaid of Ess Rúaid (ed. Osborn Bergin in *Mediaeval Studies in Memory of Gertrude Schoepperle Loomis*, 1927). LL 144a, Gilla in Chomded hÚa Cormaic's *A Rí Ríchid Réidig Dam*, adds Dagan and Cratan Cain.

LG identifies him as a son of Elatha, names the Dagda's children (including Óengus, Áed Cáem, Cermait Milbél, and Brigit), and refers to his reign (following that of Lug); LVI §32 mentions his death from a wound inflicted by Ceithlenn: §§313, 316-17; 333, 335, 344; 366, 368, 369; cf. *Leb. Gab.* §§100, 109, 117. *LG* §376 synchronizes his death with the reign of Panyas.

Keat. I: xi: 216-217 offers a different genealogy (m. Ealathain m. Néid m. Iondai). *LG* §353, LX, calls him a son of Ethliu (perhaps an error for Elatha). *1MT* identifies him as god of druidry, §20, and as battle leader of the Túatha Dé Danann against the Fir Bolg. His role in *2MT²* is restricted: he volunteers to destroy both Balor and his wife Ceithlenn, but ends by fighting only the latter (1088-1102). The dindshenchus tradition provides information about the Dagda, his unions, and his children. He is husband of the Morrígan, *Met. Dinds.* IV 196 (Odras); lover of Bóand and father of Óengus, *Met. Dinds.* II 10 23, II 18ff. (Bóand I and II). Other sons include Áed, slain by a jealous husband (Corrcend, who must carry the body until a stone of suitable size is found); Cermait, killed by Lug through jealousy, over whom the Dagda wept tears of blood, *Dinds.* §129 (Druim Suamaich), *Met. Dinds.* IV 94 (Ailech), IV 236 30; IV 238 12 (Druim Suamaig I and II), IV 268 (Codal). Another son, killed fighting to win a woman, Celg, from her father, is mentioned in *Met. Dinds.* IV 350 (Snám Dá Én). A daughter, Ainge, who has been given a washtub that leaks at high tide by her father, and whose wood for a new tub is stolen, appears in *Bod. Dinds.* §6 (Fid n-Gaibli), *Dinds.* §11 (Fid n-Gaible). In a very strange prose passage, *Met. Dinds.* IV 292 15 (Mag Corainn), Dían Cécht is also said to be a son of the Dagda, but there is no trace of this in the poetic version, III 438. With his club he rids Mag Muirthemne of a sea monster, *Met. Dinds.* IV 294 20 (Mag Muirthemne), and notes, p. 45; cf. §34 *Tochmarc Emire* in *Comp. Con. C.* The Dagda is responsible for the construction of Ailech, which he gives to his father's brother, Nét and his wife Neman, *Met. Dinds.* IV 92ff. (Ailech I-III), *Dinds.* §91 (Ailech Néit); he himself resides for a time at the Brug, *Met. Dinds.* II 18ff. (Brug na Bóinde II); *Dinds.* §4 (Dindgnai in Broga). The acquisition of the Brug by Óengus is variously described as occurring with or without the Dagda's cooperation. In *Aisl. Óeng.*, the Dagda helps his son find Cáer Ibormeith, whom he has seen and come to love in a dream. Minor appearances not involving the Dagda's family relationships include *MU²* 637 where he is one of four of the Túatha Dé Danann who stir up strife among mortals, and *Airne F.* 210, where three river sources are said to have sprung up before him (Síur, Eóir, and Berba).

His daughter Adair, wife of Éber, is mentioned in the glosses to the forty questions of Eochaid Úa Cérín, *ZCP* 13 (1919), §15, 133.

Later traditions about the Dagda are reflected in the *Acall.* which mentions his sons Bodb Derg, Midir and Áengus Óc. The three are also identified as sons of the Dagda in *OCL*, in which Bodb Derg plays a major part.

Daithe 65:256. A cupbearer.
See *Delt, *Drúcht, and note §65.
These are traditionally appropriate names for cupbearers. *BDD²* §108 mentions Delt, Drúcht and Dathen as cupbearers to Conaire. This Drúcht is also identified as

the father of Deltbanna, Conaire's butler, *Dinds.* §12 (Mag. Lifi). Another Drúcht and a Daithe are named as two of Finn's three butlers (*Duan. Finn* XII §28).

The group of names (as Drúcht, Delt, and Dathen) also occurs in *Táin* 1768 (see note 1767-1771).

*Dana or Danu g.s. Danann, Donann, *passim*. In the name *Túatha Dé Danann, "The Tribes of the Goddess Dana."

Sometimes confused with Dinann, Díanan, a daughter of Flidais, Danann appears in *LG* as the daughter of Delbáeth, son of Ogma, who bore three sons to her own father: Brian, Iuchar, and Iucharba, the murderers of Lug's father Cían (*LG* §§316; 342, 348; 368). Some strands of tradition identify Danann as the proper name of the Morrígan, daughter of Ernmas and of Delbáeth, son of Ogma (*LG* §368). Others give the Morrígan's name as Ana or Anu/Anand, daughter of Ernmas, from whom are named the Paps of Anu in Lúachair (*LG* §§314, 316; 346; 368, which also gives her name as Danann). *Leb. Gab.* places the Morrígan (Anand) and her sisters, Badb and Macha, further back in the Túatha Dé Danann genealogies, making them daughters of Dealbáeth m. Neid m. Iondai, (*Leb. Gab.* §103). Keating is ambiguous: the Dealbáeth who is father of Danann may differ from the Delbáeth m. Ealathan m. Néid who is father of her three sons (I: x: 214-215).

LG LVI §4 mentions the death of Donann at the hands of the Fomorian Dé Domnann. In *LG* §376 her death is synchronized with the reign of Lamprides. Place name traditions provide little information. *Met. Dinds.* IV 268 19 (Codal) briefly mentions a Danann and her daughter Gorm as among a group opposing the Dagda and Áed. In the Banshenchus she is a Túatha Dé Danann sorceress (*LL, Lec., D, BB, Edin.*); only the last identifies her father as Delbáeth.

*Daui or *Dui 55 g.s. Dúach, in the name *Eochaid Garb mac Dúach.

He is mentioned in *LG* in references to his son, *Eochaid Garb. His own father is said to be *Bres son of *Elatha: *LG* §§316, 337, 339 (D); 368; *Leb. Gab.* §115.

*Delbáeth 16 g.s. Delbaíth. In the name *Ériu ingen Delbaíth, perhaps also in the name of the Fomorian king, *Elatha mac Delbaíth.

There are several figures named Delbáeth in the Túatha Dé Danann genealogies of *LG*. The present one is presumably the son of Nét and father of Elatha mentioned in §§316, 339, 368. See also the references given in the entries for *Elatha, *Ériu, the *Morrígan, and *Tuirill Bicreo.

Delt 65. A cupbearer.
      See *Daithe, *Drúcht.

Dían Cécht (Díen Cécht, Dén Cécht) 11, 33, 34, 35, 55, 64, 75, 98, 123, 126; 8 g.s. Díen Cécht. Physician, father of *Míach, *Ochttríuil, and *Airmedh.

Túatha Dé Danann physician, he fits the injured king Núadu with a silver arm to replace that lost in *1MT*; his children include Cú, Cían, Cethen, Míach, and two daughters, Airmed and Etan. *LG* §§310, 314; 329, 341, 343, 346; 362, 366, 368; LIII §12 *Leb. Gab.* §104. *Keat.* I: xi: 218-219. *Leb. Gab.* §117 adds another son, Cíach.

Dían Cécht is said to be the son of Esarg m. Néit m. Indui in *LG* §§341, 368. He is called son of the Dagda in *Ed. Dinds.* §54 (Mag Corainn), a detail not found in the *Met. Dinds.* version, and perhaps simply an error. *Dinds.* §77 (Corond) is closer to *LG* but adds a generation, making Dían Cécht a son of Echtoigh m. Esoirc. *LG* §353, LX, is exceptional in naming him one of "seven sons of Ethliu." His healing of Tuirell Biccreo, son of Etan, is recounted in *LG* §319 LXVI and includes a brief sketch of *OCT*. Dían Cécht's death, of plague, is mentioned in *LG* LVI §9, and in §376 synchronized with the reign of Acrisius. He is numbered among the Túatha Dé Danann physicians and, along with his brothers Oll, Forus and Fir, establishes a healing well in *1MT* §§37, 38, 48.

In *2MT*² 20-21 he defines the possibilities of healing the wounded as in *2MT*. *Corm. Tr.* 56 identifies him as god of health and in §159 names Etan his daughter.

Cóir Anm. §157 names him "Erin's sage of leechcraft" and *deus salutis.* References to his judgements appear in *Laws* I, 18, 24; I, 24, 4; III, 362; and V, 98, 21. His healing salve is mentioned in a St. Gall incantation, *Thes.* II, 249.
See also D. A. Binchy, "Bretha Déin Chécht," *Ériu* 20 (1966), 1-65. Dindshenchus tradition adds some details about him. His harper, Coro, was given land in Corann: *Met. Dinds.* III 438 (Céis Chorainn); *Dinds.* §77 (Corond); *Met. Dinds* IV 292 14 (Mag Corainn); *Ed. Dinds.* §54 (Mag Corainn). His sons Cú and Cethen were buried at Tara, *Met. Dinds.* I 20 90 (Temair III), *Dinds.* §1 (Temair §14). He establishes a healing well, Tiprait Slainge in Achad Abla, *Met. Dinds.* IV 182 (Lusmag); *Dinds.* §108 (Lusmag); *Ed. Dinds.* §71 (Lusmag). He destroys serpents in the heart of the Morrígan's son, *Met. Dinds.* II 62 13 (Berba) perhaps an error for Mac Cécht, as in *Dinds.* §13 (Berba).

*Díanann 116 v.s. Dinand.
Sometimes confused with *Danu or Danann. *LG* identifies Dí(a)nann or Danann as a daughter of Flidais (§§317, 345, 369) and as a sister of Bé Chuille, describing both women as *bantúathaig,* "sorceresses" or "witches" (§§314, 333, 343, 366). In *2MT²* 44 their contribution to victory resembles that in *2MT*; they create the illusion of an armed host by enchanting grass and leaves. *LG* LVI distinguishes Danann/Donann (§4), killed by Dé Domnann of the Fomoire, from Dinann/Díanann/Danann who, with Bé Chuille, dies through druidry (§12). *LG* LIII distinguishes among Danann (Donand), mother of the gods (§10), Morrígu (§11), and Danand (Dinand), mentioned in the same line as Bé Chuille (§13).

Drúcht 65. A cupbearer.
See *Daithe, *Delt.

Echdam 95. One of the fosterers of *Lug.

*Edleo mac Allai 12. Túatha Dé Danann warrior killed in the first battle of Mag Tuired.
The first man of the Túatha Dé Danann to be killed in Ireland (*LG* §§310, 328, 362; LVI §2; *Leb. Gab.* §96). A pillar stone, Cairthi Aidhleo, was set up by the Túatha Dé Danann in memory of him, *1MT* §36.
LG mentions his genealogy in §§316, 343, 368 (there is some variation); cf. *Leb. Gab.* §118 (meic Aldaoi).

Én mac Ethamain (Én mac Ethomain) 62. A poet and historian.
LG mentions only an Én m. Biceoin m. Stairn m. Eidleo m. Néit (§§316, 343, 368).

*Eochaid (or *Eochu) Báethlám 61, in the name *Bresal Etarlam mac Echdach Báethláim.

Eochaid Garb mac Dúach 55 g.s. Echtach Gairuh meic Dúach. Túatha Dé Danann warrior, second husband of *Tailtiu and foster-father of *Lug.
He marries Tailtiu, the Fir Bolg queen, after the death in battle of her husband, Eochaid m. Eirc (*LG* §§311, 330, 363); *Leb. Gab.* §98; *Met. Dinds.* IV 146ff. (Tailtiu); *TMM* 65. His father's name is sometimes given as Dui Temen m. Bres m. Elathan, as in *LG* §368. For his sons, see *LG* §368, *Keat.* I: xi: 218-219. and *Dinds.* §159 (Loch n-Oirbsen). He is responsible for building the Fortress of the Hostages at Tara, *Dinds.* §99 (Tailtiu); in *Dinds.* §20 (Nás) it is he who has the wood of Cúan cleared for his wife, and he gives three rath-builders who shirk their part in the clearance the task of building the raths bearing their names: Nás, Ronc, and Alestar. He is himself buried at Tailtiu, *Met. Dinds.* IV 155 104 (Tailtiu).

Ériu (Éri) 16. Daughter of *Delbáeth, mother of *Bres by *Elatha.
In *LG* tradition she is a daughter of Fíachna. Delbaíth and Ernmas, his own mother (*LG* §§316; 338; 368; *Leb. Gab.* §101; *Keat.* I: xi: 218-219). The Banshenchus tradition either fails to mention her father (*LL, Lec., D.*) or also identifies him as Fíachna m. Delbaith (*BB, Edin.*). *Leb. Gab.* §106, however, notes that Bres gains the kingship "in right of his mother Ere, daughter of Dealbaeth."

2MT² 304 mentions Ére, Fódla, and Banbha as daughters of Fiacha mac Dealbhaoi who fight against Fomorian witches. *Met. Dinds.* IV 184 6 (Benn Codail), *Ed. Dinds.* §72 (Benn Codail), *Dinds.* §109 (Benn Codail) describe her fosterage and the remarkable growth of the mountain that parallels her own. Her marriage to Mac Gréine, one of the Dagda's grandsons (*LG* §§316, 334, 368), and her encounter with the sons of Mil, who agree to name Ireland after her, are related in *TMM*, esp. 53-58, 63-64 and in *LG* §§392, 412, 439, and LXXIV.

*Ernmas 12, 133 g.s. Ernmoiss, 137, Ernmusa, 166 Ernmais. Mother of *Macha and *Morrigan, killed in the first battle of Mag Tuired.

Ernmas appears in *LG* §§316, 368 and Banshenchus (*BB*) as a daughter of Etarlám m. Nuadat Airgetláim. *Leb. Gab.* §103 gives another genealogical tradition: *Earnbas i. Eatarlaim m. Ordain m. Iondai m. Alldaoi,* a tradition that appears in the Banshenchus (*Lec., D., Edin.*). She is killed in *1MT, LG* §§310, 328, 362; LVI §3. She is identified as mother of Badb, Macha, and Morrigan (or Ana), *LG* §§314, 316; 338 (treats Ana as separate character), 346; in §368 their father is Delbáeth m. Ogma. Banba, Fótla, and Ériu are her daughters by (her son) Fiachna son of Delbáeth son of Ogma, *LG* §§316; 338; 368. Fiachna and Ollom are identified as her sons in *LG* §§316; 338; 368 (sons of Delbáeth m. Ogma). She is mother of Glon, Gnim, and Coscar by an unnamed father, *LG* §§316, 336; 368, perhaps also mother of Bóand daughter of Delbáeth m. Elathan, *LG* §336.

Eru 95. One of the fosterers of *Lug.

Esras 7. Druid and poet from whom the Túatha Dé Danann acquired magical knowledge. See note §§2-7.

*Étain (or Etain, Etan?) 36 g.s. Étnae, 39. Étoíne, 114. Étnai. In the two names *Ogma (mac Étnae) and *Corpre mac Étoíne (or mac Étnai). The vowel lengths in §39 and §114 are uncertain, and the name intended may not be Étaín; cf. §59. See *Contribb.* E 210, 211, s.v. *Etain, Étaín*; 212, *Etan,* and citation of *Leb. Gab.* §121f, where Coirpre's matronymic is m. Eatoine (:gloine), contrasting with m. Etna in §105.

Daughter of *Dian Cécht, mother of the poet *Coirpre, *LG* §§314, 316, 333; Ogma his father, §366; she has sons Dealbáeth Dana, son of Ogma, and Coirpre (father unnamed) §368, which also cites the alternate tradition that Coirpre is son of Tuar son of Tuirend. *LG* §376 synchronizes her death with the reign of Lamprides. She appears as a poet in *1MT* §30 (no patronymic).

See also *Leb. Gab.* §104, 117. *Corm.* s.v. *Etan* identifies her as daughter of Dian Cécht, and a healer, also quoting a line attributed to her, s.v. *Torc.*

For her rape by Lug's poet see *Abcán. She appears in the Banshenchus tradition as daughter of Dian Cécht, but as mother of Mac Cécht and wife of Cermat son of the Dagda, an unusual variant tradition: *LL, Lec., D* v., *BB, Edin.*

Ethamain 62 g.s. Ethomain. In the name *Én mac Ethamain.

*Ethliu 59 g.s. Ethlend. In the name *Ogma, identified as mac Ethlend. Cf. 36 mac Étnae.

Fedlimid 95. One of the fosterers of *Lug.

Fiacha 12 a.s. Fhíochaig? Túatha Dé Danann warrior killed in the first battle of Mag Tuired, whose name is variously given as Fíachu or Fíacha; Fíachnae; and Fiachra in the sections of *LG* describing the first battle of Mag Tuired (§§310, 328, 362). The proper expansion of the name is doubtful, as this figure appears variously as Fiachna, Fíacha/Fiachu, and Fiachra (often within the same text).

His death in the first battle of Mag Tuired is mentioned in *LG* LVI §3, but as in *LG* §§310; 328; 362, and *2MT*, no patronymic is given. The career of the Fiachna who is a son of Delbáeth is recounted by *LG* §§315; 354; 367; LVI §34 mentions his death. This is presumably not the same character.

*Fíanlach 124 g.s. Fíanluig. Identified only as a son of *Crón.

*Figal 53 g.s. Figail. In the name *Gamal mac Figail, probably to be identified with the Túatha Dé Danann druid, *Figol mac Mámois.

Figol mac Mámois 80. A druid.
   The name Figol was perhaps considered reminiscent of *figel* f. (Lat. *vigilia*), "a vigil." His patronymic seems to represent a personal name extracted from the expression *fo mámus,* "under the authority of, subject to," (cf. *mámud* "subjection"), and the druid's name might be given as Vigil, son of Subservience. The doorkeeper at Tara, *Gamal mac Figail, is perhaps his son.
   The name Figol is also reminiscent of that of the druid Findgoll m. Findamnois who helps devise the stratagem through which Bres is required to drink three hundred buckets of bogwater, a feat that leads to his death, *Dinds.* §46 (Carn Húi Néit.).

Foimtinne 143. One of the charioteers of *Lug.

Fosad 95. One of the fosterers of *Lug.

Gamal mac Figail 53. A doorkeeper at Tara, perhaps son of *Figol Mac Mámois.

Glan 65. A cupbearer.
   For the names of the cupbearers, see note §65.

Glé (Gléi) 65. A cupbearer.

Glésse (Glési) 65. A cupbearer.

Goibniu (Gaibne, Gaibniu, Goibnenn) 75, 96, 122, 124, 125, 126. A smith.
   Smith of the Túatha Dé Danann, *LG* mentions him as one of the leaders of the Túatha Dé Danann, a son of Esarg m. Néit (together with Luchta, Crédne, and Dian Cécht). *LG* §§314, 343, 346, LIII §12; *Keat.* I: xi: 218-219 simply identify him as a smith. *LG* §341 and *Leb. Gab.* §104 list him among the four sons of Esarg, while *LG* §368 substitutes for Goibniu another brother, Engoba na Hiruaithi, perhaps simply another name for Goibniu himself.
   LG §353, in one version, identifies him as one of seven Túatha Dé Danann chieftains, all sons of Ethliu (as in the poetic account in LX). His death, by plague, is mentioned in *LG* LVI §9, and synchronized with the reign of Acrisius in §376. *1MT* distinguishes Aengoba na hIruaithe (§§39, 40, 48) from Goibniu. In §§48, 49 both are listed as part of the host of the Túatha Dé Danann. *Corm. Tr.* (*Nescóit*) describes the preparation of weapons for the second battle of Mag Tuired, much as in *2MT*, with the additional account of Goibniu's anger upon learning that his wife was unfaithful.
   2MT² includes references to Goibhnionn Gobha, who prepares arms for the Túatha Dé Danann: *2MT²* 25, 138, 259. *Duan. Finn.* VIII §11 mentions a *crios Goibhnionn* (of unspecified power) and lxxi (note 2) mentions the role of Gaibhdín Gabhna in Donegal folklore. In *ATDM,* 207, it is the feast of Goibniu that confers immortality on the Túatha Dé Danann. He is associated with a legal tract and craft judgements (*Laws* V 98 22); see also D. A. Binchy, "Bretha Déin Chécht," *Ériu* 20 (1966), 2.
   The glosses to the forty questions of Eochaid Úa Cérín, edited and translated by Thurneysen, *ZCP* 13 (1919), 12, list Aillenn, Cuilleann and Cairchi as his three daughters.

Ibar (Iubor) 95. One of the fosterers of *Lug.

Lúachaid? 57 g.s. Lúachadhae. In the name *Luchta mac Lúachadhae.

Luchta (also Luchtai, Luchtaine) 57, 102, 103, 122. A wright.
   The name takes various forms in various MSS.: *LG* identifies him as a carpenter (*sáer*) and as one of the sons of Esarg m. Néit (together with Goibniu, Crédne, and Dian Cécht), *LG* §§314 (Luicne); 341 (Luchtine), 343 (Luchra, Luchne); 346

(Luicni); 366, 368 (Luchraid); LIII §12; *Keat.* I: xi: 218-219. *LG* §§366, 368, *Leb. Gab.* §104 identify Indai as Nét's father; §368 substitutes Engoba na Hiruaithi for Goibniu as one of the four brothers. *LG* §353, *LX* list him among "seven sons of Ethliu." *LG* LVI §9 mentions the death of Luigne, yet another variant spelling, "by a strong fiery dart." In *1MT* §§48, 49 Lucraid *sáer* takes part in the battle, and as Luchtuinne, provides weapons for the Túatha Dé Danann in *2MT²* 28. *Corm. Tr.* (*Nescóit*) offers a version of the preparation of arms for the Túatha Dé Danann very close to that found in *2MT*. Luchta *sáer* may perhaps be associated with "Luchta's Iron" which did not burn the hand of the innocent, although its inventor is called a druid, not *sáer: Irish Ordeals* §23. Note also the adze in §17, belonging to a Mochta (for Luchta?) *sáer*, which, when heated, did not burn the tongue of the innocent. *Duan. Finn* XVI §20 mentions Luchra as Manannán's shield maker, creating the shield from the hazel split by the poison dripping from Balor's head, after Balor had been slain by Lug. For Luchta's judgments regarding his craft, see D. A. Binchy, "Bretha Déin Chécht," *Ériu* 20 (1966), 2.

Lug (also Lugh, Luch, Lucc, Luog) 4, 55, 72, 83, 88, 96, 98, 100, 102, 104, 106, 108, 110, 112, 114, 116, 118, 120, 133 (Lug-); 135, 136, 139, 146, 150, 151, 153, 155, 156, 158, 159, 163, 69 g.s. Logo, 95 and 129 Logai, 142 Lochca. Son of *Cían and *Ethne, leader of the Túatha Dé Danann in their preparations for battle, and master of all the arts.

Lug is known both by his patronymic (Lug mac Céin) and by his matronymic (Lug mac Ethnenn, or mac Ethlenn), which in time came to be considered an alternate patronymic, a process discussed in some detail by O'Rahilly, *EIHM*, 38, 310. See also Ó Buachalla, *JCHAS* 67 (1962), 77-78, n. 20, regarding the variations in Lug's genealogy. *LG* sources include §§311, 316, 330, 341; 363, 368 (adding an identification of Cían and Ethliu). *Leb. Gab.* §98 identifies him as son of Eithne i. Balair; §108 as *m. Cén m. Diancécht m. Easairg Bric m. Néid m. Iondaoi m. Alldaoi;* cf. *Keat.* I: xi: 216-217. The identification of Cían as a son of Cáinte is to be found in *1MT* §48 (Cían and Cú, both identified as sons of Cáinte). *Acall.* 2559 mentions Lug, son of Cían son of Cáinte; so also does *OCT* (*GJ* 1884), 36, where Cú and Ceithen are named as Cían's brothers in this account of Cían's murder and Lug's vengeance. *2MT²*, note 85, points out that the form Lugaidh frequently occurs in later literature instead of the earlier Lug(h). His role in this text is as prominent as that in *2MT*, although his relationship with Núadu has become more strained. A great deal of information about Lug's career is provided by *LG*, much agreeing with *2MT*: His spear (§§305, 325, 357); his fosterage by Tailtiu (§§311; 330; 363); his slaying of Balor and questions about the losses in battle (§§312; 332; 364). Other details are added: his kingship of forty years following that of Núadu (§§312, 332, 364, 366); his institution of the funeral games for Tailtiu, celebrated yearly at Lugnasad (§§311; 330; 363); his invention of assembly, horseracing, and contesting at an assembly (§§317; 349; 369). His destruction of Bres in Carn Uí Néit appears at §329; his sons Ábartach, Ainnle, and Cnú Deroil (§368); Abcán, his poet (§§316; 339; 368). Rivalry between him and Núadu is hinted in §358. He is called one of seven sons of Ethliu §353 (LX). His reign over the Túatha Dé Danann, following the death of Núadu in battle, is synchronized with the reign of Bellepares, *LG* §376. *De Gabáil in tShída* identifies Lug's *síd* as Síd Rodrubán (Fodrubain, RIA MS D.4.2), the location of which is unknown *ZCP* 19 (1931), 55.

Dindshenchus tradition provides a number of additional details about Lug. *Met. Dinds.* IV 226 14 (Tráig Thuirbe) mentions men of art who fled Tara before Lug for reasons unknown, (*Dinds.* §125 (Tráig Tuirbi), *Ed. Dinds.* §70). He is responsible for the death of various Fomorians fleeing from the battle of Mag Tuired, *Met. Dinds.* IV 282 10 (Slíab Badbgna). He fatally tricks Bres so that he drinks bogwater instead of milk and dies in Carn Uí Néit: *Met. Dinds.* III 218 43 (Carn Huí Néit). His wives are Búa or Búi and Nás, daughters of Rúadrí, *Met. Dinds.* III 40 2 (Cnogba), III 48 7 (Nás). *Met. Dinds.* III, 483, adds Echtach, daughter of Daig, from the prose dindshenchus. Banshenchus information gives Búa as Lug's wife, daughter of Rúadrach (gen.) rí Bretan (*Lec.* p. *BB, Edin.*); Nás is also identified as a wife of Lug, daughter of Rugrad rí Bretan (*BB,* H. 3.17, *Edin.*); Englecc, Elcmar's daughter, is identified as Lug's wife in several sources: *Lec.,* p. v. *D, BB, Edin.* In *YBL* col. 789-790, a text edited and translated by Osborn Bergin, *Medieval Studies in Memory of Gertrude Schoepperle Loomis* (Paris, 1927), 399-406, there is a reference to Lug's killing of Cermait Mílbél for seducing Lug's wife, Búach daughter of Daire Donn. Elsewhere, Englec is the guilty wife (*Lec.* 198b 47, Gilla Modutu), cited by Bergin, 400. Osborn Bergin's edition and translation of "A Poem by Gofraidh Fionn Ó Dálaigh," *Essays and Studies presented to William Ridgeway* (Cambridge, 1913), 323-332 provides a versified account of Lug's arrival at Tara. Another of Ó Dálaigh's poems gives a verse summary of Lug's slaying of the Dagda's son Cermait (ultimately healed by his father), Bergin, *Medieval Studies*, 400-402. Lug institutes the celebration of Lugnasad at Tailtiu in memory of his foster-mother Tailtiu or of his wives, *Met. Dinds.* III 50 41 (Nás); *Corm. Y* (Lugnasad) mentions the association of Lug and Lugnasad, without explaining the reason for its origin. He has a remarkable garment, *Met. Dinds.* III 122 21 (Dún Crimthaind), perhaps identical with *cétach Crimthainn,* cf. *Dinds.* §30, §121. *Dinds.* §82 (Druim Cliab) mentions the death of his son, Áinle. He himself is slain by the sons of Cermait, *Met. Dinds.* IV 278 (Loch Lugborta), in vengeance for their father, as in the king list of *LL* 39a, 5387. In *LG* §376, his death is synchronized with the reign of Sosares. Lug appears in various references in the sagas, especially those associated with his son, Cú Chulainn. *T. Emire* §25 names as Cú Chulainn's father Lug m. Cuinn m. Eithlenn; at §47, it identifies Lug as king of the Túatha Dé Danann after the second battle of Mag Tuired, and Taillne (=Tailtiu) as the site of his festival of kingship. *Comp. Con C.* §5 also identifies Lug as Cú Chulainn's father. In *Táin* 2322-3, Lug fights alongside his son at Sesrech Breslige. For the continuation of the mythology about Lug in the Fenian tradition, see the references given by Murphy in *Duan. Finn,* III 378, including parallels with other mythological figures including Fionn himself. For an analysis of the tale of Lug's birth in folk tradition, with reference to Welsh parallels, see W. J. Gruffydd, *Math vab Mathonwy* (Cardiff, 1928). Bardic poetry makes frequent reference to Lug as a hero, and includes details of his mythology. To give only a few examples: Lambert McKenna, *The Book of Magauran* (Dublin, 1947), 355, XXI, qq. 8-14: Lug warned of foes by a shining spot of earth; hostility to Lug on account of his Fomorian kinship.

Mac Óc 27, 28, 31, 32. Son of the *Dagda, his proper name is in fact Óengus.

Óengus, the son of the Dagda and Bóand, born at the end of a day magically lengthened to nine months to conceal his parents' adultery from Bóand's husband Elcmar, is raised by Midir who eventually brings him before the Dagda to obtain his inheritance, the Brug of the Boyne. In some versions of the incident, he gains the Brug by tricking the Dagda himself, in others the trick is played on Elcmar. These details are not mentioned at all in *2MT,* where Óengus appears only as a concerned son, anxious about his father's welfare and willing to use his quick wit to his father's advantage. In this context, he is contrasted with the ambitious Míach, whose restoration of Núadu's arm is implicitly a competitive and unfilial challenge to his father, Dían Cécht, and with the incompetent Bres, whose attempt to regain the kingdom of Ireland is carried on at his father's expense.

The name, *in Mac Óc* or *Mac Ind Óc,* given to Óengus has been variously explained. In *TE²,* in an account of his birth, his mother herself remarks, "Young is the son who was begotten at the break of day and born betwixt it and evening." The fluctuation in the form of the name, however, requires a more comprehensive explanation. O'Rahilly, *EIHM,* 516-517, suggested a popular corruption of **Maccan Oac*; Carney, in *The Poems of Blathmac, ITS* (1964), 112, however, noting the formation of compounds such as *macamrae,* "famous son," proposes, "We are then perhaps justified in regarding the Irish mythological character *Maccind Oac* as having been originally a simple expression meaning 'the fair young boy,' and to question O'Rahilly's suggestion. . . .' "

Óengus appears briefly in *1MT* §48 as a Túatha Dé Danann warrior, but has no role in *2MT²*. His genealogy is given in *LG* §§316, 340, 368; (340 adds that he and his brothers were the first men to explore a *síd* mound); *Leb. Gab.* §§104, 117. A considerable amount of information is provided about him by the dindshenchus. He is a son of the Dagda and Bóand: *Met Dinds.* III 30 74 (Bóand I), III 36 39 (Bóand II); *Dinds.* §19. *Met. Dinds. IV 92 12* (Ailech *I*), also mentions two other sons of the Dagda, Áed and Cermait; as does *IV 108 16* (Ailech III*)*. In *Met. Dinds.* IV 268 24 (Codal), Óengus is among the Dagda's host, defending Aed who has seduced Codal's wife. He resides at the Brug, *Met. Dinds.* II 10 1, 9 (Brug na Bóinde I); *Met. Dinds.* II 18 4, 23 (Brug na Bóinde II), includes an account of his fosterage with Midir.

See also the poem attributed to Cináed Úa hArtacáin on the Brug, edited and translated by L. Gwynn, *Ériu* 7 (1-238, for a verse account of the birth of Óengus, his fosterage with Midir, and his gaining of the Brug from the Dagda, an incident also detailed in *De Gabáil in tSída,* edited and translated by Vernam Hull, *ZCP* 19 (1931), 53-58. Another version can be found in *ATDM,* where as in *TE,* he gains the Brug from Elcmar, the deceived husband of Bóand.

He loves Englec, Elcmar's daughter, who prefers Midir: *Met. Dinds.* III 40 18 (Cnogba). His embroideress, Maistiu, places a cross on his tunic at his direction: *Dinds.* §32 (Maistiu). As lover of Drebriu, he seeks to protect her swine, *Met. Dinds.* III 388 42; *Dinds.* §71 (Dumae Selga). He is a leader of his people: *Dinds.* IV, 254, 24). Clidna is drowned seeking to elope with him: *Bod. Dinds.* §10, *Dinds.* §45 (Tond Clidna). He lends a horse to the eloping Eocho mac Maireda, fleeing with his father's wife: *Met. Dinds.* IV 64 101 (Túag Inber), *Dinds.* §141 (Túag Inbir ₇ Loch n-Echach), §79 (Loch Rí). Cf. *Ed. Dinds.* §55 (Loch n-Echach).

Many of these citations link him with romantic situations of various sorts, and his role in the saga literature continues the theme. His love for Cáer Ibormeith of Connacht is the subject of *Aisl. Óeng.,* and *TE,* which includes an account of his birth, emphasizes his role in bringing together Midir and Étain. In *MU* 2 576 he appears simply as a representative of the Túatha Dé Danann stirring up strife, invisibly, among mortals; In *Airne F.* §9, he is one of four members of the Túatha Dé Danann matched against four Fomoire who, having escaped the battle of Mag Tuired, work to destroy the Túatha Dé Danann corn, milk and fruit; he is also noted as the owner of a remarkable mantle §8. A gloss in *Im. Dá T.* §127 lists his three ignorances: when, how and where he would die. For references showing many aspects of the development of traditions about Óengus in Fenian literature, see Murphy, *Duan. Finn, III,* Áoenghus Óg (Index of Heroes).

See also *Abcán, *Étaín.

Macha (Maucha) 133. Daughter of *Ernmas, sister of the *Morrígan.

Daughter of Ernmas and Delbáeth m. Ogma in *LG* tradition, her sisters are Badb and the Morrígan. The three are listed among the Túatha Dé Danann, *LG* LIII §11. In the Banshenchus she is among the Túatha Dé Danann practitioners of magic (*LL, Lec., D., Edin.*). In *1MT* §29, the three are sorceresses, sending down showers and mist with rain of fire and blood upon the enemy. *2MT²* identifies Macha, with her sisters, as *bandraoithe,* but gives their father's name as Deala mac Lóich (40, 304). Her death in *2MT* is mentioned by *LG* §§312; 331; 364; *LG* LVI §7. She is identified in *O'Mulc 271* §813: *Machae .i. badb, nō asī an tres morrigan, unde mesrad Machae .i. cendae doine iarna n-airlech.* See Hennessy, "The Ancient Irish Goddess of War," *RC* 1 (1870), 32-55.

Máeltne Mórbrethach (Maoíltne, Maíltne, Maíltni, Móeltne) 151, 152, 154, 156, 157, 158. A jurisconsult.

?*Máeth Scéni (Máoth) 16 g.s. The element Scéni or Scé[t]ni may be a place name; the owner of the house is otherwise unknown.

*Mámos 80 g.s. Mámois, 83 Mámais. In the name *Figol mac Mámois.

Mathgen (Matgen) 78. A sorcerer (*corrguinech*).

LG mentions a Túatha Dé Danann druid named Math m. Umoir, §§314, 349, 369. A *Matha suí Ebraidi* appears in *LU* 2313. Marstrander, *RC* 36 (1915-1916), 353ff. comments on the proper name *Mathgen*, which could be associated with *math* "bear" and *gein* "birth", but which he prefers to link with *mathmarc*, o.m. "soothsayer, diviner." In *Lism. L.*, 1161ff., Brigit's future glory is prophesied by a druid named Mathgen.

Medol and Medón 143. Charioteers of *Lug. See note §143.

Medón 143. One of the charioteers of *Lug. See note §143.

Míach (also Míoach) 33; 34; 35, 123.
   Son of *Dían Cécht, and himself a physician, who replaces the silver arm given to Núadu by Dían Cécht with Núadu's own arm. *LG* §§310; 329; 343, 362, 368; *Leb. Gab.* §97. *LG* §310 notes that Míach receives the silver arm as his fee. *IMT* lists Míach among the Túatha Dé Danann physicians, including Dían Cécht, Airmed, and Edabar. In *OCT* (*GJ* 1884), 33ff. Míach (and a brother Ormiach) arrive at Tara, give full vision to the one-eyed doorkeeper by using a cat's eye, discover a chafer gnawing Núadu from within the silver arm, and finally restore his own arm to the king.

Minn 95. One of the fosterers of *Lug.

Morb 143. One of the charioteers of *Lug. See note §143.

Mórfesa (Mórfesae) 7. Druid and poet from whom the Túatha Dé Danann acquired magical knowledge. See note §2-7.

Morrígan 83, 84, 106, 137, 166. Daughter of *Ernmas, sister of *Macha.
   The Morrígan, a goddess of battle, is associated with a group of such goddesses, often said to be her sisters. The plural character of her identity is reflected in *Corm. Y* §697, 58, in the reference to *ūatha 7 morrígnae*.
   Despite the importance of her role in early Irish literature, the Morrígan's family history presents many questions and conflicts. Her proper name is said to be *Dana (Danann), daughter of Delbáeth son of Ogma, and of Ernmas. She is also said to be the mother (through incest with her father) of Brian, Iuchar and Iucharba. *Leb. Gab.* §103, however, names as her father Delbáeth m. Néid m. Iondai. Another tradition gives her proper name as Ana or Anu/Anand, and from her names the Paps of Ana in Lúachair. Several sources treat Danann and Anann as interchangeable forms.
   She is wife to the Dagda, although there are few references to her as the mother of his children. One son, Meche, (by an unnamed father) had a heart containing three serpents that would have devoured all of Ireland had he—and they—not been destroyed: *Met. Dinds.* II 62 6 (Berba); *Bod. Dinds.* §15 (Berba). *Met. Dinds.* IV 196ff. (Odras) calls the Morrígan the Dagda's wife in its account of her quarrel with Odras, wife of Cormac's cow-keeper Buchet (Odras is turned into a pool of water, and her herd is driven away by the Morrígan), *Dinds.* §113 (Odras). The Brug, in some accounts home of the Dagda, later of Óengus, has certain features named by association with her: the Rampart of the Morrígan, and the Paps of the Morrígan: *Met. Dinds.* II 18 13 (Brug na Bóinde II); *Dinds.* §4 (Dindgnai in Broga). *T. Emire* in *Comp. Con. C.* §50 identifies her with Badb and Bé Néid, §37 mentions that she was given Gort na Mórrígnae (Óchtar nEdmainn) by the Dagda. On the relationship between the Morrígan and the Dagda, see also Murphy, "Notes on Cath Maige Tuired," *Éigse* 7 (1954), 193. Banshenchus tradition identifies Anand as the Morrígan and as wife of the Dagda (*Lec.*, p., *BB*); Badb appears as wife of the Dagda (*Lec.*, p.) or of Indai (*D*, p., *BB*, H.3.17).
   The Morrígan's daughter Adair (by the Dagda) is said to have been the wife of Eber in the glosses to the forty questions of Eochaid Úa Cérín, edited and translated by Thurneysen, *ZCP* 13 (1919), 133. *Acall.* 5127-5128 mentions her twenty-six daughters and twenty-six sons, all warriors, but does not identify their father(s).
   For a general discussion of her character as a battle goddess, see W. M. Hennessy, "The Ancient Irish Goddess of War," *RC* 1 (1870), 32-55.

In *1MT* she acts with Badb and Macha to terrify the enemy with magic showers of fire, mist and blood §29, accompanying the host in §§39, 48. In *2MT²* they make a similar contribution, 40, and plan to give battle to the Fomorian women, 298-306.

The Morrígan plays a major role in the cycle of tales associated with *TBC*, taking the cow of Nera's son to be bulled by the Donn of Cúalnge, *RC* 10 (1889), §13, 223, and in *TBR* §7, 247, in the form of a woman satirist, she spars verbally with Cú Chulainn over driving the cow back to Connacht. She appears at many points in *TBC* itself stirring up strife, challenging Cú Chulainn, both sexually and in combat, as a woman and in animal shape, prolonging the action by protecting the Donn of Cúalnge. (For references, see *Táin*, Index of Persons, *in Mórrigu ingen Ernmais*.) She is among those seeking to prevent his death, breaking his chariot: *LL* 119. 13814-13816. Minor references to her include *Airne F.* 104, 193, where a valuable helmet is hidden from her: she is one of four Túatha Dé Danann (with the Dagda and Óengus) who drive out four Fomoire who escaped from *2MT*. In *Dinds.* §111 (Mag mBreg), *Bod. Dinds.* §2 (Mag mBreg), she helps Conaire's fool Tulchinne carry off Dil and her ox, continuing the extensive association with cattle raiding.

Another of her associations is with a particular type of cooking-pit that used a type of spit said to have been invented by the Dagda. See MacKinnon, "Fulacht na Morrígna," *The Celtic Review* 8 (1912), 74ff. and Hyde, *The Celtic Review* 10 (1916) 335ff.

Moth 143. One of the charioteers of *Lug. See note §143.

Mothach 143. One of the charioteers of *Lug. See note §143.

Núadu (Núadha, Núadae, Núadai, Núodai, Núadoo) 14, 33, 53, 70, 74, 133, 5 g.s. Núadot, 11 d.s. Núadad, 70 Núadaitt. King of the Túatha Dé Danann, replaced by *Bres after losing his arm in the first battle of Mag Tuired. The arm, replaced by one of silver, gives rise to his epithet "Silverhand" (Aircetláum, 133). Following the deposition of Bres, Núadu is again king of the Túatha Dé Danann, and is slain in the second battle of Mag Tuired.

There is general agreement about Núadu's genealogy throughout the literary tradition. Typically he is the son of Echtach *m. Etarlaim m. Ordain m. Alldui, LG* §316, cf. §§343, 368; *Keat.* I: xii: 220-221. His four sons are Tadg the Great, Caither, Cucharn, and Etarlam the poet, *LG* §368. A daughter, Echtge, is mentioned in *Acall.* 1011. His role in *1MT* and *2MT,* the invasion of Ireland and its defense against the Fomoire, is described in *LG* §§310, 312, 314; §22, 328-332, 335; 353-354, 356, 358-362, 364, 366, 370; 376; LIV §§3-6; LVI §7; LX §3; see also the Fir Bolg, section VI of *LG*. His invincible sword is mentioned *LG* §§305; 325; 357. Núadu is a major character in *1MT,* see especially §§30, 48 (his loss of an arm to Sreng) and §58, representing a tradition not found in *2MT,* that the Túatha Dé Danann cede the province of Connacht to the Fir Bolg rather than lose Núadu in the second combat to which he is challenged by Sreng. By contrast, in *LG* §353, LX he is called one of the seven sons of Ethliu. *LG* §376 synchronizes his reign with that of Belochus (after the expulsion of Bres) and with that of Bellepares, during whose reign the "battle of Mag Tuired of the Fomoraig" occurred in which Núadu fell.

In *OCT* (GJ 1884), 33, Ordan, his great grandfather, is identified as a son of Aldui, not Indui. *2MT²* 10, 83, 96, 115 passim, 208, 233, 590 also presents Núadu as a major figure, and differs somewhat from *2MT* in its characterization of him.

The Núadu of *2MT²* is jealous of Lug's ability and leaves him behind through trickery when the Túatha Dé Danann go to battle against the Fomoire because of personal jealousy (not, as in *2MT,* out of concern for Lug's well-being). The *LL* 39a list of kings of Ireland gives Núadu's reign as twenty years in length, and notes that he was slain by Balor. The dindshenchus traditions hardly mention Núadu, although *Dinds.* §11 (Fid n-Gaible) mentions a grandson, Gaible m. Etadoin meic Núadat, who steals sticks from the Dagda's daughter Ainge. *Met. Dinds.* III 400 13 (Loch Cé) and *Ed. Dinds.* §75 (Loch Cé) mention the naming of the site following the death of Nuadu's druid Cé, after the second battle of Mag Tuired. *Cóir Anm.* §154 mentions Núadu's injury, his opponent Sreng, and his silver hand. The colloquy between Fintan and the Hawk of Achill (*Anecd.* I) provides further information about the arm, carried away from the battlefield by the hawk. *OCT* (*GJ* 1884), 33, offers an account of the arm's replacement by the wandering physicians Míach and Ormiach, sons of Dian Cécht. *TMM* 59, in a somewhat obscure passage, seems to contrast *síl Núadad* with "the race of Eladen" as hostile branches of the Túatha Dé Danann. For cult sites in England associated with the god Nodens (whose name is etymologically related to that of Núadu) see R. E. M. Wheeler and T. V. Wheeler, *Report on the Excavation of the Prehistoric, Roman, and Post-Roman Site in Lydney Park, Gloucestershire,* in *Reports of the Research Committee of the Society of Antiquaries of London,* IX, Oxford, 1932. For Irish stone sculpture which appears to represent Núadu, see Ellen Ettlinger, "Contributions towards an interpretation of several stone images in the British Isles," *Ogam* 13 (1961), 286-304. For other references to the cult of Núadu, see Françoise Le Roux, "Le dieu-roi NODONS/NUADA," *Celticum* 6 (1963), 425-454.

Ochttríuil 123. A son of *Dían Cécht, and himself a physician.

Ogma (also Og(h)mae, Og(h)mai) 25, 36, 59, 72, 75, 83, 138, 162, 163, 104 v.s. Oghmau. The champion of the Túatha Dé Danann, said to have been killed by *Indech mac Dé Domnann (138), but still alive in (162-163). His full name is variously given: Oghmai mac Etnae (MS.) (36), Oghmae mac Ethlend (59), and Ogmae mac Ealauthan (138).
His identity as a son of Elatha and his death at the hands of Indech m. Dé Domnann are well established in *LG* §§312, 316; 331; 364; 368; LIII §9, LVI §8; *Leb. Gab.* §100; *Keat.* I: xi: 216-217. He appears as one of the Túatha Dé Danann warriors in *1MT,* which gives his name as Ogma (§39), Ogma mac Ethlenn (§41) and Ogma mac Eladain (§48, in a list of the five sons of Elatha). In *2MT*² he is characterized as a champion and appears frequently in the account of the fighting: 14, 242, 274, 861, 986, 990, 1007, 1010. His name is given as Ogm(h)a Graineineach mac Ealathan mic Dhealbhaoi. In *De Gabáil in tSída, ZCP* 19 (1931), 55, he is granted Síd Aircheltrai.
LG §376 synchronizes his death in "the battle of Mag Tuired of the Fomoraig" with the reign of Bellapares.

Rechtaid Finn (Fionn) 95. A fosterer of *Lug.

*Ríagal 53 g.s. Ríaghaild. In the name *Camall mac Ríagail.

Samildánach (Sam(h)il(l)dánach) 53, 68, 74; 56 d.s. Samhilldánuch. "Skilled in many arts at once," in these examples used of *Lug as a proper name.

Scibar 95. One of the fosterers of *Lug.

Semias 7. Druid and poet from whom the Túatha Dé Danann acquired magical knowledge. See note §§2-7.

Tae (Taei) 65. A cupbearer. For the names of the cupbearers, see note §65.

Talom 65. A cupbearer.

Tenda 143. A charioteer of *Lug. See note §143.

Tollusdam 95. A fosterer of *Lug.

Tres 143. A charioteer of *Lug. See note §143.

Trog 65. A cupbearer. For the names of the cupbearers, see note §65.

*Tuirill Bicreo 12 a.s. Turild Bicreo. Túatha Dé Danann warrior killed in the first battle of Mag Tuired.
A son of Etan, daughter of Dían Cécht, he is also called Delbáeth, Tuirell, and Tuirenn, and is a son of Ogma. See *LG* §§310, 348, 368; *Leb. Gab.* §116. Father,

by his own daughter Danann, of the three Dé Danann; see *Dana. His death in the first battle is found in *LG* §310, and LVI §3. *1MT* §§48, 51 mention him only as father of Brian, Iuchar and Iucharba. *LG* §319, LXVI tell the story of the murder of Cían by those three and the healing of Tuirenn by Dían Cécht, his maternal grandfather. *2MT²* mentions Dealbhaoth Dána mac Ealathan, 283, but does not expressly equate him with Tuirill/Tuirenn. *LG* §368, however, identifies "Dealbaeth Dana" as son of Ogma and also as bearing the name Tuirenn (187) although on 189, "Delbaeth Dana" figures as a son of Elatha. *MU²* mentions Delbáeth mac Eithlend (for mac Elathan?) as one of the Túatha Dé Danann invisibly present to stir up strife among the men of Ireland, 575-576. *Cóir Anm.* §155 identifies Tuirenn Beggrean as Delbáeth (without patronymic) and his children as Brian, Eoch*a*id (for Iuchar?) and Iucharba. *OCT* (*GJ* 1884), 39, gives no patronymic, but does give the full name in the phrase Clann Tuireann Beagreann, in a poem spoken by Lug, apparently equivalent to the Chloinn Dealb*h*aoit*h* of the following quatrain.

The sons themselves, murderers of Lug's father Cían and ultimately destroyed by Lug's vengeance, after completing their quest for the elaborate wergild he requires, are Brian (substituted by the editor for Úar) Iucharba and Iuchair, 36; their sister, who laments both their crime and their fate, is Ethne, 41.

See also the references given under *Delbáeth.

Uiscias 7. Druid and poet from whom the Túatha Dé Danann acquired magical knowledge. See note §§2-7.

Úaithne (Úaitniu) 163. Harper of the *Dagda.

The Dagda's harper is mentioned also in *TBFr.* 103, as present at the birth of three sons to Bóann, who named them for the three kinds of music he played during her labour, Goltraige, Gentraige, and Súantraige.

FOMOIRE

Irish tradition consistently associates the Fomoire with the sea, and Irish folk etymology interprets their name as compounded of *fo* ("under") and *muir* ("sea"). *Cóir Anm.* §234 offers "*Fomoraig*, that is, *fo-muiride*, folk who are robbing and reaving on the sea [*muir*], to them is the name." Thurneysen regards this etymology as unlikely: "Die durchgehende Schreibung *Fomore* (nicht *-mure*) macht den Zusammenhang mit *muir* 'Meer' unwahrscheinlich. Am ehesten scheint mir das Wort, das dem deutschen 'Mar' ahd. altisländ. *mara* engl. *mare* entsprach, darin zu stecken, wie in *Mor-rīgain* ['Maren-Königin'] . . . Sie wären als 'unter (seeische) Maren' bezeichnet." See also Rees and Rees, *Celtic Heritage*, 114. *Contribb.* F 286, s.v. *fomóir*, i and guttural, m; *fomórach*, o, m., cites Meyer, *Alt. Ir. Dicht.* ii 6, *Wortk.*, 86, noting that the oldest form is perhaps *fomoire* to which the genitive *fomra* occurs, and that the common Mid. Ir. form is *fomóir* while the form *fomórach* (g.sg. *-aig*) is also found in Mid. Ir. and later generally replaces *fomóir* in the plural.

The present text uses the early form, with two probable examples of the genitive *Fomra*, in §121 and §129. The exceptions are §147, *de Fomorchaib* and §51, *in slóg-sin na Fomoiridhi*, using the pseudo-etymological form found in *Cóir Anm.* §234.

The Fomoire appear variously in Irish tradition as deformed and demonic monsters, descendants of Ham who had sinned by mocking his father Noah; as raiders travelling by sea, no doubt influenced by the Irish experience of the Vikings; and as giants, their usual character in folk tradition.

On the changing character of the Fomoire in Irish tradition, see O'Rahilly, *EIHM*, 523-525, and the important discussion by Proinsias Mac Cana, "The influence of the Vikings on Celtic literature," 78-ff., especially "Lochlannaig and Fomoire," 94-97, in *The Impact of the Scandinavian Invasions on the Celtic-speaking Peoples c. 800-1100 A.D.*, ed. Brian Ó Cuív (Dublin, 1975).

Bagna (Bagnai) 128. A Fomorian leader.

In $2MT^2$ he appears as *Badhna*, 1246; his son Oghma (for Omna) mac Badhna m. Tinne Thortbhuilligh, 1239, 1252.

According to *Met. Dinds.* IV 282 (Slíab Badbgna), he was slain while in flight from the battle, and the site, lying in a range of hills in eastern Roscommon, was named after him.

Balor (also Balar, Balur) 8, 50, 128, 133, 134, 135, 55 g.s. Baloir; 133 d.s. Bolur Birugderc. A champion, father of *Ethne, son of *Dot (or Dót) and grandson of *Nét, killed in single combat with his Túatha Dé Danann grandson, *Lug.

LG §§312, 332, 364, recounts the incident, explaining the family relation, but specifies a sling-stone as the fatal weapon.

$2MT^2$ lists *Balur mac Dóit* in the Fomorian muster, 293, and gives his name as *Balur Bailcbhéimneach ua Néid Nuachrothaigh* at 1029; in this version, Balor is not slain when Lug puts out his eye (with a sling-stone) but survives to meet his grandson again at *Carn Í Néid*, where Balor is decapitated. He treacherously offers his powers to his grandson, who is instructed to place Balor's head above his own, instead placing the head on a stone—which is split by a poisonous drop falling from the head. $2MT^2$ also makes reference to his two sons, *Béluid Bháin*, 1239, 1260.

Rawl. B 502 (*Gen. Tr.* C §192) gives a genealogy that differs from *LG*: *Balar mac Doith mc. Nest mc. Silcait mc. Plais mc. Libuirn mc. Laisc mc. Innomuin mc. Galaich mc. Larcaich mc. Sithaird mc. Ollaird mc. Meircill.*

Balor's epithet *birug-derc* (from *berach* o, ā "sharp") is unusual. *Bailcbhéimneach*, missing from *2MT*, is common outside it: *Leb. Gab.* §107; *Met. Dinds.* IV 252 18 (Bréfne); *Cóir Anm.* §289 (Lecan), explaining it as "from the strength of his blows." In *OCT* (*GJ* 1884), 35, no patronymic is given, but *Eab* (=*Cab*?) and *Senchab* are also described as Uí Néit. Balor himself is described as king of the Fomoire with his royal seat in Beirbe, with a wife Ceithlenn; Bres is said to be their son.

The death of Balor at the hands of Lug, son of his daughter Ethne, is an important incident throughout Irish literary and folk tradition. *Duan. Finn.* XVI tells the story of Balor's decapitation and of the treacherous request that Lug place Balor's head above his own, emphasizing the kinship between them. (Fenian tradition also associates Balor with swine, *Duan. Finn,* XIV.)

The tale appears in poetry as an archetypal heroic conflict: see, for example, *Leabhar Branach* #32 (132-33) or *Duanaire Cloinne Aodha Buidhe* VIII, especially qq. 89, 93, 97, 109. The dindshenchus tradition adds little, mentioning Balor only as father of a daughter (by implication Lug's mother) in *Met. Dinds.* IV 162 4 (Slíab Fúait I), and in *Met. Dinds.* IV 252 18 (Bréfne) as a descendant of Ham. On folk traditions about Balor, and comparison with Welsh parallels, see A. H. Krappe, *Balor with the Evil Eye* (Lancaster, 1927).

Bres (also Pres) 14, 21, 23, 25, 29, 32, 36, 39, 40, 43, 44, 45, 49, 53, 94, 128, 149, 150, 151, 153, 154, 155, 156, 158, 159, 161, 163, 15 g.s. Bresi (also 39 and 124), 24, 25 Brese. Son of *Elatha and *Ériu, successor to *Núadu in the kingship of the Túatha Dé Danann, given the name *Eochu Bres by his father.

Most genealogies agree with *2MT* in making him the son of Elatha, although Balor replaces Elatha in this role in *OCT* (*GJ*, 1884), 35. Rawl. B 502 (*Gen. Tr.* C §191) names Bres as one of seven major Fomorian ancestors, separating Túatha Dé Danann from Fomoire before Delbáeth: *Bress mc. Elathan mc. Delbaeth mc. Deirgthind mc. Ochtaich mc. Sithchind mc. Molaich mc. Largluind mc. Ciarraill mc. Faesaim mc. Meircill . . . Noe.*

LG §316 places Bres among sons of Elatha son of Delbáeth son of Nét son of Indui son of Tat son of Tabarn (=335, with a variant making Elatha son of Nét, but Indui son of Alldui, keeping the same number of generations to Tabarn). *Leb. Gab.* §106 makes Bres son of Elatha *m. Néitt m. Ciolcaigh m. Ploiscc m. Lipairn m. Golaim m. Largaidh m. Mercill m. Sailt Claraigh m. Stairn Fiaclaigh m. Sipuirn m. Sadail m. Ucatt m. Effic m. Pelist m. Fedil m. Cuis m. Caim m. Noe.* A more usual genealogy is also given.

Traditions regarding the death of Bres vary.

LG R₁ (except Min), §312, notes the death of Bres in the second battle of Mag Tuired. R₂, §329, includes the alternate tradition that Bres died of drinking bog water, through Lug's trickery, at Carn Uí Néit, also found in *LG* LVI §11. R₃, §362, §364, simply omits any account of Bres's death. *Leb. Gab.* §106 has the *LG* R₂ version of Bres's death; *Keat.* I: xii: 220-221 mentions Bres's seven year reign, following that of Núadu, but offers no other details. *IMT* is apparently isolated, placing the death of Bres during that battle, §49, at the hands of the Fir Bolg king, Eochaid m. Eirc. In *2MT²*, Bres figures prominently as an opponent of Lug, 452, 1139-1172, and is slain by him in single combat. Dindshenchus tradition records Bres's death through drinking bog water, *Met. Dinds.* III 216ff. (Carn Huí Néit), *Dinds.* §46 (Carn Húi Néit), as does the LL 39ₐ list of Kings of Ireland.

LG §376 synchronizes his death with the reign of Bellepares. *Met. Dinds.* III 216ff. (Carn Huí Néit) places it in the reign of Nechtan *bass-chain,* overlord of the two Munsters, a figure otherwise unidentified.

Additional information regarding Bres appears in *Met. Dinds.* III 8 80 (Carmun): Bres digs Carmun's grave; *Met. Dinds.* IV 254 41 (Bréfne) mentions the death of his daughter Indusa, cf. *Dinds.* §149 (Bréfne). *Cóir Anm.* §153 reflects traditions shared by *2MT*: Eochaid Bres has the epithet *cruthach,* and is called *m. Eladhan m. Dhelbaith.* In saga tradition, Bres plays relatively little part, but in *TE²,* 143, the Dagda sends Elcmar to Bres m. Elathan in Mag nInis (Lecale in Co. Down).

On Bres's pig, see *Corm. Tr.* s.v. *Bab.*

*Coirpre Colc 147 g.s. Carpri Cuilc. A servant of the Fomorian king, *Indech mac Dé Domnann.

*Delbáeth 14, 21, 25, 128, 163. In the name, *Elatha mac Delbáith, the Fomorian king, perhaps also in the name *Ériu ingen Delbaíth.

There are several figures named Delbáeth in the Túatha Dé Danann genealogies of *LG.* The present one is presumably the son of Nét and father of Elatha mentioned in §§316, 339, 368. See also the references given in the entries for *Elatha, *Ériu, the *Morrígan, and *Tuirill Bicreo.

*Día Domnann g.s. Dé Domnann, in the name *Indech mac Dé Domnann, a Fomorian king.

*Dolb 97 d.s. Dulb. Fomorian smith.

A Dolb Drennach son of Dáilem, of the Túatha Dé Danann, appears in *Met. Dinds.* III 304 23; 306 27 (Slíab nEchtga II). He is not, however, identified as a smith, and the tribal affiliation is wrong. See also the references to a Túatha Dé Danann Dolb in *IHKS,* 230.

*Domnu g.s. Domnann, in the name *Indech mac Dé Domnann, a Fomorian king.

*Dot (orDót) 128 g.s. Doit, in the name *Balor mac Doit. See *2MT²* 293, and Rawl. B 502 (*Gen. Tr.* C §192).

In *2MT²* his son Conn Cródha, brother of *Balor, is mentioned at 284-285. See also note §128.

Elatha mac Delbáith (also Elotha(e), Elathu) 14, 21, 23, 25, 40, 128, 149, 163. g.s. Elathan 14: A Fomorian king, father of *Bres and lover of *Ériu.

Elatha's genealogy is given in *LG,* at §§316, 335, 368. There are two versions: §316 (Min.) mentions the Dagda, Ogma, Ellot, Bres and Delbáeth, the five sons of Elatha son of Delbáeth; §335 lists them as either the five sons of Elada m. Delbaith or sons of Elada m. Néit m. Indui m. Alldui m. Tait m. Tabuirn; §368 gives the version with Delbáeth m. Néit as the father of Elatha, as does *Leb. Gab.* §100. *Keat.* I: xi: 215 identifies Elatha as the son of Nét, while I:xii:222-223 interpolates Delbáeth between Elatha and Nét. In *2MT²* he is said to be *m. Dealbhaoi* and *airdrí sídhe* (231), but no further genealogical particulars are given; he is killed by Lug following a combat with Núadu (to which there is no reference in *2MT*). Bres is said to be his son (360, passim) but their personal relationship is less complex than in *2MT*. In *Met. Dinds*. III 216 3 (Carn Huí Néit) Elatha is identified as the father of Bres, but as himself the son of Nét (rather than of Delbáeth).

Eochu Bres (Eocha) 21; 23. See *Bres.

Ethne 8, 55. Daughter of *Balor, mother of *Lug, wife of *Cían.
Many sources identify Ethne as wife of Cían son of Dían Cécht, daughter of Balor, and mother of Lug: *LG* §§311; 330; 363; *Leb. Gab.* §98; banshenchus (*LL*, *Lec. p.v. D.* p. v, *BB*). *2MT²* calls her Eithne Imdhearg, inghean Bhalair, 469, 1302, 1306, in references (or addresses) to Lug. Her epithet also appears in *LG* §363 (M): *E. imderg ingin Balair Bailchbemnig*.
Met. Dinds. IV 162 4 (Slíab Fúait I) refers to a balance belonging to the son of Balor's daughter, presumably Lug; IV 278 11 (Loch Lugborta) refers to Lug as the son of Eithne, but she herself does not appear as a character. Her career after the murder of her husband Cían is described in *Duan. Finn* XLV §§6-10: Lug gives her in marriage to Tadhg son of Núadu, and she becomes the mother of Muirn, and grandmother of Finn mac Cumhaill; see also XLIV.

Goll 128. A Fomorian leader.
Goll and his brother, Irgoll, do not appear in *2MT²*, but their deaths are recorded in *Met. Dinds.* IV 282 (Slíab Badbgna): Goll m. Innig is killed by Lug while fleeing from the battle at Ros Guill, the Rosguil peninsula between Sheep Haven and Mulroy in northern Donegal. In *Duan. Finn* LXIX, Murphy discusses the mythological significance of Goll as a Fomorian name.

Indech mac Dé Domnann (also Indeach, Indeouch) 25, 50, 85, 93, 94, 128, 133, 136, 138, 147, 126, 135, Indig. g.s. Indich. A Fomorian king.
In *2MT*, Indech is slain by Ogma in a single combat in which both fall. According to *LG* §312, Indech survives the battle and it is he who gives Lug an account of the slain. No full genealogy is given, but he is uniformly said to be a son of Dé Domnann: *LG* §§312, 332 (called a druid, not a king, except in D); in 364 identified as king, but explained as "a man with arts of poetry and craft." In *2MT²* Inneach mac Dé Domhnann figures prominently; in 270-275 Ogma volunteers to destroy Indech, but fails and is himself slain, 1007, so that finally Lug is responsible for Indech's death, 1020-1022. In Rawl. B 502 (*Gen. Tr.* C §193) his genealogy is given as follows: *Indech mac Dedomnaind mc. Dicolla mc. Solaich mc. Drul mc. Tiagbaill mc. Tastaich mc. Sithchirn mc. Ballaich mc. Tabuirn mc. Sluchraim mc. Lithraid mc. Mercill. Met. Dinds.* III 84 2 (Belach Durgein), *Dinds.* §24 (Belach nDuirgein) add some interesting family gossip: when Durgen reveals her mother's infidelities, her mother persuades Indech to seek a tryst with the girl, who turns on him with her weapons and is herself slain.

Irgoll (Irgold) 128. A Fomorian leader.
Irgoll m. Innig, killed by Lug, is the eponym of Slíab nIrguill or Ross Irguill, west of Rossguill, p. Mevagh, b. Kilmacrenan.
See *Met. Dinds.* IV 282 (Slíab Badbgna).

*Lobos? 128 g.s. Lobois, in the name *Tuire Tortbuillech mac Lobois.
He is mentioned in *2MT²* in the names of his two sons, Lóman Lóm mac Lobuis, 1191, and Lópthach mac Lubuis, 915,923. *OCT* (*GJ* 1884), 35 identifies Lobus as a druid, and mentions yet another son, Liathlabhar mac Lobais. The name also appears in *PCT*, where Lóbus Laghrach is identified as a grandson of Beelzebub.

Lóch Lethglas (also Lúog, Lúoch) 136, 139, 140, 141, 142, 146, 162. The poet of *Indech mac Dé Domnann.
In *LG* §§312, 332, 364 his role as enumerator of the casualties in the second battle of Mag Tuired is taken by Indech m. Dé Domnann. In *2MT²* two figures divide the role of Lóch in *2MT*. Liath Leathghlas mac Luasgaigh, a Fomorian poet who asks the identity of the hero who wounds Balor, appears in 721. Luath Líneach, another

Fomorian poet, is asked by Lug to number the Fomorians slain in battle; Luath also composes a poem praising Balor in 1032.

*Lommglúinech 128 g.s. Lomglúinigh, in the name *Loscennlomm mac Lommglúinigh.

Loscennlomm mac Lommglúinigh 128. A Fomorian leader.

$2MT^2$ mentions Loisgionn Lom mac Lomghlúinigh: 251, 363, 450, 929, 933, 1435, and at 1216, Ludur Lunnmhór mac Loisginn Lomhglúinigh.

He is presumably to be identified with one of the seven Fomorian ancestors listed in Rawl. B 502 (*Gen Tr.* C §196), *Loiscenn Luath mac Lomgluinich m. Lomaltaich m. Lathaich ... mc. Meircill ... OCT* (*GJ* 1884), 35 mentions a Loisginn Lomghlúineach, echoing $2MT^2$ 1216 in putting the two names together, in contrast to the other $2MT^2$ passages, which make Loisgionn a son of Lomglúinech.

See also *Met. Dinds.* III 84 2 (Belach Durgein) and *Dinds.* §24 (Belach n-Duirgein) for the death of Duirgen, a daughter of Lúath m. Lomglúinigh Síl Mercill m. Smirduib, at the hands of Indech, when the girl had betrayed her mother's infidelities.

*Nét 8 g.s. Néit, 50, 128, 133, 146.

In the name of his grandson *Balor. *Corm.* s.v. *Néit* identifies him as *dia catha*; H. 3. 18, 637a names Nemon as his wife. This tradition also appears in *Met. Dinds.* IV 102, IV 114 (Ailech II and III); *Met. Dinds.* III 198 21 names Fea as his wife, as does *Dinds.* §44 (Mag Femen). Both are identified as his wives, and as daughters of Elcmar, in *LG* §§316, 338 (Badb as variant for Fea), 368. His death at Ailech is synchronized with the reign of Acrisius, *LG* §376.

For other references to this figure, see *Badb, *Balor, *Bres, *Dagda, and *Dot.

Ochtríallach (also Octríallach) 126, 128, 133. Son of *Indech mac Dé Domnann.

Ochtríallach and Olltríallach alternate as forms of the name of a son of Indech, mentioned in *LG* §§312; 331; 364. LVI §8 names him as Casmáel's slayer, and §331 mentions that he kills two Túatha Dé Danann satirists, Bruidne and Casmáel, in the second battle of Mag Tuired. In $2MT^2$ 272 Ogma promises to destroy Olltríallach in the forthcoming conflict; 969-1021 include Olltríallach's exploits.

Omna 128. A Fomorian leader.

According to *Met. Dinds.* IV 282 3 (Slíab Badbgna) an Omna m. Innigh m. Tuire. Thort-buillig was killed by Lug at Áth Omna, a ford on the River Boyle. This Omna is perhaps the "Oghma" m. Badhna m. Tinne Thortbuilligh killed by Lug at Áth Oghma for Búill, in $2MT^2$ 1239, 1252.

Rúadán 124, 125. Son of *Bres and *Bríg, daughter of the *Dagda.

Sab Úanchennach 147. Son of *Coirpre Colc, one of the warriors killed in the second battle of Mag Tuired and mentioned by *Lóch Lethglass.

Tethra (also Tetra) 25, 93, 162. A Fomorian king mentioned briefly as imposing tribute upon the Túatha Dé Danann. He does not appear in person in *LG, 2MT²,* or *1MT. Met. Dinds.* III 460 8 mentions a Tethra as the father of Smirgoll but gives no further data, nor do the Fomorian genealogies in Rawl. B 502. *Corm. Tr.* 157 identifies him as king of the Fomorians and quotes a passage found in *Im. Dá T., iter triunu Tethrach.* That text in turn, §97, glosses Tethrach as *ainm ríg Fomore.* Saga tradition makes him a relative of Emer, her father Forgall being sister's son to Tethra, identified as a Fomorian king in *T. Emire* in *Comp. Con C.* §§31, 48. A reference to Tethra's wife, glossed *badb* appears in *LU* 50a (marginalia), one to his cattle, *buar tethrach* (a kenning for waves), in *IT* III 61.20. See also the poem of Amorgen, *LG* LXIX.

Tuire Tortbuillech mac Lobois (Tuirie) 128. A Fomorian leader.

Perhaps equivalent to the Tinne Thortbhuilligh of $2MT^2$ 1239, named as the father of Badhna (*Bagna) and grandfather of Oghma (=*Omna). Perhaps, also, he is equivalent to one of the seven Fomorian ancestors of Rawl. B 502 (*Gen. Tr.* C) §194,

Tuire Torcheirnech mac. Lagais mc. Lithaich ... Met. Dinds. IV 282 4 (Slíab Badbgna) identifies Tuire Tortbuillech as the father of Indech, and the grandfather of Goll and Irgoll, Omna and Badbgna. (All are said to have been killed by Lug Lámfota.)

FIR BOLG

A full account of their invasion and conquest of Ireland appears in *LG* §§278-303, poems XLVI-LII. The *LG* tradition is expanded in *Dinds.* §78 (Carn Conoill), on the fate of the Fir Bolg royal family in the time of Cairbre Niafer. The tribal name is explained in *Cóir Anm.* §224 as "men of bags" (from the sacks in which they carried earth for the Greeks). They are often presented as ancestors of non-Goidelic peoples in Ireland (*LG* §§282, 292, 299). See O'Rahilly, *EIHM,* especially 99-101. For another perspective on their role in Irish myth, see Rees and Rees, *Celtic Heritage,* especially Ch. IV, "Coming into Existence," 95-117.

*Eochaid (or *Eochu) mac Eirc 10 a.s. Eoch*daig.* Fir Bolg king killed in the first battle of Mag Tuired.
    Accounts of the first battle of Mag Tuired appear in both the Fir Bolg and Túatha Dé Danann sections of *LG:* §§280-281; 288-290; 296-297, 299, 302-303, XLVIII §§307-308; 322; 359-360; *Leb. Gab.* §88; *Keat.* I: x: 212-213. All references identify the Fir Bolg king as Eochaid mac Eirc, as do the king list found in *LL* 39a, and *1MT*. In Eochaid Úa Cérin's poem, however, an interlinear gloss identifies "Triath mac Amuir" as the last Fir Bolg king to oppose the Túatha Dé Danann (*ZCP* 13 (1919), 132). No authority, however, is given. Amur is presumably the Umor who is father of the Fir Bolg chieftains who lead the tribe after their defeat: see, for example, *LG* §281 (Triath is not among them, however). Many sources agree that Eochaid met his death at Tráig Éothaile at the hands of three sons of Nemed: *LG* §§307-308; 360; *1MT* §54; *Leb. Gab.* §97; *Keat.* I: ix: 198-199. Eochaid is noted as first king to die by a spear-point in Ireland, *LG:* LXVIII; as first Fir Bolg king to sit in Tara: *LG* §363; and as the first man to die by spearpoint in Ireland: *LG* §363. *2MT²* mentions him in connection with Dúnadh Díbheirge, site of a Fir Bolg attack upon the Túatha Dé Danann, 1285.

Sreng mac Sengainn (Sregg mac Sengaidn) 11. The opponent who strikes off Núadu's arm in single combat in the first battle of Mag Tuired.
    Sreng is also identified as Núadu's opponent in *1MT*, where he figures prominently, in *LG* (L, a single quatrain appearing at §§290, 297), and in *Cóir Anm.* §154 (Núadu).

*Tailtiu 55:241 g.s. Taill[ti]ne in*gine* Magmóir rí Esp*áine.* Fir Bolg queen at the time of the first battle of Mag Tuired, wife of *Eochaid mac Eirc, later married to *Eochaid Garb of the Túatha Dé Danann; foster-mother of *Lug.
    Daughter of Magmóir (sometimes given the epithet Mall), king of Spain, married first to Eochaid Mac Eirc, king of the Fir Bolg, then to Eochaid Garb of the Túatha Dé Danann. The wood of Coill Cúan was cleared by her; she died in Tailtiu, and was buried there. She was foster-mother of Lug, who instituted a festival, Lugnasad, with funeral games in her memory. See *LG* §§311; 330; 363; *Leb. Gab.* §§96, 98; *Keat.* I: xii: 220-221. See also *TMM* 65-66. Banshenchus tradition agrees with *LG* in identifying her father and her two husbands (*LL, Lec., D, BB, Edin.*) These traditions also appear in the dindshenchus, *Met. Dinds.* IV 146 (Tailtiu), III 48 (Nás); *Dinds.* §99 (Tailtiu), *Ed. Dinds.* §68 (Mag Tailten). On the Oenach Tailten, held at Lugnasad in honour of Tailtiu, see especially *Met. Dinds.* IV 146 (Tailtiu). *Dinds.* §20 (Nás) adds details about the clearing of the wood of Cúan, and offers an alternate explanation of the institution of Lugnasad as a memorial to Lug's wives, Bói and Nás.

Hogan has, in general, been used as the basis of the index, and where possible an entry from the *Onomasticon* is given as headword, with occasional changes in vowel length, capitalization, and indication of lenition. The actual form found in the edition is given in parentheses if a nominative singular occurs in the text (some minor spelling variants are omitted). If there is no entry in Hogan, the headword is a nominative form from the edition, a supplied nominative (if only oblique cases appear in the text), or, if the nominative is uncertain, an oblique form from the text itself. Uncertain forms are indicated with ?. Section numbers precede the colon; line references follow. The entries *Allod Echae, *Echuinech, *Glenn Edin, *Loscondoib, *Mag Aurfolaig, and *Mag (S)cé[t]ne are based upon information kindly supplied by Dr. Alan Mac an Bhaird of the Ordnance Survey of Ireland.

Achad Abla 126. N.W. of *Mag Tuired in c. Sligo, site of Dian Cécht's healing well. On the basis of the references in *Lis. Lives*, ll. 2696ff., and since, as Professor Ó Riain informs me, Druim eitir da Loch is doubtless Drum Columb, associated with St. Finnian's (Finnbarr's) cult in c. Sligo, Achad Abla might be Ardagh in Kilmacallan, b. Tirerrill, c. Sligo, north of Heapstown. See also *Carn Ochtriallaig, *Loch Luibe, and *Tipra Slaine.

Allod Echae 84 a.s. (Also called *Echuinech, MS. perhaps Echumech). The name is obsolete, refers to Doorly townland, Kilmorgan parish, Corran barony.

Amrún Fer nDéa (Amhrún) 76 (also called *Grellach Dollaid). In Grallagh Greenan tl. in Lr. Iveagh.

Ára 13 d.s. Árainn. The context suggests that the Scottish Arran is intended, implied also by the LG passages linking the Fir Bolg of a much later period with Dun Aengusa on the Irish island, a territory which they are said to have received from Medb and Ailill (§§281, 291, 298).

Áth Admillte 85 (also called *Áth Unsen). A ford on the river *Unius, in Connacht.

Áth Unsen (Áth Unsen) 85 (also called *Áth Admillte). A ford on the river *Unius, in Connacht.

Banna 79. The Bann.

Benna Bairche (Bennai Boirche) 78. The Mourne Mountains in c. Down.

Blaísliab 78. Seems to be on the bounds of or within the territory of Ciannachta Glinne Gemin, now b. of Keenaght in Derry.

Bóand (Bóann) 79. The river Boyne.

Brí Ruri 78. Perhaps a corruption of Brí Erigi, one of the mountains defining the limits of the d. of Armagh, apparently located in c. Down.

Búas 79. The river Bush.

Carn Ochtríallaig (Carn Ochtríaldaig) 126. According to the text, the site of Dian Cécht's healing well. See also *Achad Abla, *Loch Luibe, and *Tipra Slaine. The site is at Heapstown, c. Sligo, N.W. of *Mag Tuired; it is called C. Oilltraiallaigh in a scribal colophon written in 1698 in the Annals of Loch Ce.

Conmaicne Mara 9. The land and people of Connemara, b. of Ballinahinch, c. Galway.

Connachta 84. The land and people of Connacht.

Corann 84. d.s. Corand. B. Corran, c. Sligo, but formerly contained Galenga in Mayo, Luigne, and the present Corann in Sligo.

Corcu Belgatan 9. To be associated with the Sliab Maccu Belgodon mentioned in 78. There is a Sliab Belgadain in Conmaicne Cúile Tolad (not Conmaicne Mara), at the site of the First Battle of Mag Tuired near Cong, c. Mayo (to the right of the road on the way from Cong to the village of Neal).

Crúachán Aigle 78. Croagh Patrick Mountain, 6½ miles W.S.W. of Westport, Mayo.

Denna Ulad (Denda Ulad) 78. Perhaps a "keening" for Benna Bairche, or a calque on Ard Ulad, c. Down.

Dercloch 79. Appears as Dergderc in the parallel passage in *BDD*²l. 1465, and it seems best to take the present reference as also to L. Derg nr. Killaloe, rather than to the smaller L. Derg in b. Tirhugh, c. Donegal.

Drobés 126. g.s. Drobésa. The river Drowes.

Dún mBrese 24. Near and W. of L. Corrib.

Echuinech 84. (MS. perhaps Echumech). The form represents Echainech, that is, Aghanagh, and suggests a reference to the p. and tl. in b. of Tirellill, on the W. side of Loch Arrow. But see *Allod Echae.

Ériu 9; g.s. Érionn, 31: g.s. Érenn; 125: d.s. Érinn, 126: d.s. Éri; passim.

Espáin. Espán 55; g.s. Espátne. Spain.

Falias 2, 3, 7. A mythical city in which the Túatha Dé Danann studied the magical arts.

Findias 2, 5, 7. A mythical city in which the Túatha Dé Danann studied the magical arts.

Finn (Fionn) 79. There are several rivers with this name, including the river Blackwater, Meath; the river Finn, b. Raphoe, c. Donegal; and the river Finn in the E. of Tireragh, c. Sligo, which falls into Ballysadare at Buninna.

Glenn Edin 84; d.s. Glionn Edin, 84: d.s. Glind Edind. The name, later perhaps either Gleann Eidhin or Gleann Eadain, is obsolete, but must refer to land to the N.W. of the river Unshin in Ballysumaghan parish, Tirerrill barony.

Goirias (also Gorias) 2, 4, 7. A mythical city in which the Túatha Dé Danann studied the magical arts.

Grellach Dollaid 75; d.s. Greallaig Dollaid; 76 a.s. Grellaid nDollaid (also called *Amrún Fer nDéa). In Grallagh Greenan tl., in Lr. Iveagh.

Íle 13. Islay in Scotland.

Innsi 50; g.pl. See *Insi Gall.

Insi Gall 50; d. pl. Insib Gallad; 51. Innsib Gall. The Hebrides.

Insi Mod 37 d. pl. Indsib Mod. The islands of Clew Bay, Mayo.

Laí 79. The river Lee, c. Cork.

Lige ina Lánomhnou 84. "The Bed of the Couple." According to the text, apparently in *Glenn Edin, near the river *Unius and *Allod Echae (or *Echuinech).

Loch Arbach 126 a.s. Loch n-Arboch. Loch Arrow on the borders of Sligo and Roscommon, 1 mile from Loch Cé.

Loch Cúan 79. Strangford Loch.

Loch Dechet 79. See *Loch Techet.

Loch nEchach 79. Loch Neagh.

Loch Febail 79. Loch Foyle, c. Derry.

Loch Laig (Loch Láeig) 79. Belfast Loch.

Loch Luibe 126. Given as another name for Dian Cecht's well of healing, *Tipra Sláine.

Loch Luimnig 79. The Shannon below Limerick.

Loch Mesca (Loch Mescdhae) 79. Loch Mask, c. Mayo.

Loch Oirbsen (Loch n-Orbsen) 79. Loch Corrib, c. Galway.

Loch Rí 79. Loch Ree on the river Shannon.

Loch Riach (Loch Rioach) 79. Loughrea, in p. Loughrea, c. Galway.

Loch Techet 79. Loch Dechet, now Loch Gara in cc. Sligo and Roscommon.

Lochlainn 50; 51; g.s. Lochlaindi. Used to refer to part or all of Scandinavia, sometimes including the northern part of eastern Europe as well.

Loscondoib 84; d. pl. For Lioscondoib, Lisconny townland, Drumcolumb parish, Tirerril barony.

Mag Aurfolaig 94; d.s. Moigh Aurfholaigh. The name is obsolete, but must refer to the land just to the north of Loch Arrow in Kilmacallan and Killadoon parishes, Tirerrill barony.

Mag (S)cé[t]ne 85; a.s. Maug (S)cé[t]ne. Taken as a corruption of Cétne, influenced by the reference to Scétne in the same section. The reference is thus to Magh Céidne in Ahamlish parish, Carbury barony, sometimes referred to as Magh Céidne na bhFomhórach.

Mag Tuired 1, 10, 69, 119, 126. According to Hogan, the name is "still remembered in the country and applied to 2 tls. of Moytirra, p. of Kilmactranny, b. Tirerrill, c. Sligo (on the east of Loch Arrow)."

Mana 13; d.s. Manaidn. The Isle of Man.

Márloch or Mórloch 79. Loch Ree, near Lanesborough, c. Roscommon.

Múad (Múaid) 79. The river Moy, which flows into Killala Bay.

Murias 2. A mythical city in which the Túatha Dé Danann studied the magical arts.

Neim (Nem) 79. The southern part of the river Blackwater, at Youghal.

Nemthenn 78. Nephin Mountain in p. Addergoole, b. Tirawley.

Rachra 13; d.s. Rachraind. Rathlin Island.

Ráith Breisi 25; a.s. ráth mBrese. See *Dún mBrese.

Ruirthech (Ruirtech) 79. The river Liffey, Co. Dublin.

Samair 79. The Erne, flowing from L. Erne to the sea.

Scétne 85, 94. The index to the *Annals of Connacht* lists "Fir Scédni, the McReavys (of N. Roscommon)," and the index to the *Annals of Loch Cé* includes "Feara Skene (a tribe situated anc. in the co. Roscommon, but the limits of whose territory have not been ascertained." There is a Loch Skean in N. Roscommon, very near L. Arrow.

Segais (Segois) 78. The Curlieu hills.

Sgiathia: 51. Scythia.

Sinand (Sinond) 79. The river Shannon.

Siúr (Siúir) 79. The river Suir in Munster.

Sliab Bladma (Sliab Bladmai) 78. Slieve Bloom, Co. Laois.

Sliab Líac (Sliab Líag) 78. Slieve League in Glencolumbkile parish, Banagh barony, c. Donegal.

Sliab Maccu Belgodon 78. The mountain stands in Conmaicne Cúile Tolad, near Cong, in p. Ross, c. Galway, at the site of the first Battle of Mag Tuired; it is also called Dubsléibe (Doolevy) and Benn Sléibe (Benlevy). See *Corcu Belgatan.

Sliab Mis 78. There are two well-known mountains with this name: one is in Kerry, east of Tralee, the other stands in the center of p. Racavan, b. Lr. Antrim, c. Antrim.

Sliab Sneachta (Slíab Snechtae) 78. Slieve Snaght in Inishowen, c. Donegal.

Sligech 79. The Sligo River, Co. Sligo.

Temair 3; 53; 54 d.s. Temruich, 56; d.s. Temruid; 67; 69; 72 a.s. Temair. Tara.

Tichc Maoth Scéni 16. See *Mag Scetne and *Scétne.

Tipra Sláine 123, 126. Dian Cécht's well of healing, also called *Loch Luibe, in *Achad Abla, N.W. of *Mag Tuired. Hogan cites as tipra slain, tipra slaingi.

Trácht Aebae 93. Hogan mentions a Tráig Eba, in connection with Rind Eaba, in Carbury on the coast of Sligo.

Trácht Eothaili (Trácht Eoboile) 93. Beltraw Strand to the west of Ballysadare, Co. Sligo.

Traoi 69. Troy.

Unius 84, 85; g.s. Unsen. The river Unshin, between Loch Arrow and Ballysadare.

IRISH TEXTS SOCIETY

Cumann na Scribheann nGaedhilge

Established 1898

1983

OBJECTS, SUBSCRIPTION
OFFICERS AND COUNCIL
LIST OF PUBLICATIONS

Address:
IRISH TEXTS SOCIETY
c/o WILLIAMS & GLYN'S BANK
22 WHITEHALL, LONDON S.W. 1

IRISH TEXTS SOCIETY

COUNCIL, 1983

LIST OF IRISH TEXTS SOCIETY'S PUBLICATIONS

*Out of print

*Out of print

*Out of print

35 LEBOR GABÁLA ÉRENN. The Book of the Taking of Ireland,
   Part II.
   Edited and translated by PROFESSOR R. A. S. MAC ALISTER, M.A., D.LITT. 1939

36 HULL MEMORIAL VOLUME. Fourteen County Mayo Stories.
   Edited and translated by PROFESSOR DOUGLAS HYDE, LL.D.,
   D. LITT., M.R.I.A.   1939

37* BARDIC POEMS FROM THE YELLOW BOOK OF LECAN
    AND OTHER MSS. Part I, Text.
    Edited and translated by REV. LAMBERT MC KENNA, S.J., M.A.   1939

38 STAIR ERCUIL AGUS A BÁS. The Life and Death of Hercules.
   Edited and translated by GORDON QUIN, M.A.   1939

39 LEBOR GABÁLA ÉRENN. The Book of the Taking of Ireland,
   Part III.
   Edited and translated by PROFESSOR R. A. S. MAC ALISTER, M.A., D.LITT. 1940

40* BARDIC POEMS FROM THE YELLOW BOOK OF LECAN
    AND OTHER MSS. Part II.
    Translated by REV. LAMBERT MC KENNA, S.J., M.A.   1940

41 LEBOR GABÁLA ÉRENN. The Book of the Taking of Ireland.
   Part IV.
   Edited and translated by PROFESSOR R. A. S. MAC ALISTER, M.A., D.LITT. 1941

42* BEATHA AODHA RUAIDH UÍ DHOMHNAILL.
    Life of Hugh Roe O'Donnell, Part I.
    Edited and translated by REV. PAUL WALSH, D.LITT.

43* DUANAIRE FINN, Part III. Containing Notes to all the Poems,
    Glossary, Indices, Introduction, &c.
    By GERARD MURPHY, M.A.   1954

44 LEBOR GABÁLA ÉRENN. The Book of the Taking of Ireland,
   Part V.
   Edited and trasnlated by PROFESSOR R. A. S. MAC ALISTER, M.A., D.LITT. 1956

45 BEATHA AODHA RUAIDH UÍ DHOMHNAILL
   Life of Hugh Roe O'Donnell, Part II. Introduction, Notes and
   Glossary, &c.
   Edited and translated by REV. PAUL WALSH, D.LITT. *AND* COLM
   O LOCHLAINN, M.A.   1957

46* LEBOR NA CERT. The Book of Rights.
    Edited and translated with notes, &c.
    by PROFESSOR MYLES DILLON, M.A., PH.D., M.R.I.A.   1962

*Out of print

47 THE POEMS OF BLATHMAC SON OF CÚ BRETTAN
AND THE IRISH GOSPEL OF THOMAS.
Edited and translated by PROFESSOR JAMES CARNEY, M.A. 1964

48 TÓRAIDHEACHT DHIARMADA AGUS GHRÁINNE.
The Pursuit of Diarmid and Gráinne.
Edited and translated with notes, &c., by NESSA NI SHEAGHDHA, B.A. 1967

49* BOOK OF LEINSTER TÁIN.
As edited and translated by PROFESSOR CECILE O'RAHILLY, M.A., for the
Dublin Institute for Advanced Studies, but in the Irish Texts Society
binding—Special arrangement by courtesy of the Institute, limited to
Members only. 1969

50 CATH MAIGE MUCRAIME. The Battle of Mag Mucraime.
Edited and translated by DR. MÁIRÍN O DALY 1975

51 POEMS OF GIOLLA BRIGHDE MAC CONMIDHE.
Edited and translated by DR. NICHOLAS WILLIAMS 1981

52 CATH MAIGE TUIRED. The Second Battle of Mag Tuired.
Edited and translated by DR. ELIZABETH A. GRAY. 1983

Several other new volumes are now in preparation and some of those now out of
print are to be reprinted.

*Out of print

DINNEEN'S DICTIONARY

The Society's Irish-English Dictionary (1340 pp.), *edited by*
REV. P. S. DINNEEN, D.LITT., can be obtained from any book-
seller.

Price £6.00